BALAOO

by

Gaston Leroux

Contents

BOOK THE FIRST

Chapter I

It was ten o'clock at night and it was hours since a living soul had appeared in the streets of Saint-Martin-des-Bois. Not a light showed in the windows, for the shutters were hermetically closed. The village lay as though deserted. The inhabitants had locked themselves in long before twilight; and nothing would induce them to unbolt their doors before dawn.

One and all seemed to be asleep, when suddenly a great noise of galoshes and hob-nailed shoes sounded along the echoing pavements of the Rue Neuve. It was like the clatter of a hurrying crowd; and soon voices were heard, cries and shouts and discussions between people coming none knew whence. Not a door, not a shutter opened at the loud passing of this unexpected band; but more than one ear must have been slyly listening to the tumult out of doors, for the news of a fresh calamity soon spread from neighbour to neighbour.

And yet not one went to his doorstep to know exactly what was happening. It would be time enough to learn next morning. Everybody was still suffering under the shock produced by the murders of Lombard, the barber in the Cours National, and Camus, the tailor in the Rue Verte, which had followed upon a whole series of events at one time tragic, at another grimly comic and often impossible to explain.

People no longer dared linger an the roads, where well-to-do peasants returning from the big markets of Châteldon and Thiers had been attacked by masked highwaymen and obliged to part with all their money in order to save their lives. A number of burglaries marked by extraordinary boldness and perpetrated under the very noses of the victims, who did not dare protest, had formed the basis of police enquiries which were slackly conducted and led to no serious result. The public prosecutor's staff received very little information, was confronted on every side by affrighted silence and did not think it necessary to display more zeal in hunting down the malefactors than was shown by the sufferers themselves in assisting the authorities to perform a duty intended to restore the sense of public security.

Nevertheless, when nocturnal attacks, cases of arson and thefts of greater and lesser importance were followed by those two extraordinary murders of Camus and Lombard, the police were obliged to go to work more thoroughly. They threatened the more timid natures, with a view to forcing them to speak. But these would rather have had their tongues torn out by the roots! No doubt, the police knew by this time upon whom the suspicions of the whole district rested; but they had to give up all hope of receiving evidence tending to inculpate any one whomsoever. And this added strangely to the mystery of the later crimes. The worst of it was that, side by side with dreadful acts of violence, came jests, extravagant practical jokes, each as terrifying as an attempted murder. Respectable tradesmen, walking dawn the Rue Neuve at nightfall, had received a great slap in the face without being able to say where the blow came from. Mme. Toussaint, the old gossip who contracted for embroidery, was found lying in her back-yard, yelling at the top of her voice, with her clothes in over her head and her body showing the marks of a ruthless thrashing. No one knew who had entered the yard nor how. And there were minor incidents that smacked of witchcraft. Despite doors and locks, certain objects—some light and unimportant and possessing no apparent value, others of considerable weight—disappeared as though by magic. Good old Dr. Honorat opened his eyes, one morning, to find his chest of drawers and his pedestal cupboard gone from his bedroom. True, he slept with his window open. He did not inform the police, kept his fright to himself and merely mentioned the strange phenomenon to his friend M. Jules, the mayor, who advised him to shut his window in future when he went to bed.

Lastly, no one dared go through the forest, where more things happened than were ever told. Those who came back, after seeing these things, did not boast of it, but they never ventured in that direction again. It was what was called the Mystery of the Black Woods.

Really, these hardships ought to have been sufficient. What new terror was now making the poor people of the Cerdogne country run down the usually deserted thoroughfare of the Rue Neuve? The cause of all the fuss was an apparently commonplace thing, a railway accident. More correctly speaking, however, it was an attempt upon the lives of the passengers on the little local railway that connects the Belletable and Moulins lines, on the borders of the Bourbonnais.

Criminal hands had torn up the rails at the mouth of the tunnel which opens on the Cerdogne; and, if the train, which had to cross the river by a bridge that was under repair, had not, for that reason, reached the spot at a greatly reduced speed, the catastrophe could not have been avoided. As it was, the train had a narrow escape. The luggage-van alone was destroyed. As for the passengers, some twenty in number, they suffered more from excitement than anything else. And they fled across the fields to Saint-Martin-des-Bois, spreading consternation through the village, which had already locked and bolted its doors for the night.

With the exception of two or three who had their homes at Saint-Martin, all of them went to the Roubions, who keep the inn known as the Black Sun at the corner of the Place de la Mairie and the Rue Neuve. Here, confusion was at its height. While some called for rooms, or at least a bed or a mattress, others exchanged frenzied notes on the danger which they had run.

Fat Mme. Roubion tried to please everybody, but found the greatest difficulty in doing so. One paillasse was nearly torn to pieces. And, when everybody was at last more or less comfortably housed, yet another traveller appeared, with his head wrapped in a bandage. He was the only one injured.

"Why, M. Patrice! Are you hurt?" asked Mme. Roubion, solicitously, holding out her plump hand to the new-comer.

He was a young man of twenty-four or twenty-five, with a pleasant, gentle face, a pair of fine blue eyes and a little fair moustache carefully twisted at the tips.

"Oh, it's only a scratch!" he said. "Nothing serious: it won't show to-morrow...Have you a room for me?"

"A room, M. Patrice?...Yes, you can have the billiard-table!"

"I'll take the billiard-table," replied the young man, smiling.

Whereupon Mme. Roubion went to look after M. Gustave Blondel, a traveller for one of the big linen drapers of Clermont-Ferrand, who was making his bed on the table in the pantry and threatening to kill the landlady if she did not bring him a bolster then and there.

"I'm all right here, you see, my charmer, much better than on the billiard-table in the bar-room, where all those talkers would keep me from sleeping! What do they want to go on chattering like that for?

What's the trouble with them? They know who did the business: why don't they say so?"

At the sound of these words, Mme. Roubion hastily vanished.

M. Sagnier, the chemist, had just entered the barroom. On hearing the news from the mayor, he had behaved like a hero, torn himself from the trembling arms of the beautiful Mme. Sagnier and come to offer his services. Finding no one in need of his aid, he immediately developed a very bad temper and mingled his aggressive remarks with those of the most irate of his hearers, declaring that, in the face of such outrages, it was no longer possible for a decent man to live at Saint-Martin-des-Bois or, for that matter, in any part of the Cerdogne country.

Meanwhile, M. Jules, the mayor, appeared, accompanied by good old Dr. Honorat. They came from the station, where they had received evidence from the lips of the railway-officials leaving no doubt whatever as to the nature of the outrage. They both looked as pale as if their own lives had been in danger.

"Another calamity, monsieur le maire!" said Roubion.

"Yes," replied M. Jules, in a shaking voice. "Fortunately, there have been no injuries for us to regret!"

The words were received in icy silence. And, suddenly, a voice exclaimed:

"And what about the murderers? When are they to be arrested?"

Then came an outburst. Words of applause and encouragement were flung at the speaker; but he—a peasant—had said what he had to say and remained silent. His face was crimson and his eyes avoided the mayor's.

"The police have been! If you know who the murderers are, Borel, why didn't you give up their names?" asked the mayor.

Old Borel was as clever as most people and had his answer ready:

"I've nothing to say to the police," he growled. "I'm no detective, nor no mayor neither. Everyone to his trade!"

That was what they all said: it was not their job. To the commissary of police, to the examining-magistrate, they invariably replied with the refrain:

"It's your business, not mine!...The government pays you to find out: see to it and earn your money!" with more gibes of the same sort.

They were still digesting old Borel's answer, when Gustave Blondel entered, pushing everybody aside. The commercial traveller sat down on the billiard-table, crossed his arms, looked the mayor straight in the face and said:

"What are you worrying about, monsieur le maire? What do you expect in a place where there are people whose name begins with the same syllable as vauriens?"

A murmur of assent and a few nasty chuckles followed, but the effect of Gustave Blondel's sally was interrupted by an unexpected incident. The chuckles suddenly ceased; and all now, nudging one another, stared at a new-comer who came forward while the others made way for him with astonishing unanimity.

The man was dressed in a drab corduroy suit. Long leggings came up to his knees. His shirt-collar was loose and revealed a neck like a bull's. A soft hat, which had lost all semblance of colour, was thrust back on his head, showing a tangled mass of thick red hair. The face was extraordinarily powerful and calm. The green eyes contemplated those present with a cool, bored look. The man's limbs were short and thickset, the shoulders square, the back a little bent. He carried his hands in his pockets; and his whole person gave a striking impression of brute force, quiescent, but wide awake.

He walked across the room with his even step, amid death-like silence, until he was face to face with the commercial traveller, who watched him coming; and the man had certainly heard what Blondel had said to the mayor, for he barked at him, in his rough, dull voice, full of suppressed anger:

"Vautrins, vauriens! Is that what you mean, my beauty? You needn't mind me, you know: I'm not one to take offence!"

And he moved to the chimney-place, where the mayor was standing:

"Good-evening, monsieur le maire."

"Good-evening, Hubert..."

And M. Jules had to press the hand held out to him.

The man sat down without ceremony beside the hearth, in which a fire of sticks had been lit, and called for "a glass of white," which Roubion hastened to bring him. He emptied the glass, wiped his mouth on his sleeve and, turning to Blondel, said:

"Monsieur le maire hasn't got over the last election yet!...Only, look you here, my beauty: it's all right to treat us like dirt at the meetings...but we ought to be left quiet now...What say you, monsieur le maire?"

M. Jules, feeling greatly embarrassed, gave an inarticulate grunt.

The commercial traveller had not stirred. He continued to fix an obstinate stare of dislike upon the red-haired, green-eyed man. Hubert rose and, offering Blondel his hand:

"Come," he said, "let's have no ill-feeling! Each does his best for his master: you for the King, I for the President of the Republic! If ever you want a billet..."

Blondel got down from the billiard-table leisurely, shrugged his shoulders, turned his back and went to the pantry.

"Monsieur le maire," said Hubert, in a hollow voice, "I call you to witness: that's how they treat good republicans in this place. But I'll pay him out for it at the next election, never fear!...I mark it all down on my little slips of paper, though I don't know how to write...Hear that, you others, who seemed to be enjoying yourselves, just now."

As he spoke, he cast his cold, metallic glance over all his hearers. In the depth of their being, they felt as uncomfortable as if they were before a magistrate.

His coolness in enlisting the mayor on his side with a word, as though, after the forced intimacy of the election, the mayor had necessarily become his accomplice and his friend, brought the beads of perspiration to M. Jules' bald forehead.

The man flung four sous on the table and walked back to the door with his calm gait. On the threshold, he stopped and turned:

"I'm going back to my brothers," he said. "By the way, I've been to the tunnel and seen the damage. The man's a damned blackguard who did that job. I shall tell Élie and Siméon as much, presently. What I say is, we shall have to find the beggar who plays us these tricks, or life won't be worth living for decent men."

And he disappeared under the black cavity of the archway.

The room at once emptied, as though the man's departure had restored everybody's liberty of movement; and they all took advantage of it to escape from a place where the visit might be repeated at any time.

Roubion and his wife, assisted by the servants, carefully locked the doors of the bar-room: the door into the archway and the door opening straight on the street.

No one remained in the room except young Patrice, to whom the landlord and his wife had said good-night. Nevertheless, though he was alone with his billiard-table, he heard a noise close beside him. He perceived that some one was undressing in the pantry. The door between the two rooms was closed, but a communication remained in the form of the little open window of the serving-hatch. And he at once recognized the voice of the commercial traveller, who, stooping to the opening, said:

"Good-night, M. Patrice. If you want anything, you can call to me through here...This is rather like a confessional-box, isn't it?"

These details were destined to be impressed on Patrice' mind for all time, though he did not suspect their importance at the moment. He answered Blondel politely and hoisted himself on to the mattress which had been laid over the billiard-table. When they were both lying down, they began to talk:

"Why didn't you go to your uncle's for a bed?" asked Blondel.

"I knocked at the door and called out. They were all asleep, I suppose, and I didn't like to wake them."

"Is Mlle. Madeleine well?"

"Thank you, I hope so."

"When is the wedding to be?"

"You had better ask my uncle."

Blondel saw that he had been indiscreet. He changed the subject; and they now started discussing the outrage and the recent murders, which the commercial traveller flatly put down to the score of the brothers Vautrin.

"Oh," said Patrice, "at Clermont-Ferrand, we think—just as they do here—that you can't explain everything with the Three Brothers."

"You can explain everything with the Three Brothers and the sister," said the commercial traveller.

"The incredible part of it is," Patrice insisted, "that no trace of the murderers was discovered in either Camus' or Lombard's case."

"Possibly," replied the other, "but one thing is certain, that, if Camus and Lombard had not opened the door on the night of their murder, when they heard the sound of moans in the street and the voice of that little savage of a Zoé...they would be alive now. It was the sister who lured them on..."

At that moment, the two men ceased talking, as though by a sudden accord. And each of them sat up in bed, pricking up his ears. Moans came from the street.

"Do you hear?" asked Blondel, in a husky voice.

Patrice had not even the strength to reply. He heard the commercial traveller get up, jump to the tiled floor of the pantry and enter the bar-room with every precaution.

"One would think they were murdering somebody outside the door!" said Blondel.

Patrice, whose occupation was that of first clerk to his father, a solicitor in the Rue de l'Écu at Clermont-Ferrand, had always been more or less timid by nature. He shuddered as he slipped down from

11

his billiard-table. With a choking throat and a moist forehead, he admired the courage of Blondel, who walked up to the door of the barroom that opened on the street whence the moans had come.

The traveller had pulled on his trousers, but kept his handkerchief knotted round his head by way of a night-cap. The great, fat fellow, with his bare feet, his night-shirt hanging loose round his waist and the two corners of his handkerchief sticking out above his forehead like horns, looked the picture of absurdity; yet Patrice did not think of laughing.

The moans had ceased abruptly. Blondel and Patrice looked at each other in silence, by the dismal light of a lamp over the billiard-table, the wick of which had been turned down. All the mysterious tragedy of which Camus and Lombard had been the victims passed before their eyes. The thing had, begun like that, with moans, in the case of both the unfortunate men.

And suddenly they turned their heads. The door of the staircase leading to the upper floor opened; and Roubion appeared, carrying a revolver in his hand:

"Did you hear?" he asked, in a whisper.

"Yes."

Roubion was a fine, big chap, built, like his wife, on huge lines. He was trembling like a leaf. All three remained for moment behind the street-door, listening to the silence of the village night, which nothing more disturbed.

"Perhaps we were mistaken!" said Roubion, with a sigh, after a good deal of hesitation.

Blondel, who had recovered all his composure, shook his head, by way of denial:

"We shall see about that!" he said.

"What!" protested the innkeeper. "You're not going to open the door, surely?"

Blondel did not answer and went and stirred the fire, which gave a little glow. It was a cold night, although summer was not far off. Soon, all three were sitting round the chimney, where Roubion warmed them some wine in a sauce-pan.

"All the same," said the commercial traveller, "if we could manage to catch the scoundrels here and now, it's a stroke of business that would be worth doing!"

"Hold your tongue, Blondel!" said Roubion, peremptorily. "Don't meddle with that...it would bring you bad luck!"

"Certainly," said Patrice, "it's none of our business."

"Remember Camus and Lombard!...If they had not opened their doors!..."

Blondel, who was on the road at the time of the two murders, asked for details.

Roubion went back to the door, listened and, hearing nothing, returned more or less tranquillized:

"This is exactly what happened," he explained. "Lombard and his old aunt had gone to bed after bolting all their doors and windows, as we now do every evening at Saint-Martin. Lombard's bedroom and his aunt's were both on the ground-floor. The barber was sound asleep, when he was awakened by the old lady standing at the foot of his bed and whispering to him to listen to what was going on. Lombard listened. Some one was wailing and lamenting in the street. It sounded like dying moans mixed with little plaintive cries. Lombard got up, lit his candle and took his revolver from the drawer of the table by his bedside. You know how careful we are at Saint-Martin; and we are right to be, unfortunately. The aunt whispered to Lombard, 'Whatever you do, for God's sake, don't open the door!' Lombard, without opening the door as yet, decided to speak: 'Who's there?' he asked. 'Who's that crying?' A voice answered, 'It's me, Zoé. Pity in the man's house!'"

"What does that mean: 'Pity in the man's house'?" asked Blondel, interrupting him.

"Oh, it's one of Zoé's expressions. The chit lives like an animal, either in her brothers' den or in the forest; and, as her brothers always talk slang among themselves, the result is that she speaks a language different from that of other people."

"So, you see, it was she," said Blondel. "There's no mistake about it."

"Wait!...It was only half-past ten. In spite of all that his aunt could say, Lombard opened the door. He looked out into the street. It was a bright night. He saw nothing and was very much astonished. The moans had stopped. Fearing a trap, he was careful to keep on the threshold, called Zoé, received no reply, closed his door again very cautiously and went back to bed, saying, 'It's another hoax. There's no sleeping in peace, these days, at Saint-Martin-des-Bois!' The aunt also went back to bed, but, after this disturbance, did not sleep. She lay awake all night."

"Oh," said Patrice, "she must have gone to sleep, or she would have heard!"

"She swears she never closed her eyes. And the door between their two rooms was left wide open. In the morning, she got up as usual and went to open Lombard's shutters. When she turned round, she was greatly surprised not to see him in the recess where the bed stands. The bed-clothes were flung back as if Lombard had just got up. Not knowing what to think, she opened the door leading to the hair-dresser's shop and gave a terrible yell: the poor barber's body was swinging in the middle of the shop, hanging from the brass lyre that serves as a chandelier. They thought at first that it was suicide; but Dr. Honorat and the divisional surgeon agreed that the hanging had been preceded by a terrible strangling and all so suddenly that the unfortu-nate man had no time to say, 'Oh!' or the old woman would have heard. What seemed the great mystery from the very first was how the body could have been carried into the shop and hanged...It was found that there was not a trace of footsteps in the shop, which had been freshly sanded on the evening before. Lastly, a fact which proved from the start that Lombard had not hanged himself was that there was no chair or stool lying on the floor beside him."

"Ah, well!" said Blondel, jerking his head. "Men are tired of life have more than one trick in their bag!...What about Camus?"

"The same story. He too heard moans in the middle of the night and recognized Zoé's voice. Camus was a friend of Lombard's: they were the only two lame men in the parish; and this had brought them together. He thought it a good opportunity to discover the barber's murderer and avenge his death. He took a weapon, opened the door and, like the other, saw nothing and heard nothing more. But, when he had shut his door, he did not go to bed. He wisely lit all the lamps in his shop and, with his revolver by his side, sat down by his till and started doing his accounts. He then told his little assistant, the young lad whom you know, to go upstairs to bed. Well, the next morning, the assistant, on returning to the shop, uttered a piercing cry. His master was hanging from the iron bar from the ceiling that holds the yard-measure with which he used to measure the cloth for his customers. The revolver was lying on the till. The till had not been touched. Ca-mus' throat showed the same marks of strangling which were found on Lombard. And, in the tailor's shop, as in the barber's, it was impossible to discover any marks of steps, any footprint allowing a plausible ex-planation of the method of the crime. People said and people are still saying, 'The Vautrins! The Vautrins!' Well, the Vautrins themselves took little Zoé to the examining-magistrate; and she had no difficulty in proving that she was far from the spot of the murder at the time when it was committed and that somebody must have imitated her voice."

"And where was she?" asked Blondel.

"She was helping monsieur le maire's servant to wash up her plates and dishes. There was a big dinner at M. Jules' that night."

"There's a fine alibi for you!" sneered the commercial traveller.

"M. Blondel, you are blinded by politics!"

And Roubion poured them out some more hot wine.

"And the Vautrins? Were they examined?"

The magistrate wanted to question them. Their answer was that little Zoé had spoken for all the family and that they were not going to have any dealings with the police at their time of life. Then they sent M. de Meyrentin, the examining-magistrate, an extract from their judicial record, which in fact is absolutely blank, and with it they enclosed a request that he would just kindly leave them alone!

"What cheek!" exclaimed Blondel.

"Listen!" said Patrice.

The moans had begun again.

The three men all stood up. Patrice tottered on his legs and nearly dropped when he distinctly, most distinctly, heard the fatal phrase:

"It's me, it's Zoé. Pity in the man's house!"

Roubion, with his hand clutching his revolver; turned as white as a sheet. Blondel said, in a whisper:

"That's Zoé's voice, there's no mistake about it. I know it."

And he slipped behind the door.

The moans had come nearer still. It was as though the three men heard them in their ears, as though somebody quite close, quite close, had whispered the moans to them. They heard the sound of oppressed breathing and the strange phrase of despair:

"Pity! Pity in the man's house!"

Blondel sprang round and ran to the wall-rack. He seized a cue by the narrow end.

"Oh no!...Don't open the door! Don't open the door!" stammered the innkeeper. "It's the Lombard and Camus trick!...That's how they were murdered!...Don't open the door, or we're done for!..."

He rattled out his words and trembled so violently in his fright that he disgusted Blondel, who growled:

"Oh, are you all cowards in these parts? It's one of two things: either they're murdering the child, or else they're getting at us!...Or it may be," he added, feverishly wiping the streaming perspiration from his forehead with his shirt-sleeves, "it may be Hubert coming to take his revenge...But there are three of us, what!&...And you have your revolver, Roubion!"

"Don't open! Don't open!" said Roubion again.

It was now as though Zoé were sobbing outside the door, or as though she were on the point of death.

"But we must find out what it is!" protested Blondel, still wielding his billiard-cue.

Then he asked, in a powerful voice:

"Who's there? Who's crying'?.. Is it you Zoé?..."

There was no reply but a hoarse groan.

Suddenly he drew back the bolt and turned the key of the door.

"Where are the ruffians?" he growled, putting his head outside.

At last, he took up his stand on the threshold, with his billiard-cue in his hand.

This corner of the Rue Neuve was well lit by the light of the street-lamp at the corner of the Place de la Mairie. Nevertheless, Blondel distinguished nothing; and the moans had ceased. He beckoned Patrice and Roubion, who joined him, mastering the unendurable anguish of which they were now ashamed.

As a matter of fact, they felt angry with themselves for being such cowards. As Blondel had said, there were three of them, not to mention that the inn was full of visitors who would hasten at the first call; at least, it was to be hoped they would!

"Do you see anything?" asked the commercial traveller. "I can see nothing."

"No, nothing!...There is nothing!...There's nothing to see!"

"Here, wait a second till I go to the corner of the lane...over there..."

"M. Blondel, you mustn't!...You mustn't!..."

But, by this time, the other was in the street. He made no noise, walking barefoot on the cobbles, and thus slipped to the corner of the lane on the left, where he looked and listened, without venturing down it...The he came back and went off to the right, as far as the Place de la Mairie.

The light of the gas-jet flung the huge shadow of Blondel, still armed with his billiard-cue, upon the opposite wall. A silence that was incomprehensible, after those recent moans, hung over the village; and this seemed to Patrice more terrifying than the moans themselves. The moans must have been heard in the neighbouring houses: opposite at the Bouteillers'; next door, at Mme. Godefroy the postmistress'; but nothing had stirred on either side. The fear that reigned supreme at Saint-Martin-des-Bois allowed no doors to be opened to the voices of the night...And the moon might cast the dancing shadows of the three

Brothers in the streets, or send sprawling the less formidable, but equally mysterious, shapes of lifeless things—such as the shapes of the chimney-pots, for instance, which are more terrifying than any, with their caps upon their heads—but people were not inquisitive enough to look at them at night!...No, no, there was nothing inquisitive about the people of Saint-Martin-des-Bois!...

The three men closed the inn-door just as Mme. Roubion, "feeling more dead than alive," joined them. She too had heard noises, but would never have thought that Roubion could have the imprudence to allow the door to be opened. And she dragged him away, pushed him up the staircase, beating him as she went and carrying with her the key of the street-door, to make sure that they did not open it again.

When Blondel no longer heard them, he turned to Patrice, who did not know what to say or do:

"You're too impressionable, my lad," he said, "you'll never get to sleep in here. I only laugh at this kind thing you see. One discovers all sorts of coincidences, once things are over; and the Vautrins are capable of anything: I saw the way they went to work at the last elections! The point is to know them. If they want to deal with me, let them come! I'll sleep behind the door, in your place, on the billiard-table. I'll wait for them."

Patrice, looking a little shamefaced, replied:

"Perhaps we had better not go to sleep at all!"

But the other had already caught up Patrice' blankets and was carrying them to the pantry. And he returned with his own things and threw them on the billiard table.

Patrice let him have his way and was not at all sorry to move farther from the street and from that door against which he still, at moments, seemed to hear a rustling.

They drank one last bowl of steaming wine, shook hands and wished each other good-night. Patrice tried to make some excuse for himself, could not find his words, was afraid of appearing a coward. The other pushed him along:

"Go on, my lad, go on!"

Then Blondel climbed on to the billiard-table, muttering:

"That's how boys are brought up nowadays; their parents make school-misses of them!"

When his head was on the pillow, he lit a cigarette and sent the smoke up to the ceiling.

Patrice could see him clearly through the little open door of the serving-hatch. The solicitor's clerk, on his mattress on the pantry-table, was lying with his head on the same level as the head of Blondel, on the billiard-table. And, suddenly, what Patrice saw through the little square of the hatch filled him with a horror so great that every hair on his head stood on end.

He continued merely to see Blondel's face; but what a face! Never was hideous terror printed on human countenance in features more atrociously distorted. With his eyes starting from their sockets, with his mouth open, but incapable of emitting a sound, with his whole face dreadfully convulsed, Blondel was staring fixedly at the ceiling.

Patrice could not see what Blondel saw; and, awed as he was, his terror was but the reflection of the other's terror.

Patrice tried to make a movement to rise...Yes, he had the strength and also the pluck, for he needed pluck to move; and something abominable must be happening on the ceiling of the other room; and the sense of his own safety was ordering him not to stir a limb...

Was the movement which he made perceived?...Were they trying to with fright too?...For, from the ceiling of the other room, he heard a hoarse and formidable voice utter his name...yes...yes...his name...Patrice!...And that certainly was a frightful command, a threat that nailed him to his place!

This time, he stirred no more; and, with eyes full of horror he continued to gaze at the little square of the serving-hatch that framed the terror-stricken and apparently hypnotized face of Blondel...

And, all at once, the young man saw, in that little square...saw coming down from the ceiling, which he could not see...saw two clutching hands under two shirt-cuffs, which made two very clear white patches in the half light...saw two terrible arms which fell upon Blondel, which clutched him by the throat and which rose to the ceiling holding that throat captive.

And Blondel had not even said, "Oh!" Already his head was falling back, his head of which Patrice was never more to forget the eyes, starting, jutting, enormous, as though ready to slide from the sheath of their reversed lids.

Lifted by the murderous hands, the head and then the whole upper part of the body disappeared from the frame of the serving-hatch; and next came the legs, which left the billiard-table and rose, hanging side by side, towards the ceiling!...

Oh, horror!...Oh, horror!...Oh, to cry out!...To cry out! Patrice can't...he can't...because he is too much afraid!...Yes...he's a coward...he's a coward!...Ah, to move...to run...to fly!...Patrice' legs are of lead, of lead!...Ah, he succeeds in stretching one of them out of bed...one alone, noiselessly...But what can he do with only one leg out of bed?...And he feels that he will never have the strength to put the other out...If he could only put the other out...and run away, run away on his legs of lead!...But, once more, in a hoarse whisper, over there, from the ceiling, comes a monstrous chuckle in which he distinctly hears his name:

"Patrice!"

The other leg has that moment come; and there he now stands, with his feet on the floor, on the tiled floor, but his back glued to his mattress...Yes, his name uttered up there, from the ceiling, has glued him irremediably against the improvised bed...

Why has his name been uttered?...

The man on the ceiling evidently knows, evidently, absolutely knows that he, Patrice, is there, since he calls him by his name and, very charitably, warns him not to move...

Thereupon, he does not move...He obeys...

And suddenly the breath ceases...the enormous breathing from the ceiling!...And he hears it no longer...he hears it no longer!...

And he no longer sees anything above the billiard table, through the little window of the serving-hatch...

Yes! Yes!...He does see something. He sees something coming back, coming a little lower: Blondel's two feet, which swing...and swing...and swing...and then, gradually, cease their swinging...and at last remain motionless, toes downwards...

There is nothing now in the bar-room of the Black Sun but a profound silence, those two motionless feet above the billiard-table and, in the pantry, Patrice Saint-Aubin, who has fallen into a dead faint...

And perhaps also the murderer.

For if he entered when the door was opened, he must needs now go out.

Chapter II

They are early risers in the village. That morning, the inhabitants of Saint-Martin-des-Bois put their noses out of their windows even earlier than usual. They were eager to know the exact reason of the disturbance during the night. They soon heard about the outrage at the Cerdogne Bridge and were already asking one another for details from door to door, when they saw big Roubion running like mad towards the Cours National. They tried in vain to stop and question him. Then they followed him to monsieur le maire's door, where he rang with all his might. M. Jules, still more than half asleep, came to the window. He saw Roubion standing utterly distraught and went down to let him in. Three minutes later, they both came out again and M. Jules looked as terribly flustered as big Roubion himself. They walked with great strides towards the Black Sun, without answering anybody who spoke to them. Ten or twelve persons came after them, recruiting others as they went along. But all had to wait outside the door of the inn, while the mayor and Roubion entered by the great archway.

Almost at the same time, good old Dr. Honorat appeared upon the scene, having been fetched by an ostler from the Black Sun. Dr. Honorat went into the inn, but the ostler remained with the crowd and told them what had happened. That was how Saint-Martin-des-Bois learnt that Blondel, the commercial traveller, had been found hanged, like Lombard and Camus. And soon the whole village was standing in front of the inn, filling the Rue Neuve from one side to the other.

To avoid this crowd, which was kept outside the barroom door by the crier—nicknamed Daddy Drum—the visitors who were in a hurry to leave the inn and the village went out at the back, by the side of the Parish School; and this also was the means of exit adopted by the mayor and Roubion, who, three-quarters of an hour later, left by a roundabout road for the station, where they were to meet M. Herment de Meyrentin, the examining magistrate of Belle-Étable.

M. de Meyrentin, who had been informed during the night of the fresh outrage on the line between Saint-Martin and Moulins, was expected by the half-past six train. No trains would run beyond Saint-Martin until after the line had been repaired.

While waiting for the magistrate's arrival, the mayor and Roubion walked up and down the platform, with their heads sunk on their chests, their hands behind their backs, exchanging their thoughts in a low voice as though they feared that they might be spied upon and overheard. They were speaking of the Vautrins.

M. Jules admitted that the Three Brothers were not a credit to the district and that they might be held responsible for a good many minor misdeeds, but he maintained that they were incapable of murder. Big Roubion had a curious way of replying, in a hollow voice, "Mind what you're saying!...Mind what you're saying!" which gave the impression that he knew more than he could tell. This time, he abandoned his customary prudence. Had Mme. Roubion been there, she would have pinched his arm for him.

The mayor, nodding his head, contented himself with saying that those horrible crimes were becoming more difficult to explain. Lombard and Camus had never injured anybody. They had no enemies. They were on neither good terms nor bad with the Three Brothers. Lombard used to shave them for nothing, once a year; and Camus, with whom they had a small account, had never sent in his bill.

"May be!" said Roubion, after casting a glance round him. "But the Three Brothers were on very bad terms with poor Blondel!"

"Oh, politics!" growled the mayor.

"Well, believe me, monsieur le maire, you will see that you made a great mistake in bringing them into' your politics..."

"They brought themselves in without me," replied M. Jules, greatly incensed.

Meanwhile, Dr. Honorat arrived and joined them; telling them that he had sent Patrice, whose condition no longer gave cause for anxiety, to his uncle, old Coriolis Saint-Aubin. Patrice had remained as though stupefied and had merely shaken his head in reply to the questions put to him.

Blondel's body had been laid on the billiard-table; they were careful not to touch it more than could be helped. The doctor had refused to take any observations before the arrival of the magistrate. He had ordered rest for Patrice. Besides, it was the magistrate's business to question him; and nobody else's.

"'You did quite right," M. Jules agreed. "And then, from what I could gather out of his monosyllables and gestures, he did not see the murderer."

"Whether he recognized the murderers or not," said good old Dr. Bonarat, "I hope that, after what took place last night between Blondel and Hubert, they will not be spared..."

"The magistrate will please himself," retorted M. Jules, who was becoming more and more tetchy.

"The magistrate is in the hands of the deputy. You will see, they'll want to 'give them another chance' again!" moaned Honorat.

"Oh, but look here, my dear doctor, if you know anything, say so! Don't behave like the peasants!..."

"I have every reason to be at least as careful as they are. I am often on the roads at midnight, all by myself, in my gig, and am more exposed than anybody to the wicked attempts of wicked fellows."

Nevertheless, he could not refrain from saying that he had more than once come upon the Vautrins in suspicious circumstances, hiding themselves in order to drag to the Black Woods a cart covered with branches and containing "what they had chosen to put there!"

The mayor snarled:

"You ought to have looked; it might have been your chest of drawers."

Honorat grabbed the mayor's hand:

"Come, come, M. Jules!...You know as well as I do that they are the only people capable of such acts!..."

The mayor stopped both Honarat and Roubion and, taking each by a button of his overcoat:

"I tell you once more that I know nothing about it; and I do know nothing about it...You're beginning to annoy me!...One thing which you may as well know is that we have discovered marks that cannot have been made by the Three Brothers!..."

"Which are those?"

"The marks on the neck, to begin with..."

"Oh, tut!" growled Honorat. "You're trying to humbug me now. I've seen those marks on the neck myself..."

"You've seen nothing!..."

"What's that?"

"Oh, the magistrate is sure to speak to you about it to-day and Roubion can be trusted not to talk! I'm sick and tired of having 'The Vautrins! The Vautrins!' hurled at my head...No, doctor, you have seen nothing!..."

"But I was the first to examine the necks of Lombard and Camus."

The mayor interrupted him:

"If I may say so without offending you, if you had taken as long to examine them as the medical expert who was appointed afterwards, you would have perceived that the terrible marks of strangulation were made upside down!"

"What? Upside down?"

"It is so incredible," continued M. Jules, "that I am not surprised that you did not observe it. You saw the prints of the fingers and that was enough for you: 'Murder,' said you, 'strangulation.' How could you be expected to observe that the print of the thumb was at the bottom and that of the other fingers at the top? To do that, you would have to imagine that the crime was committed by a murderer working with his head downwards!"

The doctor and Roubion looked at the mayor as though he had suddenly gone mad. Honorat ended by shrugging his shoulders:

"If I did not make those observations, it must have been because I considered them superfluous. Strangulation with the fingers was a certainty. But it's true that I should never have imagined the crime to be committed by a murderer with his head downwards: it was easier and simpler to picture the murderer coming up from behind and dragging his victim's head down backwards."

"The enquiry has shown that position to be impossible," said M. Jules, roughly.

"Then what?" asked Roubion, timidly.

"Then don't come bothering me with the Three Brothers! Did you ever see them walk head downwards?"

Roubion and the doctor once more exchanged glances.

"Ah, but look here!" exclaimed good old Dr. Honorat, folding his arms. "What's your examining-magistrate after? And what does he think?"

"You had better ask him!" replied the mayor, as the train entered the station.

The first person to alight was M. Herment de Meyrentin. He jumped out on his short legs and seemed to come rolling towards the authorities waiting for him. He was as round as a top. He had a good-natured, genial face, brightened by a little turn-up nose and also by the sense of his high responsibility in all this criminal business at Saint-Martin-des-Bois. Behind him came his clerk, a tall, gawky, elderly man, dressed in a huge frock-coat, in which he limped along with difficulty.

The mayor, Roubion and the doctor made a rush for the magistrate, who spun round two or three times on his own axis before stopping. He did not give them time to say a word. He seized hold of the mayor:

"I say, M. Jules, you never told me that! It seems that, some years ago, all the dogs in your district were found hanged!..."

"Yes, monsieur le juge, but allow me..."

"Is it true? Yes or no?"

"We have serious news..."

"There is nothing more serious than that!...Is it true or not?"

"It is quite true..."

"And nobody ever knew how?"

"No, monsieur le juge."

"For, after all, those dogs did not hang themselves of their own accord!"

"No, monsieur le juge...Monsieur le juge, there has been a fresh murder!..."

"Eh?..."

"Yes, Blondel, the commercial traveller from Clermont-Ferrand, was found hanged last night, at Roubion's..."

The magistrate looked at them:

"The devil!" he said; and he began to spin round again. "Come!"

They followed him. All of them climbed into the omnibus of the Black Sun, which contained no other passengers. Here, before anything else, M. Herment de Meyrentin handed M. Jules a sheet of letter-paper and said:

"Read that aloud."

M. Jules read it. It was a last word from the divisional surgeon, who said:

"The wounds on the throats of Lombard and Camus look as if they had been made by some one walking upside down." And the note ended:

"Imagine the murderer coming towards his victim, not walking on the floor, but walking on the ceiling; and you will have those wounds."

"There! What did I tell you the other day? I didn't invent it, you see!" said M. Herment de Meyrentin, taking back his note with a little movement of pride.

M. Jules gave a sigh. The doctor and Roubion lowered their eyes, dumbfoundered, flabbergasted. The magistrate's clerk scratched the tip of his long, aggressive nose.

Five minutes later, all four entered the bar-room of the inn. The window-shutters were still closed; and the sound of an impatient crowd penetrated from the outside.

The two billiard-lamps had been lit. The first thing that M. de Meyrentin saw, on entering, was, lying on the billiard-table, the life-less body of Gustave Blondel, the linen-draper's traveller from Clermont-Ferrand and one of the political agents of M. le Comte de Montancel, whom he knew well. He leant over the corpse.

M. de Meyrentin at once observed on the poor fellow's throat the terrible prints, the marks of "upside-down strangulation," of which Lombard and Camus had died.

He drew himself up, settled his double eye-glass on his little turn-up nose and looked up in the air.

What was he looking at? Every eye had followed the direction taken by his.

But there was nothing to be distinguished above the shaded lamps.

"Open the windows," ordered M. Herment de Meyrentin.

Roubion and the servants hastened to obey the instruction. The shutters were flung back. The daylight streamed in and a hundred heads pushed against the windows and the door to see. At first, there was nothing but cries of pity for the fate of Blondel, whose body the people saw covered with a sheet.

And then they noticed that the magistrate was looking up in the air. They did likewise. And everyone saw what M. de Meyrentin saw, as, with outstretched arms and open mouth, he continued to stare at the ceiling.

There was but one cry:

"Footprints on the ceiling!"

Chapter III

Yes, fully-outlined footprints showed on the white plaster of the ceiling. The feet went to and fro, returned to the point whence they started and went back to the metal stem supporting the billiard-lamps from which the unfortunate commercial traveller had been found hanging!

The noises and cries were almost immediately succeeded by a stupefied silence. And then a few comments arose from the crowd peering through the windows, while M. de Meyrentin stood without moving and contemplated that trail, which was surely the strangest trail in the world.

"D'you mean to say the murderers walked like flies?" said one.

"As they never left any marks on the ground, they must walk somewhere!" said Mother Toussaint, that old gossip who was always the first to arrive when there was anything on hand.

"The footsteps are quite plain...that's because it was raining yesterday," said old Fajot, who always wanted to be cleverer than anybody else.

But some one remarked:

"Faith, that's a fine joke to play on the police!"

And at once there were spiteful, hostile laughs. It was obvious that the business of the footprints on the ceiling was assuming the appearance of a gruesome jest, almost an insult to M. de Meyrentin. And prudent allusions were made to "the others":

"Ah 'they' know their way about! 'They' know their way about!..."

"Seems Blondel told them what he thought of them, yesterday."

"He won't tell them so to-day...It's best to mind one's business..."

And they called out to the magistrate, who was still looking in the air, as they might to a dog:

"Go find! Go find!"

"Silence, all of you!" ordered Daddy Drum, in his voice husky with liquor.

At a sign from the magistrate, Daddy Drum closed the windows.

Then they shifted Blondel's body a little to one side and M. de Meyrentin climbed up on the billiard-table and made a careful and prolonged examination of the footprints on the ceiling. It was a long foot with a large heel and a well-developed great toe. These details were visible although the feet had been placed there not quite bare, but clad in socks. The man who had walked on the ceiling had taken the precaution to take off his shoes, so as not to make a noise; and he had certainly removed them before entering the house, for the footprints on the ceiling were still quite wet with the black mould in which he must have walked outside. Here and there, the socks showed the cross-work of the coarse wool and the darns. M. de Meyrentin pointed these out to M. Jules. The mending, instead of being correctly done, displayed a rough and very peculiar "whipseam," a sort of round patch, the size and shape of a five-franc piece, joined on to the heel and "whipped" anyhow, all round.

"Joke or no joke," said M. de Meyrentin, "with a clue like that for us to go upon, the man who played the joke will pay for it with his head!"

And he jumped down to the floor and spun upon his own axis several times to express his satisfaction.

"Gentlemen," he announced, in the most serious tone, "we must look for the man who walks upside down!"

"How does he manage when he takes a drink?" asked Michel, the driver of the Black Woods diligence, in an undertone.

Michel had just arrived and was poking his cap cautiously through the pantry-door. Fortunately, the magistrate did not hear him. He was asking Roubion if he knew of any black mould anywhere around the inn. Roubion took him to the back of the building; and there they were able to trace distinctly, in the middle of the lane, the same marks of footsteps which they had seen on the ceiling. The marks stopped suddenly, between two high walls without doors or windows. It was impossible to understand how those marks were not to be found anywhere else.

"The joke continues!" chuckled M. de Meyrentin, with a knowing little air. "And now let's go to M. Saint-Aubin."

The others had already given M. de Meyrentin a detailed account of how they had found Patrice in a faint in the pantry, though it was understood that he was to sleep on the billiard-table. This sort of transposition of bodies seemed to interest the examining magistrate greatly.

Patrice's uncle, M. Coriolis Boussac Saint-Aubin, owned the largest and oldest estate in that part of the country. It was also the most sequestered, standing at the end of the village, almost on the edge of the woods.

Roubion and the mayor took leave of M. de Meyrentin when he raised Coriolis' knocker. Old Gertrude came and opened the door. She said that M. Patrice was "resting." The good woman seemed quite upset. The doctor said a word to reassure her.

Then Coriolis appeared upon the scene, in the devil's own temper, shaking his long white locks, hardly civil to the magistrate, complaining at being bothered with all this business and bitterly regretting that his nephew had come to disturb him at Saint-Martin without his permission.

"I want to see your nephew, at once, please!" said M. de Meyrentin, incensed at this reception.

"He's asleep."

"Wake him up."

Thee uncle turned his back on him. But a young girl with a sweet, engaging face and eyes still red with weeping intervened:

"Come with me, monsieur le juge..."

When they entered the bedroom, they found Patrice tossing in a feverish sleep, waving his arm as though to ward off some frightful vision and uttering incoherent words. They arrived just in time to hear him cry:

"Pity in the man's house! Pity in the man's house! Why did you call me: 'Patrice!'"

M. de Meyrentin could not help giving a start.

The doctor said:

"It will be better to wake him and let his mind recover its balance. Dreams like that can only do him harm."

M. de Meyrentin made a sign to the doctor to hush and once more listened to the sleeping witness. But Patrice now uttered none but unintelligible sounds.

The magistrate turned to Coriolis:

"You were not expecting your nephew?" he asked.

"He pretends that he sent me a telegram during the day. I did not receive it. That explains why nobody opened the door when he knocked last night."

"M. Bombarda," said M. de Meyrentin, to his clerk, "go and ask Mme. Godefroy, the postmistress, if she received a telegram for M. Boussac Saint-Aubin."

The clerk limped off in his long frock-coat.

And Patrice woke up.

M. de Meyrentin welcomed this awakening eagerly. At last, perhaps, they would know, know what the thing was that walked on the ceiling, with hands that strangled!

The first thing that the young man saw, on opening his eyes, was the sweet face of Madeleine.

Like himself, she was fair, with blue eyes. They had loved each other for many years, ever since the time when, quite young, they used to meet, during the holidays, at the house of Patrice' father in the Rue de l'Écu at Clermont-Ferrand; for Coriolis' daughter had been brought up in France while her father was doing business at the other end of the world, at Batavia, where he was French consul. Patrice was sorry when Uncle Coriolis returned from the Far East and retired to his estate at Saint-Martin-des-Bois, where he led the life of a bear. The uncle did not care for his nephew's visits and had told him as much. He accepted the engagement in principle and had spoken a word or two about it to old Saint-Aubin of Clermont; but, meantime, he insisted that they were not to "bother him."

Patrice was still looking at Madeleine, in fond admiration, when Dr. Honorat spoke, to introduce the magistrate to the young man. Then he recommended Patrice to be calm and, above all, to recover possession of his wits. In short, the time had come for him to act with courage and not to be afraid to tell the police all that he had seen and heard. The safety of the whole district depended on him.

The examining-magistrate was marking his approval of these last words by nodding his head, when the long, black, limping clerk returned from his errand. He was in a great state of fury. His raised fists threatened no one knew whom; and he spoke so fast that his hearers did not understand a word of what he was saying. They seemed to gather that he had received a slap!

"A slap?" asked M. de Meyrentin, astounded.

"Yes, a slap in the face!"

And the magistrate's clerk cut so queer a figure as he spoke that Mlle. Madeleine could not restrain a smile, while old Gertrude burst out laughing.

"There's nothing to laugh at!" declared the clerk, angrily. "A regular slap in the face! To me! But it won't end there, I can tell you!"

"Come, come, M. Bombarda, first tell us how it happened."

M. Bombarda rubbed his cheek, gave Gertrude a fierce look and said:

"I was coming back from the post-office and was just about to leave the Rue Neuve for the road. I was walking as fast as I could and, as I did so, brushed past a man in front of me who seemed to want the pavement for himself. I hardly touched him. I apologized and was going on my way when—whoosh!—I received a slap!...But such a slap!...Monsieur le juge d'instruction, it was a slap that hurled me against the wall and made me see stars!...I was just meaning to go for my assailant, when I saw that he had disappeared as if the earth had opened under his feet!...I could not make out where he had got to...I hunted for him, I shouted, I threatened him!...It was well for him that he did not show himself, for he would have had something to remember me by...But what a slap!...To me!...Look, my cheek is still quite red!...But I shall find my man all right; and, once again, I sha'n't let it end there!"

"Yes, yes, yes," said M. de Meyrentin. "A slap! I see! Well, we'll talk of it later!...For the moment, M. Bombarda, sit down and take out your note-book!...But, first, what did the postmistress say?"

"She said that she received a telegram for M. Coriolis yesterday and that she gave it to M. Coriolis' man-servant, who had just come into the office to stamp and post his master's letters."

"Then why didn't Noël give me the telegram?" exclaimed Coriolis. "I can't understand it. Go and ask him, Gertrude."

The old woman went out and returned almost at once, striking her forehead with one hand and waving the blue paper of a telegram in the other:

"Oh, my memory! &...My poor head!" she said. "I'm becoming good for nothing! You had better get rid of me, my dear master!...Noël gave me the telegram for you. I put it in my pocket and forgot all about it until this moment...Oh, it doesn't do to grow old!..."

"That'll do," said Coriolis, snatching the telegram from her. "Go away."

Gertrude made herself scarce. Coriolis read the telegram and the examining-magistrate asked to see it.

"My nephew's telegram seems to worry you?" asked Coriolis.

"Very much so, monsieur, and I will tell you why. The question of knowing whether your nephew was expected at Saint-Martin or not is particularly important because we have to solve the problem which of the two they meant to murder last night: the commercial traveller or M. Patrice!"

Madeleine gave a cry of horror and turned as pale as Patrice himself, who received the magistrate's supposition as he would a stunning blow. The blood buzzed in his ears and he thought that he was about to relapse into the state of coma from which he had just emerged. As for

Coriolis, he scorned the idea that anyone could be sufficiently interested in his fool of a nephew to want to murder him. He shrugged his
shoulders and uttered this scathing sentence:

"He has nothing to do with our local differences and never leaves
his mother's apron-strings."

The doctor muttered his regret that M. de Meyrentin should behave so tactlessly towards an invalid and translated his thoughts by
saying, aloud:

"Be gentle with him!"

This was not at all the intention of the magistrate, who had had to
be gentle with everybody up to now and who thought this a good opportunity to make a powerful impression on the young man and to get
something out of him at last.

He politely ordered everybody out of the room, except the clerk,
and remained face to face with Patrice, who stammered:

"Kill me!...But I know nobody here...and I have no enemies,
monsieur le juge!"

"We always think we have no enemies," retorted M. de Meyrentin, sententiously, "and it is at the moment when we think ourselves
safest that we are hit in the dark. Tell me all that you know, all that
you have seen, heard and...and suspected. Fear no reprisals of any
kind: I shall act with the greatest prudence. Not a soul shall hear what
must remain our secret until the moment when the criminal is punished
and, therefore, made harmless. So trust me, M. Saint-Aubin, and speak
out!"

Patrice described the incidents of the night as we know them, as
circumstantially and accurately as possible. He felt a need to explain
things to himself. Gradually, as he spoke, the magistrate's supposition
appeared more and more plausible to him; and he shivered at the bare
thought.

When he had finished, he looked at M. de Meyrentin with anxious
eyes. The magistrate tugged nervously at his pepper-and-salt whiskers;
and his little eyes glittered with anger through his gold-rimmed
glasses.

"Is that all?" he asked, harshly.

"I have told you all that I saw and heard," sighed Patrice.

"So you saw nothing more? So you did not have, I will not say
the courage, but the curiosity to drag yourself to the door of the hatch
and look to see what was happening on the ceiling?"

"Monsieur, I was paralyzed; and, when all my pluck was gone, I
had even less curiosity!"

M. de Meyrentin had the greatest difficulty in restraining the expression of his disappointment.

"And so you let the poor man die..."

"But, monsieur le juge..."

"In your stead!" continued the magistrate, fiercely. "Yes, in your stead! For the other thought that he had hanged you, monsieur, and that is all about it!...Wait now! Don't go and faint!...All hope is not lost...Answer my questions. It had been publicly understood that you were to sleep on the billiard-table?"

"Yes, monsieur."

"You entered the inn with your head bandaged; and Blondel, before going to bed, put a handkerchief round his head!"

"Yes, monsieur."

"Are you quite sure that you heard your name uttered from the ceiling?"

"Yes, monsieur, very plainly, worse luck!"

"Wait!...Wait!...In the state in which you were, you may not have been able quite to realize things...You speak of a huge breath, of a monstrous breathing in the midst of which you heard your name pronounced: 'Patrice!'...Are you quite sure that it was the breath that spoke?...For there was the breath on the ceiling and there was the hanged man...It may have been the hanged man, it may have been Gustave Blondel who, knowing that you were in the next room, gave a last groan: 'Patrice!'"

"Monsieur, it was unlikely. He would have called out, 'Help!' and not 'Patrice!' I did not know M. Blondel well. He would not have called to me by my Christian name."

"That's true enough," assented M. de Meyrentin, growing more and more irritable, for the witness' evidence seemed to contradict a theory on the murders at Saint-Martin-des-Bois which he had now entertained for some days.

"It's quite true!" he resumed, after a pause. "So it was the breath—I give that name to the thing on the ceiling which you did not see, but heard—it was the murderer who spoke!...And the murderer had a huge breath, which evidently came from his difficulty in breathing upside down...And the murderer spoke: 'Patrice!' In what tone did he say, 'Patrice!'?"

"Oh, monsieur, I feel pretty certain that it was in a tone of hatred!"

"You see! And who is there that calls you by your name of Patrice?"

"No one, except my father, my mother, my Uncle Coriolis and my Cousin Madeleine!"

"I see."

A momentous pause, during which the magistrate reflected and bit his lips...

"And you are sure that, behind the door, you heard, 'Pity! Pity in the man's house!'?"

"Yes, we heard those words plainly."

"And what do the words mean, in your opinion?"

"Why, monsieur, I don't know!"

"Nor I either, monsieur," said the magistrate. "And the murderer wore cuffs, you say? What sort of cuffs?"

"Oh, I can't tell you positively. I saw some white linen coming beyond the sleeves."

"What I want to know is what sort of idea you had when you saw what you did of the murderer coming down towards Blondel's throat."

"Oh, I did not have much of an idea at that moment, but, all the same, I realized that it was two arms that were coming to strangle Blondel."

"You saw those arms up to where?"

"Up to the elbows, at least."

"Would you know them again?"

"Upon my word, I can't say...the sleeves were dark...As you know, it was not very light on the other side of the hatch..."

"Which explains why he hanged the other in your stead: the fact is becoming more and more certain to my mind...Think it well over. Concentrate your thoughts upon it. Help me with all your might, with all your intelligence..."

"But, monsieur, I can't understand it, I can't under stand it at all!..."

"Nor I either, monsieur!..."

"But, when all is said and done, monsieur le juge, how did the murderer get in? How did he get out?"

"That's what I was going to ask you," said M. de Meyrentin, rising from his chair. "Well, as soon as you are able to get up—and I hope that will be at once—just stroll round to the inn and, in my name, ask Daddy Drum, who is keeping the door, to show you the footprints which the murderer left behind him."

"Oh, so he left footprints?...On the floor of the bar-room, I suppose?"

"No, monsieur!...On the ceiling!"

Chapter III

With these words, M. de Meyrentin took leave of the unfortunate Patrice, who began to cry like a child.

Luckily for the young man, old Coriolis and Madeleine soon succeeded in convincing him that M. de Meyrentin was the biggest fool living. The uncle, especially, was furious with the examining-magistrate. None of the Saint-Aubins, whether of Clermont or Saint-Martin-des-Bois, had ever been mixed up in the politics of which Blondel was, beyond a doubt, the latest victim. In the Rue de l'Écu, they went in for respectable law-practice and nothing more; and, on the other hand, Coriolis contended that, during all the years since his return from Batavia, he had no interest in anything beyond his absorbing study of the bread-plant, an uncommon, starchy vegetable which he had brought back from the Far East and of which he had the patriotic intention of giving his country the benefit. This way of living was not calculated to create mortal enmities; and Coriolis and his household passed almost tranquilly through that horrible period during which the Cerdogne country went in a state of constant terror. He was persuaded that "they" would never do him any harm.

"They," to Coriolis as to everybody else, stood, of course, for the Three Brothers. But he overwhelmed them with kindnesses, had never troubled them for the rent of the hovel which they occupied on the edge of the wood...and, as the manor-house in which he and Madeleine lived was situated in a rather lonely spot, he did not hesitate to have it guarded by the three good-for-nothings. Now this was a stroke of genius. Old Coriolis still chuckled when he thought of it. To be protected by thieves: there was an idea for you!

"They're safer than the gendarmes," he would say to people who were surprised that he had given the Vautrins the right to walk about his property with their guns on their shoulders.

The old man himself did not shoot. It was as though he had presented all his game to the Three Brothers, who otherwise would certainly have taken it without his permission. And he paid them into the bargain! But, at any rate, he enjoyed peace and quiet and was able to sleep soundly. And here was this fool of an examining-magistrate, who knew nothing of the habits of the district, pretending that they had tried to kill his nephew!...

He made the said nephew get out of bed...and briskly, at that, to change his train of thought. He sent him into the garden, where Madeleine was waiting for him. Coriolis, who was in a hurry to go back to his bread-plant, left them to themselves. Madeleine at once said:

"I have been thinking over what that silly man said to you. It's one of two things: either the murderer knew you, or he did not. He knew you, because he called you by your name, telling you not to move from where you were. And, as he knew you, how could he make so great a blunder, at the moment of strangling and hanging you, as he thought? Was it light enough to see in the room?"

"Certainly, it was pretty light...The proof is that I saw Blondel's face distinctly."

"Then he must have seen it too; so set your mind at ease, Patrice. And tell me how my aunt is. Don't think any more about this horrid business. It's all a matter of political revenge, which doesn't concern us."

"The Vautrins again, eh?"

They were passing by the railed gate that opened on the fields.

"Take care! Don't speak so loud. There's always one of the albinos prowling about near here. What a scourge for the district!"

They stood for a moment at the gate, looking at a little roof that rose out of the ground, on the other side of the road. It was where the Vautrins lived.

Hubert! Siméon! Élie! The triplets whom Mother Vautrin had brought into the world, at one birth, like a litter of wolves, the three who at first, as little chaps, had amused the country-side and who were now its terror. Everybody had long ago proclaimed himself their friend, so great was the fear which they inspired. And, even now, those who met them on the roads showed every eagerness to shake them by the hand. Only, people preferred not to run across them in the evening; and those who came to Saint-Martin-des-Bois avoided the way that led by the skirt of the forest, near the low-roofed roadside cabin where old Mother Vautrin lay paralyzed, dying by inches and telling horrible stories about the father, who had been to penal servitude.

This last detail had not prevented the Vautrins from cutting a figure in local politics. And it was no secret that, during the last three parliaments, by distributing prospectuses and professions of faith in all the villages in the division of Belle-Étable, creating disturbances at public meetings and making a stay in the district impossible to rival candidates, who considered their very lives in danger, the Three Brothers had contributed largely to securing the election of a deputy who was a credit to the constituency and the budding hope of the Chamber.

They themselves might have achieved respectable positions in the district. But they did not care about that. We must do them the justice to say that they had tried. They accepted posts under Government in reward for services rendered. They allowed themselves to be appointed telegraph-messengers. People still trembled at the recollection, at Saint-Martin and in the Cerdogne plains. The brothers used to put off until the middle of the night the delivery of a telegram received at six o'clock in the evening, waking people out of their beds, clamouring for supper and going away with a five-franc piece easily extorted from the pusillanimous ratepayers. Unfortunately, they took a dislike to the face of the inspector and they sent in their resignations after Hubert had promised that exalted functionary to get him sacked, a promise which was faithfully kept.

No, those fellows were born to work just as and when they pleased. They would take on a job when the fit seized them, at vintage-time, for instance, when they got blind drunk on the thin wine of the hill-side. The rest of the time they managed to occupy themselves in the "Black Woods," those great forests of firs, beeches and oaks, covering the whole bulk of the Montancel, where they reigned as uncontested masters.

Though their dwelling, on the edge of the road to the woods, was a wretched one, they were said to be well-off and to hoard the fruit of their robberies at the bottom of the mysterious quarries of Moabit, which explained the failure to find any traces of those robberies among the receivers of the neighbourhood. As for them, they let people talk. One would think that it amused them to be the terror of the country-side; and, in the tap-rooms, they sometimes went so far as to encourage the tattle:

"Well, what do you say of us? Have we been misbehaving again to-day? Done something fresh, eh?"

The people told them, joined in the joke, like cowards. The Three Brothers banged the counter with their great fists, declared that "that was a good 'un," swore that it would not prevent them from laying down their lives for the Republic and went out on the road, almost always shouldering a gun and grinning from ear to ear. At such times, they were so funny that they would have made a corpse laugh. But when, suddenly, they became serious, then they were terrible to behold. All three resembled one another, with the same gait and the same tricks of manner. Hubert, however, was the strongest and biggest. Siméon and Élie were of a much fairer red. These two were known as "the albinos."

Patrice drew Madeleine from this vision:

"How can you stay in such a part? Oh, how I long to take you away, my dear little Madeleine! Hasn't your father said anything to you yet? I never dare speak to him, he's always so cross."

"I'll tell you a secret: papa is tired of this part as well."

"I can understand that!" said Patrice, approvingly.

"And we are going away before long."

"Really?"

"Yes. We are going to settle in Paris. The wedding will be in Paris."

"I hope to goodness it will be soon...and I sha'n't bring you back to Saint-Martin in a hurry!...I don't know what your father means to do in Paris, but anything is better than staying here...What are you waiting for, before leaving?"

"Papa has still a few experiments to make with the bread-plant. He says it is not quite ready yet," said Madeleine, blushing slightly and turning away her head.

"Oh, I hate the very name of that bread-plant! My opinion is that your father's a bit cracked, like everybody who has a fixed idea in his head. He thinks he'll make his old plant take the place of everything else. He'll soon find out his mistake, like all inventors. However, he's not a bad sort; and that's the main thing."

They were walking along, leaning towards each other prettily, exchanging their confidences and feeling happy and at ease in that paradise of a neglected garden in which things grew anyhow; for Coriolis refused to keep a single servant to help old Gertrude look after his big manor, except his native "boy," a tall, very quiet lad, as gentle as a lamb, who did not speak twenty words a day and who had been brought from the Far East together with the bread-plant. He was known Noël.

Now, Noël had no time to attend to the garden. He spent his days with his master, at the far end of the property, in a corner where stood a rather weather-beaten building, with a conservatory in front of it. This was where the curious plant was tended which Patrice had only once or twice set his eyes on, without understanding the least thing of what his uncle was doing.

The building was surrounded by a wild orchard closed with a door through which no stranger was ever admitted. All this part of the domain was reserved for the experiments of which Coriolis kept a record from day to day, writing it up in the evening in his study and afterwards locking it carefully in his safe. Coriolis' study was right at the top of the manor-house, in the belvedere-turret. Here the old man would sit and write throughout the night, after devoting the daylight hours to his work in the orchard.

All this at first seemed very mysterious to Patrice, especially during the earlier period, when his uncle used to display such ill-humour at his visits to the manor, two or three times a year, and when he was absolutely forbidden to enter the orchard. During the last three years, however, this prohibition had been less strictly enforced; and, now that Patrice was able to walk with Madeleine where he pleased, anywhere in the grounds, including even the building in the orchard when his uncle had finished work, he consoled himself with a reflection that settled the matter:

"Madeleine's father is an old lunatic, with that bread-plant of his!"

The two young people had not yet kissed. They remembered it suddenly and called each other's attention to this lovers' omission; and Patrice, very properly, as behoves a good little solicitor's clerk from the Rue de l'Écu, imprinted a chaste salute on Madeleine's brow.

Forthwith, there was a clap of thunder!

Madeleine started visibly, turned a little pale and looked at her sweetheart with anxious eyes, while Patrice raised his to the sky, which was without a cloud.

"This is too much," he said. "That's the second time it's happened."

"What?" asked Madeleine, ingenuously, blushing all over her face without apparent reason.

"Why, that it thunders when I kiss you!"

Chapter IV

"I don't know what you mean, Patrice," she said. "It's a heat-storm," she added, "for there are no clouds in sight. Perhaps we had better go indoors."

"You remember the last time I came," he said. "I was saying good-bye in the porch. Your father said, 'Come, give her a kiss.' I stooped to kiss you, when bang!—there came a clap of thunder as though the house had been struck by lightning. And I never gave you that kiss. Your father literally flung me out, shouting, 'Quick! Quick!...There's a storm coming...Run to the station!' And he slammed the front door in my face...Outside, there was no storm at all!..."

"Oh," said Madeleine, toying with a flower which she had picked, "we never mind that here! It often thunders, just like that, in the Black Woods. It's the forest that causes it. Papa says that it's 'forest electricity'."

"Forest electricity? I never heard of that sort of electricity."

"Papa tried to explain it to me, but I couldn't understand. It seems that, in Java, the forests thunder like that all the time...Listen, the storm is passing away. Can you hear it, Patrice?"

A very distant rolling was now coming from the forest, whereas, a little while ago, they could have almost thought that a thunderbolt had fallen close to where they stood. And they turned their heads towards the gate, through the railings of which they could see the edge of the Black Woods.

At that moment, they saw an unusually fair-haired face pressed against the railings, a face covered with patches of light-red hair, a motionless face with two pink eyes that stared at them with indecent persistency. The young man made an angry movement towards the gate, when the albino's voice rooted him to the spot:

"Don't move any nearer, M. Patrice!"

These words and the way in which his name was pronounced sounded fearsomely in the young man's ears. He stopped, with a beating heart and the blood throbbing at his temples. Madeleine had taken his hand and did not move either, but stood watching the albino.

The man quietly inserted the barrel of his gun through the railings of the gate and fired in their direction. The two young people uttered a cry of terror. A thrush fell dead at their feet.

"Well, what's the matter?" asked the sportsman, coolly. "You're not hurt, are you?"

"No, but whoever heard of shooting like that under people's noses?" said Madeleine, angrily.

"Eh, I never missed my shot yet, Mlle. Madeleine. So what are you afraid of?"

Patrice, still trembling all over his body, had stooped to pick up the bird.

"Poor thing!" he muttered.

"I'll give it to you two sweethearts for your lunch...Good-bye, Mlle. Madeleine; good-bye, M. Patrice."

And, when Patrice made as though to fling the bird through the railings, the girl prudently stopped his violent impulse.

"Good-bye, M. Élie, and thank you!" she said, in a husky voice.

The albino had already disappeared behind the gate. Patrice was on the point of speaking, but Madeleine put her little hand on his mouth, a little hand that shook most terribly. She did not remove it until she no longer heard the other's footsteps on the pebbles of the path. The she said:

"Oh, how he frightened me with his gun!"

"And with the words he said!" whispered Patrice.

"I can still see his gun passing through the railings," said Madeleine. "You know, darling, if he had shot at us, he would have hit me first: I put myself in front of you..."

It was quite true. Patrice had not noticed this movement of heroism at the time. He took Madeleine in his arms. Some one gave a cough, behind them. It was Noël, whom Coriolis had sent for them.

"The master wants you," he said, in his rather hoarse voice.

And he turned back, with his hands in his pockets and bent mopishly. They followed him to the orchard.

"What a life for you!" said Patrice. "Between your monomaniac of a father, that stupid old Gertrude and that lad whom I have never seen laugh." And he pointed to Noël's stooping figure. "The natives of Haï-Nan are a melancholy lot; and cultivating the bread-plant does not seem to raise this one's spirits."

"You don't know Noël," said Madeleine. "When he likes, he can be the best of company: ask Gertrude. There are days when he makes us laugh like mad."

"That's all right. But I've always seen him fit to die of weeping."

"He's like that when we have people here. He is shy."

"He is very fond of you..."

"Yes. He's particularly frightened of papa..."

"Does your father treat him harshly?"

"Very; he has to. It seems you have to act like that with those' boys' from the Far East; otherwise you get nothing out of them..."

"I have never been able to judge of his character," said Patrice. "We say, 'good-morning' and 'good evening'; but I come here so seldom..."

"Oh, he's becoming quite civilized now! He eats with Gertrude in the kitchen...But formerly papa had his meals sent in to him in his room, at the end of the orchard...because of the bread-plant, which couldn't be left, at that time..."

They had reached the door of the orchard. Noël, who seemed to be moping more and more, held it open for them, very humbly. They passed through.

"He hasn't improved in his looks!" said Patrice to Madeleine.

"Oh, do you think him ugly?" said Madeleine, quickly. "Have you looked at his eyes? I have seldom seen such intelligent eyes."

"That's true," Patrice acquiesced, not wishing to contradict her. Coriolis stood before them, at the door of the conservatory. He looked anything but pleased. He glanced at the two of them and then at Noël, whose attitude of utter dejection would certainly have provoked loud laughter in any whom it did not almost move to tears.

"I sent Noël to fetch you," said old Coriolis, knitting his brows-- an habitual trick with him, which no longer frightened any one but Noël--"because I thought I heard a thunder-storm; but I may have been mistaken. A man can't trust his ears at my age..."

Patrice listened in amazement at the tone in which he spoke of the storm; and his surprise knew no bounds when he heard Coriolis ask him, roughly:

"Well, the two of you!...I don't suppose you'd tell me a lie!'...Has it been thundering, or has it not?"

"I didn't hear it," replied Madeleine, with the greatest effrontery.

And she shot a glance at Patrice that he was not to contradict her. Unfortunately, the young man was already saying, without disguising his astonishment:

"Thunder!...I should just think it did!...I thought a thunderbolt had struck the house!"

Madeleine had flushed to the roots of her hair. Coriolis wagged his forefinger at her, sternly:

"That's very wrong of you, Madeleine!...You know I don't like it!...What would become of us, if I went by what you said?"

"But, papa, I assure you I didn't notice it...It must have been because one of the albinos fired a gun and frightened me..."

"Élie again I suppose," growled Coriolis.

"Yes, papa, Élie...He had the impudence to shoot a thrush in the garden, while we were there!"

"Here it is," said Patrice, showing the bird which he had brought with him.

"The villain!" mumbled the uncle. "I shall have to tell him to do his 'game-keeping' a little farther off, if he doesn't mind...We've seen too much of his face lately..."

Madeleine, whose embarrassment continued, said:

"You are quite right, papa, but I have already sent him word by Zoé."

"What did you tell her to say?"

"That he must shoot a little farther away, that his gun frightened me. He answered, through his sister, that he was watching over us closer than usual because the district wasn't safe, since the murders."

"And what did you say in reply to that?"

"Nothing. I sent him a bottle of rum. He'd had nothing from us for a long time."

"You did quite right, Madeleine. We must have patience with those scamps for just a little longer. You haven't told Patrice?..."

"No, papa, I have told him nothing," said Madeleine, with the most delightful composure.

"How she can lie!" thought Patrice.

And he thought her all the more charming.

"Well, tell him that we are going to settle down in Paris. Yes, my dear Patrice, in Paris."

"Then you have finished your work on the bread-plant, uncle?"

"Yes, nephew, it has attained its majority!...Now go and take a turn, you two, before lunch. I have something to say to Noël."

The young people left the orchard. Patrice was astonished, on passing Noël, to see the poor fellow tremble like an aspen-leaf. Five minutes later, when Patrice and Madeleine went to Gertrude's kitchen to ask what there was for lunch, they heard terrible cries of distress in the distance.

"What's that?" asked Patrice, with a shudder.

"Nothing," said Madeleine, pinching her lips. "I expect Noël has done something silly again and papa is punishing him."

Patrice turned to old Gertrude, in his surprise, and saw that she was crying.

"Oh dear, he'll kill him!" she said, blowing her nose. "There's no sense in beating a grown-up lad like that."

"You know that papa is always angry when he hears the thunder!" said Madeleine, who seemed cross with Patrice and was almost as much upset as Gertrude.

"So that's why you made signs to me," said Patrice, "and why you told your father a fib about the thunder..."

"Yes, that was why, Patrice..."

Patrice was going to apologize, but he was interrupted by the arrival of a little girl of thirteen or fourteen, black as a mole, with a pair of glorious eyes. She was dressed in a wretched, short, patched skirt, which showed her skinny calves. Panting, she asked:

"Is that Noël screaming? Is the master beating him again?"

"Yes Zoé," said Gertrude. "It's a pity..."

"Oh, I thought there would be trouble, when I heard the thunder!" said Zoé.

"Come and help me scour my brasses," said Gertrude.

The housekeepers of Saint-Martin employed that chit of a Zoé at such jobs, from time to time, in order to curry favour with the Three Brothers.

Chapter V

Patrice was sent for, that afternoon, to attend the magistrate's enquiry. He was re-examined by M. de Meyrentin in the bar-room of the inn and stood staring long and stupidly at the marks of footprints on the ceiling, at the curious pattern of those socks and at their curious whipseam.

Monsieur le juge seemed more and more puzzled, especially after a little incident, ludicrous enough in itself, which nevertheless kept his mind strangely busied. After lunch, while monsieur le juge was having forty winks in his bedroom at the Roubions'—just half an hour's siesta, no more I—somebody had stolen his watch. True, he declared that the watch was made of brass and that the thief had been sold; but the fact remained that he thought of nothing else, for, on the floor of the room in which he had gone to sleep, M. de Meyrentin had perceived the marks of the feet on the ceiling!...Who could that invisible person be, who hovered around them in the twofold guise of a criminal and a practical joker, making fools of one and all?

Patrice, on his side, returned to the manor-house, more terrified than ever at what he had seen and heard; and the evening-meal was very gloomy in consequence. He could not get rid of the sight of Blondel's corpse; and he was haunted, in his inner consciousness, by the constant refrain:

"It's you who ought to be in his place."

Gertrude waited on the party in silence. Suddenly, she resolved to address her master:

"Zoé's here, sir."

Coriolis deigned to wake from his dreams and to look at his old woman-of-all-work:

"Oh!...Well, have you spoken to her?"

"Yes. She says she would go to the ends of the earth with you, sir. Only she hasn't dared mention it to her brothers yet."

"You can leave her brothers to me...I'll grease their palms; and, anyhow, they won't be sorry to see the child make a move. The great thing is that she likes the idea...Did you tell her that she would be going to town?..."

"Yes, yes, she said she would go wherever you wished, sir. When I told her that we were leaving the country and that she would most likely never see us here again, she cried: she's not a bad sort of girl, in spite of the shocking example she's had set her. And she's not really lazy. She can work when she likes to and when she's not taking it into her head to go running about the woods. We should soon train her in town, especially if she saw no trees and as soon as she was away from the forest...Well, you'll speak to her yourself, sir. I've kept her to dinner...What do you think she asked me? She begs you to forgive Noël."

"Let Noël out," said Coriolis, giving Gertrude a key. "He's in the black hole. I think I hit him rather hard. But it's his own fault. He ought to have more sense, at his age."

"Oh, he takes it very much to heart, sir, when you're cross with him. Zoé will be so pleased. He always makes her laugh."

And she went off with the key. A few minutes later, Zoé was heard screaming with laughter in the kitchen. Coriolis looked at Patrice:

"Do you hear them? It's Noël amusing them," he said. "Oh, he never bears malice. He wouldn't hurt a fly! But he needs a beating from time to time."

"Aren't you afraid of his going and complaining to the village constable?" asked Patrice.

"He? He'd give his life for me! I saved his life, when he was a child, at Batavia. He'd have died of starvation, but for me."

"Does he never hanker after his country?"

"He does nothing but speak of it," said Gertrude, changing the plates.

"That's always the danger with those exotic servants," said Patrice, sententiously. "You can do what you like with them; they are regular slaves; but a time comes when there's no holding them. They must and will go home again."

"Where have you seen that?" asked Coriolis, with obvious annoyance.

"Well, at Clermont! Near us, there was a lady who had been to Russia and who brought a nana back with her for her children. It worked very well for a couple of years; and then, when the lady did not go back to Russia, the nana died."

"I dare say she was consumptive!" Coriolis burst out, with a loud, aggressive laugh. "But Noël's well and strong, you see."

"Oh, I didn't say it to annoy you, uncle, but just because I always see Noël looking so awfully sad!"

"That's a look he keeps for strangers, so now you know; and that's enough about it!"

"Very well, uncle."

At that moment, Zoé was heard yelling and screaming in the kitchen.

"What's up now? What's happening?" cried the uncle.

And they all rushed to the kitchen, where they found Zoé in tears, by herself.

"What's the matter? Where's Noël?" asked Gertrude.

"Oh, it's nothing!" said Zoé, between her sobs. "Noël pulled my hair!"

"What did he pull your hair for? Have you been teasing him again?"

"No, I told him that he was nice-looking and he thought I was poking fun at him..."

"He was quite right. You're always chaffing him. You'll end by making the boy's life a misery," said Coriolis emphatically, forgetting the drubbing which he himself had just administered to Noël.

They finished their dinner. It was now dark. Uncle Coriolis thought that Patrice must be feeling tired and told him to go to bed. The young man obeyed, said good-night and held out his hand to Madeleine.

"You can kiss her!" said Coriolis.

Patrice put his lips to Madeleine's forehead. And he could not help thinking to himself:

"It's sure to thunder!"

But Madeleine received Patrice' kiss and there was no thunder. The young man had tried, at the same time, to seize Madeleine's hand in the dark and to press it tenderly, in the manner of sweethearts, but the hand seemed to avoid his grasp. He felt much upset, thought Madeleine very unkind and went up to his room quite sadly.

"If you want anything," his uncle cried after him, "knock on the ceiling. Gertrude's room is above yours. Good-night! And mind you lock your door."

"That's all right, uncle..."

The first thing he did in fact, when he reached his room, was to lock the door. Then he looked under the bed, in the wardrobe, in the cupboards, everywhere. Lastly after putting out his lamp, he cautiously opened his window, peered into the outer darkness and listened to the shadow of the forest.

His bedroom was on the first floor, in the left wing of the house. On his right, in an angle of the building, he saw the belvedere-turret, the top room of which was already lighted for Coriolis, who had settled down to work, as usual.

In front of Patrice was the yard, with the outhouses, the stables, buildings that now served no purpose save for the household washing and for storing apples. A little to the left, almost beneath him, was another little building, the wood-shed, with its dark archway. It was a dusky night; and he was only just able to distinguish, in the distance, the shadow of the house in which the bread-plant lived, to the right of the garden, contained within its high walls. But suddenly the house lit up, a window gleamed. It was obviously Noël going to bed. And then, almost immediately, the light went out.

A gentle breeze, coming from across the fields, carried the haunting fragrance of the earth to Patrice' nostrils. Had Patrice been a poet, he would have revelled in the peaceful silence of nature and breathed the soul of the night with joy. But not only was he no poet: he was a lad who had every reason, for the moment, to be obsessed with other things. To begin with, there was the terrible adventure of the night before; and then there were the brutal suppositions of the examining magistrate, which kept on returning to his mind, in spite of all that Coriolis and Madeleine could say. Lastly, there was something which he was unable to define exactly and which was due to his general dissatisfaction with the day which he had passed.

The fact was that he was displeased with everybody here: with his uncle, with Gertrude, with Madeleine. After what had happened to him at the Black Sun and the hideous dangers which he had been through, he could not understand that he was not the constant, one and only object of their thoughts.

Now all of them—Madeleine as well as the others—seemed to be thinking of something else the whole time, in the orchard, in the garden, at table, or when amusing themselves for a moment with their poor butt of a Noël, whom Coriolis treated so savagely. And Madeleine seemed to him more distracted than ever, with her thoughts far from him, even when he was walking alone with her, talking of their future.

It was not the first time that, after spending a few hours at the manor-house, he had had this curious feeling that its occupants were thinking of something of which he could not even suspect the nature; but the feeling had never been so acute nor so painful as to-day.

These reflections passed through his mind as he stood at the window; and then, suddenly, he caught his breath. He had seen a white form, a form so light that its movement made no sound, glide quickly along the wall in the shadow of the outhouses. He had a fluttering at the heart which made him think that he was going to faint again. He managed to keep his feet, however, and leant back in a corner of the window, invisible from the outside. The 'white figure had disappeared under the arch of the wood shed and he distinctly heard Madeleine's voice answer, in a whisper:

"Are you there, Zoé?"

Then there followed, in the shadow of the wood-shed, a curious dialogue which Patrice, where he stood, could distinguish plainly and which was not exactly calculated to set his mind at rest. Zoé and Madeleine thought themselves safe from any eavesdropping; but the open arch of the woodshed sent their voices up to Patrice like the horn of a gramophone.

"You've got to tell me the truth," insisted Madeleine. "It was Élie who did it, was it not?"

"I assure you, miss, I don't know. I would tell you, if I did. I always tell you everything, but those are things I never know. They don't trust me. They tell me about their pranks, true enough, me and mother. But things like this nobody ever knows, not mother, I nor anybody..."

"I want to know, Zoé, I must know. I shall not be easy in my mind until I do..."

"Why, miss? They say it's politics..."

"Who says so?"

"Everybody."

"And your people at home, do they say it's politics?"

"They haven't spoken about it before me. Only, mother, when she heard of it, said to me, 'They say that Blondel's been killed like Camus and Lombard. You know, Zoé, I'm afraid your brothers are doing something silly...'"

"You see, Zoé?...Well, next?"

"Next...next...Listen, miss, you won't tell anyone, will you? This is for yourself alone."

"Yes, yes, go on..."

"Well, yesterday evening, yesterday evening, before the murder, Hubert came home in a rage. He was swearing, he threatened to set fire to the village to make people stop their tongues. He had been to the Black Sun and had words with Blondel. They had both insulted each other. It wasn't the first time either: they nearly fought at the elections..."

"Hubert is only too glad to fight with anybody. It means nothing..."

"Do you think so, miss? That's all right, then. He frightens me, though...When I heard him shouting like that, I went to bed..."

"Is that true? Did you go to bed?"

"I swear I did, miss. I told the magistrate so this afternoon..."

"Still, it was your voice that made them open the door...You must know who it is that imitates your voice..."

"How can I tell?"

"You must have a notion. It can't be difficult for your brothers to imitate your voice..."

"I don't know anything about it. I don't indeed."

"You went to bed, you say...And did Hubert go to bed too?"

"You must never tell...No, he spent the night out of doors, with his gun; he went poaching in the forest...Don't tell, or he'll kill me..."

"Are you sure that he went poaching?"

"I think so. He came home in the morning with a couple of hares and a roebuck. He certainly didn't buy them in the town."

The voices were silent for an instant and then Madeleine resumed:

"Did Hubert go poaching all by himself?"

"No, he met Siméon and they came back together."

"I see...Now, listen to me, Zoé...and don't tell me any lies..."

"Oh, Mlle. Madeleine!"

"What was Élie doing all that time?"

"I don't know!..."

"So you won't tell me the truth'!...Very well, we're going away and we'll leave you behind...I don't want to have anything more to do with you!..."

"Oh, please, miss!..."

"You're not such a dainty bit of goods as to make us want to take you. It's no use giving you clothes: you wear them once and then there's nothing left of them but rags...You're only a little forest gadabout...You're never happy except when you're climbing up the trees...I've no use for you...You'd better go back for good to your birds and your squirrels and don't let's talk about it any more...Good-bye, Zoé!..."

But Zoé's voice was raised in entreaty:

"Oh, miss, you wouldn't do that!...It would kill me!...I don't care a rap for the birds and the squirrels and, if it gives you any pleasure, I promise I'll never speak to them again or tear my dress either...if only you'll take me along with Noël!"

"Are you very fond of Noël?"

"Oh, yes!..."

"Well," said Madeleine's voice, slowly, "we will take you with us and Noël, if you tell me what Élie was doing last night while Blondel was being murdered at the Black Sun...Do you understand me, now? Do you quite understand?"

"Oh, yes, miss...but I swear to you...I don't know!..."

"Very well!...That'll do!...Good-bye, Zoé!"

"No, no, listen!...I don't know, because Élie did not come home last night!..."

"Ah, you see!...That's something, at any rate!...He did not come home last night!...And you don't know what he did during the night?"

"No, I swear I don't!"

"Well, you've got to know, that's all!"

"Then you think it was he who killed Blondel?...What does it matter to you, miss, seeing that it was politics?"

"I'll tell you one thing, Zoé: I don't believe it was politics."

"Tell me what you think, then, and perhaps I shall understand."

"I think that Élie made a mistake when he murdered Blondel and that he intended to murder M. Patrice!"

"Oh, oh, oh!...I understand, miss, I understand you now!...Oh, what a terrible thing!...Oh! Oh!"

"Have you quite understood?"

"Yes."

"Then what will you do?"

"There! I promise to find out what Élie was doing on the night of the murder and to tell you everything!..."

"Mind, you've got to know by to-morrow! You saw Élie to-day: what did he say to you?"

"He said I was to bring some more ribbons..."

"I knew it! My hair-ribbon has gone...I noticed it, Zoé!...Give me back my ribbon, you little thief!"

"He thrashes me, when I don't bring him what he asks for..."

"Give me back my ribbon!"

"Here!...But Noël and I have no luck, either of us: we're always being beaten!"

"You can't care much about your brothers then."

"That depends on the day. Sometimes I don't."

Patrice, pale as death, listened, but heard no more. Soon he saw the two shadows gliding out of the wood-shed, taking a thousand precautions not to be seen. High up, on the right, the lamp burnt in the belvedere, lighting the waking hours of the man who was to introduce the bread-plant into France...

Patrice closed his window and sank into a chair. He could no longer doubt the hideous fact: they had wanted, they still wanted to murder him!...And the reason was simple enough: he had a rival!...

It was a rude shock for a young man who had always dreamt of leading a calm, prosaic life. He found himself crushed under the weight of this romantic and dangerous position; and, though his love for Madeleine was greater than anything, greater even than his fright, he resolved to leave the district the very next day, the examining magistrate notwithstanding.

Fortified with this decision, he rose from his seat. He felt that he must speak to Madeleine at once. He went downstairs.

Chapter VI

Patrice, hearing Zoé's voice in the kitchen, pushed open the door.

Gertrude was busy with her pots and pans. Zoé, sitting at the big round table, was darning stockings and socks, a pile of which lay in the basket beside her. Patrice looked into the basket without seeing. Suddenly, he saw!

It contained the sock of "the man who walked upside down!" He saw the piece of stuff, the size of a five franc piece, stitched to the sock with a whipseam.

And he flung out his hand to take it, thought he had taken it.

But he found Zoé in front of him, pale in the face; and, with a quick movement, she pushed the precious basket behind her.

Patrice was dumbfoundered by Zoé's attitude, but, above all, he regretted his own imprudence. Of course he was wrong to put the Vautrins' sister on the alert; but how could he imagine that she would know the value of the object that had suddenly attracted his attention? No, she could not possibly even suspect it; else would she have been foolish enough to darn those telltale socks, so to speak, in public? But then why had she leapt up in such a hurry, why had she moved the little work-basket out of Patrice' reach? Why was she so pale? And one more formidable question forced itself upon him: what were the socks of "the man who walked upside down" doing in Coriolis' house?...

All these questions, which remained unanswered, only heightened the importance of obtaining possession of the whipseam; and, pushing Zoé away, Patrice once more put out his hand to the basket. But the girl, nimble as a monkey, was by this time at the other side of the table, with the little basket in her hands.

"What's the matter with you, Zoé? Why won't you let me look at your work?" asked Patrice, in a panting voice, endeavouring to overcome, his agitation.

"My work's my own," said the girl, compressing her angry lips. "I don't like having my work touched. It makes me lose my stitches and then mademoiselle scolds me..."

"Whatever's the matter?" asked Gertrude, leaving off scouring her sauce-pans to interpose in a quarrel which she did not understand.

"The matter's this," said Patrice, in so threatening a tone that the cook, who at first thought that he was joking, began to shake on her old legs, "the matter's this, that I want to see what's in that basket!"

And he pointed with his excited finger to the work-basket in Zoé's hand.

Gertrude, who was standing behind Zoé, had only stretch out her arm to take the basket. The girl, who was not prepared for this move, screamed and let go the basket, but first, with her deft hand, snatched away the sock which Patrice wanted; and, as she still had the second sock of "the man who walked upside down" on her other hand, Patrice no longer coveted the basket itself. He chased Zoé, who ran round the table. Neither of them laughed; both rather glared at each other like enemies longing for each other's blood.

"Give that here!" he stormed.

"No!" yelled the girl. "It's mine! It's my work! It belongs to me!...Take what's left in the basket, if you want to!...I'll tell Mlle. Madeleine you took it!"

"Why won't you give me those?...The pair of socks you have in your hand: I'm not asking for the others..."

"Because I tell you this is my own work!...I won't have you go showing it to Mlle. Madeleine; so there!...She pays me to do the mending of the house and she'd give me the sack if she knew that I spent my time here darning my brothers' socks and stockings..."

"Ah, you see, the little baggage!" yelped Gertrude, unable to contain herself at this confession.

"Are those your brothers' socks?" asked Patrice, trying to steal up to Zoé.

But the other retreated:

"Of course, they're my brothers' socks!..."

"Well, give them to me and I sha'n't say a word to Madeleine."

But he received no reply. Zoé was in front of the kitchen-door to the yard. She darted out.

He flew after her. Zoé knew the way in the dark better than he did. He heard the quick patter of her wooden soles on the dry earth...She was still inside the grounds...He must prevent her from getting out. She was no doubt making for the little door, near the orchard, that opened on the woods.

Patrice ran across everything, without bothering about the path, trampling the plants under his winged feet, and he reached the little door just in time to see Zoé slam it in his face...But he pulled it open again; the child could not be far...And he saw her, twenty yards ahead of him; but to catch her was another matter...

She had taken off her clogs and was running barefoot. Now Zoé, barefooted, was a little bird. Patrice puffed and panted to no purpose; but he was determined to catch her: it was his one thought, his one object...He did not reflect that she would soon gain her lair, take refuge in her burrow, nor that this burrow was also that of the Vautrins, before which people generally passed—and then only when absolutely necessary—without making a sound or turning their heads.

Zoé was now near the dread hovel that squatted below the level of the road, with the eye of its window gleaming into the night. And Patrice did not notice that he was at the Vautrin's, until Zoé had opened the door of the cabin and flung herself inside, leaving him standing breathless on the bank, which she had leapt at a bound like a goat.

He now realized his imprudence. He had not even a weapon on him. And he had hunted the sister of the Three Brothers to her very lair. The child would, of course at once tell them of the incident of the whipseam. That amounted to informing them that Patrice no longer doubted the part which they had played in the murders at Saint-Martin-des-Bois, that he was following up the evidence by every means in his power, that, in any case, he had declared war against them...He felt that they would soon come out to look for him; and, if they found him...!

These swift reflections affected him all the more inasmuch as fitful sounds of voices now came from the cabin. Patrice turned from side to side, not knowing what to do nor where to conceal himself. He was standing against the house, at that moment; and the door had opened, casting a square patch of light upon the road. He had no time to reach the screen of poplars which surrounded the Vautrins' plot of ground at a few yards' distance. There was nothing but the house to hide him. If one of the brothers went round it on one side and another on the other, he was caught. Luckily there was the roof. It was a thatched roof, which, at the back, at the side opposite the road, sloped down almost to the ground. He hoisted himself upon it, lay flat and crawled up to the chimney. Soon, he heard Élie's the voice of one of the brothers replying to it. As he had feared, the two Vautrins were going round the house. He saw them, one coming along the road, the other taking a few steps within the allotment. Fortunately, the night was very dark. Zoé cried:

"He's gone back, let him be!...It's not worth while: leave it to me. I'll tell him a tale to-morrow."

And, suddenly, below him, a loud, rasping voice, obviously the mother's, grated:

"Come in! Come in! You can find him when you want him!"

The two men took a last glance around them and went in; the door was shut and the patch of light on the road disappeared.

Patrice was preparing to slide down from his roof, when he again plainly heard the rasping voice, saying: "But; Zoé, what made him run after you like that?"

And Zoé answered:

"He must have seen something, or he wouldn't have asked me for the sock!"

"Show it to me," said the gruff voice.

Surprised at hearing so distinctly what was said inside the cabin though the door was shut, Patrice examined the roof around him. A ray of light filtered through the thatch, almost under his elbow. It must be through this that the voices reached him. There was an opening where the thatch had worn away. He softly separated the old, rotten straw and was able not only to hear, but to see.

The ramshackle dwelling had no upper floor and no-ceiling. It was just a large cabin, divided into two rooms by a partition. Behind the partition, no doubt, was the room of the Three Brothers. What Patrice saw was the common living-room, with the chimney-place, a sort of recess, in which lay Mother Vautrin—old Barbe—impotent and helpless. A straw mattress on an iron frame, in a corner, must be Zoé's bed. He saw a rough table, some stools, a large, plain deal sideboard against the wall, a row of painted earthenware bowls on the mantel-shelf. Guns and game-bags hung on the walls. There were no boards, or tiles: the floor was just beaten earth. On the table stood a big loaf of bread, some heavy, deep plates, pewter spoons and forks, a bottle and glasses. A stew-pan simmered noisily on the hearth.

Patrice recognized the two albinos, who had resumed their seats at the table, with a knife in one hand and a slice of bread and meat in the other. They had begun their supper; but the plates and spoons had not been used. They had obviously not touched the soup. And yet it was late; but Hubert had not come in and they must be waiting for Hubert.

The was a candle on the table. Its light did not reach as far as the recess, but the flame in the hearth at times lit up old Barbe's horrible face, which rose out of the darkness in ghastly relief. The fiendish brilliancy of that witch-like glance was not to be withstood; and every-body knew that it made even Hubert lower his head. Oh, that ugly mug of Barbe's! The face of an antique mask, with hollows and protuber-ances that were always on the move, dead flesh astir around the one tooth that lingered in the yawning cavity of the mouth. No one had ever seen Barbe with any other covering to her head than the tangled locks of her white, hempen hair, which with an unconscious action, she kept on pushing back behind her ears, where they refused to stay because she was constantly shaking her head and tossing herself about on the bed which she never left. Such movements as she made were livelier even than Zoé's. Only, her legs were no longer able to bear her. She always had a stick near her, which she flung at her offspring whenever the fit seized her, at random. And the boys tamely brought the stick back to her. Zoé did not love her mother, for she got the stick oftener than fell to her rightful share; but Hubert and the albinos re-spected her, because she told them stories of the penal settlement where the father had done time, stories of which they never wearied.

When Patrice put his eye to his improvised peep-hole, he at once saw the old woman bending over the sock which Zoé held out to her. He recognized the whipseam. Barbe's head and Zoé's were brought still closer together; and then came a spell of silence, during which the albinos, who were attentively watching the scene in the recess, hushed the sound of their jaws. Then Zoé asked if she should bring the candle, to which the old woman replied that it was not worth while. Thereupon Zoé stood away from Barbe. The old woman chuckled in so gruesome a fashion that Patrice, on his thatch, shivered to the very marrow of his bones. And the albinos also began to chuckle. Zoé was the only one not to laugh. She pocketed the sock, while Barbe yelped:

"'Tain't yellow, it's red!"

Patrice was wondering what meaning to attach to this strange sen-tence accompanying the disappearance of the whipped sock in Zoé's pocket, when the door opened and Hubert walked in. He had his hat pulled over his eyes, carried a big cudgel and seemed very tired. He wore a smock-frock that came down to his knees.

He slammed the door to, with the heel of his boot, and stood be-fore them, without moving, with his hat over his eyes:

"Good evening, mother," he said. "Come on, you others! What's the matter with giving me a hand?"

The two albinos went up to him, slipped their huge hands under his smock and produced a number of packets of tobacco, which they found under the belt.

"That's the result of a glass on Mother Soupé's zinc counter," said Hubert, in explanation. "The shop had just got its stores in. I helped the old girl check them."

He spoke without stirring, his elbows glued to his body:

"Higher up," he instructed his brothers, who were still fumbling under the smock-frock for plunder.

Élie and Siméon pursued their quest up to the arm-pits and fished out two bottles of fine white wine, which they uncorked then and there in order to appreciate the aroma, giving their noses to the necks. They corked them up again and smacked their gluttonous tongues with the air of men who know a good thing when they see it. The old mother also asked for a smell:

"Where did you get that?" she asked, with sparkling eyes.

"It ought to be pretty good" replied Hubert. "I met the cellar-rat[1] and he knows."

"Did you show him your swag?" she asked, in astonishment.

"He showed me his," Hubert answered. "I met him at the corner of the Rue Verte. He was going along the wall, without stopping to ask his way of anybody. You know how he walks when he's going home at night: he keeps his fore-paws as stiff as if they were made of wood; and I'd said to myself before now, 'There's more in this than meets the eye: what does he hold his arms like that for?' So I went straight up to him, said good-evening, very politely, and shook him warmly by the hand. But he thought I shook it a bit too warmly and said, 'Not so hard!' I at once put my hand under his arm-pit. By gum! He had his bottle there...and one on the other side as well! Then I said, 'That's a nice thing, Mr. Inspector! Is that the way you look after the interests of the Republic! I'll bet you've taken a bribe from a reactionary! There's none but a rank monarchist would dare to buy the conscience of a decent man like yourself with two bottles of white! I'll tell our deputy, I will!' He handed me over the bottles and promised me two more like them, every month, to hold my tongue...And now let's have our soup, children."

He had flung his hat into a corner and Patrice obtained a close view of the terrible red head, with the green eyes, of which the cottagers dreamt at night. Hubert slid a stool between his legs and bent over the steaming plateful which Zoé handed him. Blowing upon it to cool it, he went on:

"Ay, that's all mug's talk! But I've a better yarn to tell you! To every dog his bone! Some coves spend their day in jawing: not me! I listen...and with both ears too! He learns most who lives longest!...How goes it, my birdlet?" he asked, catching Zoé a terrible clout, which set her whimpering. "Don't you like it? Why, I'm making kind enquiries after your health!"

"What are you knocking her about for?" asked Barbe. "She'll tell you. I saw her carrying on with Balaoo this afternoon, down Pierrefeu way."

"She's all right," said the mother, "and Balaoo wouldn't hurt a fly!"

"May be! But I've a sister and I want her to keep straight and do us credit! If not, we'll have a job of it getting her married!"

"That's true enough; but I tell you she's all right. Show Hubert your sock," yelped the old woman from the recess in which she lay.

The girl took out her sock and Patrice saw Hubert bend over it and examine even the other side of the wool. And Hubert gave the sock back to Zoé, who put it in her pocket, and Hubert said:

"'Tain't yellow, it's red!"

And the others once more roared with laughter.

"Lucky that we're not reckoning on her for her dowry," said Hubert, after emptying his porringer, which he lifted up to his heavy animal jaws. "But never you mind, my birdlet: you look to your morals and your virtue; and we can take you to the notary for all that, before we go on to the priest...Gentlemen!" he said, solemnly, placing his elbows on the table. "I told you there was a stroke of work to be done. Who's in it? Who speaks first?"

"Yo know the albinos aren't talkers," said the mother, "and they go where you go, like dogs. So fire away, cockie!"

Hubert turned to Zoé:

"I'll thank you to go into the woods and count a hundred!"

The girl was frightened at Hubert's attitude and did not wait to be told twice. She opened the door of the cabin, went out and shut it behind her. Patrice thought of following her and was thanking his stars for giving him the opportunity of at last obtaining possession of the precious sock, when; thrusting his head forward, he caught sight of the child and saw that she did not move away from the house, but, on the contrary, remained by the door, with her ear to the latch. He stayed where hewas ans, puzzled by Hubert's last words, began once more to look and listen. Hubert had drawn himself up like an animal stretching itself, lifted his clenched fists to the rafters, and dropped back with his elbows on the table and his chin between his enormous hands:

"Two hundred thousand!" he said.

The albinos started; and old Barbe jumped with excite ment on her truckle-bed.

"Yes," continued Hubert, without waiting to enjoy the effect produced. "Yes, but there may be claret!"

"Pity!" muttered Barbe. "I think there's been too much bleeding in these parts lately!...You'll see it'll lead to trouble!...As your late lamented father said to me on his death bed, 'Don't you go in for claret![2]"

"I know what you mean to say, mother," said Hubert, "but you express yourself badly. Camus, Lombard and Blondel were not bled, but nicely throttled and hanged, by one who knew his business. Struck me as quite uncalled for, all the same. Because you have a few words with a man on politics, that's no reason to wish him dead. Else, of course, one'd go cooking everybody's goose!"

"Well, Hubert," said Barbe, shaking her horrible pate, "no one's calling you to account, but remember that I couldn't live without the lot of you...You could be masters of the whole country if you chose, but there are ways and ways; and slanging Blondel in a public-house, just before his death, is not the way to ease your old mother's mind."

Hubert looked at the old woman and then leered at the two albinos, who gave him a leery look in return.

"I never laid a finger on him," he said. "But may be there are folk who are after revenging family-quarrels...In any case, it was pretty work. The beak can't make head or tail of it. And then the footmarks on the ceiling: that was funny, if you like!"

"Don't you be too funny, Hubert. Your late lamented father used to say that, if he'd always kept serious, he wouldn't have had to spend twenty years in quod before settling down respectably here!"

"That'll do, mother! You've no more sense than the hind-legs of the sergeant of gendarmes. You'd send me to the scaffold if anyone heard you!...I don't like unnecessary words...Listen to the albinos: they're not jawing!"

Siméon and Élie had not uttered a word since the three murders at Saint-Martin were first mentioned. They were satisfied to look at their brother with stealthy curiosity or to look at each other, exchanging quick glances that would have given cause for reflection to anyone who noticed them. The Three Brothers seemed mutually to suspect one another of those crimes, or else each wanted to make the others believe that he suspected them of crimes which he had perhaps committed himself. No one ever knew the whole truth with the two albinos, who were always silent and reserved; and there were a good many matters on which Hubert had long given up trying to make them open their lips. Nor did Hubert tell all that he himself did. There was a natural and indissoluble partnership between them, there were common interests that bound them together in life and death; but this did not prevent each of them from having his own little private affairs which had nothing to do with "Three Brothers Ltd."

The strange murders of Camus, Lombard and Blondel had formed the subject of more than one conversation and more than one silence among the Vautrins; and it was not at all surprising that the allusion to those astonishing and still quite recent crimes should stop the conversation for a moment, even when it promised to be as interesting as that which Hubert had started.

Old Barbe was the first to revert to it, for the three others seemed steeped in thought, filling and emptying their glasses silently. Hubert now appeared to be hesitating. He said, in answer to Barbe:

"It's a big risk, but nothing venture, nothing have."

"Tell us, anyway."

"Well listen...I was at Mother Soupé's, checking her fresh lot of tobacco with her."

"She sent for you, of course!" grinned Barbe.

"I don't think!...But she's too polite to refuse the Vautrins' services, that's certain sure!"

"If you'd only hold your tongue, mother," said Siméon, "we might get to learn something."

"We were at the counter, in the corner of the shop, when Switch came in and asked for half a noggin and there was another came in with him, a skinny little bloke whom I didn't know by sight. He took white wine, that one did. I soon grasped, from their bragging, that the little 'un was a clerk in the works t'other side of the Montancel, where they're driving a tunnel. D'ye twig? There's no railway there. Well, they're building one, you know. If you don't know, you can take it from me; and there are five hundred workmen, that's something, five hundred workmen who've got to be paid...in ready money, mind you! Here, Élie, you're good at figures: just tell me how much that makes, at six or seven francs a day."

"If they got ten francs, that'd be a hundred and fifty thousand francs a month."

"Well, old chap, what the contractors want at the end of the month is two hundred thousand..."

"Then there are more than five hundred..."

"Well, it seems there's important works over there: the little bloke who came in with Switch complained that they were miles from anywhere, that it was no catch, no getting there..."

"But," Siméon broke in, "those works were to have been done ten years ago..."

"Can't help that: they were started two months since. And, every month—do you follow me, you two? Are you listening, mother?—every month, the workmen have to be paid. To pay them, you want money; and where do you find money?...You find it in the banks..."

"Do you want to rob the bank at Clermont?" asked Barbe, whose face, fierce with greed, was now stretched towards the three men.

"What rot will you talk next, mother? There are times when you seem right off your chump," said Hubert. "Can't you let the bank be? The money's got to leave the bank, that's sure. The workmen aren't going to the bank for their money, are they? That'd cost too much in fares."

"Have you learnt the road the wages'll travel by?"

"Now you're asking questions."

"And how did you find out?"

"Well, I followed Switch and his pal without their knowing. They went to Mathieu's to take a glass. The little bloke had his back teeth well afloat. He did nothing but prate about the works and about everything. I listened to them, ay, in a corner where they couldn't see me...and I now know which way the wages go," Hubert concluded, lowering his voice in a sinister fashion.

The two others simply said:

"Ah!"

Barbe could stand the tension no longer: she beckoned to Hubert, to come nearer her bed; and the brothers went with him. And all four of them, mouth to ear and ear to mouth, said things which did not take long to tell, but which, unfortunately, Patrice could not hear.

When the secret palaver was over, Siméon drew himself up and asked:

"And what did Switch say to that?"

"Oh, Switch didn't seem to like it!" replied Hubert. "I think he'd have liked to be rid of the job. The little 'un stayed on and slept at Mathieu's. Switch said to him, 'and now, old man, you go to bed. You're drunk. To-morrow morning, you'll be glad to think that you've only been speaking to an honest man.'"

"Switch doesn't half fancy himself!" Élie spat out.

Chapter VI

The three men had gone back to the table. There was a long pause. The old woman's head had withdrawn into the shadow, at the back of the recess, and was no longer visible. Everybody was thinking.

"Well, who speaks first?" Hubert said, at last. "I'm waiting to hear you."

And his green eyes wandered round those in the room, from the recess to the table.

"There's sure to be claret," said Barbe's voice, from the depths of her cave.

"And what about it?" asked Hubert, peevishly.

"What about it! What about it! It's much better not to lose our position in the country for a job that mayn't come...Our deputy would never forgive us...And we have Zoé's future to think of...We've all we want here," said Barbe. "And, if you lads got pinched, I should kick the bucket before the week was out!"

"You never think of anyone but yourself, mother," growled Hubert. "All right, we'll say no more about it!"

"I didn't say so!" Siméon declared, sententiously.

"Nor I," said Élie.

"And suppose there's claret?" the mother insisted.

"Well, there'll be claret, that's all!" concluded Hubert, lighting his pipe.

Zoé's voice was now heard at the door, asking leave to come in.

"Come in!" cried the mother.

"Where were you?" asked Hubert.

"Behind the door," said the girl, "listening to you. Better me than the gendarmes!"

And, when they all raised their hands to clout her, she rapped out, hurriedly:

"P'raps there wouldn't be any claret with Balaoo! Remember Barrois' trunk!"

"The kid's right!" said Hubert. "We ought to see Balaoo at once."

"That's easy enough," said Zoé. "He's at his own place."

"Let's go there now."

"Yes, let's go."

"You're never going to leave me all alone!" whined Barbe.

"Business is business!" said Hubert. "No one'll eat you! Come along, Zoé."

"Oh, it's no use taking me!" said Zoé. "The porter has orders not to let me in. I'm not on the best of terms with General Captain!"

"Come on, all the same!"

62

They took down their guns, went out and crossed the road, with the girl. Zoé led the way over the fields. Patrice saw their dark outlines entering the forest.

He climbed down from his roof and returned to Coriolis'. That night, he was not disturbed by any sounds outside. He was so tired that he even dozed off from time to time.

[1] "The cellar-rat" is an inspector whose duty is to superintend the manufacture of alcohol in the distiller's districts. He examines private cellars and takes stock of the produce of the stills.— Author's Note

[2] Blood—AUTHOR'S NOTE

Chapter VII

Patrice was out of bed at four o'clock in the morning. He dressed in the dark, so as not to arouse the suspicions of anyone in the neighbourhood.

To see the magistrate and then be off: that was the great thing. The rest was mere politeness. And he continued to think that his safety depended on the swiftness of his departure.

The threat of the albinos, after his imprudent pursuit of Zoé, still rang in his ears:

"We'll find him to-morrow!"

Now to-morrow was to-day!

And he tied his neck-tie inside out.

Then he wrote a line to Coriolis and Madeleine and left it on his table, where it would be seen.

An ostler was opening the yard-gate when he reached the inn. At the same moment, Michel, the driver of the Chevalet diligence, came up, went straight to his little office in the yard and turned over the pages of the register containing the names of the passengers who had booked their seats. Patrice booked one for himself, inside. It would be time enough later to show himself on the top, when they were far away...

Having done this, he felt easier in his mind and asked for the magistrate.

A sleepy little scrub of a chambermaid, who was still rubbing her eyes, told him that M. de Meyrentin was already in the bar-room, which had been closed to all comers since the tragedy. Patrice went there, expecting to find the examining-magistrate at breakfast, instead of which he discovered him perched on all-fours on the top of a cup-board near the door that opened on the street.

Patrice did not waste time in astonishment at this very extraordinary position for a. magistrate:

"Monsieur!" he cried. "You were right! There's an accomplice!"

"I should think so, young man!" chuckled M. de Meyrentin, from the top of his cupboard. "Of course there's an accomplice! I'm following up his traces now. I told you that the murderer could only have come in through the door and that, as he could not have entered by the bottom of the door, he must have got in by the top...The murderer—we'll call him the accomplice, if you like; any way, the man whom I believe to be the instrument of the Three Brothers—climbed over your heads to this cupboard, where he crouched down...No wonder you couldn't make it out...You see, I am continuing my enquiry upside down and what I don't find down below I discover up above. There are traces of the murderer everywhere, on the top of the furniture. There are three big pieces of furniture, two cupboards and a sideboard, on which some strange individual has literally moved about, leaping from one to the other with amazing ease and agility...And now listen to me carefully..."

And M. de Meyrentin, to tell his story to Patrice more comfortably, invited him to stand on a chair, while he himself sat down on the top of the cupboard, with his legs swinging to and fro.

"But it's you I'm asking to listen to me!" the young man ventured to sigh.

"Will you listen to me, or will you not?" roared M. de Meyrentin, giving two loud kicks with his impatient heels to the panels of the cupboard. "Listen, M. Saint-Aubin: you can't understand yet...and I dare say I look very queer to you on the top of my cupboard...but there's nothing queer in life: everything is natural, everything is linked up...Be quiet! Don't interrupt! Listen to me!...I'm going to put a momentous question to you...do you understand? Mo—men—tous!...Listen to me carefully, M. Saint-Aubin, and then answer me: are you sure, are you quite sure...that the murderer, yes, the murderer...Now, think!...Take your time! There's no hurry!...Are you quite sure that you heard him speak?..."

"Why, of course I heard him!..."

"Think!...Think!...Try and remember!...It may have been an illusion of your ears...And tell me, tell me carefully: you are sure that he spoke?"

"Why, yes, yes, yes!..."

"Oh, what a pity!...What a pity!...What a pity!..."

"But what do you think?..."

"Nothing, since you say that he spoke!"

"You are talking in riddles, monsieur le juge," said Patrice. "And I don't understand you. But I will tell you something that's quite clear:

last night, I ran after the Vautrins' sister, who was mending a sock with a whip seam that bore a striking resemblance to the pattern which you were examining on the ceiling when I came in!"

"Oh, really? Very interesting, very interesting!" said M. de Meyrentin, fixing his eye-glasses on his nose and looking down at the young man at his feet. "And why was she running away?"

"Because I tried to take the sock from her."

"Then she knew the value of it?"

"I doubt that, because she was mending it before people...But the fact is that she ran away to where she lives and showed the sock to her mother, who uttered a strange sentence which I have remembered because it was repeated by the Three Brothers: "Tain't yellow, it's red!'"

""Tain't yellow, it's red!'" exclaimed the magistrate, jumping down to the floor like an india-rubber ball and bounding up again under Patrice' nose. ""Tain't yellow, it's red!' You heard that? And at the Vautrins'?...You've been to the Vautrins'?...And they let you get away alive?..."

"Monsieur, I was on the roof!"

"Aha! So you approve of my system!...Monsieur, there's nothing like conducting one's enquiries upside down!...But tell me everything, tell me all you saw, heard, thought, guessed, felt, everything..."

The other told him everything, in full detail. The magistrate took hurried notes. He did not interrupt Patrice once, until the young man began to talk of the job which the Three Brothers were preparing, the two hundred-thousand-franc job. Here, M. de Meyrentin could not refrain from displaying his delight and satisfaction...Ah, at last!...They would have them!...They would catch the Vautrins in the act!...And high time too!...And quite easy and simple!...They had only to make discreet enquiries from the Montancel railway-contractors about the road by which the wages would be conveyed...and to lay the trap...Not one of the villains would escape!...They'd bag them all: the Three Brothers and the accomplice...and the rest, if more there were...the whole gang of them!...They would purge the district, in short! M. de Meyrentin would have embraced Patrice, had his magisterial dignity not prevented him...

"And what do you say the accomplice' name is?"

"Something like...something like Bilbao."

"Bilbao? That's a Spanish name...However, we'll see...But, above all, not a word, young man, not, a word to anybody!...Why, you're a hero! A hero on the housetop, on the Vautrins' housetop!...But there! Let's hope that that job is not meant to come off at once!...They must have time to prepare it...and I too!...You don't remember anything that could put me on the right track, I suppose?.."

"The fact of their going to see their accomplice in the forest last night proves..."

"Why, of course! Of course! It must be coming off to-day...It's a great pity you couldn't hear, all the conversation...What we must do is to find the little man...you know, 'the little bloke' at Mathieu's— without a word to Mathieu himself—the little bloke who was drunk and who told everything to the other one...It's unfortunate that you can't remember the name of the other one, the man to whom the little one told everything..."

"Oh, but I remember now!" said Patrice, suddenly. "Hubert called him Switch..."

"Switch?" said M. de Meyrentin, giving an emphatic start, while his expression grew more and, more quizzical. "That's capital...Switch!...I congratulate you...Switch!..."

"Do you know him?" asked Patrice.

"Ye-es, slightly," replied the magistrate, evasively.

"And now, young man, I must go; I have not a moment to lose."

"I am going too, monsieur le juge, and I have not a moment to lose either. I confess to you that, after my pursuit of Zoé, I don't care to stay in the Vautrins' neighbourhood. And, as the trains don't suit, I am taking the diligence..."

"Oh, is that settled?" asked M. de Meyrentin, with a certain surprise.

"I have just booked my seat."

The magistrate seemed to be turning something over in his mind. Then:

"Very well," he said. "Good-bye, monsieur."

And he gave him his hand. But Patrice held it for a moment:

"You appeared to understand that sentence, "Tain't yellow, it's red,' and you have not told me what it means..."

"Oh, it's a private matter! Good-bye."

And he walked away, leaving Patrice to wonder whether the magistrate was not making fun 'of him.

Patrice called for a bowl of milk; and presently the time came when the diligence was due to start. But he perceived that it was not yet ready. It had been brought out into the yard, but the horses were not harnessed to it and it stood on three legs, or, properly speaking, three wheels: the place of the fourth was taken by a jack. And the young man learnt from the angry passengers that Michel, the driver, had discovered, at the last moment, that the fourth wheel had broken down. He had sent it to the wheelwright, who promised that it would be ready in an hour but no sooner, for it wanted three new spokes.

The driver walked across the yard. He was in a vile temper and only grunted in reply to the questions put to him by the passengers. Patrice asked him very politely if he really intended to start in an hour and received so surly and unintelligible an answer that he felt utterly cast down. His stay at Saint-Martin-des-Bois had proved unpleasant up to the very last moment. He would not forget his holiday in a hurry!

To while away the time, he tried to see M. de Meyrentin again; but Roubion told him that the magistrate had gone to wake up Mme. Godefroy, the postmistress.

The hour passed and the five disconsolate passengers grouped around the great motionless diligence were informed that the wheelwright wanted another hour to fix a piece of wood to the felloe. They thereupon decided to abandon their journey for that day.

Patrice, in spite of his reluctance to change his plans, seeing that the diligence was playing him false and more firmly decided than ever to get away, resolved to run to the station, where there was still time for him to take the train. On reaching the station, the first person he saw was Zoé, who seemed to be looking out for his arrival.

After what had happened the night before, he felt certain that she was there on his account and that, failing to see him at the manor-house, she had told her brothers, who had sent her to keep a watch on him. For aught he knew, they might at that moment be busy wrecking the line somewhere, with a view to causing his death. After all, the mystery of the former attempt had not yet been cleared up; and the most that the examining-magistrate allowed to leak out was that he had found a few footprints near the Cerdogne tunnel which were exactly like those on the ceiling in the Black Sun.

Clear-sighted as were Zoé's eyes, Patrice succeeded in eluding them and returned to the inn in an unspeakable state of collapse. Heavens, how he wished himself back in his dark and quiet little office, with its blotting-pad and its inkstand, in the Rue de l'Écu! He swore that he would never leave it again, except to get married; and even then...!

An hour elapsed, during which he did not catch a glimpse of M. de Meyrentin, look for him as he might. At last, the wheel arrived and, together with the wheel, a fresh array of passengers, newly alighted from the train, who were taking advantage of the delay of the diligence to make use of this unhoped-for connection with the Chevalet district.

There were fourteen of these new passengers. Never had the yard of the Black Sun contained such a crowd. It did not occur to Patrice to feel astonished at this rush of travellers nor at their curious demeanour. And yet, for common people who had done a journey together, was it not difficult to understand that they had nothing to say to one another? There were peasants among them who wore their smocks very clumsily: for instance, they did not know where to find their pockets, as though they had forgotten where they were put. Then again, these yokels were sad-looking men, with white faces or yellow, never red and wrinkled, like the ordinary faces of the Morvan peasants.

They asked no questions of Roubion. He, on the other hand, asked questions of them, but they only gave vague answers and turned their backs on him. Roubion felt so greatly puzzled that he went and woke up Mme. Roubion, who sat down at her window, in her nightgown, with her hair in curlers, to watch the departure of those extraordinary customers.

Patrice, who had retired to a corner of the room, left it only to take his seat in the diligence. When about to do so, he was alarmed at the crowd that filled the inside, especially as two more passengers appeared at that moment, carrying between them a small portmanteau which seemed to be very heavy. They packed themselves and the portmanteau into the coach and, strange to say, none of the occupants protested against the introduction of that luggage into a space already so well filled.

Patrice had come down from the step. Mme. Roubion called out to him:

"Why don't you go outside, M. Patrice?...The weather's fine!..."

The young man raised his flushed face. How loudly she had bawled his name! It must have been heard all over the village...as far as the Vautrins', at the end of the road...

He made a hasty reply, for politeness' sake, and, so as not to attract attention to himself, scrambled up to the top, which was empty, whereas the inside and the coupé[3] were crammed. And he flung himself into a corner of the tarpaulin, out of the way of the trunks which Michel, assisted by the ostler standing on a ladder, was strapping down.

The horses were put to and stood shaking their bells impatiently.

"It'll be a nice time to get there!" grumbled Michel, adding, between his teeth, "If we get there at all!..."

Chapter VII

But Patrice did not hear him. He thought only of concealing himself, he wondered if he would pass unperceived when the diligence entered the forest near the Three Brothers' cabin.

A start was made at last, amid much horn-blowing, whip-flourishing and jolting over the cobbles of the Rue Neuve, and the vehicle lumbered off at a slow trot.

Before they entered the forest, Patrice ventured to glance at the Vautrins' shanty: it was closed and there was nothing suspicious on that side; but his eyes, looking up higher, at the manor-house, saw the dainty figure of Madeleine waving her handkerchief from the little door that opened on the woods.

Patrice felt a pang at his heart: not that that organ swelled straightway with immoderate love, but rather with a sudden fear produced by this imprudent act.

"Well," he said to himself, "I don't call that at all clever of her. I should have thought that she knew better!"

However, he recovered his composure in the forest. Every yard that took him farther from Saint-Martin added a trifle to his peace of mind.

It was not to last. They had not gone much over a mile through the trees, when Michel gave an oath and pulled in his horses, one of which had suddenly shied:

"Oh, it's that Zoé!" snarled Michel through his toothless gums.

Zoé!...So she was everywhere...everywhere that he, Patrice, was! She was pursuing him...Perspiring with fright, he huddled under his tarpaulin, but she most certainly saw him, for she called out:

"Ah, good-morning, M. Patrice!...So you are off!...Where are you going?..."

And, when the other failed to reply, she yelled a "Good-bye!" to him, accompanying the salutation with a fit of laughter that sent a cold shiver down the young man's back. Long after Zoé had disappeared from sight, pursued by a parting cut of Michel's whip, Patrice beheld her ominous little figure skipping in the white dust of the road.

"Do you think that we shall reach Saint-Barthelemy before dark?" Patrice asked the driver.

"Not before ten o'clock to-night!" replied the other, ill-temperedly, cracking his whip. "We sha'n't be at Mongeron, for lunch, till two."

The prospect of travelling part of the night through the forest was far from delightful to Patrice, who relapsed into his very gloomiest thoughts.

Michel was clearly not a talkative person. He did not even turn his head when the young man spoke to him; he seemed very busy with his horses and also with the road, which he watched carefully and constantly with his little red lidded eyes. Patrice was surprised at being alone on the roof, when there were so many inside, and imparted this reflection to Michel, who replied, drily:

"That's their business!"

Most of the passengers stepped out when the diligence began to toil up hill. Only the two travellers with the portmanteau did not stir from their corner on the back seat, near the coupe. They had put the portmanteau under the seat. Michel remained on his box and Patrice did not get down either. He felt not the least inclination to stroll along the roadside and gather wild flowers.

The journey continued thus, monotonously and with out incident; until Mongeron, where they arrived at two o'clock and where a cold lunch was served.

Patrice had thought, for a moment, of sleeping at Mongeron and resuming his journey next morning in a hired carriage, so as to avoid going through the forest at night; but he ended by preferring the risk of travelling, even at night, as one of a numerous company to that of staying in that lonely inn right in the middle of the woods.

Nothing happened during lunch. When the diligence started, the passengers took the same seats as in the morning. They were chattier now and, when climbing the hills, began to talk to one another like old friends. They even looked as though they were exchanging confidences around the diligence, which they were careful to keep in sight.

Patrice more than ever regretted the fatal notion that had made him hit upon this way of escaping from Saint-Martin. The high-road, since he had seen Zoé, now appeared to him the most dangerous of all, especially since it was beginning to grow dark. They had long ago come to the tall, thick trees which gave this southern forest its gloomy name of the Black Woods. The daylight made its way with difficulty through the dense foliage. And, under the great trees, what a silence! The crack of Michel's whip alone from time to time awakened the echoes of that wilderness.

However, Michel was no longer so silent as in the morning. The Mongeron innkeeper had given him of his best and filled his drinking-can with good white wine. Patrice heard him talking to himself at intervals, with many a knowing head-shake. He seemed to have resigned himself to something known to himself alone and kept on saying:

"Go ahead!...Go ahead!..."

Chapter VII

It might be six o'clock in the evening when they arrived at the Côte du Loup, so-called because the hill is overhung by a rock which, with a slight stretch of the imagination, almost resembles the shape of a wolf. The coach was once more emptied of its passengers; and Michel, dozing on his box, was letting the reins drag on the horses' cruppers, when he was suddenly roused from his slumbers by a voice that shouted to him from the road:

"Don't go to sleep, Switch!"

Patrice's own eyes were suddenly opened!...Switch!...Who had shouted, "Switch?"...And whom was it meant for?...He bent over the road and saw standing by the horses a man who, until then, had stayed inside the coach on all the hills, one of the two who had hustled him on the step, in the morning, as they were lifting in the small, heavy portmanteau. He was a little wizened chap, with a cap on his head, and his appearance corresponded pretty closely with the description which Hubert Vautrin had given when telling his brothers about "Switch and the little bloke."

The little wizened chap had his nose in the air and was looking up, half-jestingly, at the driver, who playfully gave him one with his whip between the legs.

Patrice moved his eyes from the road to the box of the diligence:

"What!" he said, with an agitation which he did not strive to conceal. "Are you Switch?"

Michel did not reply.

"Excuse me, monsieur," Patrice insisted, "but are you Switch?"

"What's that to do with you? My name's Michel Pottevin, but they can me Switch, in these parts, for fun. It's a nickname like, which Mother Vautrin gave me, as a lark, in the old days. We used to dance together, at Saint-Martin Fair, before she lost the use of her legs. She's no good at that now. Seems that, in her jargon, 'Switch' stands for 'the driver.' Perhaps it means that because of my whip: true enough, I always look as if I had a switch in my hand, same as a man who goes fishing. Is that all you want to know? Are you satisfied?"

Patrice was unable to reply at once. The wizened little fellow in the cap had scrambled up beside Michel and was whispering in his ear. The other shrugged his shoulders. The little chap got down again and Switch said:

"Well and good, if it suits you. I'm not keen on it, myself!".

A strange gleam suddenly lit up the situation in Patrice' bewildered brain. Was there ever such luck as his? Here was he taking the diligence to escape adventures and finding himself let in for one of the most dangerous affairs imaginable since the attack on the Lyons mail: a coach-robbery! How was it that he had seen nothing, guessed nothing since the morning? His brain must be full of past events, not to have noticed what was being plotted around him! Oh, he was sure of it now! The two-hundred-thousand-franc job was to come off presently, at once, perhaps!...Yes, yes, it was quite simple, too simple!...The heavy little portmanteau contained the cash to pay the workmen; and it did not take much to guess the kind of cashiers that all those passengers were!...He understood it all: the two and a half hours' delay of the diligence; M. de Meyrentin's persistency in remaining with Mme. Godefroy, the postmistress, whom he had gone to pull out of bed, immediately after his conversation with Patrice!...Ah, the magistrate had taken all the time he wanted, after contriving the trick of the wheel, to arrange for the protection of the two hundred thousand francs!...It was he who had sent to the prefecture, by special train, for all these sham peasants, with the aid of whom he hoped to lay hold of the Vautrin gang, the whole gang, the Three Brothers and the mysterious accomplice!...

Patrice's only hope now was that the plan might prove too simple. He thought that the Three must already be warned and that it was not for nothing that Zoé had kept watch at the station and in the forest. They would never dare risk it. And Patrice was now crossing the Black Woods guarded by a whole regiment of detectives...

The poor lad tried to screw up his courage with these arguments, for he was utterly down-hearted. The last discovery had done for him. And, above all, he was angry with M. de Meyrentin for not warning him.

It grew darker and darker. It was not yet night, but the dank dusk that fell from the arch of gloomy verdure under which the coach was now driving was more impressive than night itself, for the darkness did not seem natural, but rather contrived with sinister intentions by the evil genii of the forest.

"Don't be silly, get back inside!" said Michel to the little wizened man, who was trotting along, cracking his jokes, under the horses' noses. "I don't like the Côte du Loup!..."

At these words, the passengers on the road manoeuvred so as to keep closer around the diligence, gradually, without any apparent order. It was easy fat Patrice to see that the approaches to the carriage were well guarded. Those gentry were ready for all eventualities, with their hands in their pockets or under their smocks, doubtless concealing their weapons.

"Mr. Switch," said Patrice, creeping nearer to the driver, "it was I who spoke to M. de Meyrentin, the magistrate, this morning!"

This time, the other turned right round on his seat: "Ah, it was you who discovered the job got up by the Three Brothers, was it? Well, you've done a pretty thing, my boy, you have!" said Switch, lighting his pipe. "I can't congratulate you."

"What makes you say that?" asked Patrice, taken aback.

"Why, you must be fond of whacks to mix yourself up with such things!...Well, there, you're a plucky one!...I don't care, after all...I'm all right with them; they won't hurt me...and I sha'n't do anything to make them, you take my word....But, as for you, my lad, since you've chosen to prate, you'd be better off if you were safe at home!"

"Then I oughtn't to have said anything?" asked the young man, not knowing which of his saints to invoke and mechanically wiping the perspiration from his forehead.

"You'd have done wiser not to," said the other.

"Not as far as you're concerned, at any rate! If I'd said nothing, you would have been much more certain to be attacked and there would have been no one to protect you!"

"It's not me," replied Michel, logically enough, "it's not me they'd have attacked: it's the cash-box of those contractor-chaps; and a fat lot I care for the cash-box of those contractor-chaps!...There may be a million inside, for all I know!...It's not for me, is it?...The others would have taken it away quietly; and I should have gone my road, that's all, see?...Now, let's understand each other...I know nothing: it's you who know all about it...The judge says to me, the Vautrins are going to do so-and-so!...I, I don't say no, I say nothing!...It's the first time they've been informed against...and it's you who've had the cheek to do it!...Well, my lad, I hope it may bring you luck!..."

All these words of Michel's, while giving Patrice a sense of the magnitude of his courage and the immensity of his imprudence, filled him with the greatest confusion.

He felt a fool and bitterly regretted interfering in this matter of the two hundred thousand francs which might turn out so badly for him.

"But, when all is said," he sighed, "you surely don't believe that the Three Brothers will dare to attack us, protected as we are!"

"I don't say that they will," the driver retorted, obstinately, "but I don't see why they shouldn't, if they want to!"

"Do you think they won't realize that all this pack of sham peasants are only coming with us to protect the cash?"

"Oh, if it's they who are to do the job, you may be sure they know all about it by now!...They must have watched us from more than one corner of the road!..."

"Can they follow us as easily as all that?"

"Oh, they're as quick as quick can be!...There's not a quicker animal in the forest, that's sure...They'll have seen us from in front, from behind and from both sides; and they have cross-roads which take them all round is without our suspecting it for a minute!...Yes, my gentleman, you might almost say it was they that made the forest and not Providence!"

"I've heard a lot about what they do in the forest..."

"And about what they don't do, I expect!...I wasn't born yesterday—you're so something more of a chicken—and it's longer ago than yesterday since people began to speak of the Mystery of the Black Woods!"

"What's the Mystery of the Black Woods?"

"You'd better ask the people who sometimes travelfrom the Chevalet country to the Cerdogne country. They may answer...but there's not one who'll ever complain, you bet your boots!"

"Is it truee what they tell about travellers being stopped by a gang of masked highwaymen?"

"Oh, that's very old, very old!...That's a worn-out trick, the trick of the black masks...Nowadays, when people travel by diligence, they feel almost comfortable...provided they behave properly to the Wolf Stone."

"What do you mean by behaving properly to the Wolf Stone?"

"Have you a five-franc piece about you?"

"What for?"

"Give it to me!" said the other, taking the coin which Patrice produced from his pocket.

And he threw it to the little wizened man, who stood in the midst of the group, cap in hand. The little man picked up the five-franc piece, without asking for explanations, and climbed the bank a few steps away. This bank was surmounted by the enormous Wolf Stone which was seen so clearly from the bottom of the hill. He hung on to the slope and emptied the contents of his cap into a hollow in the stone, which emitted a silvery sound. Then he threw the five-franc piece in and scrambled down again.

Patrice watched this performance without understanding a bit of it. His eyes wandered from the Wolf Stone to the passengers and the driver. Michel chuckled with delight at seeing his mystification:

"What you have just seen, young gentlemen, is the wolf's pence"—"Click, clack!"--with the whip--"that's it: the wolf's pence"—and he gave another "Click, clack!" for the wolf's pence.—"Catch the idea? You don't? Well, when a traveller has paid his wolf' spence, he can feel more or less comfortable between Cerdogne and Chevalet, young gentleman!...Now that you have given your five francs, I could tell you to set your mind at rest, if this was an ordinary day. But to-day it's another pair of shoes: there's the matter of that wages chest downstairs, young gentleman!"

"Then is that the Mystery of the Black Woods?"

"Part of it..."

"So they'll come presently and fetch the wolf's pence? The men below have paid so as not to rouse the Vautrins' suspicions, I suppose?" added Patrice, knowingly.

"No names, please: they don't like that!...They come and fetch the wolf's pence when they feel inclined. Sometimes, the pence remain in their hollow stone for a fortnight at a time...and nobody dares touch the money. Travellers go and look at it sometimes out of curiosity, on their way out and back again, before adding their own contribution...Oh, they've seen funny things, believe me, things which can't be explained and which prove that the forest does whatever those beggars want it to!"

"For instance?" asked Patrice, looking forward more confidently to the end of the journey, for, the more he saw of his fellow-passengers, the more he felt persuaded that they knew what they were about: he had watched them for some time moving among the bushes that lined the road, with an easy daring that reassured him where he sat, on the roof.

Old Switch stood up on his box, blinked his eyes and looked at something in the distance behind him. Then he sat down again and said:

"There, I expect it'll be all right, to-day!...I'm just as pleased, you know!...Well, what are you staring at me like that for? Perhaps you'd like me to tell you the story of Barrois' trunk?..."

"Barrois' trunk!" thought Patrice. "Why, that's what Zoé was talking about!" And he said, aloud, "If you do, I sha'n't regret my five francs."

For Patrice, without being stingy—far from it—had a thrifty mind.

"The story's well known in the Chevalet country," said the other, nodding his head, "and in Cerdogne too, believe me; but the people are

76

shy with strangers; and the story of Barrois' trunk is one which they tell among themselves, like all the stories of the Mystery of the Black Woods, which might put things into the heads of the police, see?...And there's no need of police. Who could do their work in the forest better than those who look after the wolf's pence? But they've got to be paid, that's only fair...Well, it's because of somebody who not only refused to pay, but stiared to steal the wolf's pence, that the trouble with Barrois' trunk came about!...Yes, young gentleman."

"But is it a real story, which really happened?"

"It happened just behind me, where you're sitting, young man...on the exact spot!...Well, there, you've heard speak of Blondel, the man who was murdered the other day at Roubion's?"

Had Patrice heard speak of Blonde!...He gave his name; and the driver knew his connection with the tragic adventure of the unfortunate commercial traveller.

"Well, this Blondel who was murdered—I don't know by whom: it's none of my business—had a friend on the road, like himself, who thought himself very clever and made fun of him because Blondel had told him that, each time the Chevalet people passed the Wolf Stone, they paid their wolf's pence, to bring them luck. Blondel himself gave his half a franc like the others, when he took the Chevalet diligence, and made no secret of it either...I must tell you that, at that time, he hadn't had any political troubles with the Three Brothers: between you and me, politics are enough to make the best of friends quarrel, aren't they?...Well, Blondel's friend, a certain Barrois, Désiré Barrois, started betting that he'd go past the Wolf Stone and never give his half a franc and that nothing would ever happen to him. Now this Barrois had just taken on the business of a firm at Cluse for the whole of the countryside. It was very rash of him to behave as he did, for he would often be wanting the diligence. And here's what happened to him, true as you're sitting there, my dear sir!—Now then, Nestor, keep quiet, can't you? Did you ever see such a brute? Look at him! Look at him putting back his ears! You know I won't have it; Click, clack!—The first time Barrois went past the Wolf Stone—it was on the way back from Saint-Barthelemy; they were coming down the hill and the diligence had stopped for the passengers to go and put in their pence—Barrois, seeing this, bellowed like a bull: it was a disgrace, he was in a hurry, coaches had no business to stop when going down hill and so on and so on! But he wasted his breath: the others had sent round the hat and emptied the collection in the hollow stone up there...Then Barrois climbs up to the stone and sees the treasure. There was quite twenty-five or thirty francs, which proved that the wolf hadn't passed for quite three days. Barrois picks it all up and puts the cash in his pocket: 'That'll cure you,' says he. 'Each time I come this way, I'll do the same. When you know that it's I who take it, you won't put any more in. So you've something to thank me for.' The others grumbled, but, as they had done their duty, as far as they were concerned, they washed their hands of it, see?...Next day, Barrois, who had put up at the Black Sun, received a note, signed 'The Wolf of the Black Woods,' saying that if he didn't put into the wolf's hollow as many pieces of gold as he had taken out coins of all sorts, he'd smart for it! '...Barrois was obstinate and put in nothing; but, a little later, here's what happened, on my word of honour: going to Mongeron, on business, he opened his trunk of samples to show his goods to the innkeeper, a big trunk which had made the journey here, where you're sitting, sir...Well, the trunk, which was full when he put it on board, in front of all of us, at Saint-Barthelemy, was empty, oh, absolutely empty, not so much as a watch-chain left—I forgot to tell you that he travelled in watches and jewel-lery—and there may have been thirty thousand francs' worth when he started! What do you say to that?...Barrois went clean off his head, for it was a mystery, a real mystery of the Black Woods...and something more than an ordinary trick of the wolf!...When Blondel heard this at the Black Sun, he began to chaff Barrois and said, Well, what did I tell you? Now, there's nothing for it but to put your pieces of gold, as the wolf said, into the stones and put back your empty trunk on the top of the diligence: then perhaps it'll be full again. There's mercy for the re-pentant sinner!'...No sooner said than done. Next day, Barrois takes the diligence to go back to Saint-Barthelemy and puts his trunk there, where you are, and then sits down beside me. Then, when we're near the Wolf Stone, he scrambles down and goes and leaves his gold pieces: three hundred and sixty francs in ten-franc pieces—the wolf didn't say in his note that they must be twenty-franc pieces—after which he gets up beside me again; and, on reaching Saint-Barthelemy, we take down the trunk!...Oh, the excitement!...It was so heavy, there was no moving it; in fact, it was too heavy for jewellery...He opens it: what do you think's inside? Stones!...The stones they break on the roads!...We've seen the heap from which the wolf took the stones to fill the trunk...What do you think of that for a mystery? How did the wolf know when the time had come? No one ever knew; and that's what they call the story of Barrois' trunk...And believe me, ever since that day, everyone has paid his wolf's pence and never touched the money in the hollow of the Wolf Stone...Barrois' gold coins even

78

stayed there for more than three months, yes, sir, as an example to everybody...and then the wolf took them, like the rest...and then Barrois, who had taken to his bed, died...There's the story of Barrois' trunk, as I saw it happen with my own eyes, sure as I'm called Switch! And, if you ask me, I should say the wolf has watches enough to tell him the time from now till doomsday!"

Patrice thought to himself:

"For all that, they stole the magistrate's watch as well!..."

The driver would have liked to sit and enjoy the effect produced by his story, but his horses were taking up a lot of his attention, though they were going at a foot's pace and he was not worrying them and they knew the hill. Nestor was particularly restive; and Michel flicked him over the ears with his whip.

Patrice was still pensive:

"Do you usually get down, when you're going up hill?"

"Yes, certainly."

"You and the outside passengers?"

"Nearly always."

"And, those two times, when that happened with the trunk, did you all get down, on the hills?"

"Yes, I'm sure we did, for, the second time, we chaffed Barrois when we saw that his trunk was still in its place. But, though we got down, we never lost sight of the coach and the women remained inside. Well, nobody saw anything."

"Very well," said Patrice, after turning the matter over in his mind, "very well, the trunk was taken from the top during the journey and put back without you noticing it, while you were climbing the hills. How could that have happened? There's only one thing I can think of, which is that, in certain parts of the forest, where the trees form an arch over the diligence, somebody bent down from the top of that arch and took the trunk and put it back again a little farther on: there's your whole miracle for you! But it would take a very clever, very strong and very active person and one who knew every inch of the forest..."

"Oh, as for that, sir, the wolf of whom I speak has all those qualities!"

"Mr. Switch, have you ever heard in the forest of a certain Bilbao?" asked Patrice, who, for some moments, had been thinking of the queer name mentioned by Zoé at the Vautrins', a name which he could not remember exactly.

"Bilbao?...Wait a bit!...Never...no, never...Bilbao?...Wait!...No, but sometimes one hears a call in the forest at dusk, near the Pierrefeu clearing—yes, I've heard a call something like this: Baoo!...Baaoo!...Perhaps it was Bilbao."

"And you've never seen him!" asked Patrice. "I don't even know if he's flesh or fish!" replied Switch.

"Well, it may have been he who played the trick with Barrois' trunk," said Patrice. "And it's he the Three Brothers are relying on to lift the contractors' moneychest! It's a good thing, for them that they've put it inside and that it's guarded by fifteen detectives: Bilbao will have had his trouble for nothing."

Michel looked at Patrice as though all this was Greek to him:

"But who is this Bilbao?" he asked.

"He's the accomplice of the Three Brothers!"

The driver chuckled:

"They're quite smart enough to have invented that accomplice!" he said.

Patrice was struck by these words and by the tone of conviction in which they were uttered. It was not the first time that he heard this opinion expressed. As far as he could make out, the peasantry, from Saint-Martin to the Chevalet country, were all persuaded that the Three Brothers could do without accomplices of any sort.

Suddenly, the driver flung himself back, holding in his horses, which seemed ready to run away and were neighing madly:

"Oh, oh!" said Michel, in a low voice. "Look out! They're not far off now!"

"How do you know?" asked Patrice, beginning to shake with fear.

"Look at my horses," said Switch. "I can't hold them. They always behave like that when the others are near: my horses sniff as if they smelt a wild animal!..."

Patrice, greatly alarmed by what Switch was saying, leant over the side of the coach to see what was happening on the road. The detectives, surprised at the disorderly conduct of the team, had run up beside the carriage. They too seemed impressed, as though they realized that the decisive moment was at hand and the attack about to be delivered. Perhaps they had seen or heard something. They exchanged swift words, in a low voice. Brief orders were given.

Other figures sprang up in the twilight, in front of a bush, and gave a faint whistle, to which the people of the diligence replied. Patrice thought they were a reinforcement from the Chevalet district who must have watched the roads throughout the day.

This fresh little band arrived without hurrying, like peasants returning home, though there was no such thing as a cottage within five or six miles.

Patrice' idea must have been correct, for, on coming up to the diligence, all these people mingled, in the dark. And the horses once again snorted and Switch found such difficulty in holding them that a voice from the road asked him what was the matter with the brutes to make them so very restive.

Michel did not reply.

At a given moment, Nestor reared and neighed and the two other horses[4] neighed in concert and gave every sign of the most intense terror. They swerved to one side and the diligence drew almost right across the road. Patrice, holding on to the hand-rail, peered at everything around, as well as the falling darkness would permit.

He was overcome with a terrible sense of fear when he saw the confusion that reigned below. A group of detectives, acting on the order of one of their number, were preparing to re-enter the conveyance; the little wizened man in the cap had put out his hand to seize the bridle of Nestor, who was neighing more and more intractably, when suddenly, with an incredible wild fury, the whole team darted forward, bounding, flying along the road amid shouts and cries of despair.

The horses carried the great jolting body of the diligence at full speed, as though it weighed no more than a feather, far, far from the detectives, who panted after it in vain and soon lost sight of it...

Patrice thought that his last hour had come. He had the greatest difficulty in keeping his seat on the top of the coach. Clutching the iron rail, he turned to Michel.

He saw the back of the driver sitting so still and straight and calm on his box that Patrice could not understand it, could not understand it. Michel was driving his horses on a light rein, not with the ludicrous effort of a coachman trying to master his animals and failing, but with the stately pride of a victorious competitor in an ancient chariot-race. What did it mean? What did it mean? Had Michel lost his head? And Patrice shouted:

"Michel!...Michel!..."

The driver turned round. It was not Michel!

And, in fact, it was hard to tell who it was, for he wore a black mask on his face. This was the crowning terror. Incapable even of yelling out in fright, Patrice, jolted to and fro by the demon chariot, fell upon his knees.

Chapter VII

"Don't move, Patrice!" said the black mask, in the voice of Blondel's murderer.

Patrice was bereft of the strength to make the slightest movement save those enforced upon him by the alarming bounds of the diligence. A jerk more powerful than the rest sent him rolling to the feet of that hell's own coachman, who now was standing straight up above the runaway team. The driver must have hands of iron to make animals mad with terror keep the road at such a pace....And Patrice could see that that devil of a driver used only one hand, only one, to his three horses...where as the other...the other hand descended...descended slowly—while the driver calmly resumed his seat—descended slowly—ah, it was the same long arm at the end of which appeared the dazzling white cuff, the cuff that made that arm appear so much longer, through the little serving-hatch of the bar-room—slowly but surely the hand descended to Patrice' throat, even as he had seen it descend to Blondel's throat through the little aperture of the serving-hatch...

And Patrice felt a grip of iron clutch his throat...

And he gurgled...and his eyes almost burst from his head, from his head which was now raised to the level of the head with the black mask...

O hideous, O hideous death-agony, during which he still had just time to shrink before the fiery glance of hatred that gleamed through the eye-holes of the black mask...

And he heard, he could just hear, he heard a voice from under the black mask—the same voice that had murdered Blondel—ask:

"Shall you go back to the man's house?"

And, as the grip round his throat was slightly released, Patrice was just able to gasp out a single word:

"Never!"

But this word which he gasped out to the man in the black mask was marked with such an accent of sincerity that it saved Patrice' life. The terrible driver ceased strangling him—there was just time and the eyes veiled their terrible glitter. It even seemed to Patrice, for so far as one can realize such a thing at such a moment, that the terrible driver was chuckling, under his mask.

In any case, what Patrice did see was that the demon driver took off his cap to him, very politely, and put it on again at once.

Then, as the diligence slackened its pace, for the horses were out of breath, and skirted the tall forest trees, the man in the mask grasped a branch, hooked himself onto it as though by magic, swung his heels, turned an astounding somersault and disappeared in the dark leafage above.

[3] The coupé is a half-compartment in front of the main body of a French coach or diligence and immediately behind or under the driver's box.—TRANSLATOR'S NOTE

[4] The usual French diligence is drawn by three horses driven abreast.—TRANSLATOR'S NOTE.

Chapter VIII

The diligence stopped almost at once. Patrice was saved. But the heavy little portmanteau with the two hundred thousand francs was gone. There was nothing left in the coach but Patrice, half-swooning, on the top and, inside, the contractors' agent, who, when M. de Meyrentin's detectives at last joined the phantom diligence, had just enough strength left to tell them how he had been robbed in the simplest fashion by a gentleman in a black mask who had sprung upon him and calmly placed the muzzle of a revolver to his forehead. The agent had not had the pluck to resist him. Besides, the man had already flung the portmanteau on the road and jumped out after it.

The clerk had hardly finished his short and distressful tale, when old Switch came running up. The driver was safe and sound. He related, with great excitement, how he had suddenly felt himself lifted from his box by an irresistible force. And, before he could say a word, he was up in the trees, in the arms of a masked gentleman, who had let him down without ceremony, but very carefully, in the road and, taking off his hat, had wished him a good journey, whereupon Switch had hurried to take a cross-road and catch the diligence at the top of the hill. As for the detectives, they were in dismay. They declared that they would never dare return to duty nor even go back to the prefecture. They were condemned to, public ridicule for all time.

The reader will not be surprised to hear that, on learning of the failure of his expedition, M. de Meyrentin was so much upset that he was promptly laid up with jaundice. And it was while he was keeping his room that, by the irony of fate, the Three Brothers were arrested!

The thing happened in the stupidest fashion. The most monstrous and also the most mysterious tyranny that a small district was ever doomed to undergo seemed—I say, "seemed "—to have come to an end because two gendarmes happened to pass along the road at the moment when the Messieurs Vautrin were sending the dirty soul of Bazin the process-server to the great hereafter...Say what you will, there was nothing ill-natured about the Three Brothers; and, as long as you did not resist them, they did you no harm! But you mustn't resist them! That fool of a process-server would have been living to this day if he had handed over his money-bag nicely and quietly. A blow is so soon given. They had not measured the consequences. And Bazin the process-server died of the blow.

It was very unlucky for him that the Three Brothers were not carrying their guns that day when he met them. He would have given them anything without protest and would still be serving his writs. It was unlucky for the Vautrins too, who had to yield before the threat of the gendarmes' revolvers without making the least show of a fight.

The Three Brothers were sent to Riom for trial; and the proceedings were hastened. Now that they were no longer feared, everybody rose up against them and they were charged with all the crimes committed in the department during the past ten years, all the crimes that had not been brought home to their authors. The murders of Lombard, Camus and Blondel were ascribed to them, of course. And it was partly their own, doing, for they defended themselves slackly, not feeling at all sure that one of them was not the culprit and refusing at any cost to accuse one another.

For the rest, they adopted an heroic and cynical attitude, boasting of the misdemeanours which they had committed beyond a doubt and parading their contempt for humanity in general and the government in particular. They could not forgive the government for not finding some quibble to save them from the assizes; and they loudly proclaimed that, if ever they recovered their liberty, they would not be such fools again and would vote for the King. And so they were closely watched.

The question of an accomplice was raised at the trial. The public prosecutor would not hear of it, the presiding judge neither, both of these luminaries considering that the case was quite clear without an accomplice and both agreeing with the prisoners, who themselves swore that they had never had an accomplice.

But M. de Meyrentin urged the other point of view. And he spoke of a certain Bilbao.

Patrice also, who of course was called as a witness, timidly mentioned the name of Bilbao, without, however, insisting when the prosecuting counsel strongly suggested that he must have dreamt it or made some mistake.

Zoé was called and, like her brothers, replied that she had never heard the name in her life. She would have been implicated in the charge but for the mayor, who repeatedly declared that she was employed at his house on the nights when the crimes were committed. She was left at liberty out of pity for old Barbe.

And the Three Brothers were sentenced to death without further ado...

But they were not yet executed...

M. de Meyrentin remained persuaded of Bilbao's existence; and the reader who is curious to know all that he was thinking will accompany the worthy magistrate to Saint-Martin-des-Bois, to a little road-labourer's cottage standing on the bank of the road that runs at the back of Coriolis' property.

He has been there since last night, in hiding, simply waiting for M. Noël to return home...

The reason why M. de Meyrentin did not take upon himself to contradict the public prosecutor too openly on the question of the accomplice was that, to his mind, the question was still too far from being solved.

To-day, it is solved; at least, so he thinks.

It is solved, thanks to his patience, thanks to a number of nights spent in the little labourer's cottage, with one eye on the Vautrins' cabin and the other on Coriolis' manor-house, while the magistrate kept repeating to himself, "'Tain't yellow, it's red!" which is pure slang for "It's not gold, it's copper!" a phrase which corresponded curiously with something at the back of M. de Meyrentin's mind when Patrice came and reported it to him. Had the magistrate not been robbed of a watch which was not entirely free from alloy?

How easy it now was to understand Zoé's flight with the sock in which she had hidden the watch! Well, this watch could only have been given to her by "the man who walked with his head down," by the mysterious accomplice.

Zoé, therefore, was the friend of the accomplice, so much his friend that she mended his socks. It was Zoé therefore that he must keep his eye on. And he kept his eye on her, while his heart beat at the thought of what he was about to discover...

M. de Meyrentin was inclined, for a time, to believe that the extraordinary accomplice was neither more nor less than some animal trained by the Three Brothers, hidden by them in the forest and serving them blindly in their comic or tragic enterprises. This, moreover, seemed to correspond pretty closely with what people ventured, from time to time, to reveal to him about the mysteries of the Black Woods.

Throughout the district, the legend of destructive and bloodthirsty animals, werewolves, monsters that devoured children and cattle, had never entirely died out. At the time of the wholesale hanging of the dogs, all the peasants had agreed in contending that it was a trick of the "Pierrefeu Beast," which did not want to have the dogs barking at it when it came walking into the village to perpetrate same villainy. M. de Meyrentin, on the other hand, at once, an learning the facts, imagined that it was a trick of the Three Brothers, who had thus rid their animal of the scent and barking of the dogs.

But what manner of animal was it? It could barely be built simply on the lines of the famous Gévaudan Beast?[5]

M. de Meyrentin had scarcely dared reply to his own question, after a great deal of hesitation:

"It must be a monkey!"

For at least four hands were needed by the individual who, hanging to the roof, found means, by clinging to the top of an open door or cupbaard, to make his way into Lombard's or Camus' or Roubion's premises. He would need four hands to hold on to iron supports or rails or lyre-shaped gas-brackets, with his head dawn, while strangling his unfortunate victims who were too much terrified to utter a cry!

Lastly, it was on the top of the furniture where Patrice had discovered him that M. de Meyrentin thought he had traced the whole course taken by the murderer along the ceiling. Springing with absolute precision on his fore-hands, the marks of which had remained in the dust on the furniture, he had flung his hind-hands on the ceiling to obtain a fresh impetus; and those hind-hands were clad in socks which, in their turn, left their prints on the ceiling, the footprints of the man who walked upside down!

The man who walked upside down was therefore a monkey!

But Patrice had said:

"He speaks!"

And the whole theory had fallen to the ground, all the more so as M. de Meyrentin could not conceal from himself the difficulty of having his monkey version accepted, short of producing the monkey in a cage in the public prosecutor's office at Belle-Étable!...

He looked upon all these inferences as admirable in principle, but so exceptional in practice that he dared not state them plainly to a soul. And he himself put them on one side, to hunt about nearer at hand, among mankind, for the exceptional sort of acrobat who could take the place of the monkey in his mind.

Meanwhile, to keep a watch on Zoé, he hit upon devices worthy of a Red Indian. But Zoé went hardly anywhere, except to Coriolis', and home again. She was seen now and then with M. Noël, Coriolis' man-servant, a tall, quiet fellow who ran his master's errands, without loitering to talk to the village-gossips, and who took off his hat politely to the people in the street. This M. Noël was also the only person who sometimes crossed the Vautrins' threshold, no doubt out of charity for old Barbe, now that her sons were sentenced to death.

Well, one day M. Noël appeared to have been in the forest, for, on the skirt of it, he met Zoé leaving Coriolis' place; and M. de Meyrentin, who was in his little cottage, clearly heard Zoé say to M. Noël:

"Madeleine's been asking for you, Balaoo!"

Balaoo!...Bilbao!...

A great light, a first-class illumination blazed up in the examining-magistrate's heated brain!...He reflected that Noël had been brought from the Far East: what nimbler, more active, more acrobatic person could you hope to find than a Chinese or Japanese?...

One day, the magistrate was lucky enough to discover some prints left by M. Noël's shoes and corresponding exactly with the prints of soles which he had found on Lombard's roof, near the chimney, in the soot—on the lot where the murderer, no doubt, had gone to put on his shoes after the crime—and corresponding also, as far as possible, with the footprints on the ceiling&helli...

There was no doubt left...

Ah, Noël, with his sly, melancholy airs: what an impostor! Coriolis must be as ignorant of M. Noël's crimes as Patrice himself. And Patrice, on his side, could know nothingof the hatred with which he had inspired M. Noël.

Well, M. de Meyrentin would deliver all those people from a danger. He would make a scoop which would very much annoy Mr. Public Prosecutor, but which would cover him, M. de Meyrentin, with glory: he would arrest the accomplice of the Three Brothers...

He remained two days at Belle-Etable, to make all his preparations, without a word to a soul, and returned to Saint-Martin, accompanied by two gendarmes who were to await his orders, at the corner of the forest and the Riom Road.

And he went off to ensconce himself, for the last time, in his labourer's cottage, waiting until he was sure that M. Noël was at Coriolus' before performing his duty as a magistrate.

Now M. Noël did not give a sign of life. And it was beginning to grow dark.

Perhaps Noël had not left the manor-house.

M. de Meyrentin walked out of his cottage and deliberately went and rang the bell of the little door that opened on the woods.

Coriolis came and opened the door himself.
"M. Noël, if you please," said the magistrate, raising his hat.
"Come in, M. de Meyrentin," said Coriolus, crimson in the face.
And he closed the door.

[5] The so-called bête du Gévaudan was a ferocious animal, prob-ably a very large wolf, which appeared in the dense forests of Gévaudan, in Languedoc, about the year 1765, and whose devas-tations occupied the attention of France for some considerable time.—TRANSLATOR NOTE.

BOOK THE SECOND

BALAOO HAS THE TIME OF HIS LIFE

Chapter IX

When Balaoo appeared on the edge of the forest, the autumn sun, which was setting behind the little village of Saint-Martin-des-Bois, sent its last rays shooting down upon him. And Balaoo, dazzled, immediately went back under wood, to wait until it was quite dark, for he would have done anything rather than face a member of the Human Race in his tattered overcoat and his torn trousers.

Not to mention that he had lost his hat. This careless attire and the job which he had just pulled off at Riom led him to avoid the highroad and to look askance upon the passers-by. He sat down quietly in the middle of a thicket and leant against the trunk of a beech to put on his boots, which he usually took off when he was going through the forest and sure of not meeting any of the Race.

The fact was that he had been taught never to attract attention either by his get-up or by his wild-man's gestures. Since he had had explained to him what a pithecanthrope[6] was, he accentuated the gentleness and shyness of his manners, for he wished on no account to be confused with a member of the monkey race, who are so rude and ill-bred. It was quite bad enough to be taken, because of his almond eyes, his slightly flattened nose and his face with the broad flat surfaces, for a native of Hal-Nan, whom Dr. Coriolis, who had been French consul at Batavia, had brought back from his travels and taken into his service as his gardener.

So Balaoo put on his boots. As he found some difficulty in forcing in his hind-hands—for Balaoo could say what he liked: pithecanthrope though he was, he had more of the monkey than the

man about him, since he had four hands, which is the obvious characteristic of the quadrumana—he heaved slight sighs, in other words, he
gave forth growls which the inhabitants of Saint-Martin-des-Bois had
more than once taken for the premonitory sounds of a storm.

Moreover, it was one of his favourite amusements to imitate the
thunder with his reverberating, rolling voice, when far away from men,
to frighten them. He distinctly remembered seeing his father and
mother filling the whole family—his little brothers, his little sisters,
his old aunt and him, Balaoo—with unspeakable delight by striking
their chests, down yonder, in the heart of the Forest of Bandong, not so
very far from the bamboo villages built hanging over the swamps.
They thumped their chests like men-singers about to raise their voice;
and they brought forth the thunder. Oh, it was quick work! Hidden
behind the mangroves, they at once saw the bravest members of the
Human Race, even the very Dyaks, who are armed with bows and ar-
rows, run like water-rats in search of a shelter, of a well-fortified
kampong, behind which they heard them call upon Patti Palang Kaing,
the king of the animals, himself. What fun they had in those days!
Balaoo had his boots on. He reflected that, now, when he mimicked
the voice of the thunder, he was scolded on returning home. And there
was cause for it, no doubt; for, after all, he ran the risk that, one fine
day, it would be discovered that the thunder was he! And his master
had told him flatly that he would not answer for the consequences. The
members of the Human Race, if they found Balaoo out, would treat
him like a gorilla or a common gibbon. He would be popped into a
cage...and a good job too! He had better bear that in mind.

What he had in mind at the moment was the stroke of work which
he had done at Riom. And, when, by the last glimmer of daylight, he
saw two gendarmes pass along the road, the short hairs on the top of
his head stood up and began to move swiftly to and fro, an unmistak-
able sign of terror...or of rage.

He considered that the gendarmes did not go away quick enough.
He was late: he had been away two days. He wished himself home
again. What would his master and Mlle. Madeleine say? He could hear
their reproaches now: they had had to look for him, to call after him in
the forest. All the same, before he went in, he must go and tell Zoé of
the stroke of work which he had done at Riom.

The road was free. He crossed it at a bound and ran across the
fields to the cabin of the Three Brothers Vautrin.

It stood midway between the forest and the village, all by itself,
on the roadside, with a screen of poplars behind it. It consisted of but

one floor, covered with a thatched roof, from which rose a single chimney sending its smoke straight up into the peaceful evening. There was no light at the window. When he opened the door, a figure sitting huddled in the chimney-corner asked:

"Who's there?" He replied:

"It's I, Noël."

Balaoo's voice was both dull and guttural, rasping out the syllables low down in the throat. Bottles and bottles of syrup had been used up in the effort to "humanize" that voice. It was a little painful, a little startling, but not unpleasant to listen to. And, even with that voice, as he possessed the genius of mimicry, he managed to imitate a number of other voices and to excite sympathy for an incurable sore throat. When he tried to soften it, when speaking to young ladies, it produced a queer piping sound which roused laughter; and he hated that. He went about saying that he owed that curious lack of control over his vocal organs to the excessive use of betel in his youth; but, of course, he had given up chewing since he entered the service of his kind master, Dr. Coriolis!

"It's I, Noël."

The figure in the chimney-corner rose and another dark figure, in a recess in the wall, sat up on end. Mother Vautrin, the old paralyzed woman, and little Zoé looked at him with questioning eyes.

Zoé struck a match. Balaoo knocked it out of her hand and put his foot on the burning wood. He said there were gendarmes on the road and he did not want to be seen in the cabin. The old mother moaned in her dark corner; and the breath rattled in her throat, for she was very ill; but the first words uttered by Balaoo gave her relief:

"They will be here, in a cart, at eleven o'clock tonight...Have everything ready..."

Zoé was on her knees, kissing the pithecanthrope's boots:

"Have you saved them, Noël?...Have you seen them?...Are they coming, all three of them?"

And she named them, to make sure that not one would be missing: "Siméon? Élie? Hubert?"

Balaoo growled:

"Yes, Siméon, Élie and Hubert!"

"You've done it, Noël, you've done it?"

She continued to drag herself at his feet, but he pushed her away with his heel. The girl irritated him: when brothers were at liberty, she was always complaining about being beaten; and, now that she heard that they had been rescued from prison, she was licking his boots for joy.

"Quick!" he said. "Let me get back. What will they say to me at home?"

The child burst into tears:

"Mlle. Madeleine has been looking for you all day. She went all over the forest calling out, 'Balaoo!...Balaoo!...Balaoo!...'"

"Oh, bad luck!" said Balaoo, giving himself a great blow, on the chest, which resounded like a gong.

And he left without even taking leave of the old woman, so great was his hurry to get away.

Once outside, he sniffed the air. It no longer smelt of gendarmes. He went through the vineyard, by a path which he knew well, from taking it a hundred times when he had leapt his master's wall to fetch the Vautrins and go with them in search of adventures or to have "a rare old spree" in the forest. And he at once reached the back of the Coriolis estate, by the little door opening on the woods. He carefully sniffed the path leading to the station, but it did not smell of railway-passengers. Then, trembling, he gave a tug at the bell. It tinkled so loudly that Balaoo almost fainted.

Footsteps creaked upon the dead leaves on the other side of the wall. Balaoo fell on his knees upon the stone threshold. The door opened and Balaoo at once felt a hand seize him by the ear.

"You rascal!" said an angry young female voice. "I'll make you pay for this!...Two days and two nights out of doors...and in such a plight!...A nice thing!...I could cry, to look at you!...I have cried, Balaoo, I have cried!...Oh, don't you go crying, you; don't you begin! You'll bring the whole village round you!...You young scamp, you!...All your clothes in rags!...Your new trousers!...Your Paris over-coat!...You've been climbing the trees, sir, you've been larking in the moonlight!...And you've upset papa most terribly!..."

Dragged by the ear, docile, repentant, snivelling and with his heart throbbing loudly with remorse, Balaoo let the girl lead him to his quarters. But, on reaching the end of the kitchen-garden, where he was supposed to work with M. Coriolis, in the greatest mystery, at the different transformations of the bread-plant, and opening the door of his room, he found himself in the presence of Coriolis himself. He at once made a movement as though to return to the friendly forest at a bound.

Coriolis' face was colder, deader than marble.

Balaoo knew that expression. He dreaded nothing on earth so much as the sight of it. He would have preferred beatings and even the whippings with which he was tamed in his early youth to the silent reproach of those fixed eyes, of the haughty and contemptuous mask assumed by one of the Human Race who had obviously made a mistake in thinking that there was anything to be made out of a mere pithecanthrope.

And Coriolis' lips—if they moved at all, for there were days when they remained closed as though human speech would be disgraced by conversing with a pithecanthrope—Coriolis' lips were perhaps about to ask him, in front of Mlle. Madeleine—oh, the shame of it!—how his friends were, the great wild-boar of the Crau-mort and the wild-sow, his good lady, and the little wild boars, their children; and had he brought a message from the family of wolves that lived on the table-rock of Madon? Oh, horror! He who used to visit the brothers Vautrin, before they went to prison! And who was treated by them as an equal, as one of the same race! And even that he must not say, of course, because his master had remarked to him, one day, after meeting him on the road with his three chums, that he would rather have seen him in the company of hyenas, and jackals! So that he no longer knew where he was! After all, they belonged to the Human Race, they did!...'

Coriolis moved his lips:

"Turn round!"

Balaoo did not obey.

But Balaoo did as though he had not heard. He knew that his overcoat was nothing more than a rag and that the seat of his trousers was hanging down behind. He could never display such a sight before Mlle. Madeleine.

Coriolis took a step towards Balaoo, who began to tremble in every limb. Madeleine interposed with her gentle voice, with her gentle face of entreaty. She had understood Balaoo's shame. She wanted to spare him the disgrace. His eyes filled with tears. Oh, he loved her, he loved her, he loved her! Goodness, how he loved her!...

But the doctor commanded:

"I want him to turn around!"

Then the soft voice said:

"Turn round, Balaoo dear!"

Ah! "Balaoo dear!" She could do what she pleased with him, when she dropped his man-name and called him by that which his father and mother had bestowed upon him in the Forest of Bandong: Balaoo!...

Balaoo dug his toe-nails into the soles of his boots and turned round.

Then a laugh which he had never heard before echoed through the room.

He spun round furiously. There stood a man whom he recognized at once from meeting him sometimes in the village street. He was the friend of the man who limped and whom he, Balaoo, could not stand at any price, the friend of that M. Bombarda whom he smacked in the face whenever the opportunity offered. He was the friend also of the gendarmes who had taken the Three Brothers to prison. Had he come to take Balaoo to prison too? What was he doing here?...

It was the first time that Balaoo had had the honour of having a stranger brought to see him! It was the first time that he was receiving a guest under his roof, that people condescended to introduce one of the Race to him in his own apartments!

By Patti Palang Kaing, his king, his god, the man had laughed at the condition of the pithecanthrope's trousers! But Balaoo spun round so quickly and so furiously that the man's laughter broke off in the middle and the man himself, terror-stricken, rushed to take refuge behind the table.

"Don't be afraid, monsieur," said Coriolis. "He's not dangerous. He wouldn't hurt a fly!"

"A fly!" growled Balaoo, within himself. "A fly indeed! Better ask Camus, the tailor in the Cours National, who was always making fun of me, better ask him if I wouldn't hurt a fly!"

"Come here, Noël," said Coriolis.

And, as Balaoo came forward, quivering with anger, Coriolis, with his grand white beard, resuming his kinder manner, gave the pithecanthrope a friendly little tap on his raging cheek. Balaoo drew in his dog-teeth and wiped his forehead with his handkerchief. It was high time. Another minute and the stranger would have taken him for a brute.

The visitor said:

"It's extraordinary! I have seen monkeys at the music-hall, but anything to equal this...never!"

Balaoo clenched his fists to his mouth to prevent the thunder that swelled his chest from bursting.

Coriolis said:

"Never use that word in his presence."

"What word?"

"Monkey."

"Oh, does he understand as much as that?"

"You need not ask if he understands: look at the face he's pulling!"

"Yes, he frightens me," declared the visitor, stepping back in alarm.

"Once again, you have nothing to be afraid of. You have vexed him by using that word, but he wouldn't hurt a fly..."

"Oh, he understands anything!" continued Coriolis.

"And you say that he speaks?"

"He speaks better French than our peasants. Speak, Balaoo, say something." Balaoo, seeing himself treated, in front of one of the Race, like an interesting animal at a fair, turned his poor face, wrung with shame and despair, to her who always, at his worst trials, had been his supreme consolation and who sometimes, when his brain relapsed into animal darkness, had proved herself his saving star.

Madeleine, seeing his anguish, gave him a smile and uttered these words:

"Book of etiquette, paragraph ten."

The pithecanthrope at once turned to the visitor:

"I have not had the honour of being introduced to you, monsieur," he said, in a roar that made the house shake again.

"Oh!" exclaimed the visitor. "Oh! Ah! Ah!..."

And he opened, the wide eyes of one who is ready to rush away in fright.

But Coriolis was not satisfied:

"Politely," he said. "Politely. In your gentlest voice."

"Come, Balaoo, in your gentlest voice," insisted Madeleine, in her own gentle voice.

And Balaoo repeated the sentence—"I have not had the honour of being introduced to you, monsieur"—in the piping voice that made all the young ladies laugh, excepting Madeleine.

"But it's marvellous," shouted the other member of the Race. "It's marvellous, marvellous!...I can't believe it!...He can't be a pithecanthrope!..."

"He's not one any longer," Coriolis assented. "He's a man."

At these words, Balaoo raised a proud and triumphant forehead.

Coriolis proceeded to make the introductions in the terms prescribed in the book of etiquette:

"I have the honour to introduce to you M. Noël, my valued assistant in my work on the bread-plant." And, turning to Balaoo, "This, my dear friend, is M. Herment de Meyrentin, the examining-magistrate, who is very anxious to make your acquaintance. Pray sit down, gentlemen."

The "gentlemen" sat down.

"You know what a magistrate is, my dear Noël?" asked Coriolis, with an important air.

"A magistrate," replied Balaoo, with an air of equal importance, "is a man who sends thieves to prison."

"And what is a thief?" M. de Meyrentin ventured to ask.

"A thief," said Balaoo, imperturbably, "is a man who takes things without paying for them."

And he closed his eyes to escape the visitor's curious scrutiny:

"That magistrate's a great bore," he thought. "Is he never going?"

"May I give you some tea?" said Madeleine, in her musical voice.

Tea! Balaoo, utterly dazed, opened his eyes again. Madeleine handed him a cup and he stirred the sugar in the fragrant brew with the tip of his silver-gilt spoon.

Only, just before drinking, believing that no one was looking at him, he swiftly dipped his hand into the liquid and sucked his fingers, pithecanthrope-fashion. That was a thing he could not resist.

Coriolis and M. de Meyrentin, who were carrying on an eager conversation between themselves, did not notice the ill-bred action; but Madeleine saw it all and silently scolded Balaoo with a threatening forefinger. Balaoo glanced at her out of the corner of his eye and gave a sly grin. Then, when Coriolis looked at him again, he drank like a man and put his cup down prettily on the tray.

Next, Balaoo crossed his legs, swung one foot with a careless grace, threw himself back in his chair with a smirk and sat smiling fatuously. Suddenly, M. Herment de Meyrentin stooped, took Balaoo's right hand and examined it attentively:

"But these are not the hands of a..."

Coriolis cut him short: "Hush," he said. "I warned you not to use that word...and I have already told you of the work to which I have devoted myself for the last ten years. You can do anything with electrolytic, depilatory creams and a little patience. Look at his face: wouldn't you say he was a Chinese or a Japanese, just a trifle sunburnt? Who would ever take him for a quadrumane? You can use that word: he does not understand it."

"A quadrumane? A quadrumane?" repeated Herment de Meyrentin, rather irritably. "I've seen only two hands so far..."

"Balaoo, take off your boots." Balaoo thought that his ears must have deceived him. But no, Coriolis repeated the hideous command.

Chapter IX

Take off his boots! He, who has always been forbidden to show his shoe-hands! And who had been brought up to loathe and abominate his lower extremities! And who had never revealed this mystery except before the brothers Vautrin, in the depths of the forest, on days when he had gone hunting without leave and taught them to build invisible little huts in the trees!...

No, then, no, he would not take off his boots! The disgrace was too great, when all was said! And he stood up, with his hands in his pockets, whistling a tune, as though he had forgotten all about it. To his surprise, the others said nothing. They watched him as he walked, for Balaoo was walking up and down, with a thoughtful brow, as we sometimes do when we have something that preoccupies our mind. He forgot that he had no seat to his trousers. A scrap of conversation between his two visitors reminded him of it:

"You see, he has no appendage like that which we see in the lower quadrumana: no tail and no callosities. Note also that the bones of the ischium, which forms the solid framework of the surface on which the body rests when sitting, are less developed than in the quadrumana endowed with ischial callosities and are shaped more like those of a man. Lastly, he walks, as a rule, slowly and circumspectly; and I have taught him to give up his habit of waddling..."

Just then, in his annoyance, Balaoo began to waddle from side to side.

"You'd *better* waddle!" cried Coriolis, angrily. "I'll send you waddling in the streets of the village; and the school-children will laugh at you, Balaoo!"

Balaoo thought to himself:

"Ask Camus and Lombard, who were found hanged, why I put them to waddle at the end of a rope!"[7] But Balaoo's trials were not over. After taking off Balaoo's boots himself, Coriolis took his shoe-hands in his own, human hands. Balaoo turned away his head so as not to witness a sight that, disgusted him. But he could not help hearing.

"You see," said Coriolis, "that the great toe of the foot, which is smaller than in a man, makes up for this by being much more flexible."

"I hope he's not going to tickle me!" thought Balaoo.

M. Herment de Meyrentin nearly swooned with delight, when he saw, at last, the feet of the man who walked upside down.

"I see! I see!" he cried. "It's incredible: a quadrumane, a quadrumane that talks!...Oh, it's simply incredible!"

"All animals talk," said Coriolis, "but the quadrumane, which is one of the higher animals, possesses a greater variety of distinct sounds than the other beasts to express desire, pleasure, hunger, thirst, terror and so on: very distinct sounds and invariably the same. These utterances, therefore, from a language. In my pithecanthrope, which is the chief of the quadrumana, the one most nearly related to man, I have discovered as many as forty distinct sounds."

"And you went on the principle that, if an animal can pronounce forty sounds, it can pronounce every sound?"

"Open your mouth, Balaoo," said Coriolis.

Balaoo, who was ready to die of shame, had no time to protest. Coriolis, after holding his shoe-hands, was now holding his two jaws, without any antiseptic preliminaries, and working them on their coronoid processes as though he were setting a wolf trap. Balaoo foamed at the mouth; and his large, round, gentle eyes shed tears as they contemplated Madeleine, who was sadly watching the operation. Even so the sufferer who is having a tooth extracted gazes mournfully and gloomily at the staunch friend who had accompanied him to the dentist's.

"He has magnificent teeth," said M. de Meyrentin.

"Never mind the teeth, my dear sir," said Coriolis, impatiently "Just look at that pharynx! I have always said and I have always writ- ten, 'Every faculty, functional and anatomical, moral, intellectual and instinctive,' depends upon the strueture; and, as the structure tends to vary, it is capable of improvement.'"

"He doesn't see that he's spitting in my mouth!" thought Balaoo.

"You have perfected the pharynx," said M. de Meyrentin, "altered the back of the throat, worked at the vocal cords; and that was enough, you say, to enable you to turn a monk...a quadrumane, I mean, into a man?"

"Why not?" said Coriolis, letting go the jaw for a moment. "It is not difficult to show that no absolute structural line of demarcation, wider than that between the animals which immediately succeed us in the scale, can be drawn between the animal world and ourselves."

"All the same, my dear sir, there is an immense gulf between the monk...the animal, I mean, and man."

"No one is more strongly convinced than I am," answered Corio- lis, continuing to quote the late Professor Huxley, "of the vastness of the gulf between civilized man and the brutes. No one is less disposed to think lightly of the present dignity or despairingly of the future hopes of the only consciously intelligent denizens of this world; but, even from this intellectual and moral point of view, I contend that, by modifying the structure, it is possible to fill up the gulf."

"What you say fills me with admiration and, at the same time, with terror."

Within himself, the magistrate thought:

"It's you who will be filled with terror, presently, when I tell you what your advanced theories have brought you to!"

For M. de Meyrentin, the cousin of the great Meyrentin of the Institute, had remained an idealist and an anti-Darwinian, like the pride of the family.

"Nonsense!" said Coriolis, aloud. "What is it that makes man what he is? Is it not the faculty of speech? Language enables him to note his experiences; language increases the scientific assets of the generations that follow one upon the other. It is thanks to language that man is able to link together more closely his fellow-creatures distributed over the face of the globe. It is language that distinguishes man from the rest of the animal world. This functional difference is immense and the consequences are extraordinary. And yet all this can depend on the very slightest alteration in the conditions of the back of the throat. For, what is this gift of speech? I am speaking at this moment; but, if you change in the least degree the proportion of the combined forces at present in action in the two nerves that control the muscles of my glottis, I become dumb at once. The voice is produced only so long as the vocal cords are parallel; they are parallel only so long as certain muscles contract in a similar fashion; and this, in its turn, depends upon the equal action of the two nerves of which I have just spoken. The least change in the structure of these nerves and even in the part from which they spring, the least alteration even in the blood-vessels involved, or, again, in the muscles which the blood reaches, might make us dumb. A race of dumb men, deprived of all power of communicating with those who can speak, would be a race of brutes."

"Just so, just so," said the magistrate.

"It goes without saying," continued Coriolis. "Don't scratch yourself, Balaoo!"

Balaoo, who hought himself unobserved, was covered with shame.

"Well, what I have done is the opposite of one aiming at producing dumbness: I have aimed at increasing the scope of an organ which was already capable of emitting certain sounds of speech. I have held all those nerves, all those muscles, all those arteries in my forceps, for the greater glory of my demonstration."

Balaoo, who had been under an anæsthetic during the operations, listened to all this with a very casual interest.

"And I have succeeded in producing the necessary parallel position of a quadrumane's vocal cords. Open your mouth, Balaoo."

Balaoo opened a terrible wide mouth, which Coriolis at once turned back under the lamp, and asked himself when on earth this awful torture was coming to an end.

"Look, my dear sir, look...there...you can still see the scars..."

"It's astounding, it's astounding!...And he now talks like a man...But has he also retained the power of emitting the animal sounds which he used to?"

"Yes, but it takes him a greater effort than it did. Speak as you used to, Balaoo."

Balaoo, by way of revenge and of joking, began to speak as he used to in the old days, but as he used to when he was angry, that is to say, when his voice could be heard for a mile around:

"Goek! Goek! Goek!...Ha! Ha! Ha! Hâââ!...Hâââ!...Hâââ!... Goek! Goek!..."

The magistrate, Coriolis and Madeleine put their fingers to their ears and made violent signs to Balaoo that that was enough. He ceased; but Coriolis explained what he wanted:

"Talk as you used to, but not so loud. We can't hear ourselves speak."

Thereupon Balaoo "talked" as he used to, but mezzo voce, while Coriolis expatiated on the virtues of the pithecanthrope's throat:

"You see," he said, to Meyrentin, "how the capacious membranous pouch, situated beneath the throat and communicating with the vocal organ, with the laryngeal ventricle, swells. Look at it: it swells and swells and swells! The louder he speaks and shouts, the more it swells; and then it resumes its normal shape when he stops."

"*Goek! Goek! Goek!*" said Balaoo, more and more embarassed by the singularly persistent gaze of the man who sent thieves to prison.

"And what does '*Goek*' mean?" asked M. de Meyrentin.

"It means, 'Go away,'" said Balaoo, who was not without a sense of humour.

"Why," observed M. de Meyrentin, "it's almost like the German '*Geh weg!*'"

Balaoo did not know German and declined to pursue the subject; and M. de Meyrentin stayed on.

Chapter IX

Balaoo heaved a sigh: he had never suffered so much in all his life. A hand took his tenderly. Oh, Madeleine! And Balaoo's heart began to thump inside his breast. Ah! M. de Meyrentin was getting up. Did he mean to go, this time?...Did he?...Yes, yes, at last!...He offered Coriolis "all his congratulations"...like an ass, like an ass!...He seemed to be fairly laughing at Balaoo and to be planning something which Balaoo couldn't make out: one must always be careful with those people who send thieves to prison...And it was foolish in any case, of M. Herment de Meyrentin to appear to make little of Balaoo, for this business might turn out badly too!

The magistrate said, with icy deliberation:

"All my congratulations, my dear sir. You have made a man-child. What with science and your scalpel, you equal the Creator!"

Coriolis thought that he was exaggerating and told him as much. M. de Meyrentin confessed that he was exaggerating. With an insolent glance at Balaoo:

"Yes," he granted, "it's true. The Creator made them handsomer."

He uttered this in front of Madeleine. Balaoo, at first, choked. His astonishment paralyzed him, stupefied him. Coriolis, seeing the pain which his visitor had given to his pupil, to the child of his creating, tried to speak a word of comfort:

"Yes, the Creator has made handsomer men," he said, "but none gentler, better, more loving, or more faithful. This one has amply rewarded his old master for all the trouble which he gave him at first; for I admit that it was difficult, during the early years, to make him forget his games in the Forest of Bandong. But now he is absolutely, as I contend and am prepared to prove, a member of the human race."

At this speech, which ought to have touched him, M. Herment de Meyrentin grinned like a fool and, pointing to the torn overcoat and trousers, said:

"Humph! He still indulges in a little prank at times!"

Balaoo could have wept, but he controlled his tears in the presence of a stranger. And kind Dr. Coriolis gave the magistrate his answer:

"I have known men's children who were not more than seventeen years old and whose parents would have been thankful if they had spent their time climbing the trees after apples and tearing the seats of their trousers in the process. It is not for me to advise you, my dear sir, to consult the records of the criminal courts. You know as well as I do how some men's children employ themselves at seventeen, with knife in hand!"

"The master's right," thought Balaoo. "I have never struck anyone with a knife. That's all very well for men-children, who have no strength in their hands."

"In your part of the country, M. Coriolis," said the magistrate, in a tone of voice that made Balaoo look asquint, "people don't use the knife in committing murder. They strangle their victim. Their fingers are all they want."

Balaoo blinked his eyes and thought:

"What made him say that, I wonder?"

Corlolis, pointing to Balaoo's hand, observed:

"There's a hand that wouldn't hurt a fly!"

"You insist upon that fly of yours," thought Balaoo, timidly, with lowered eyes, for he was an admirable dissembler, "but I, who wouldn't hurt a fly, would not at all mind strangling this distinguished visitor!"

M. Herment de Meyrentin, remembering that his illustrious cousin in the Academy had always combated the Darwinian theory with rather antiquated arguments about the impossibility of indefinite reproduction among mixed species, refused to leave without a Parthian shot to give Coriolis something to think about. What right had the imprudent doctor to let loose the evil instincts of the Forest of Bandong upon civilized human society? Well, he would be punished for it before supper by the arrest of his pithecanthrope, whom M. de Meyrentin fully intended to come back and fetch with his posse of gendarmes. And, in his finest, throatiest voice, the magistrate let fly:

"I congratulate you, my dear sir. All you now have to do is"—here de Meyrentin's features widened into an infamous smile—"to get him married. He will soon have attained the legal age. I hope that you are already thinking of the young lady whom he will lead to the altar. Mlle. Madeleine will be bridesm..."

M. Herment de Meyrentin was unable to finish either his smile or his sentence, for he felt round his throat the grip of two clutches contracting with a force that was positively alarming to a member of the Human Race who still hoped to spend many a year upon this earth, utterign foolish and unseemly words. He gurgled, he struggled, he choked! Balaoo squeezed and squeezed. Coriolis and Madeleine uttered yells of terror and hung on to Balaoo to make him let go. Coriolis seized a poker and rained blows with it upon Balaoo. The blows sounded as though they were striking a drum; but Balaoo felt nothing. Madeleine wept and sobbed and prayed and raved; but Balaoo heard nothing. He squeezed!

And he did not stop squeezing until M. Herment de Meyrentin stopped struggling. That would teach the gentleman to think that Balaoo, who wouldn't hurt a fly, was not handsome and to make fun of him in front of marriageable girls! A nice thing the gentleman had done for himself: he was dead!

Dead was M. le Juge d'Instruction Herment de Meyrentin, first cousin of the illustrious Professor Herbert de Meyrentin, member of the Institute, secretary of the moral and political science section! A whole family cast into mourning! A most distinguished family! That was all that remained of that mighty exemplar of human power, an examining-magistrate! A rag, a doll broken over a pithecanthrope's arm!

Balaoo flung that offal to the ground. He was astounded to see kind Dr. Coriolis glue his ear to the thing's chest. There were some people who didn't mind what they touched! But where was his little sister Madeleine? Balaoo looked round for her and discovered her standing flat against the wall, with her mouth wide open and her eyes glittering with fright.

"It's clear to me," thought the pithecanthrope, "that I've made a blunder here. They don't look a bit pleased!"

Coriolis rose to his feet as pale as death:

"Wretch!" he raved. "What have you done? You have murdered your guest!"

"Tut!" thought Balaoo. "Why do they get into such a state? What worries them is the corpse, I can see that! And I expect they are afraid of the commissary of police, who always arrives when you hurt a member of the Human Race. For instance, you can murder my friend Huon, the great old bachelor wild-boar, who was nicely killed with a stab in the heart in the presence of everybody, and nobody to say a word against it, or my friend Dhol; the big old lusty wolf, whom they riddled with bullets because he ate a six-months' baby that hadn't yet learnt to say 'Papa' and 'Mamma,' but you've no right to strangle one of the Human Race, just like that, with your hands. It's the law. All right! All right! I'll take away the corpse; and no one will be any the wiser. I'll hang this one too: that will be a good trick!" So thinking, Balaoo took M. Herment de Meyrentin's big, flabby body by the hind legs and dragged it to the door. Coriolis tried to stop him, but Balaoo shouted, "*Goek! Goek!*" in so loud a voice that Coriolis soon saw there was nothing to be done with the pithecanthrope at such a moment. Balaoo was all on edge, excited, glorying in his terrible work. He wouldn't hurt a fly; but, for all that, Dr. Coriolis realized that it would be unad-

visable to part him from his prey, which the pithecanthrope was dragging behind him with a pride as conscious as that of a Roman general
carrying the *spolia opima* in his triumph. Oh, what a lofty brow was
Balaoo's and how well fitted to wear the laurel-crown! There is a Roman general in every monkey!...And bang! One good kick with his
shoe-hand to the door; and it opened wide to let the procession
through.

Madeleine was powerless to stir a limb and Coriolis was still
shaking like a poltroon when Balaoo, with his burden, solemnly made
his way under the branches of the neighbouring forest.

[6] From the Greek pithekos, ape, and anthropos, man: an animal
half way between a monkey and a man and marking as it were
the transition between the former and the latter. Scientists, including Gabriel de Mortillet in the first place, have discovered in
the tertiary strata the traces and the fossilized remains of these
intelligent animals, as well as the proofs of their intelligence.
Others, relying on traveller's tales, declare that this species of
ape still exists and that a few specimens can be found in the
depths of the forests of Java. Dr. Coriolis is not the only one who
has hunted for them there.—AUTHOR'S NOTE.

[7] This was a terrible thing for Balaoo, who did not know that
Camus and Lombard were lame and who believed that they
made fun of him by imitating his waddle as they walked along
the street, which was his reason for hanging them!—AUTHOR'S
NOTE.

Chapter X

There was to be a gathering that evening at Mme. Roubion's, at the Black Sun; for, since the Three Brothers had been arrested and the streets become safe, or nearly so, at night, people in the village had once more taken to sitting up. At nine o'clock, Mme. Mûre, a little old woman in a cap who lived at the third house in the road leading to the station, slipped her embroidery-case into her hand-basket, together with some poppy-heads, of which she proposed to crush and eat the seeds in the course of the evening, and lastly a few walnuts, of which she knew Mlle. Franchet to be inordinately fond. Now Mme. Mûre and Mlle. Franchet had not been on speaking terms for five years past; and it would be a treat for Mme. Mûre to see Mlle. Franchet watch the others feast on Mme. Mûre's walnuts.

Having filled her basket, Mme. Mûre cautiously opened her door. The church-clock struck the hour. More doors opened in the direction of the Cours National. Other little old women poked out their caps in the moonlight, hesitating to cross the threshold, having lost the habit of leaving the house after supper. True, people were nearly easy now that those horrid brothers Vautrin were comfortably stowed away in prison and about to pay their debt to society; but, all the same, it was impossible to throw prudence to the winds from one day to the next.

Ohoo! Ohoo! Shadows on the road, swinging lanterns as they went: it was M. Roubion and his inn-servants to summon the embroiderers to sit up with the Empress of Russia's gown.

The little doors opened wider: the little white caps ventured forth, hand-basket on one arm, foot-warmer hanging from the other. Oh, they knew better, in this harsh weather, than to go out without their warming-stools, the coals in which, for years and years, had scorched the skin of their legs to such good purpose that many of them, no doubt, had nothing but a pair of burnt sticks to show under their skirts.

Ohoo! Ohoo! They pattered and clattered along, after carefully locking their doors. It was the last evening which they were to spend on the Tsarina's gown; and they would not have missed it for the empire of All the Russias. Two hours' work and it would be done; the contractor was coming to Saint-Martin next morning to fetch the dress. At least, so Mother Toussaint, the forewoman who had arranged with the contractor, said—the old gossip!—perhaps to stimulate their zeal.

The procession went flapping and clapping down the Rue Neuve. Shutters were flung back against the walls as it passed. More than one would have loved to be invited to go and see the Empress'gown and not all who had been long in bed were yet asleep.

Big Roubion increased his pace. No one wanted to loiter. They trotted and trotted. It was cold; and the women had lowered their hoods over their caps; and their shoulders shivered, in spite of all, less with cold than with fear, at the thought of the Three Brothers, who loomed large in the shadows of the night.

There was a full gathering at Mme. Roubion's for the last evening with the Empress'gown. The embroiderers worked in the large summer dining-room, which was used for the commercial travellers in the fine season, but closed in winter. The wonderful gown lay spread at full length on the leaves of the dining-table; and each of the needlewomen took her seat. Two of them made the eyelets, another the raised spots, another finished a rosette, another worked at the scalloped edges and two assistant hands, working side by side, sewed on some old lace. Mme. Toussaint, that old gossip, supervised everything and worried everybody. Mme. Roubion, with her enormous head resting on her capacious bosom, had eyes for none but her guests. After the bar-room was closed, monsieur le maire arrived, accompanied by Mme. Jules, his spouse; M. Sagnier, the notary, and madame, who possessed such beautiful false pearls; and M. Valentin, the chemist, and madame, who was the only lady in the neighbourhood that used make-up—and such a lot of it!—and who was also the only lady that could boast of having had an adventure, last autumn, at the manoevres, with a cavalry-officer. All these fine folk had come to admire "the masterpiece of French industry" before its departure for the Russian court.

Now this dress, which, at any other time, would have kept twenty talkative women wagging their tongues for an hour, left the ladies very indifferent in ten minutes or even less. To begin with, they thought it too simple in its immaculate splendour. It was an all-white dress, of embroidered cloth, and Saint-Martin-des-Bois could not picture the Empress of Russia other than adorned like a reliquary and swathed from head to foot in gold, precious stones and silver lace. Mme. Jules considered it hardly even a dress for the seaside. The embroiderers could have boxed her ears; and Mme. Toussaint, the old gossip, felt that she would like to scratch her eyes out. The ladies gradually left the summer dining-room to join their husbands in the bar-room, where they found the gentlemen sitting round the fire, cracking a bottle of old wine and discussing the Vautrin case. Oh, how that case had been discussed since the arrest! But it was apperently always new; and, now that "they" were going to be guillotined and that there was no longer any reason to fear them, people were almost proud of having been so afraid. Nevertheless, no one was willing to admit his terrors. On the contrary, each vied with the other in trying to show that it was he who had "handed over the Vautrins to the public vengeance." Through the half-open door, the embroiders, who also thought of nothing but the Three Brothers, heard the chemist and the notary each boasting of his courage at the trial, where they had smashed the ruffians with their evidence. True, by that time, the verdict against them was certain, because they had been captured red-handed: the gendarmes had appeared in the road at the moment when Élie, Siméon and Hubert were taking Bazin the process-server's money-bags from him, after stunning him with that little pat on the head of which he died. However, it must be admitted that, in order that this verdict might be far-reaching and allow none of the three prisoners to escape, M. Sagnier and M. Valentin had taken advantage of the Bazin murder to saddle the Vautrins with all the suspicious matters that had distressed the district for the past ten years.

The chemist and the notary each enlarged upon the merits of the civic heroism displayed by himself at a time when no one else seemed to retain a proper sense of his duty; monsieur le maire knew what was meant!

All this self-sufficiency and self-conceit ended by annoying the people present, down to the needlewomen in their work-room; and even Mme. Mûre coughed as she swallowed her poppy seeds. As for Mlle. Franchet, that worthy could not keep from chuckling and spluttering into the bowl of mulled wine which Mme. Roubion had brought her, with a word of warning not to stain the Empress of Russia's gown. They knew and everybody knew that those two who were now posing as dare-devils had been very meek and mild indeed while the Vautrins were about.

Had the needlewomen been in monsieur le maire's place, they would soon have made them put a stopper on their loquacity. The same thought occurred to monsieur le maire himself. It was not a very happy thought, however; for, when he reproached the gentle men, not without a touch of irritation, with having waited so long to accuse men of whose crimes they were cognizant, he was told, in reply, that, "but for the fortunate incident of the murder of the process-server, where the Vautrins were caught red-handed, there would have been every reason to pity decent people who were so ill-advised as to inform against such powerful election-agents as the brothers Vautrin."

The mayor bit his lips and Mme. Jules, his spouse, made a sign to him not to go on embittering the conversation. Nevertheless, he retorted that he was not the only one to be elected to the municipal council with the Vautrins' aid. His two subordinates protested loudly and called Heaven to witness that they had had no finger in that pie and that, at any rate, they had never been mixed up in the dirty jerrymandering of the general elections; and they didn't mind saying so; and, if anyone chose to take offence, that was his affair.

M. Jules, the mayor, of course, could not take this insult lying down; he did his best to pass it off by saying that, if anyone had the right to boast that he had brought the truth to light, it was good old Dr. Honorat. Ah, there was one who had spoken out! And said useful things too! He had supplied the proof of the murders by speaking of the rope with which the men were hanged.

"Agreed," retorted Mme. Valentin, the local lady who had had that adventure with the cavalry-officer, "agreed; but, as M. le Vicomte de la Terrenoire"—the officer in question—"said at the trial, considering that Dr. Honorat examined the bodies in the commissary's presence, why did he not then call the attention of the police to the kind of rope with which the men had been hanged and which he thought that he had already noticed at the Vautrins' on the day when he was called in to attend Zoé?" And she concluded, "If Dr. Honorat was more useful than anybody afterwards, he was more prudent than all rest of us before!"

To this, Mme. Jules, the mayoress, replied:

"He had the right to be, or, at least, he had every excuse. Dr. Honorat drives along the roads, night and day, all alone in his gig; and an accident is easily met with. What could he have done against those three ruffians?"

"He preferred to nurse them," hissed long, lean Mme. Sagnier, the lady with the false pearls, between her teeth. "It was he got them sentenced to death," resumed the mayor, in an authoritative tone, "and, I repeat, he showed courage in doing so, for, as long as I live, I shall never forget Siméon jumping up from his seat in the dock, shaking his fist at Dr. Honorat and shouting, 'You'd better mind yourself, for, if ever I get out of this, my first visit will be paid to you!' It was enough to give one the shivers. Well, Dr. Honorat did not turn a hair. He's a brave man, I tell you."

The two others raised their voices in protest:

"And what about us, weren't we threatened? Élie and Hubert said to us, 'You are liars; and, the next we meet you, we'll break your heads.' Those are the very words."

"I had to keep my bed for a fortnight after," declared Mme. Valentin."

"So had I," said Mme. Sagnier.

There was an embarassed silence, which was interrupted by fat Mme. Roubion, who went round among the company with her bowls of mulled wine:

"That's not the point," she said. "What's the use of arguing, now that their business is settled? When are their heads to be cut off? They ought to have been cut off here; but, as the thing's arranged to take place at Riom, has monsieur le maire thought of engaging a window?"

"Look here," said M. Jules, roughly, "I'd rather talk about something else..."

And, for the next five minutes, they talked about nothing at all. Everybody sat steeped in thought and one and all had the same thought: they would not be really easy in their minds until the Three Brothers were dead and buried. There was only one fear, that the President of the Republic might commute the sentence of one of them; and, after all, people had been known to escape from prison. You never could tell...

Mme. Roubion made a fresh effort to dispel the figures of the Vautrins:

"You know Mlle. Madeleine Coriolis is to be married soon?" she said.

"Oh, nonsense!" said Mme. Valentin. "To whom?"

"Why, to M. Patrice Saint-Aubin, her cousin from Clermont."

"There was a rumour of it," said Mme. Sagnier, "but they have lots of time before them. He is quite young still."

"Quite young?"

"He's twenty-four," said Mme. Roubion, "and he has just passed as a solicitor. His father is anxious to make over his practice to him. He wants to see his son fixed up and married and settled behind his papers in the Rue de l'Écu before his death, for the old gentleman does not think that he has long to live."

"He's right there," declared the chemist. "You can't be too careful. One never knows who's going to live and who's going to die."

"They say the Saint Aubin boy is rich enough for two," said Mme. Valentin. "Has little Madeleine any money?" All the company were of opinion that she had not. Dr. Coriolis, an old eccentric, who used to be consul at Batavia, might have made his fortune in the Malay Archipelago, but the general view was that he had returned from the Far East with nothing but a fatal passion for the bread-plant, which had made away with his last shilling. Did anyone ever hear of such madness? To try and make a single plant take the place of bread, milk, butter, cream, asparagus and even Brussels sprouts, which he pretended that he was able to make out of the waste! And for years he had been living with his hobby, at the bottom of his immense garden surrounded by tall walls behind which he lived in a state of almost complete isolation, seeing nobody and refusing to be assisted by any one except his gardener, a boy whom he had brought with him from the East and who seemed greatly devoted to him. He was a very nice young fellow, that Noël, that they must say: a little shy, never talking to anybody, but always bowing to everyone most politely. When he crossed the street; for his master sometimes sent him on an errand, he nearly always carried his hat in his hand, as though he lived in fear of "offending somebody."

"He's not what you would call good-looking," said M. Roubion.

"He's not ugly either" said Mme. Valentin. "Only, he's rather flat-faced." "He's like all the Chinese," said Mme. Roubion, pedantically, having seen "Celestials," as she called the inhabitants of the Celestial Empire, at the Exhibition of 1878. "They are not handsome, but they look very intelligent and not the least bit ill-natured. My opinion is that he's a Celestial."

And Mme. Jules summed up the general view on Noël by asserting that "he wouldn't hurt a fly."

In the summer dining-room, the needlewomen, seated around the Empress' gown, ceased to listen to the ladies' and gentlemen's conversation as soon as they had finished talking about the Three Brothers. These alone had the gift of interesting Mme. Toussaint, Mlle. Franchet, Mme. Boche and Mme. Mûre, though on this subject the good women were inexhaustible, always finding new things to say and even repeating the old things over and over again, without ever wearying. They were fellows who were not satisfied with being highway robbers, said one, but who did wrong for its own sake, in other words, for their pleasure. Mme. Boche told how she had nearly died of fright, last year, one evening when she was closing the shutters of the little shop where she dealt in groceries, haberdashery, deal boards, laths and coals. She maintained that one of the Vautrins had hidden on the roof of her house—Mme. Boche's roof almost touched the ground—and snatched off her cap and wig. She was almost sure that she had recognized Élie, unless it was Siméon, unless it was Hubert, but it was certainly one of the Three Brothers, who, when they were not murdering people on the roads, spent their time frightening old women. Oh, the Vautrins had broad backs! Mme. Mûre shed tears over the decease of a poodle which met its death in a very curious way, one evening when it was barking too loudly at the heels of the Vautrins, who were preparing some trick. It suddenly ceased barking. Mme. Mûre went out into the yard and found her dog hanging from the rope of the well. This suicide, which was at least as difficult to explain as Camus' and Lombard's, had been as it were a signal for the suicide of all the dogs in the village at that time. It was a regular epidemic. The dogs were all found hanging from the well ropes, So much so that, since then, Saint-Martin-des-Bois had given up keeping dogs.

Mme. Toussaint shook her fat chops and her flabby chin under her mob-cap:

"And, then, if they had only been satisfied with the dogs!" she said. "Those wretches need not have thrown my little cat Mirette into the pond, with a stone round her neck, for us to know them for savages. Their reputation was made!"

In short, "life had become a hell;" but, since "they" had been in prison, people had recovered their peace of mind to some extent and the old ladies of Saint-Martin were once more beginning to enjoy life.

It was at that moment, just as the several visitors at the Black Sun were expressing their contentment with a state of quiet to which they had long been unaccustomed that a mad sound of galloping was heard on the rough cobbles of the Rue Neuve. This galloping was accompanied by the noise of a light vehicle, a noise which could only belong to Dr. Honorat's gig. Everybody recognized it; and the proof was that everybody cried:

"There's Dr. Honorat!"

But what had happened? Why that din? Why that hurry? Had his horse taken the bit between its teeth and run away? Had the doctor dropped the reins?

Mlle. Franchet cried:

"Perhaps he's been murdered!"

But everyone was at once reassured, at least in so far as Dr. Honorat's existence was concerned, for he was heard shouting, in a hoarse voice:

"Open the door!...Open the door quickly!..."

M. Jules, the mayor, M. Roubion, M. Sagnier and M. Valentin drew their revolvers, without which they had not sallied forth for many a long day; and the ladies, seeing their husbands produce those lethal weapons, began to tremble and were unable to utter a word.

"What's the matter?" asked Roubion, putting his ear to the door.

"Open the door, can't you? It's I, Dr. Honorat! Let me in, Roubion, let me in!"

"Are you alone?" asked Roubion, prudently.

"Yes, yes, I'm alone, let me in!"

"You can't keep the doctor standing at the door," Mme. Roubion declared. "Let him in."

Everybody at once fell back, while the needlewomen, leaving their work, gathered anxiously in the doorway between the bar-room and the summer dining-room.

Roubion opened the door.

Dr. Honorat, who had fastened his panting horse to the ring in the wall, burst into the room like a whirl-wind. Roubion bolted the door behind him and all clustered round the doctor, who had promptly sunk into a chair. He was deathly pale. He was hardly able to speak. His eyes were wild and staring. He managed to groan:

"The Vautrins!...The Vautrins!..."

"What about them?...What about the Vautrins?..."

"The Vautrins are here!..."

Everybody shrieked. Fear sent its gust of madness over them, flinging up their arms in meaningless gestures, tossing the company this way and that way, making them writhe and twist as though they had all suddenly lost their mental balance:

"Eh?...What?...Where?...The Vautrins?...What's he talking about?...The man must be mad!...Where did you see them?..."

"At their own place!" gasped the doctor. "At their own place!...In their house!..."

"He's been dreaming!...He must have been dreaming!..."

The chemist and the notary were now as pale as the doctor. They did not believe him. They did not think that such a thing was possible; but, all the same, from the very moment of his stating the incredible horror, it left them as though stunned, with arms and legs paralyzed, throats dry and hearts beating like mad.

The nameless terror depicted on their faces seemed rather to exhilarate monsieur le maire who, after a rapid examination of conscience, arrived at the conclusion that, throughout this business, he had preserved so prudent an attitude that he had nothing to fear from the vengeance of the Three Brothers. He showed the coolness which should never desert a chief magistrate in the presence of his fellow-citizens. He silenced the silly moans of the needlewomen and the incoherent questions of the ladies.

"Come, doctor," he said, "don't lose your head like this. Are you quite sure that you saw them?"

"As sure as I see you now."

"In their house, by the roadside?"

"In their house. They had not even drawn their window-curtains. I was coming down the road, on my way back from my rounds. My mare was going at a slow trot. I saw a cart outside the Vautrins' door and a light in the windows; and I seemed to hear voices. I had a sort of feeling that I should come upon something unexpected. And I was not mistaken. I was just passing the door, when the door opened and I saw, as plainly as I see you, Élie, Siméon and Hubert quietly carrying a chest out to the cart. I at once whipped up my mare; and she galloped off. But they had caught sight of me and recognized me, they shouted after me, 'See you soon, doctor!' I thought I should go mad!...Oh, I thought they were behind me; and I rushed on like the very devil. I felt that I was done for, if I did not reach Saint-Martin before they did. For they are coming!...They are coming!..."

"Don't talk nonsense, doctor," monsieur le maire broke in, speaking in his most serious tone. "If it's really they, then they've escaped from prison and will never dare come here."

"I tell you, they are coming. They told me so in court! I'm a dead man!..."

As he spoke, good old Dr. Honorat, decent man, who, perhaps, before this fatal meeting, had taken a pint of old wine more than he need have on his rounds—for he did himself pretty well—Dr. Honorat, I was saying, noticed the white faces of M. Sagnier and M. Valentin and had the satisfaction of remembering that they too had been threatened at the trial; and he put his satisfaction into words:

"And you too, M. Sagnier!...And you too, M. Valentin!...You are both dead men!"

M. Sagnier shook his head and said, in an expiring voice:

"It's not true, what you're saying; it's impossible!" M. Valentin shared this opinion. He whispered:

"How can they have got out of Riom gaol? It's impossible!"

This was clearly the key-note of the situation; and everybody repeated:

"No, no, it's quite impossible!"

Monsieur le maire smiled at seeing people so frightened: "Come, ladies," he said, "pull yourselves together. Our worthy doctor has been imagining things. Give him a glass of mulled wine, Mme. Roubion; that will do him good."

"I don't want anything," said the doctor; and his eyes wandered more wildly than ever over the company.

Monsieur le maire shrugged his shoulders and, seeing Mme. Toussaint, Mme. Mûre, Mme. Bache and Mlle. Franchet gathered round him like so many hens who had sought refuge under their rooster's wing, he packed them back to their work. Clucking with anxiety, they returned to the summer dining-room; but no sooner were they there than they uttered such screams that it was now the turn of those in the bar-room to go after them. They found Mme. Toussaint, the old gossip, indulging in an orthodox fit of hysterics. The Tsarina's dress had disappeared!...

Chapter XI

What had become of "the masterpiece of French industry?" Obviously, some one had stolen it. But who? And how? No one had remained in the summer dining-room while they were all flinging themselves into ecstasies of horror at Dr. Honorat's impossible story. On the other hand, there was no way into that room except through the bar-room; and nobody had seen anybody. On the other hand, again, the windows looking on the inner yard of the inn had remained closed. On the other hand, once more, you can't carry off an Empress of Russia's gown as you would a pocket-handkerchief.

The mystery surrounding the incident was so profound that nobody doubted that "there were Vautrins at the bottom of it." It resembled too closely a number of other indoor disappearances which had never been explained and which had always been put down to the Three Brothers. No one now doubted that Élie, Siméon and Hubert were back and that they had performed the miracle of escaping from the executioner's knife with the one and only object of rushing to Saint-Martin-des-Bois and stealing the Empress' gown. And, if M. Jules, the mayor, who had always had a sneaking kindness for those scamps, because of the relations which they kept up with the elected representatives of the nation, if M. Jules still hesitated to yield before the evidence, his hesitation did not last long. For there came a fresh knock at the door of the Black Sun; and the person who knocked seemed in as great a hurry to obtain admission as Dr. Honorat himself had been. An awful silence at once reigned inside the inn, for all were wondering if they were about to hear the voices of the Three Brothers. But no, it was the trembling voice of an old lady entreating to be let in; and everybody recognized Mme. Godefroy, the Saint-Martin postmistress.

"An official telegram! An official telegram for monsieur le maire! Open the door, M. Roubion, it's very urgent. O Jesus, Mary, Joseph!"

Mme. Godefroy's terror must have exceeded all bounds for that respectable functionary to neglect the last counsels of prudence and to dare invoke the saints of the Roman and Catholic paradise within two steps of her lord and mayor, who had distinguished himself by his stalwart paganism at the time of the separation of Church and State.

"Monsieur le maire is here, Mme. Godefroy," Roubion shouted, through the door.

"I know that," replied the other. "Let me in."

The mayor, greatly perturbed, said:

"An official telegram? Push it under the door, Mme. Godefroy."

"Never will I push an official telegram under the door!" declared the unhappy woman. "I must deliver it into monsieur le maire's own hands..."

"Let her in," said M. Jules, heroically.

The door was half-opened and Mme. Godefroy appeared.

She wore the same mortal pallor, the same wild, staring eyes that had marked the entrance of Dr. Honorat. A yellow paper shook between her fingers. Monsieur le maire took it from her and read the contents of the official telegram aloud:

"*Prefect* PUY-DE-DÔME *to Mayor* SAINT-MARTIN-DES-BOIS.

"Three brothers Vautrin escaped to-day from Riom gaol; take necessary steps."

The mayor, who had no armed forces at his disposal, beyond his beadle and his town-crier Daddy Drum, flung a lifeless, circular glance at those around him. The poor people seemed to have lost the power of breathing. M. and Mme. Sagnier and M. and Mme. Valentin held each other clasped in a tight embrace, forming two couples similar to those in the pictures representing the early Christian families thrown to the lions. Dr. Honorat, in his chair, gave not a sign of life. The band of little old needlewomen clustered round buxom Mme. Roubion; who, with her two hands laid flat on her enormous breast, made a vain effort to control the beating of her heart. And the terror was so great that Mme. Toussaint herself, who was supported by Mme. Boche, who was supported by Mme. Mûre, who kept a tight hold on Mlle. Franchet's hand, Mme. Toussaint herself had ceased her lamentations on the disappearance of the Empress of Russia's dress.

Monsieur le maire read the official telegram for the fifth time, without deriving from it the inspiration that would have saved him at this difficult moment. For everybody was relying on him. He kept on repeating:

"Take necessary steps...take necessary steps...he's a nice one, the prefect!...What necessary steps would he have me take? It's for him to take the necessary steps...He ought to have sent us some gendarmes by now...He must have known that 'they' would come back here..."

Three loud bangs on the bar-room door...Everybody gave a fresh jump. And a voice in the street said:

"Quick, quick! Let me in!...It's I, Clarice. Open the door, in Heaven's name!"

"Camus' clerk! We ought to put out those lights. We shall have them all coming here," cried Roubion.

But the other kept thumping at the door for all he was worth:

"Let me in! Let me in!..."

They opened the door, but swore that this was the last that they would admit. He was even more scared than the others; and he had every reason to be. He had not seen the Three Brothers, but he had bumped up against M. de Meyrentin's body hanging on a tree on the Riom Road. Oh, how they all screamed! The Vautrins were beginning their revenge! Lord, what would happen next?

The cries were followed by general consternation, by mute despair; and then this assumed yet a fresh shape as was to be expected. While monsieur le maire was reflecting upon the melancholy of the situation, without being able to come to the slightest decision, he suddenly saw a furious spectre brandishing its fists in his face.

It was Dr. Honorat, shouting at him: "This is all your fault!"

It needed nothing more to inspire the rest with courage.

The notary and the chemist attacked the mayor at once; of course, it was his fault! But for him, none of this would have happened! But for him, those ruffians would long since have relieved the country of their presence! But they had found a mayor to encourage them, to reward them! Every time they committed a misdeed, a crime, the mayor gave them money! And that, no doubt, was how they had escaped, by bribing their warders with the gold of the municipality and the elections!

The wretched mayor could not get a word in edgewise. Everybody was now shouting:

"You have made yourself their accomplice, their accomplice!"

Dr. Honorat, with his eyes starting from his head, let fly the word:

"Murderer!"

And they made so great a noise that they did not hear some one rapping, this time at the gate of the yard, with the heavy knocker.

Mme. Boche it was who went and listened in the passage. She returned, waving her arms, while her legs gave way beneath her:

"Hark! Hark!"

All were silent; and, as the knocking had also ceased, everyone heard a rough voice in the distance calling monsieur le maire.

This time, there was no mistake about it: Hubert, the eldest of the three Vautrins, was outside! They knew his voice; and, as he was the most dreadful of the three, there was a general rush to the darkest corner of the bar-room. The women began to squeal like cats that were being skinned alive. But monsieur le maire, whom madame was holding back by the skirts of his jacket, broke away from the trembling band and said to the innkeeper:

"Come, Roubion, we must find out what they want. You've never had any bother with the Vautrins; have you?"

"Never! Never!" proclaimed Roubion, hurriedly, with obvious satisfaction. "No, no, there's never been anything between us."

"I won't have you go, for all that," whined Mme. Roubion.

"Then I shall have to go alone," said the mayor, laughing.

At that moment, the knocking at the gate started afresh.

Roubion pulled himself together:

"Monsieur le maire is right," he said to his wife. "They can't mean harm to people who have never done them any. I never refused them a glass of wine when they came here. What do you imagine they could do to us? Perhaps they want a drink..."

"You're not going to let them in?" sobbed Mme. Valentin.

"No," said the mayor, "but we can talk to them."

"I'll open the spy-hole in the gate and we shall soon see what's up," said Roubion.

"It's quite true, I've never failed them. I've always treated them well. Why should they wish us harm?" argued Mme. Roubion. "If they're thirsty, we can always hand them a bottle through the spy-hole. So let's all go together."

"That's it," said the mayor. "We'll all go together." Nevertheless, none except the mayor and Roubion, followed by their wives, left the bar-room and ventured under the archway of the yard. And even then Mme. Jules and Mme. Roubion remained at the entrance to the archway. As for the others in the bar-room, they did not make a movement. The women had ceased squealing. There was not a sound heard but their heavy breathing.

The mayor and Roubion were away for at least five minutes, which seemed an eternity. They returned at last, still accompanied by their wives. When they entered the bar-room, the others saw, by their awe-struck faces, that they had no good news to tell. Dr. Honorat, the chemist and the notary kept their eyes fixed on monsieur le maire, waiting for him to speak. And no prisoner in the condemned cell, watching the magistrate who comes, at break of day, to tell him that his petition for mercy has been rejected, ever felt greater terror in his heart.

"But at least tell us what it is," said Mme. Sagnier, with chattering teeth.

"Well, it's like this," said the mayor, mopping his forehead with his handkerchief. "I saw Hubert through the spy-hole. He wants us to hand Dr. Honorat over to him."

The doctor, on hearing these words, gave a great jump in his chair; and there was a long pause, at the end of which monsieur le maire said:

"I did my duty; I refused."

"Quite right!" said M. Sagnier, who had meanwhile recovered his voice. "Quite right! We are armed. We will defend ourselves here to the death and until the arrival of the gendarmes, who can't be very far off."

"M. Sagnier is right," said M. Valentin, of the pale face. "The ruffians are asking for the doctor because they know that he's here; and, presently, when they know that we are here too, they will ask for us as well, What do they take us for? We won't allow ourselves to be killed like sheep!"

Mme. Sagnier and Mme. Valentin said nothing, but began to glare angrily at Dr. Honorat, who had not spoken a word and who, according to them, should have given himself up at once, to save the rest.

Mme. Godefroy vanquished the tyranny of her nerves, which condemned her to a trembling silence, and asked:

"What answer did he make?"

"He said," replied the mayor, "that he would go and consult his brothers; and he went away."

"Did you think of telling him," asked M. Sagnier, "that they were running the greatest danger by remaining here, that the gendarmes were on their way and that they'd do better to, clear out to some other part of the country?"

"I said all that," the mayor declared, stiffly, "but he told me to mind my own business."

"He has gone away," said Mme. Roubion. "Perhaps they will not come back. Perhaps all of you had better go home."

But one and all protested. They were quite agreed not to leave the inn before daylight and especially before the arrival of the gendarmes who were sure to be sent to Saint-Martin-des-Bois.

"Hark! They haven't gone far!" said Mme. Boche.

The knocking was renewed. The mayor once more drew himself up, like a hero marching to his death, and, with not a sign of weakness, stepped towards the archway. M. Roubion wanted to go with him again; but, this time, Mme. Roubion curtly ordered her husband to stay with her:

"Don't you go mixing yourself up in other people's affairs!" she said.

M. Roubion did not care to dispute the matter and acquiesced.

Mme. Jules sighed out her husband's name and took three steps in his wake:

"What a business!" she moaned. "What a shocking business! It's hard indeed to be mayor under such conditions." And, gazing severely at the down-hearted band, "Monsieur le maire is the only brave man here," she said.

The brave man returned. This time, he was almost as pale as the others. They awaited the decree. He spoke:

"Hubert says that he has consulted his brothers," he intimated, in a flat and shaky voice. "They are all three agreed to murder everybody here, if we don't give Dr. Honorat up to them. I replied that we were armed, that we would defend ourselves and that we would not give up Dr. Honorat."

Hereupon the pack of sempstresses began yelping: they had never had any differences with the Three Brothers; and, if the Three Brothers knew that they were there, they would certainly let them go without hurting them!...There was no need for them to stay in the inn! Who knew what might happen?...As the Three Brothers only wanted Dr. Honorat, the needlewomen ran no risk in going home. They wanted to go home.

"The doors shall not be opened without my orders," said the mayor. "Besides, you would never get out. Hubert, Élie, Siméon and little Zoé are watching every exit. Hubert told me again and again that they would murder anyone who tried to leave. And they know quite well that you are here."

"And what about us? Do they know that we are here?" asked the chemist and the notary.

"Yes, they do."

"And...and...and did they say nothing...about us?"

"No."

"It's only Dr. Honorat they're after, that's quite clear!" said Mme. Sagnier, with a fierce glance at the unfortunate man.

Chapter XI

"Yes, yes," repeated the notary and the chemist, between their teeth, "it's only Dr. Honorat they're after."

"But what do they mean to do?" asked Mme. Roubion, who began to cry like a little girl.

Her example was immediately followed by Mme. Boche and Mme. Toussaint, while Mme. Mûre and Mlle. Franchet still retained a particle of dignity and became reconciled in the moment of misfortune after an estrangement that had lasted for five years:

"There, Mlle. Franchet, there, they won't hurt us!"

"We needn't fear, my dear Mme. Mûre. They would be ashamed to!"

"You ask me what they mean to do: upon my word, I don't know!" confessed the mayor, with a submission to the inevitable that was not without dignity. "Perhaps they merely wanted to frighten us...I hope so, but one can never be sure of anything with those fellows!"

Just then, a great commotion was heard in the street, accompanied by shouting and swearing. It was as though they were dragging a lorry to the door of the Black Sun. Those inside could distinctly hear the sound of shutters clapping against the walls of the houses opposite and Siméon's loud voice ringing through the echoing night:

"Hi, you, up there! Hide your ugly mugs, or I'll pepper them with lead."

The threat was no sooner uttered than it was followed by the report of a gun which woke up the whole village.

The needlewomen fell on their knees. Mme. Mûre and Mlle. Franchet, who were regular church-goers, began a Hail Mary. The sounds from outside bore evidence that the whole of the Rue Neuve was in an uproar; but the windows half-opened by the terror-stricken onlookers must have been closed again at once, for the threats of the Three Brothers had ceased. Nothing was now heard but the movement of their heavy shoes over the cobbles of the road and up and down the pavement. What were they doing? That was what all the people inside the inn were wondering. All were sweating with anguish and trembling with despair. However, the notary and the chemist, assisted by the mayor, the Roubions and some of the women, had made a last heroic effort and pushed the billiard-table against the door leading to the archway, through which they dreaded to see the ill-favoured features of one of the Vautrins appear at any moment. They worked thus for the general safety without making any demands upon Dr. Honorat, who had lost the last shred of resemblance to anything human and who sat huddled in a chair, in a corner, like a lifeless thing. All of them gave him a malevolent look as they passed and controlled themselves so as not to load him with insults. The chemist's wife, who was braver than the others, because of her adventure in the cavalry, manifested the general feeling towards the wretched doctor by spitting on the floor in his direction. Mme. Jules had caught the contagion of Mme. Roubion's tears. The sobbing of these two, combined with the mumbled prayers of the others, ended by irritating the mayor, who was pricking up his ears to try and discover what was happening in the street. Taking the name of the Lord in vain, he swore at them to stop; and, having thus restored silence, he put a chair on a table and scrambled up to peep through the fanlight above the window-shutters. From here, he was able to look into the street. What he saw, by the flickering flame of the lamp that was supposed to light that corner of Saint-Martin-des-Bois, seemed to fill him with fresh terror, for he was unable to control an excla mation which increased the excitement of the besieged.

He disregarded their requests for explanations and sprang from the chair to the table and thence to the floor with the nimbleness and agility of a youth of twenty:

"Oh no!" he cried. "We can't have that!"

"What? What?"

"We can't have that! We can't have that! Let me be, all of you, and hold your tongues!" This with a terrible oath. "No, we can't have that!...Keep quiet, keep quiet, will you? I must go and talk to them."

And, pushing aside the woebegone wretches who pressed round him, he leant against the bar-room door that opened on the Rue Neuve and glued his ear to it, after giving three great thumps on the shutter with his clenched fist:

"Hullo, you, out there!" he shouted. "What are you doing?"

The noise outside ceased as had that indoors.

The mayor resumed his position and called the Three Brothers by their names. Then some one was heard approaching the shutter from the street.

"Who's there?" asked the mayor.

"It's Hubert," said a voice.

"I'm the mayor speaking."

"What can I do for you, M. Jules?"

"What are you doing out there, in the street and at the corner of the square?"

"We're putting down some straw, Mr. Mayor, some nice, dry straw, which looked like spoiling in the Delarbres' loft."

"What for?"

"To send you to blazes, Mr. Mayor, since you refuse to hand over that old Honorat."

At the announcement of this fresh and imminent catastrophe, the cries were renewed in the bar-room of the inn. A fierce gesture of the mayor's demanded silence.

"You wouldn't do that, Hubert. You wouldn't do a thing like that...Oh, he's not answering! Shut up, all of you, can't you!...Hubert!...Hubert!..."

"What is it, Mr. Mayor?"

"You surely won't do that?"

"Oh, won't I just! Here, Zoé, give me the matches..."

Fresh cries, fresh roars in the bar-room.

"Hold, your blasted tongues, will you?...Hubert!...Hubert!...You can't do that...There are women in here, women and girls!..."

The last word referred to Mlle. Franchet, who would never see fifty-five again. But Hubert's tremendous voice now filled the whole street. Men have since said that it was heard from one end of the village to the other.

"We don't care a hang about the women. It's Dr. Honorat we want..."

Then, pushing his mouth against the door, he sent a hideous threat through the key-hole:

"You shall all go through the mill—the notary and the chemist and the notary's wife and the chemist's wife—if you don't hand Dr. Honorat out to us...Give us Honorat and all will be forgiven and forgotten..."

This time, the ruffian was so near that there was no mistaking what he said. It seemed to Sagnier and Valentin as though his voice were drilling the words of temptation into their ears. At the same moment, a great flame lit up the fan-light; fear and cowardice began to do their work; and the two men made a rush for the limp rag of a doctor huddled in his corner. And they had no difficulty in dragging with them the women, who were already raving at the thought of being burnt alive.

But great was the assailants' amazement at finding themselves confronted by a victim who defended himself tooth and nail! The doctor had not understood at first; but, feeling the hands that clutched him and hearing the mouths that roared, "Out of this! Out of this!" he had no doubt left of the fate that awaited him. And he recovered his strength in the presence of death. It was a merciless battle. The notary, the chemist, the women no longer even thought of turning him out.

Instinctively, they revenged themselves on his person for their own cowardice, treating him as a coward because he had not the pluck to save them all at the cost of his own skin. In the rear of this onslaught, the front of the inn began to blaze. The wood crackled and the whole house was lit up through the fan-lights. Outside, there were more cries, gun-shots; and suddenly came the mournful sound of the alarm-bell tolling over the village and across the fields, proclaiming the disaster, summoning help. The fierce and callous voices of the Three Brothers and the shrill voice of little Zoé rose above all the other noises. With the aid of a thick plank, which they used as a battering-ram, the Vautrins were now trying to drive in the bar-room door, while the Black Sun was already wreathed in clouds of smoke.

The women at last let go of the doctor, who, covered with blood, with his clothes torn from his back, crawled under the billiard-table. Followed by the men, they rushed into the yard. There was no way out of the yard save through the great gate under the archway. And this road was closed to them.

Roubion did nothing but shout:

"Why don't the fire-brigade come?...They're burning down my house!...My house is on fire!...Why don't the firemen come?" forgetting, for the moment, that he himself was the captain of the fire brigade and that the engine was locked up in his own shed.

The three inn-servants, in their night-attire, were asking for explanations in tragic sentences, accompanied by murderous threats. Not realizing what was taking place, they had attempted to escape by the Rue aux Navets, where they were shot at the moment they put their noses outside. They had only just time to slam and barricade the door. They had recognized the Vautrins' voices; and fear now sent them tearing around like squirrels in a cage.

The whole troop once more gathered round the mayor and called upon him to get out of their plight without delay. And they might all have flung themselves upon him, as they had upon the doctor, if the glow in the sky, which lighted up the whole of the inn-yard, had not suddenly faded, as though it had been blown out.

The noises outside had ceased. The alarm-bell stopped ringing. The terrible battering against the bar-room door was heard no longer. This instantaneous calm, the dark and peaceful night surprised everybody. They stood for some time without speaking, without shouting, not knowing what to think. At last, the mayor's voice was heard saying:

"They have burnt a few trusses of straw to frighten us and they have gone away..."

Mme. Roubion thought and said:

"Perhaps the gendarmes have come..."

M. Roubion, following up his idea of getting rid of the whole crew, the primary cause of the tragedy, made a suggestion:

"There may be a way for all of us to get to the town-hall. We should be safe there. Come up with me to the hay-loft."

They followed him, scrambling up a wooden staircase, with a greasy rope for a rail.

"Mind and don't strike any matches!"

They were in utter darkness, groping and feeling for one another, stumbling at every step. At last, the hatch for hoisting the fodder was cautiously opened by Roubion; and a slice of the outer dusk, less black than that of the loft, stood out against the dense gloom inside. They had forgotten Dr. Honorat. No one knew what had become of him and nobody worried.

Roubion leant out of the hatch. He looked down at the lane that separated the inn from the town-hall, which was shrouded in darkness and gave no sign of life. Roubion—who saw nothing at all—said, in a low voice:

"I see the schoolmaster! He's making signs that we can get down this way. Who'll go first? The Vautrins will never imagine that we can get out here. And they will still be watching at the doors when we are far away."

"That's not a bad idea," said the mayor.

"Well, set them the example," said Roubion. "There's a rope and pulley: that's all you want."

The mayor declared that it was his duty to be the last to leave, like a captain on board his ship. But they explained to him that it was "not the same thing." In fact, it was "just the contrary." The first to leave was the first to take a risk. If he saved himself, then everybody was saved. He decided to venture, after fondly embracing Mme. Jules; and this was the road by which they all left the inn, men and women alike sliding down a rope. It formed the staple subject of conversation in the village for many a long day. Mme. Mûre had not practised this form of exercise for over sixty years; and I fear that it will leave her with a rick in her back for the rest of her life. To this day, when she speaks of it, she says, thinking of the Vautrins:

"There are men who behave worse than savages." M. Roubion was the last to let himself down.

When the little band were all below, the mayor said: "And now to the town-hall, all of you!"

"Don't make a noise," Mme. Jules advised them.

But nobody dreamt of making a noise. They tried to get in by the back of the building, but they shouted to the schoolmaster in vain.

"He must have gone back to bed again," thought M. Roubion, aloud.

They decided to go round and reach the municipal sanctuary through the square, unless they should see anything to arouse their suspicions on the road.

A silence quite as impressive as the recent uproar weighed heavily on the village; and they pressed against one another, holding their breaths and walking on tiptoe. And even now no one troubled to think what could have become of Dr. Honorat.

As they were about to enter the square, gliding along the walls and keeping in the shadow, suddenly, as though with one accord, they stopped. Not a cry did they utter, not a movement did they make, nothing that might betray them. What they saw in the circle of light cast by the lamp at the corner of the Rue Neuve had struck them dumb and powerless, as though by lightning. Élie and Siméon passed, dragging after them Dr. Honorat, with a gag in his mouth and his hands tied together. Behind them walked Hubert and little Zoé. Hubert carried a gun on his shoulder. Little Zoé carried two.

Chapter XII

Balaoo, after rolling the Empress' gown very tidily under his arm, sat down on the edge of the forest. The darkness was absolute; the last lights were extinguished in the windows of Saint-Martin-des-Bois. He sat and thought. He sincerely regretted his mishap with the distinguished visitor who had called to see him. Not that he suffered pangs at so unceremoniously and without previous warning killing one of the Human Race who had insulted him; but he feared that he had caused great pain to his dear little Madeleine. What a queer face she put on, when he was proudly dragging by the hind-legs that M. Herment de Meyrentin who would never make fun of him again! And what terrible eyes his kind master Coriolis had made at him! What desperate grimaces! What a business!...

No, on thinking it well over, he positively preferred not to go home that evening. And yet it was not that he did not want to be good. He knew quite well that, when he spent the night in the forest, Madeleine was sad all the following day, because it grieved her to think that he would never be anything more than a horrid wild beast. Ah, what would she say now that she knew that he had killed one of the Race? Balaoo scratched the short bristly hairs on the top of his head. O perplexity!...

It was to purchase his forgiveness and to secure a welcome at Madeleine's hands that Balaoo had purloined the Empress' gown just now. After hanging M. Herment de Meyrentin's corpse, from the first tree in the forest on the Riom Road, in the dead man's own necktie as was right and proper, Balaoo had been three times round the Coriolis estate, listening for a sound, a call. Ah, if he had suddenly heard Madeleine's voice in the dark, calling him by the name which he bore in the Forest of Bandong—"Balaoo!...Balaoo!...Balaoo!"—how he would have flown to her! How gladly he would have returned at once to his human dwelling!...But no, he heard nothing. No one was calling him. Everything seemed dead in Coriolis' house since he had killed that visitor, that M. Herment de Meyrentin, without a word of warning.

With bent back and hanging head, dragging his feet and carrying his hands in his pockets, Balaoo had entered the deserted village, wondering what he could do to atone for his offence, when he met the little frightened troop of needlewomen, with their galoshes and foot-warmers, going to the Black Sun under Roubion's escort. He smiled, without exactly knowing why: perhaps because he recognized Mme. Mûre and Mme. Boche, on whom he had played many a practical joke in his time. He heard them talking about a wonderful dress, a dress of the kind that was only worn among the emperors of men, the dress of the Empress of Russia. Balaoo's curiosity was roused. He wanted to see that "masterpiece of French industry." He removed his shoes and tied them round his neck by the laces. He was quite comfortable now; and it only took an acrobatic leap or two over a couple of walls and a roof to bring him to the fan-light of that summer dining-room where Mme. Toussaint was spreading out the marvel. Balaoo made up his mind the moment he set eyes on it. The dress would suit Madeleine "to perfection." And, at the first opportunity supplied by the absence of the needlewomen, he pushed open the fan-light, held on to the window by his hind-hands, took a swing; seized the coveted object with his fore-hands flying, leapt back through the fan-light and vanished over the roofs with the Empress' gown.

He ran straight to the little door at the end of Coriolis' garden, his own private door, and was on the point of ringing. But, suddenly, his hand, which was already on the bell-pull, rose and scratched the bristly hairs on the top of his head. He remembered the law, the lessons in the law which Madeleine had given him:

"One must always pay for things before taking them!"

And Balaoo had just taken something without paying for it; for, to Balaoo, stealing and taking meant the same thing; and the question of payment before taking possession was only a matter of politeness invented by the members of the Human Race, who refused to do anything like other races. And Madeleine would not be pleased. She would send him packing, with his Empress' gown. And that would make two bothers instead of one. Sorrowfully, he moved away from the little door at the end of the garden and made for the open country.

So there he stood, on the edge of the forest, with the Empress' gown under his arm. Hearing a noise in the distance, from the Rue Neuve, he said to himself that they must have discovered his theft and that Mme. Boche and Mme. Mûre were rousing the whole village in order to tell the story of that strange event...Unless, indeed, it was some one in the neighbourhood who, coming home by the Riom Road, had bumped up against the distinguished cqrpse of the distinguished visitor whom he had strung up by his necktie on the first branch of the first tree on the left of the road. If so, M. Jules had been told by this time and the man who played the drum would be harnessing his cart to go and fetch the commissary of police, as they always did when there were dead people hanging at the end of a rope...Unless, again, they had learnt that Élie, Siméon and Hubert—with his, Balaoo's, assistance; but no one would ever know that!—had escaped from Riom prison, a thing which would certainly annoy the members of the Race, for the Three Brothers were feared by everybody.

Ah, Balaoo had done some pretty work that day! It was a red letter day in his life. He ought to have been well pleased with himself...But no, he was not: since Madeleine was unhappy, Balaoo was sad.

However, he could not remain all night on the edge of the forest, whining like a baby, and it was not healthy to sleep in the open air; so he got up to go to his home in the forest, his little set of chambers in the Big Beech in the Pierrefeu clearing.

It was a very dense forest, which had never been disfigured except by the necessary high-roads running from town to town. Apart from these gashes, which are inevitable in the forests of the Human Race, there were no carriage-roads, good, bad or indifferent: merely a few small foot-paths used by poachers and animals; and even then you had to know where to find them! And those woods went on for ever in the direction of the rising sun. Oh, there was plenty of room to walk about, even for a Balaoo who had known the Forest of Bandong! True, all that tangle of hornbeams, ashes, big oaks and big beeches; all that collection of thousands of pine trees standing bolt upright; all that which went to make up the Black Woods was but a shift for Balaoo, "as who should say a park." And, when one of his friends in the underwood, such as As the fox, for instance, put on side about the thick yoke-elm where his hole was, Balaoo had great fun telling him stories of the giant creepers of the tropics, roaring with laughter as he did so.

Thus, last time that the other came to look him up at the Big Beech, Balaoo spoke out pretty freely:

"As, you're just a new-born baby. If you had seen, as I have, the flowers of the cocoanut-trees and the trees with three feet[8], in which we build our huts above the thick water of the swamps; and if you had seen the wall of giant creepers, strung from tree to tree, which, for a hundred thousand years, have kept the members of the Human Race from penetrating to our village, you would never again dare mention your hole of a house protected by the yoke-elm of Saint-Martin-des-Bois...That As," thought Balaoo to himself, "who puts on such a lot of side in Europe, would bring a smile to the lips of an elephant at home." And he added, aloud, "Besides, you see, just look at this: when anyone wants to enter my Forest of Bandong, he has to make a hole in it, like a tunnel. It's quite unlike the forests over here."

As did not insist, knowing that he would not get the better of Balaoo, remembering the proverb:

"A traveller may lie with authority."

As understood all that Balaoo said to him, because the pithecanthrope took care, when talking to animals, to drop the language of men which he had learnt from Coriolis and Madeleine. He never waited to be asked, but always, very amiably, put himself on an equality with them, as between beast and beast, and communication was at once restored between animal instincts. This, however, did not prevent him from preserving his human dignity and even thinking his human thoughts, while expressing himself to the others in the usual terms employed by the animal race. And he acted in this way even with General Captain, who spoke men's words without understanding them and understood only animals' words.

General Captain was the parrot he had stolen from Mlle. Franchet and carried as a slave to his hut in the forest, to serve as his hall-porter. Balaoo had the greatest contempt for General Captain, being of opinion that there was nothing sillier for an animal than to insist on talking men's words when he does not understand what they mean.

Thus thought Balaoo in the dense forest, as he walked, without a road and without compass or matches, through the dark, moonless night to his hut in the Big Beech, which might be described as his bachelor's chambers. Thus thought Balaoo, his heart heavy with his misdeeds, carrying the Empress' gown, done up in a neat parcel, under his arm.

A voice from high up in the air disturbed his meditations:

"Hullo, Polly!"

"The idiot!" said Balaoo, aloud, shrugging his shoulders.

The voice at once continued, in the dark trees:

"Well I never! Did you ever? What next? What next? What next?"

"Stop playing the fool, General Captain!" commanded the pithecanthrope, in a rough, animal voice, employing animal sounds that produced an immediate effect.

General Captain ceased pretending to be a man and, from his perch on a branch so high that none of us could have seen it from below, even had it been daylight and even had we had Balaoo's eyes, he humbly bade his master welcome, like the humble porter-parrot that he was and in the parrot tongue, which Balaoo understood quite well, for almost all animals understand one another's language.

Balaoo gave a grunt or two and asked how it was that the parrot was not asleep, at that time of night. General Captain replied that he was awoke by a great light shining over the village:

"You can't see it from below," the bird-porter explained to the pithecanthrope, "but I can see it clearly. The sky is quite red, a glorious, bright red, as when the sun rises in my country."

Balaoo grinned, for he knew General Captain's high-flown pretensions. The bird, who lied like a lawyer or a dentist, used to declare that he had seen as many countries as Balaoo himself, though he was unable to name them. As a matter fact, he was only able to brag from hearing a Brazilian parakeet describe his equatorial feats of prowess at the Marseilles bird-fancier's where General Captain had been landed as a youngster. Balaoo always shut him up by saying:

"Oh, drop it! I have known parrots in the Forest of Bandong. They were not a yellowy-green like you, but had bright-red wings and bright-blue heads and gold round their necks. You don't even know; General Captain, how the parrot-mothers of the Forest of Bandong get the gold into their little one's necks. Why, old chap, it's by feeding them on the yolks of eggs! There's nothing like yolk of egg to make you gold in the neck. That's the way they produce canary-yellow in the Forest of Bandong, General Captain!"

Whereupon the general would make no reply, because everybody knew that he was not fed on the yolks of eggs at Mlle. Franchet's.

For the moment, Balaoo climbed the tree, feeling uneasy at what the parrot had told him about the fire. The Big Beech in the Pierrefeu clearing was at least three hundred years old. It was a world, a nature, a universe in itself. It was the finest tree in the forest, stood nearly a hundred and sixty feet high and was over six feet in diameter. Balaoo took the greatest pride in it, although he never omitted to tell any of his forest friends who congratulated him upon it that the tree was nothing compared with those in the Forest of Bandong and that his father and mother, before slinging their house in the mangroves in the swamps, had begun, when they were quite young, by living in a eucalyptus-tree which was over fifteen hundred feet high—so he said—and thirty feet in diameter. However, he consented to be satisfied with his tree, for he liked its smooth, clean bark, its silky branches, its polished leaves, which looked so shiny after the rain; and he ate its fruit. But he took care to throw away the rind, nature, whose voice was always whispering in his ear, having told him that it contained the worst of poisons, the one that gives epilepsy and makes you look like a tipsy man.

Balaoo, when he moved in, had driven all the animals from the tree, excepting the little birds, whose nests he respected with the greatest care. But he had sent a family of crows about their business, with such honours as were due to them; for their croaking deafened him and disturbed his midday slumbers. The crows thought themselves quite safe up there, on the top floor, where they sat and laughed at men; but they were nicely caught, one fine spring afternoon, when they saw a man come walking up the trunk as easily as up a staircase, who, after greeting them with a stately wave of his straw hat in his right hand, with his left sent the clumsy tangle of twigs and branches which that wretched family dignified with the sweet name of nest flying right across the tree-tops.

As I said, Balaoo kept the little birds with him, in his tree. This was not from any excess of sentiment, but because he loved a good omelette, a fact of which the little birds became aware, in course of time, and left him, for all his consideration in not driving them away.

Balaoo, after climbing ten flights of branches, arrived at his little set of pithecanthrope chambers. The hall-porter was standing at the door, with his beak wide open, gazing towards the distant blaze. Balaoo shaded his eyes with his hand and looked. The fire was flaring in the very middle of Saint-Martin, by the Place de la Mairie. He at once felt reassured. As long as Madeleine's home was not in danger, nothing else mattered. His thoughts turned instinctively to the Three Brothers, who loved to play tricks on the members of the Human Race, like real pithecanthropes, and he said to himself that this great glare was perhaps an invention of theirs.

The sound of the alarm-bell filled his ears with a noisy and unpleasant booming. General Captain thought aloud that they were ringing the bells for the midnight mass to which Mlle. Franchet went once a year. Balaoo called him a fool and told him to hold his tongue. All this fuss and bustle in the village worried him. He was still thinking of his hanged man, of Madeleine's grief, of Coriolis' anger. When the light fell and the alarm bell ceased, he went indoors and struck a match.

He lit a candle, which had not cost him a large sum, any more than the candlestick. We may safely say that Balaoo had furnished his flat without going to great expense. The grocers', drapers' and other shops in the village had supplied him, in due course, with all he wanted; and he had provisions in his larder; for his hut, which he had built very neatly, solidly and comfortably, in the pithecanthrope style, with reeds, leaves, ferns and branches, was divided into two rooms, after the fashion of men. In the back room, he heaped up the fruit of his industry and the produce of his thefts; the front room, which was always very clean and nicely kept and almost decorative, contained the essential articles of furniture, that is to say, a mat; a chest of drawers filled with a few changes of clothes and linen, but especially plenty of well-starched collars and cuffs, for which Balaoo entertained a perfect passion: this chest of drawers had once belonged to Dr. Honorat; a pedestal cupboard, from the same source; a cabinet-photograph of Madeleine; and that was all. No bed. It was bad enough to have a bed, with sheets and blankets, in his rooms in the house at the village. Here, when you wanted to sleep, you lay down on the mat; and the same when you wanted to talk. Balaoo hated arm-chairs, of whatever style or period. This does not mean that he was averse to decorative art: for instance, he had hung his walls with picture-placards advertising the best chocolates and the daintiest biscuits. The owners of the Black Sun Inn had long misses a gorgeous cardboard poster, on which a young and lovely female, in short skirts, was pictured lifting her little finger as she sipped a glass of golden yellow bitters. This work of art, which had once adorned the Roubions' summer dining-room, now figured in Master Balaoo's picture-gallery, at his country-house in the Big Beech at Pierrefeu.

General Captain was attached to this palace, in the office of hall-porter, by one leg. His duties consisted not only in cleaning the whole establishment, with a deft beak, during his master's absences, but also in admitting visitors and giving them beech-mast while they waited. For Balaoo, when in the mood, was at home to his friends of the woods and the underwood. For those who were heavy in their haunches, he had contrived a system of little notches cut into the trunk so as to form a staircase. He had taken the idea from General Captain's perch at Mlle. Franchet's. Balaoo, who had never seen a lift, was very proud of this piece of work, which allowed even his friend Dhol, who had never left the level of the ground, to walk about Balaoo's tree as though he were at home and to give himself the airs of a jaguar, airs which, I am bound to say, looked absolutely ridiculous in a wolf.

Balaoo, as we have seen, struck a light. He next unfurled the splendours of the Empress' gown before General Captain's fascinated gaze. Then, after shaking it, as he had been taught to shake out stuffs, in order to remove the folds, he hung it on a nail. This done, he lay down dreamily on his mat, his brain afluster with the day's events.

He longed for quiet; but General Captain never ceased asking him questions, to which, for that matter, he did not reply.

The Empress' gown puzzled the hall-porter. He wanted to know if Balaoo had brought the garment for his own use and if he should soon see his master walking about in that fine white dress. He turned it with his beak and managed to tear a bit of lace from it, for which he got a box on the ear.

"You needn't be angry," he said, hurrying out of reach. "I am sure it would suit you beautifully. You ought to have a necklace of beads to go with it, like Mlle. Franchet."

Balaoo was filled with concentrated fury at the idea that anyone could conceive him decked out like that old faggot of a Mlle. Franchet. General Captain, who was too stupid to notice his master's bad temper, went on jabbering like a parrot:

"I hear that beads are much worn by the monkeys." At this word, Balaoo pushed two fingers into his nostrils and sat up on his hind-quarters, a bad sign.

"A parakeet in the Cours Belzunce at Marseilles told me that, on the Equator, the macaques"—O fool of a General Captain, to use that name before Balaoo!—"have hairs behind their ears and rings and bracelets of yellow gold on their feet and necklaces of rare pearls round their necks."

Balaoo withdrew the fingers from his nostrils, a sign that he had overcome his anger and recovered his spirits. One can't lose one's temper with a General Captain. And he said:

"General Captain, I suppose you don't know what a jacare is?"

"A jacare? No, Balaoo, I don't."

"A jacare is a sort of crocodile who lives in the Forest of Bandong. When the Java panther begins to eat him by the tail, he does not move a step; when the Java panther has eaten half of him and satisfied his hunger for the day, the panther goes away, but the jacare remains. Yes, I give you my word, he remains waiting for the panther to come back, next day, and eat the other half. Isn't he a fool?"

"Why do you tell me that?" asked the hall-porter, aghast.

"So that you may know that, in the Forest of Bandong, everything is finer and grander than here. Thus, for instance, the jacare is an even bigger fool than you. But don't go building on it, General Captain!

True, I sha'n't ever eat you by the tail; but my friend As, if I gave him leave, might be less squeamish."

At that moment, some one scratched at the door. Balaoo told his servant to open it, for he recognized a friendly scratch; and, as luck would have it, As the fox walked in, carrying a chicken between his jaws and waving a greeting with his arched brush.

Balaoo at once ordered him to go outside and leave his prey on the door-mat—Balaoo had recognized one of Mme. Boche's chickens—and reproached him with his carnivorous instincts. As put the chicken carefully in a corner, within easy reach. His snout was covered with blood and feathers and he stretched it out on his paws with the air of a philosopher who claims the right to live as he likes and who can listen to the observations of others with equanimity, having his belly full and his dinner provided for the morrow. He let the virtuous Balaoo talk and descant upon the peaceful charms of a vegetarian diet; and, at the moment when the other least expected it, let fly an argument which, in a manner of speaking, struck the pithecanthrope all of a heap:

"You boast of being a man," said As, "and you don't even eat chicken!"

Balaoo said nothing, for a series of moments that, to himself, seemed endless. Would no fit answer ever occur to his brain? It was really not worth while going through a course of study, learning to read men's words on wooden cubes and to write them first with a pencil and then with a pen and ink, only to allow one's self to be flummoxed like that by a simple As. At last, he sat up, with glittering eyes, gave a cough and declared:

"I wouldn't hurt a fly for the sake of food! True enough, I kill; but I kill because I'm annoyed and I never kill to eat: I call that disgusting; and you can take it straight from me."

"Then you don't like those who kill to eat," said As. "If so, why do you like the Three Brothers, who kill to eat?"

Balaoo retorted:

"I saw them kill the process server; and they did not eat the process-server."

"Yes, but they kill us, here, in the forest; and they do it to eat us."

"You flatter yourself," said Balaoo, shrugging his shoulders. "The Three Brothers never eat fox. Men don't eat fox. You are not even good to eat for those who eat everything, which is far from saying that the Three Brothers won't kill you, for they don't like chatterers and windbags."

"I know more than you think about them," said As, in a tone of vexation. "As I was going through the Rue Neuve, I saw them dragging one of the Race along ; and they had put a piece of white stuff, like that which you use to wipe yourself with, in his mouth; and they were kicking him to make him go faster. I ran away, because they had guns on their shoulders. They can do what they like, for all I care: they are no friends of mine; but, as you are so thick with them, you might tell them to leave me alone. Last year, I came home to find that they had set fire to my hole. They thought that I was there."

"People who lead the life which you do must be prepared for everything," replied Balaoo, sententiously, without making any promise. And he thought it his duty to add, "There are good and bad sides to forest life. And now, As, old chap, let me get to sleep."

"It's easy to sleep," said As, who understood that he was being shown the door, "when one is the friend of men and has an easy conscience, like yourself. By the way, Balaoo, there's a man hanging from the first tree on the left on the Riom Road; you ought to go and cut him down."

Balaoo sprang at As' paw and nearly broke it:

"Who told you that?"

"No one told me: I saw it!" said As, releasing and licking his paw.

"What did you see?" growled Balaoo.

As gave a glance to make sure that the door was open:

"I saw you putting his tie straight!" he flung to Balaoo, jumping out of the little set of chambers in the Big Beech at Pierrefeu.

Balaoo ran to the door, but the other was far away.

His nasty, sniggering laugh was heard in the dark and leafy distance.

Balaoo, choking with anger, could find nothing better than a word in man-language to express his animal wrath:

"Filth!" he shouted, in his terrible voice of thunder, into the black night of the forest.

[8] The mangroves.—AUTHOR'S NOTE.

Chapter XIII

On the day after that night of terror, at early dawn, the troops sent from Clermont-Ferrand began the famous siege of the Black Woods. It took no less, from the start, than a regiment of infantry and a squadron of cavalry, with M. le Vicomte de la Terrenoire at their head, to ring the space in which it was thought that the Three Brothers might have taken refuge. The police-officials of the chief town of the department, including M. le Prefet Mathieu Delafosse, were taken over the scene of the crime, heard the story of the tragic night from the mayor's own lips and made their preliminary arrangements in concert with the military. On the other hand, the sub-prefect and the deputy for the arrondissement of Tournadon-la-Riviere, who were too deeply compromised with the Three Brothers, were requested, by the government to keep in the background.

M. Mathieu Delafosse was upset, to begin with, by the undoubted fact of the kidnapping of Dr. Honorat and showered reproaches on the mayor of Saint-Martin for not interfering when the ruffians were passing under his nose with their unfortunate victim, to which M. Jules replied, with no little common sense, that, if he had given the least sign of life, the result would have been a great massacre of his fellow-citizens and that, taking one thing with another, they could congratulate themselves on being let off, after such a night, with the disappearance of Dr. Honorat, who, at any rate, was an unmarried man.

These sage words did not, for the moment, have the effect of cheering monsieur le prefet, who felt a secret fear that the Three Brothers had seized upon the doctor's person only with the object of holding him as a hostage, thus complicating a task which was difficult enough in itself. However, upon reflection, the fact that the three ruffians had already killed M. Herment de Meyrentin gave monsieur le prefet some little hope. Those scoundrels were thirsting for blood; and Dr. Honorat also was probably dead by this time. If that were so, there was no need for the authorities to hold their hands lest they should thereby be giving the doctor his quietus!

"They are impulsive brutes," thought M. le Prefet Mathieu Delafosse, recovering his serenity. "They've killed him without thinking that they had the price of their ransom in their hands."

Once this idea, that Dr. Honorat's sufferings were at an end, had taken definite root in the brains of the first magistrate of the department, it was resolved to "go strenuously to work."

There would be no shrinking from extreme measures.

The government was very much annoyed by this fresh bother, because of the rumour which began to be current that the Three Brothers, who were known for political agents, had held their tongues throughout the trial on the part which they played in the elections, only because they had been promised an absolute chance of escape.

And that escape had been neatly carried out indeed! It could not be explained except on the assumption that a helper had come from the outside, working at his leisure, undisturbed by the warders. The warders themselves declared that they could make nothing of it. The commission of enquiry came to no conclusion and declared itself powerless to explain the escape by ordinary human means. The Three Brothers, confined, in one cell and guarded by five armed policemen, had flown as though on wings. When it happened, the warders were playing cards in the cell, as usual, all seated round a table, while Siméon, Élie and Hubert stood behind, advising them. When the game was finished and the players raised their heads, they looked in vain for the prisoners, who had disappeared. Two of the bars at the window had been twisted out of shape with an effort which no man's arm was capable of making. It was through this aperture that they had flown away. And there was really no other word for it: they must have skimmed across the roofs like birds. In short, the whole thing resembled a dream; and the ministry, who would certainly have to answer questions, could hardly come down to the Chamber with such a fairytale! And so the prefect and his staff were given clearly to understand that, since it was impossible to explain the escape, they must absolutely find the fugitives, alive or dead, so that any idea of complicity might be removed.

"Strenuous measures, major, strenuous measures!" said M. Mathieu Delafosse to the Vicomte de la Terrenoire, whom he found prancing on his sorrel outside Mme. Valentin's windows, with all the village round him. "You will please trot down the Tournadon-la-Riviere Road with your men, till you come to the Grange-aux-Belles, and there join the detachment which is marching from the Chevalet side. That is the only road still open. It must be barred to the ruffians. You will then arrange with Colonel du Briage and drive the quarry between Moabit and Pierrefeu. And be sure to tell the colonel to send his whole regiment into the woods and to make his men beat all the bushes and hunt about everywhere. And, if the scoundrels defend themselves, they're to be shot down like rabbits. Send me a message by one of your troopers, when you're nearing Moabit, and we'll enter the forest in our turn. Do you understand? Good-bye and good luck to you!...I shall go straight back to that old Vautrin hag, who may end by telling us something. When I think that they had the cheek to come home and fetch their belongings. What belongings? More politics, that's certain! There was nothing found when the place was searched...And what's become of the Zoé girl? The old woman says that she went scouring the forest with them. It seems hardly likely: she would be rather in their way..."

"Little Zoé knows the forest as well as they do," said monsieur le maire, who had now arrived, "and she climbs the trees like a monkey. I tell you, they're not caught yet! You would have done better to keep them in your prison, monsieur le prefet."

The prefect pretended not to hear and, followed by the whole village, turned towards the Vautrins' cabin, where paralyzed old Barbe lay moaning in her recess by the chimney. The mayor and his two deputies sadly closed the procession.

The other actors in last night's tragedy did not think of putting in an appearance. One and all were laid up with a feverish chill, including even Mme. Godefroy, the postmistress, though there was plenty for her to do. All the heroes and heroines of that fatal night wished themselves miles away, down to Mme. Valentin, who carefully kept her little powdered and painted face hidden behind the lace curtains of her dainty bedroom, although her maid told her that M. de la Terrenoire had passed under her windows on horseback to say good-bye before setting out for the war.

The only people who could have told the truth about the events of the night were either invisible or silent. And the population had embroidered on the terrible adventure to its heart's content. Some went so far as to say that the Vautrins had loaded with chains at least half a score of prisoners, men and women together, and carried them off to the forest with Dr. Honorat and that the Three Brothers had started operations by slitting the tongues of everybody in the big room at the Black Sun.

Citizens who had had the courage to peep through their shutters on that accursed night had seen things fit to make you shudder. Mme. Toussaint, they said, who had tried to defend her Empress' gown, had been dragged three times round the Place de la Mairie by the hair of her head.

The news soon spread all over the department. People struck work for thirty miles around. Peasants came across the vineyards waving their arms and asking, as soon as they were within earshot, if "they" had been caught. Their curiosity outweighed their very fears.

No, no, the Three Brothers had not been caught.

And what beat everything was that old Barbe, on her truckle-bed, laughed in her sleeve at all the questions which the prefect put to her. She was prouder than ever of having brought into the world that fine progeny which was keeping the whole Republic busy and upsetting an entire department. And she sent a cold shiver down the back of all who had entered her cabin by the way in which she said:

"Ah, good! They've taken Dr. Honorat, have they? I wouldn't be in his skin for a trifle!"

And she went on, in the hearing of the thunder-struck authorities:

"Oh, the lads! When I think that I had all three of them 'in one litter!' There aren't many mothers like me in the world! I ought to have had a decoration. Ay, on the christening-day, I thought they were going to fork out the legion of honour! The mayor gave me a kiss. Yes, M. Jules, that's how the mayors used to carry on with Barbe, in those days. They christened the three of them together. They put three pillows in a basket, my word they did, with the three laddies on top of them, squealing like calves. And they carried the three kids in the basket to his reverence, who put salt on their tongues. There were three godfathers, who all gave their names. And, in the evening, the whole village was drunk and the mayor and the priest too!...That's how people carried on in those days, M. Jules!...So don't you go hurting my boys! Old Barbe couldn't get three more like them nowadays!"

And then she stopped and refused to answer any more questions.

Suddenly, there was a great commotion in the road outside the Vautrins' house. Everybody was pushing and jostling to see a white thing coming down the middle of the road, from the forest.

It suggested an apparition of the Virgin Mary. A white, ethereal shape came gliding and floating towards the astounded crowd. Nobody dared take a step in its direction. Everyone marvelled what it could be. The pious crossed themselves. It was like a miracle, that beautiful lady in white, erect and buoyant in the middle of the road!...

She advanced with no apparent movement of her feet. Monsieur le maire and monsieur le prefet, alarmed and curious like all the rest, had gone to the window. And, suddenly; a voice cried:

"Why, it's the Empress' dress!"

And every mouth repeated:

"It's the Empress' dress! It's the Empress' dress come back!"

But the Empress' dress was not returning alone; and soon they were able to see that the Empress' dress was returning on the shoulders of little Zoé! Yes, as I live, it was Zoé, in the Empress' gown, giving herself the airs of the Queen of Heaven as she came down the road! The stupor was so great that not a cry was heard, not a laugh. And yet it was enough to make a cat laugh to see that little black sloe of a Zoé, who was usually no bigger than a shrimp, now looking ever so tall in the white trailing gown of the Empress of All the Russias!

She wore that gown, which was not yet stitched, like a cope, with the back panel falling in an immense long train over her heels; and she had passed her bare, skinny, grubby arms through the holes that were waiting for the sleeves. Her towzled blue-black hair hung down her shoulders and flowed in inky waves over all that as yet unspotted whiteness.

Zoé wore a serious face, as though in church. And her eyes insulted all the bystanders.

She at once addressed the mayor:

"Monsieur le maire," she said, boldly, in her little shrill, vinegary voice, "I have come from my brothers, who have something to say to the President of the Republic. They want him to give them a pardon."

The ambassadress rattled out her message loud enough for everyone to hear. Then she took breath and gave a little cough, putting her hand before her mouth like a well-bred ambassadress, or like a schoolgirl trying to remember the exact words of her lesson.

This quiet self-assurance took everybody aback. She continued:

"If the President of the Republic does that, my brothers will never be heard of any more. They will do nobody any harm and they will leave the district."

Then an angry, threatening voice arose. It was M. Mathieu Delafosse, recovering his wits:

"And, if your brothers do not receive their pardon, what will they do then?" he asked, furious at seeing all his apprehensions justified, for he guessed that there was a hostage behind this move.

Zoé coughed, blushed slightly, gave a kick to the train of her lovely dress and said:

"If the President of the Republic does not give them their pardon, they will kill Dr. Honorat."

Loud rumours at once arose and the prefect again regretted that the worthy doctor had not already departed this life. He was heard growling in his moustache: "A nice business! We're in for blackmail now!" He left the Vautrins' house at last and walked up to Zoé. The others formed a circle round them on the road.

"Don't touch me, mind!" said the girl. "My brothers said that, if anyone touched me, they would kill Dr. Honorat first and set fire to Saint-Martin afterwards."

Fresh rumours, which the prefect silenced with a gesture:

"No one's going to touch you, child," he promised, with sudden gentleness, "but you must tell us where Dr. Honorat is."

"He's with my brothers."

"And where are your brothers?"

"With Dr. Honorat," replied the girl, wiping her nose on a corner of the Empress' gown.

The mayor now came forward:

"Zoé," he said, "I promise that you shall not be hurt. Go back quietly to the forest, where your brothers are waiting for you, and tell them that they have nothing to gain by behaving as they are doing. The President of the Republic has not yet taken any decision about their pardon; but they must remember that they can't hope to save their heads by setting fire to the village and murdering Dr. Honorat. Of course, we can't promise anything; but, supposing one of them was to have been pardoned a couple of days ago, he won't be now, unless, of course, they all three surrender of their own accord. Tell them to think of that. Do you understand?"

"I can't understand a word of what you're saying!" declared Zoé, whereat everybody laughed, in spite of the gravity of the position.

The mayor, flushing pink under the humiliation, retorted, roughly:

"Don't you understand that, if the President of the Republic was thinking of pardoning one of your brothers...?"

"That's no good," said Zoé, interrupting him bluntly.

"What they told me was, 'All or none!'"

More rumours in the crowd.

"This obstinacy won't serve their turn!" exclaimed M. Mathieu Delafosse. "You go and tell them, child, that you've seen the prefect and the gendarmerie and the police and all the soldiers from Clermont...and that orders have been given to fire on them, if they don't surrender."

Zoé coughed, with her hand before her mouth, and asked:

"Is that your answer?"

"Our answer is that they must surrender and then the President of the Republic will see what he can do. If they listen to reason and don't hurt Dr. Honorat, the chances are that they won't repent it...You tell them that."

"I don't mind," said Zoé, nodding her head, "but that's no answer..."

"Tell them, all the same," said the mayor, "and you'll see, it will make them think, if they have any sense...Be off, now. How is Dr. Honorat?"

"Oh, he's all right!"

"What does he say?"

"He doesn't say anything."

"Mind they don't put him to pain!"

"Oh, he's tied up, so that he can't run away! Apart from that, no one bothers about him!"

"But surely you give him something to eat?"

"Oh, we gave him his feed this morning, but most likely he's not hungry: he never touched his pan!...So that's all you have to say to me?...Well, then, good-bye, gentlemen all; see you later!"

And she turned back, in her Empress' gown, while no one ventured to utter a reflection upon the manner in which she had obtained possession of that sumptuous garment. Nobody cared to fall out with the Vautrins.

A few voices were even uplifted in praise of Zoé's appearance in that get-up. Some one said:

"It suits her jolly well!"

She dissappeared as she had come, erect and proud as a lady, not deigning to turn her head, sweeping all the dust off the road...

It goes without saying that none dared follow her. The edge of the forest was dangerous, notwithstanding the presence of a company of infantry which was flaunting its red trousers on the grass, waiting for orders to march ahead. Other soldiers, farther away, continued the chain of posts; but, as the officers said, "it would need two divisions and more to make sure of preventing the escape of those beggars who know every bit of timber in the forest."

Colonel du Briage had drawn up his men on the other side of the tall trees of Pierrefeu, but hesitated to push his way into the woods. As a matter of fact, he hated this police-work and only performed it grudgingly. He had told the Vicomte de la Terrenoire, who was riding

144

at the head of his squadron from one end of the district to the other, linking the different units of that curious besieging army, that he would talk to the prefect first, for he had no intention of accepting the slightest responsibility in the matter.

The episode of Zoé's embassy delayed operations still longer. The prefect telegraphed to the minister of the interior and was waiting for the minister's reply, which had not yet arrived at three o'clock.

At three o'clock, on the other hand, Zoé once more appeared on the edge of the forest. She was still wearing her Empress' gown and was still bareheaded, in spite of the blazing sun. She passed through the soldiers, who could not refrain from cracking a few jests at her, which made her knit her young brows, for no one had ever had a word to say against Zoé's morals.

She walked into the Rue Neuve. The whole village was around her in a second. She said that she had brought the answer of the Three Brothers and that she wanted to speak to the mayor. They told her that the mayor, the prefect, the chief detective of Clermont, Colonel du Briage himself and two majors had just finished luncheon at the Black Sun.

She entered the Black Sun and, a minute after, was shown into the room where the civil and military authorities were sitting.

There were clouds of tobacco-smoke, a profusion of bottles and liqueur-glasses and, on the top of all, any number of stupid remarks, stupid because they were futile and could lead to nothing until the minister's reply came. However, in the absence of the minister's reply, they now had Zoé.

It was the prefect, of course, who put the questions: "Come here, child," he said, as though he were speaking to a little shy girl.

But there was no shyness about Zoé. She walked up to him, carrying in her hand a parcel wrapped in a newspaper.

"You've seen your brothers? And you're back already? Then they are not far away," said the prefect.

"You see for yourself that, if we had wanted to capture them, they would have been in our hands by now. But it's better that they should come back of their own accord. I hope they understood that?"

"Here's their answer," said Zoé.

And she held out her parcel to the prefect, who asked: "What's that?"

"Look inside and you'll know," she said, with her usual coolness.

Chapter XIII

After turning his eyes over all those present, to express his astonishment, M. Mathieu Delafosse took the parcel from Zoé's hands and began to undo it.

Everybody's curiosity was excited to the utmost when, after the first wrapper had been removed, another appeared all covered with blood-stains. The prefect opened it quickly and at once put the parcel on the table, uttering an exclamation of horror as he did so. The others, who stood bending over him, all gave a cry of horror with him. The parcel contained a finger.

When the excitement had more or less subsided, M. Mathieu Delafosse, pale in the face and gnawing his moustache, began to question Zoé:

"What's this you've brought us, you unhappy girl?"

"It's one of Dr. Honorat's little fingers," replied Zoé, placidly, wiping her nose again on the Empress' dress.

"Have your brothers cut off the doctor's finger?"

"Well, it's not yours, monsieur le prefet, and it's not mine!"

"Oh, so it's Dr. Honorat's little finger, is it?"

"I know it is," said the mayor. "I can tell it by the ring."

And he pointed to the gold ring which had been left on the finger as though to prove its genuineness.

"But this is abominable!" exclaimed the prefect, turning paler and paler.

"Why shouldn't they cut a finger off people who want to cut off their heads?" asked Zoé, logically.

"And can you tell me, you little wretch, why they have committed this horrible cruelty?"

"It's like this, they say it's to show you that they're prepared to go to all lengths with Dr. Honorat, if the President of the Republic won't give them their pardon. They told me to tell you that they'll give the President of the Republic until the stroke of twelve to-morrow. If, at the stroke of twelve to-morrow, the President of the Republic has not pardoned them, they'll cut off the doctor's other little finger and make you think again. I'm only telling you what they said. Lastly, on the day after to-morrow, they'll kill him outright and send you the pieces; and they'll resume their full liberty; and you'll be responsible for whatever happens...That's all I have to say. Can I go back?".

At that moment, the prefect was handed an official telegram. It was the long-expected answer. M. Mathieu Delafosse opened it eagerly and read it at a glance. Then he indignantly gave vent to his dissatisfaction:

"Well, this beats everything!"

And he passed the telegram to the colonel and the mayor, who read:

"Impossible for government to treat with people who have placed themselves outside the law. The law cannot give way; but act cautiously, for sake of Dr. Honorat."

"That doesn't help us much!" said the mayor. "It amounts to this, monsieur le prefet," explained the colonel, "that the government leaves the entire responsibility for the operations with you. I will do what you tell me, but there must be no misunderstanding: I want precise orders; and, for the rest, I wash my hands of it."

"But what am I to do? What am I to do? You see for yourselves they mean to kill him!" exclaimed M. Mathieu Delafosse.

"That's certain!" declared Zoé, whose presence had been overlooked by all of them.

The prefect was ashamed of betraying his weakness and embarrassment before an agent of the enemy. He got out of his difficulty, for the moment, by a display of anger:

"What's still more certain," he cried, "is that your three brothers, if they act like savages, will obtain neither pardon nor pity and that they will be massacred by the troops before dark. Those are the orders."

"No," said Zoé, shaking her head. "If those were the orders, you wouldn't be so puzzled. However, what am I to tell them?"

"Tell them to set Dr. Honorat free."

"That's no answer. You won't be satisfied till they've cut off his other little finger. So I'm to go?"

The mayor said:

"We might telegraph the story of the little finger to the minister. Perhaps that will make him come to a decision."

The prefect acquiesced:

"I'll do so at once."

And he called for a pen and ink.

"Listen, Zoé," he said. "I'll keep you here until I receive an answer from the minister. You go into that room next door. We must get the matter settled one way or the other."

"You'd better get it settled as fast as you can," said Zoé, "for they're beginning to lose their patience in the forest."

Zoé went into the next room and the prefect wrote out his telegram. When the telegram was dispatched, they resumed the discussion.

Suddenly, the noise of a great altercation came from the next room. They heard a voice yelping:

"Give me back my dress! Give me back my dress, will you, you thief, you sister of murderers!"

And the door opened and Zoé came and took refuge with the officers and claimed their assistance and protection against Mother Toussaint, who wanted to strip her as naked as a worm. Mother Toussaint had learnt from public rumour that her Empress' gown was on Zoé's back and that Zoé was walking about, doing the grand in her property. She forthwith forgot the terrors of the night and her wholesome dread of the Three Brothers, ran to the Black Sun like mad and went for Zoé, who was at a loss to understand the reason of this rating.

Zoé defended herself with indignation, opened wide innocent eyes before the mayor and the prefect and called heaven to witness that the gown was really and truly hers and that she had never stolen a thing in her life.

Losing his last shred of patience at an incident which he considered of no importance at such a moment, the prefect asked the girl where she had got that work of art. When the child replied that a passer-by, whom she did not know, had made her a present of it in the forest, there was a great burst of laughter, which carried the day. The mayor himself tried to make Madame Toussaint understand how very much out of place her claim was at a moment when they were engaged in saving a man's life. Lastly, the chief-detective reconciled everybody by dogmatically stating that the child had not been seen to steal the dress and that, in the matter of personal property, possession is nine points of the law, whereupon Mme. Toussaint was turned out of the room and advised to seek her remedy in the law-courts. And thus was settled the fate of the Empress' gown, which remained on the back of little Zoé, Queen of the Forest at Saint-Martin-des-Bois. While this was going on, the government's second reply arrived. It was as categorical as the first and ran:

"Abominable savagery. We repeat law cannot give way. Finish business to-day certain and telegraph report. Debate set down for to-morrow. Act cautiously, for sake of Dr. Honorat."

As we may imagine, these fresh instructions did not relieve M. Mathieu Delafosse' perplexity. More than ever, the whole burden of this extraordinary adventure was left upon his shoulders. It was for him to make the best he could of it.

He concealed his discomfiture beneath an air of haughty decision:

"Tell your brothers," he said to Zoé, "that the government refuses to recognize them except to receive their submission. Once again, they must surrender and the President of the Republic will see what he can do. He will give them till ten o'clock tomorrow morning to think it over. And Dr. Honorat's death won't keep your brothers from being guillotined: on the contrary! And now be off!"

She went away, pouting.

As soon as she was gone, a council of war was held at Roubion's. The prefect had his plan. As his orders were to act quickly and cautiously, he would skilfully combine ruse and force. He had already begun to realize this Machiavellian scheme by sending word to the Vautrins that they would be left alone until ten o'clock next morning. Ostensibly, the troops guarding the skirt of the woods would be ordered to pile their arms. They would encamp where they were, cook their suppers and appear to settle down with the sole object of quietly spending the night there. Then, at two o'clock in the morning, they would all make a start. The Three Brothers could not be very far from Saint-Martin, as was proved by little Zoé's journeys. The circle hemming them in could be narrowed during the night by the soldiers slipping under wood, with the wariness of Red Indians.

This circle, according to the prefect's calculations, must have as its centre the Moabit clearing, so called because it had once served as a retreat to a Jew of the name of Moab, who was crossed in love and who lived there, far from the world, in some quarry-pits disused since thousands of years, covered with luxuriant vegetation and, at that time, known to him alone.

An ordnance-survey map was brought and spread upon the table; and they worked out the plan of operations until dinner-time, after which everybody, knowing exactly what he had to do, returned to his post. The mayor had sent the crier round the village to announce that it would be dangerous to walk about the streets and in the country after eight o'clock at night; and he advised his fellow-citizens to go to bed early and not to trouble their heads about anything that might happen outside their doors. They could sleep with easy minds: their safety was being cared for.

That night, nobody went to bed at Saint-Martin-des-Bois. Every inhabitant was posted behind his shutters. Those in the Rue Neuve could see the light burning in monsieur le maire's office in the town-hall and tried to give a name to the fitful shadows that slipped across the square, doubtless coming for orders. At midnight, three cloaked forms were seen to leave the municipal buildings, avoiding the light of the street-lamp. It was M. le Prefet Mathieu Delafosse, Colonel du Briage and the chief-detective of Clermont. As for the mayor, he had declared that he would not leave the post of honour, but stay in his office, ready to grapple with events!...

Chapter XIV

While the civil and military authorities were studying M. Mathieu Delafosse' plan of attack at Saint-Martin, the slanting rays of the autumn sun were gilding the tops of the trees round the Moabit clearing, where the Three Brothers lay sleeping, with their loaded guns by their side, under the tall ferns and in the heart of the inextricable tangle of shrubs which made an inviolable sanctuary of this forest corner. Remnants of victuals, with bottles lying on the grass or thrusting their necks from the game-bags, showed that folk lacked nothing at Moabit. They were gathered like animals that had eaten their fill. The strongest of the three was Hubert, square-built, as it were chopped and carved out of the wood of the forest. A magnificent, unkempt beard, a bush of tawny hair, swept from his mouth to his stomach and half hid his shaggy chest. He was snoring; and yet it would have been hardly safe to say that his pupils were not keeping guard under his slightly raised eyelids. It must have been with those lads' eyes as with their ears; it was likely that, trained by the very animals which they hunted, their senses were never entirely at rest. It was known that all three could see better in the dark than in broad daylight and that they brought the instincts of tiger-cats to help them follow the trail. They were fellows who were never happy among men, with their eternal game-laws; and in reality they enjoyed themselves in decent society only at election-times, which are heavenly times on earth.

They slept; but Dr. Honorat did not sleep. Seated at the foot of the oak to which he was firmly tethered by one ankle, he was still, though he suffered great pain from the loss of his little finger, thinking of the skill with which the amputation had been performed. This secret admiration had not, as will be believed, come to him at once. It was preceded by a feeling of the deepest horror; and it is useless to attempt to describe the frenzy of alarm with which the excellent man had seen the operator, armed with his knife, come up to him. His anguish can be easily imagined; and, in spite of the abject cowardice displayed by the worthy doctor on the previous night, when the Vautrins were besieging the Black Sun, it would be unfair to despise him altogether. The poor man knew that, from the instant that the Three Brothers escaped their gaolers, he himself was doomed to suffer martyrdom. His evidence was designed to send the Vautrins to the scaffold. He had a pretty shrewd notion of what they would say to him, now that they were free. And that was more than enough to make a man lose his nerve!

And yet, though it threw him into a blue funk, Dr. Honorat kept his wits sufficiently about him to admire the neatness of an operation that had deprived him of a finger. And the doctor set great store by his finger!

Élie had cut off the finger; Hubert, who knew the virtue of herbs, had dressed it properly and bound up the bleeding stump; Siméon had explained:

"You understand that, if we meant to hurt you, we should not cut off your finger. Follow my argument: you represent to us the most precious thing in the world, our lives. We shall restore you to your friends on the day when the President of the Republic announces in his official gazette that our death-sentence has been commuted into anything he pleases. The hulks! We're not there yet! But one can't take too many precautions against the guillotine. Well, old codger, there you are; we're taking a finger off you just to stir the President up and make him leave our three heads on our shoulders. When he gets that by post, he'll see that we're in earnest and that it doesn't do to trifle with the Three Brothers!"

"And, if he won't give in?" asked the prisoner.

"Oho! Why, if he won't give in...next day, we'll send him a bit more!...."

"Oh, indeed?...A bit more?" stammered the poor doctor. "A bit more?...And, if he won't give in then, what will you send him on the third day?"

"Oh, on the third day, blow me tight, I think you might begin to say your prayers!...But there are chances that neither you nor we will be reduced to such sad extremities. Let us hope for the best, doctor. A little finger, delivered by post, makes a big impression."

And, upon my word, the doctor ended by saying as much to himself! What a glorious thing it would be if he got out of that tight place with the loss of a little finger! And he could not conceive that the public authorities, when confronted with his little finger, would hesitate for a moment to make the necessary sacrifices to recover possession of a worthy country practitioner, whose premature disappearance would have been a disgrace to any civilized nation. He had not, therefore, felt unduly perturbed when he saw Zoé go off with her brother's last instructions and with his little finger wrapped in a paper parcel. And he also thought, in the secret recesses of his being, that the government, which was born tricky, could always promise those scoundrels their lives...and change its mind at leisure...

So he sat down, patiently, at the foot of his tree, to which he was tied by the ankle with so cunning a knot that it would have been vain for him to try to discover its mystery. Moreover; he knew that the Three Brothers would be down upon him at the least suspicious movement...

Élie was the first to straighten himself. A glance at the prisoner, who had not stirred, sitting on the grass, against the trunk of his tree; and Élie stretched himself with a yawn, displaying an enormous pair of jaws and a splendid set of teeth.

The yawn woke the others, both of whom sat up, wide mouthed, tiger-jawed.

"Oho!" growled Hubert. "It's late; and the child's not back."

Unhooking his clasp-knife from his belt with a fierce gesture, he said no more.

A sigh came from the foot of the tree, a shudder, every sign of cowering fear.

"Yes, old codger," snarled Hubert. "If she's not back in an hour...your time's up!"

Inarticulate syllables at the foot of the tree, a stammering, a terror-struck mouthing and jabbering.

"What are you saying? I can't hear, doctor. Why don't you speak up?"

"Ah," grinned Siméon, ominously, "he spoke better than that at the trial!"

"The swine!"

"No one can tell what he was trying to say," remarked Élie, contemptuously. "He's dribbled it into his beard. Call that a man!"

"No, he's not that!" Hubert assented. "Now Balaoo: there's a man for you. But this one's worse than nothing: he doesn't count!...The others won't even have him as a swap for us!"

"Ay, it would be better if we, had the President of the Republic!" thought Siméon, who had greater powers of imagination than either of the others.

"Oh, they won't dare touch us, now that we have got clear with the State papers!" retorted Hubert.

"Bah, a deputy's, not the State!" said Élie, with a contemptuous smirk. "Because he owes his situation to us, that's no reason why the Republic should divorce us from the widow!"[9] "The swine!" said Hubert. "He'd never have got in but for us."

And all three, yielding once more to the fascination of the elections, began to talk voting-papers and registers and committees, just like so many town-clerks. The doctor, s'itting with his cord round his leg at the foot of his tree, could not bÉlieve his ears! Here, in the depths of the forest, were these three wild beasts antici pating the chances of a candidate for the next par liament and calmly casting up the likely number of votes before sharpening their knives to cut him, the doctor, in o pieces and sending him by post to the President of the Republic! What a sight! What a prospect! Was it not enough to make anyone mouth and jabber?

Suddenly, Hubert was on his short, thick legs with an alarming bound:

"That's all neither here nor there. The kid's not back!" The doctor at once found his voice; and what he had to say came straight from his throat, proclaiming the anguish that stifled him:

"Perhaps she's stopped to play on the road!"

"If that's so," said Siméon, facetiously, "you shall give her her smacking."

"It's getting dark," said Élie, deliberately, "but there's no danger at our place. If there was any danger, Balaoo would be here by now."

"Ah, there's a man for you, there's a man!" Hubert repeated, enthusiastically.

"You'd better give him our sister for a wife," grinned Siméon, drawing himself up on his enormous feet and swaying from one to the other, like an opossum.

"Why not?" asked Élie.

"Soon as he likes," said Hubert. "When shall we have the bans?"

"I believe there's nothing the kid would like better," said Siméon, whistling down the barrel of his gun.

"He's not hunch-backed, the citizen; and he's not bandy-legged; and he's no slouch on his feet!" declared Élie, squinting at his brothers.

"He needn't show his feet to monsieur le maire!" declared Hubert, peremptorily, tossing down a dram. "And it's not with his feet that a man swears to make a woman happy."

"Well, if you like, we'll mention it to him, next time we have the honour of receiving him at our table," suggested Siméon.

"Talk of the devil, there he is!" said Hubert, with his nose pointing up to the tree-tops.

And all three, with their loud, jolly voices, shouted:

"Halloa, Balaoo!...Halloa, Balaoo!...Halloa, Balaoo!..."

"Whom are they halloaing to?" Dr. Honorat wondered, seized with a fresh sense of anxiety.

No one had appeared in the little clearing. The others were looking up at the sky. Honorat could see nothing. He thought that they must be having a joke with him. Were they expecting a visitor in an aeroplane?

"Well, what's he waiting for?" asked Hubert.

"He's spotted that there's somebody here," said Élie.

"Can't you see he's putting on his socks?"

The doctor took his spectacles from their case and, more dismayed than ever, fixed them on his perspiring nose. And, in fact, right up on high, between two branches, he caught sight of a party sitting at his ease and pulling on a pair of socks.

"Well, Balaoo," cried the Three Brothers, "shall we see you to-day or to-morrow?"

"Coming, coming!" replied Balaoo, in his soft, gong-like voice.

And Dr. Honorat, unable to believe either his eyes or his spectacles, saw a gentleman walk down from the top, from the very top of the tree, as comfortably as though he were walking down from the top floor of a house: a highly respectable gentleman, upon my word, except that he was walking on his socks and carried his boots slung over his shoulder. He walked down from up there with his hands in his pockets and his hat on one ear, from branch to branch, all the way down the trunk, just as an ordinary person walks down a staircase, without hurrying. Dr. Honorat had never seen anything like it, except in the circus at Clermont, with Japanese acrobats walking straight up and down a pole. Who was this acrobat? Eh? Why? What? The doctor was not mistaken!...It was he!...He recognized him beyond a doubt!...There was no mistake about it!...It was M. Noël!..."How are you, M. Noël?..."

The prisoner in the heart of that deep forest, at the mercy of three ruffians who might rob him of his life from one minute to the other, looked upon Balaoo in the light of a saviour. The new-comer's kind, flat, placid face and his round, good-natured eyes gave the doctor confidence. Of course, he was not expecting M. Noël, especially by such a road, and he remained absolutely astonished, while attempting vaguely to explain the anomaly by the circus tradition of the facility of the yellow race for climbing slippery poles. In any case, his eyes did not deceive him: there was M. Noël; and the doctor, in his present plight, was determined to accept the most unhoped-for and even the most ridiculous assistance.

Balaoo, on touching ground, gave him a little wave of the hand and said, "How do you do, doctor?" from a distance, in a casual and patronizing tone that did not reassure Dr. Honorat quite as much as he expected. M. Noël, Dr. Coriolis' gardener, whom he had sometimes seen passing through the village, lonely and saturnine, seemed on the best of terms with the Three Brothers. They shook hands all round and exchanged congratulations. Then, taking no notice whatever of the doctor, they moved away and sat down in a circle, as though for a palaver.

Dr. Honorat, more and more puzzled, tried to hear what was said at this secret council in which, for aught he knew, his fate was being decided; but the voices did not reach his ears.

The news which Balaoo brought his friends was this: "I have just come from the top branch of the Big Beech at Pierrefeu. No one has entered the forest yet. *Tourôô!...Tourôô!*[10] Still, there are a lot of red trousers in the fields. They don't look as if they were preparing for battle. They are all eating and smoking, lying on the grass, like cows...I saw Zoé this morning: she told me she was going to Saint-Martin. She went back again in the afternoon. Aren't you afraid that the people of your Race will hurt her? I called out to her that it was rash, but she wouldn't listen. Has she come back? No?...Now here's what I heard in the forest: As told me that they are going to attack you from every side at the same time. As is giving the alarm to all the animals, like the funk that he is. All the inhabitants of the forest have gone to their homes and are lying low and barricading their doors and shivering. I'm keeping a look-out; and I can see that this is all cowardly animals' fuss, for the red trousers are sprawling on the grass like cows. *Taurôô! Taurôô!*"

The Three Brothers in turns questioned Balaoo about the distribution and attitude of the troops and asked what the officers were doing and whether there was much movement at Saint-Martin. He replied to the best of his ability, saying that he would return to his post before nightfall and that they could go to sleep in all security: he was there as a sort of night-watchman, he added. Then he looked in the direction of the doctor and asked what they meant to do with him. Were they going to eat him?

The others began to laugh. Balaoo retorted, with a serious face, that he had only asked the question because he knew that they ate all the game which they caught and had heard As say that the Three Brothers had killed the process-server to eat him.

Hubert answered that he was keeping the doctor as a hostage, whereupon Balaoo wanted to know what a hostage was. But the other had not time to explain: the branches of the hornbeam nearest to the group parted and Zoé's wide-awake face appeared, smiling all over. She cast her eyes around her, saw that all was well and dropped into the midst of the circle like a grasshopper. Her skin was almost bare, with just a few rags and tatters as its covering.

Balaoo gave her an angry look:

"What have you done with the Empress' dress?" he asked.

Zoé blushed and tried not to answer.

But Balaoo persisted and growled again:

"What have you done with the Empress' dress?"

"I've put it away," she ended by explaining. "I don't want to spoil it: it's not a forest dress."

"*Woop! Woop!* Please, please!" said Balaoo, in the pithecanthrope monkey-tongue, for he was very fond of showing the Three Brothers and their sister that he knew foreign languages. "*Woop! Woop*! I told you, I don't want to see you naked, like an animal. You disgust me, Zoé. Put on your dress, or I'll go away, sure as my name is Balaoo!"

Zoé vanished behind the hornbeam and, five minutes later, appeared in the clearing with the gorgeous white dress on her back. The brothers, who did not know of this acquisition, uttered shouts of delight and were lavish in expressions of their admiration. Hubert laughed till he cried, at seeing his sister dressed as an empress in the middle of the Moabit clearing. Siméon and Élie, the two albinos, slapped their thighs. Zoé walked up and down, indifferent as a queen.

"So help me, where did you get that?" asked Hubert, choking with laughter.

"I gave it her," said Balaoo. "I felt sorry for her, when I saw her passing this morning in her rags. I won't have her going along the roads with nothing on her back: it's indecent. I happened to have a dress up at my place, so I dropped it over her shoulders from the top of the Big Beech at Pierrefeu. It fits her like a glove. *Tourôô! Tourôô*!"

The others "could not get over it" and turned and twisted their sister about, to take the thing in. So she had gone to see the prefect like that, like a real lady, what! She had swaggered round Saint-Martin-des-Bois in that rig-out! What a sensation she must have made! They were proud of her; they could have kissed Balaoo, had Balaoo been willing.

"Why didn't you let us see it sooner?" they asked.

"You had it when you came back this morning!"

"She's a secretive kid," said Élie. "Every time Balaoo gives her something, she keeps it to herself, as if we were likely to steal it."

"It's a dress," said Siméon, speaking with a purpose—a purpose so clumsily emphasized that everybody understood what he meant"—it's a dress which she is quite right to be careful with. She couldn't hope for a grander to wear on her wedding-day."

Zoé at once ceased parading her finery and turned as red as a peony. Balaoo gave a growl and, without ceremony, spat at Siméon's feet: an invariable sign of his displeasure. And, lest there should be any doubt about it, he grunted:

"I don't like people to talk about marriage in my presence!"

There was a chilly pause. Hubert thought it wise to say, in a soft voice:

"There's nothing to upset you, Balaoo, in that remark. Zoé will have to marry some day."

"That's her business!" jerked Balaoo, with swelling cheeks and temples.

"And you too, Balaoo! You must, you know, someday!..."

"I!" roared the pithecanthrope, springing up. "I! Marry! Marry a man-girl! Never! Never! Never!...Phoh! Phoh! Goek! Goek! Tch! Tch! Phoh! *Phoh! Phoh! Phoh!*...A man-girl, indeed!..."

He struck great blows on his chest, which gave forth sounds like a drum, and moved away from his man friends.

"Have you left your sweetheart in your own country, Balaoo?"

"Yes...perhaps...in the Forest of Bandong," lied Balaoo, with a steaming breath and a voice thick with sobs.

He moved still farther away, flung himself suddenly with his face to the ground and his head in his hands and lay long motionless.

The others did not seek to interfere:

"He is dreaming of the Forest of Bandong," they said.

"Let's get to business."

And they now first thought of asking Zoé the result of her negotiations, so sure were they beforehand that the enemy, whose obstinacy they had learnt to know at the time of the elections, would never accept their conditions on receipt of the first little finger!

[9] La veuve, the slang term for the guillotine.—TRANSLATOR'S NOTE.

[10] A monkey-word expressing satisfaction and equivalent to "All right!"—AUTHOR'S NOTE.

Chapter XV

Night fell over the forest. It was agreed that they should cut off the doctor's second little finger at the first rays of dawn and that Zoé should take it to the prefect at ten o'clock, the time fixed for the morrow's decision. Once the government saw how ready the Three Brothers were to cut the doctor into pieces, it would be only too eager to meet the gentlemen's views.

The doctor prepared to spend another sleepless night. He was warned of the fate that awaited him and suffered all the pangs of anguish. He refused his food. He had a temperature, which is easy to understand, and was reduced to a little heap of terror, at the foot of the tree, in the silent darkness.

Never had the forest been so quiet at night. The animals had disappeared; and the leaves scarce ventured to stir, as though frozen hard in the humble expectation of what was coming.

Élie, Siméon and Hubert dined heartily, with Zoé to wait on them. Balaoo all the time lay flat on the ground. When Zoé asked if he would take anything, the only answer she received was a stiff clout. In such cases, it is no use insisting; and Zoé, with tears in her eyes, went and sat in her corner, reflecting that Balaoo was anything but kind to her.

By this time, the Moabit clearing was nothing more than a black hole, fearsome as a cave and deep as well. You had to throw your head back to see the blue night and the stars up in the sky. And you had to know the place well to venture your groping steps there. It was as treacherous—even to animals that were not used to it—as the quicksands by the sea. You never knew that the creepers on which you trod were not going to give way and swallow you up for good. A simple carpet of moss, which nobody would suspect, might prove to be a curtain just flung across the breakneck entrance to some deserted quarry which had not been worked since the early days of French history and which was used by the Three Brothers as a store-house to keep their savings and provisions, amid countless skeletons of animals.

In point of fact, Élie, Siméon and Hubert disappeared suddenly, without the doctor's being able to tell how, and this long before the night was at its darkest. Zoé alone remained to watch the prisoner. As for Balaoo, he rose to his feet in the gloom, preparatory to returning to his barbican in the Big Beech at Pierrefeu.

"Are you going, Balaoo?" asked Zoé, with tears in her voice.

"Yes," he replied, quite pacified now and a little sad, "I am going. It is safer. If there's anything fresh, I shall thunder; and then you must all keep still as mice in your hole. If the men come this way, I shall strike my breast three times, like this..." And he gave three terrible blows on his chest, which sounded like a bronze bell. "That will mean, 'Look out, at Moabit!' Do you understand?"

"I understand," said Zoé. "But they won't have the face to do anything before ten o'clock to-morrow. They promised me."

"One never knows, with the people of your Race!" Balaoo grunted.

"Ah, yes, I know that, at heart, you despise us," murmured Zoé.

"No, not your brothers, because they are of the Race without belonging to it and they can see in the dark. I took to them at once. And also they have noses that smell everything in the forest and would never confuse the trail of a rabbit with that of an elephant, like the rest of the Race, who don't know anything except how to read a book. I wonder what they would do if they had no books, what Coriolis, my master, would do! Whereas your brothers don't want anything. They are like the animals, who know everything and are not to be humbugged, in the forest. I like your brothers very much. They would have been as happy as could be, if they had been born in the Forest of Bandong."

"You are always talking of your Forest of Bandong. Do you regret it so?"

"Sometimes."

"And me?" Zoé ventured to ask, in a trembling voice. "Do you like me?"

"You don't count: you're a man-girl!"

"But I say, Balaoo: I know a man-girl who has only to walk in the forest and cry, 'Balaoo! Balaoo!' for Balaoo to come hurrying from any distance as fast as ever he can."

"Now look here," panted Balaoo, angrily, "look here and just listen to me: you'd better not speak of that one and never mention her name before me. You'd soil it by merely sending it through the dirty little lips of the dirty little man-witch that you are! You go and talk to men: men will understand you and put you in their back-yards, if that's what you like; but don't you talk to Balaoo!"

Zoé stood crying in the shade. "Why are you crying, Zoé?"

"You don't expect me to laugh, do you, after what you've said to me? I thought you had become my friend again, because you gave me the dress. What are you here for, if you're never happy except with her?"

"You dirty little man-witch; you forget that I came to the forest to defend your brothers against those of the Race."

"And also because of the man you hanged."

"Who told you that? As?"

"I don't understand the language of animals as you do, Balaoo. I only understand them when they don't speak. And there are plenty who know me in the forest and come and sit in my lap and smicker to me; and we understand one another without speaking. I have friends in the forest. Why, I have only to show myself by the big fir-thicket, with my hands full of nuts, to have squirrels climbing all over me! But, as for your friend As, I despise him too much to associate with him. One evening, when we met in Mme. Boche's yard, he tried to nod to me, on the pretext, no doubt, that he had seen you and me together; and I threw a big stone at him which nearly broke his paw."

"What do you think about the hanged man?" asked Balaoo, feeling bored.

"I think that you hanged him as you hanged Camus and Lombard, after settling their business. You can't pretend it wasn't you: I was there when they were cut down. I recognized the mark of your long thumb. A thumb like that is called a murderer's thumb, among us. I don't care, mind you: I like you as you are. And that's why I said nothing when my brothers were accused and even when they were sentenced. Their three heads, you see, are nothing to me compared with one smile from you, Balaoo. But you never smile to me, now; and you're always laughing at me...I put on your Empress' dress only so that you might think that I looked nice. But you laughed at me, like the others. And yet you will never know what I did for you at the time of Blondel's death..."

"Hold your tongue, will you, you filth!" roared Balaoo.

"Oh dear! Oh dear!" sobbed Zoé. "The things he says to me!"

"Why do you speak of that? I never speak of it to myself: surely, there's no reason why you should...Lombard and Camus had made fun of me. I played with their throats and they died. And I don't regret it. But Blondel had done me no harm..."

"And what harm had Patrice done you?"

Balaoo began to storm from the bottom of his pithecanthrope chest. His whole thoracic cage rumbled with distant thunder.

"Never mention him to me!" he sent hissing through his terrible jaws.

"Not him, nor her!...I know!...I know!..."

Zoé sniffed, wiped her nose with the Empress' dress and said, in tones of damp despair:

"You tell us that you're only happy with us in the forest; and, all the time, you're lying!...You thinking of no one but her...The reason why you're here now is that you daren't go back to your house in the village, because she'd reproach you with the man you hanged: she thinks he's your first, Balaoo!...If she only knew!...If she only knew!...I saw you dragging him by the hind-legs, from the garden-door to the forest...Oh, that was a fine piece of work you did; and how pleased they'll be with you in your house in the village! No, don't come to me with your tales. Don't tell me that you love my brothers. And you've no need either to call me a filth, like Siméon. You don't go home, because you daren't, that's all!"

"It's true," said Balaoo, "it's true. But, as for the men I've hanged, the only one I regret killing is Blondel, which proves that I'm not a bad sort!..."

"Who said you were a bad sort?"

This ended their conversation; but Dr. Honorat had heard every word of it. With his cord round his foot and his hair-standing erect with horror, he had listened to that curious talk and wondered if he were dreaming. But, alas, since they had cut off his dear little finger joints, he had lost the right to doubt the reality of his portentous adventure! And this adventure was now complicated by an unparalleled revelation of crimes and criminal complicity that seemed incredible to one who, from time to time, in the village-street, had come across the whimsical and inoffensive figure of M. Noël, the man-servant and gardener of that old eccentric of a Coriolis.

Apart from the fact that the doctor was unable to understand the greater part of the conversation—just the part that puzzled him more than all the rest: what did they mean with the reproaches which each addressed to the other in regard to their race and their association with the beasts of the forest?—M. Noël now inspired him with the same fear as a monster and appeared to him like the beast in Revelation, with the shadow of his rude and superhuman strength cast by the light of the moon, which now hung like a lamp, right over the middle of the clearing. And he had the strength left to withdraw his cowering fear to a distance of at least eighteen inches, which was a praiseworthy feat, considering that his fear had never weighed so much as at this moment.

But nothing could stir in the forest unheard by Balaoo, even when he was not listening:

"Some one's moved!" he said, without getting particularly excited, so greatly depressed was he by the words of that little man-witch of a Zoé.

"It's the doctor," said Zoé, mopping her nose and eyes and all her moist little face with the Empress' dress.

"What do they mean to do with him?" asked Balaoo, for the sake of saying something.

"They mean to kill him for speaking ill of them to the jury...It'll do them no good. One never has any peace with them. I'm beginning to have enough of it. We've had murders enough, as it is."

"Yes, yes," muttered Balaoo, fed up with his last hangings. "Murders enough, as it is...Where are you going, Zoé?"

"I'm going back to the quarry...This is the second night I've had no sleep...Good-night, Balaoo..."

And Zoé, in spite of the full moon shining straight upon her, suddenly disappeared before the doctor's eyes, as though the earth had swallowed her up.

Amid this appalling nightmare, Dr. Honorat heard one phrase sounding and resounding in his ears:

"Murders enough as it is!"

Zoé had uttered it and gone, but M. Noël had repeated it and stayed. Who could this person be, who walked about so easily, with his hands in his pockets, on the tree-tops in the forest? The Three Brothers must have great confidence in him, not to hide their secrets from him!

Meantime, he heard M. Noël calling:

"Zoé! Zoé! What about the doctor? Are you leaving him to himself?"

Zoé's voice rose from somewhere close at hand, from a tiny bush not large enough to hide a pair of lizards; Zoé must be underground:

"That's all right!" she cried. "They've tied him with a poacher's knot...Good-night, Balaoo."

And, from that moment, an immense silence filled the moonlight.

For ten minutes, the pithecanthrope stood motionless as a statue. He stared at the doctor, who pretended to be asleep. Persuaded that the prisoner was sleeping, he sat down with infinite precautions, hardly displacing the air as he moved. He took off his socks, his hat, his over-coat, his jacket, his neck-tie and collar, his shirt, his trousers. At last, as in the days of the Forest of Bandong, he sat quite naked under the moon.

The doctor looked at M. Noël's feet. A monkey! M. Noël was a monkey!

He nearly swallowed his tongue in the effort not to cry out. Oh, there was not a doubt of it, because of the feet, the shoe-hands, the lower hands with which he hung to the nearest branch and swung, gleefully, upside down, as in the days of the Forest of Bandong! And then he let go and hung on with his upper hands and, swinging here and swinging there, caught hold with his lower hands, in mid-air, and thus flew from tree to tree across the clearing, the Trapezium King of the forest, under the silent moon.

Suddenly, a last bound brought him seated in front of the doctor, who pretended to sleep and who had his back so close against the tree that he seemed to form part of the trunk, Balaoo contemplated the prisoner, with one elbow on his left thigh and his cheek in his right upper hand, in the attitude of a member of the Race who is thinking. What was Balaoo thinking of? Why those sighs? Why that trembling, that movement of the lips? What was the man-phrase that escaped from that animal mouth?

"Murders enough as it is!"

Balaoo craftily imagined that, if he saved one of the race, Made-leine would perhaps forgive him for dragging his distinguished visitor by the hind-legs to the tree where he hanged him. And, as I live, here was Balaoo undoing the poacher's knot and, abandoning his pithecan-thrope attitude, tapping Dr. Honorat on the head:

"Hop!" he said, rudely. "Get up!"

Get up! The quadrumane was telling him to get up!

The quadrumane was releasing him! Already, in his stupid brain, apt to draw hasty and sentimental inferences, the doctor was setting animals above men, because of this one generous act. Nothing could please him better than to get up. Unfortunately, he was unable to get up, because the monkey, with his human way of expressing himself, had given him a blow on the head more powerful than one adminis-tered with a quarter-staff! Balaoo lifted him up, Balaoo made him take a drain of the fire-water left over from the banquet, at the bottom of a flask. The doctor sighed, leant on the arm of the dear, kind quadrumane, took a few steps, felt his assurance return and suddenly thought that perhaps he might recover his strength and not die after all!...

He collected the last remnants of that strength and, hanging on to the quadrumane, who led the way, walking erect, ever so erect, while he, the man, was nearly crawling on all fours, he dived under the trees. Sometimes the quadrumane took him in his arms and carried him into the trees...and he made no more resistance than a babe in the arms of its nurse. Oh, the dear, kind quadrumane!...

At last, they came to a foot-path...Balaoo put him down...Yes, yes, the doctor remembered stories of "wild men of the woods" in books of travel. After all, once that eccentric of a Coriolis had a wild man of the woods living with him, perhaps there was nothing so very extraordinary about the adventure. True, this particular wild man of the woods talked. Well; why shouldn't he have been taught to talk? Scientists had been known to say that it was not impossible. At any rate, the great thing for good old Dr. Honorat was to get out of his perilous predicament as quickly as he could.

Balaoo, on reaching the path, pointed to the direction in which the doctor was to go and himself turned back, solemnly, without even waiting to be thanked.

Released! The doctor began to run like a madman, like a madman, like the madman that he was certainly in a fair way to become.

For how long did he run? He could not be far from the high-road now. He was saved! Suddenly, he stopped short: some one had tapped him on the shoulder. He recognized the quadrumane's touch. He turned round, greatly annoyed. Balaoo was standing behind him:

"You never told me," said Balaoo, quite as much out of breath as the doctor, "you never told me you were a *postage*!"

A dismayed silence on the doctor's part.

"You must come back, as you're a *postage*!" continued Balaoo.

A despairing silence on the doctor's part.

"They can't hurt my friends as long as you're a *postage*. So come back at once."

A comatose silence on the doctor's part.

Silence gives consent. Balaoo tucked Dr. Honorat under his arm; and a quarter of an hour later found the doctor once more sitting at the foot of his tree, with the poacher's knot round his foot and all the tribe of Vautrin gathered round him, trying to make him understand that Balaoo' would never have let him loose if he had for one moment suspected the real value of a *postage*!

166

But Dr. Honorat was never again to understand anything in this life...Dr. Honorat had dropped asleep with the peaceful sleep of child-hood...Dr. Honorat was mad. "*Phoh! Phoh!...Hack! Hack*!"

Friend Dhol came up, yellow-eyed, his tail between his legs, chat-tering his wolf's teeth. Hubert snatched at his gun, but Balaoo struck down the barrel:

"What's the matter, Dhol? Can't you stop those teeth of yours?"

"Can we come here?" Dhol asked Balaoo, in three words of wolf. "The Race are on their way. Is there room for Mother Dhol and the little ones? We don't know where to go in the forest."

Balaoo, who knew all the forest languages by heart, understood all that those three wolf-words implied. Behind the branches, a little beyond Dhol's tail and levell with the moss, was a great pair of yellow eyes, as wide as goggles, belonging to the mother, and, close beside them, six little piercing stars and, around all that, a great sound of chattering teeth. It was the terrified Dhol family, following its head.

"We have been to the Big Beech at Pierrefeu," Dhol explained, "but it's not safe. The people of the Race who are hastening from every part of the forest cannot be very far away. I spoke to General Captain, who told me that you were with the Three Brothers at the Moabit clearing, so I thought you might say a good word for us to the Three Brothers. The people of the Race will never come so far. We should be quite safe here, Balaoo, if you don't mind."

All this was said in three or four or five wolf-words at the most, words in which people of the Race, who only know how to read books, would have heard nothing but "*Hack! Hack*!" and understood nothing at all, of course.

Balaoo spoke to the Three Brothers and they had a serious discus-sion as to what to do. Dhol was the first scout to announce the enemy's attack. They showed their appreciation by allowing him to tuck away his family in a little corner of Moabit, on the express understanding, however, that they were not to bite Zoé's bare legs.

Dhol had not finished settling down, when friend As showed his anxious mask. Balaoo learnt from him that all the animals were trem-bling with fright in their lairs and that they did not even dare remain there, at least not those who, like As, had seen men firing their holes.

Never had so many men been known to go hunting, especially at night. No one knew what it meant, but it was most alarming. It was no good their hiding: they had reckoned without the moon and they could be seen gliding like snakes through the grass. And besides they could be scented from a distance, for the wind was blowing straight from Saint-Martin-des-Bois.

All this was useful information for the Three Brothers; and Balaoo imparted it to them. As also received permission to curl himself up in a corner of Moabit; but he chose the opposite corner to that of the Dhol family, with whom he was on bad terms. As had no family; he had been a bachelor all his life.

Élie, Siméon, Hubert, Zoé and Balaoo held a palaver in the centre of the clearing. They were all of one mind that the members of the Race who made use of speech to tell lies and break their promises were more contemptible than the cow in the fields, who knew no better than to let herself be milked by hired hands.

At that moment, a family of roe-deer, the buck—a six-pointer—his doe and their little fawn, arrived from the opposite side to Saint-Martin. They stopped at the edge of the clearing with their legs all atremble, not knowing where to go, already showing the white of their scuts, turning tail because of the men. But where were they to flee? There were men everywhere!

Balaoo whistled to them; and they shook with fright as he went up to them with soft words. He wanted to question them also, but had not time. A great noise approached from the distance. The whole forest seemed to rustle with thousands of wings and thousands of legs; and the branches on the ground crackled like burning wood. And, suddenly, Moabit was filled with an innumerable horde of panic-stricken animals. They darted blindly into the forest and ran round and round, like the horses in a circus under the ring-master's whip. The rabbits arrived in battalions. They were thick underfoot. And all the boughs of the trees were full of birds. An old stag lifted desperate antlers to the moon. A pair of wild-boars with their young were so frightened that, neglecting all caution, they slid into the bottomless pit of an abandoned quarry.

Balaoo in vain tried to calm them all by declaring that the members of the Race would never, never dare venture above the Moabit quarries. There was nothing but moaning and wailing all over the ampitheatre; and this partly because of the presence of the Three Brothers, which they could have well dispensed with. Yet the whole forest knew that the Three Brothers never killed animals when Balaoo was there. Hubert silenced Balaoo, when he was renewing his attempts to give confidence to the crowd, and whispered in his ear:

"I can see you've never served in the army. 'They,' will go where they are told to go. That's their orders; And you'll see, they will come here."

"So much the worse for them," said the pithecanthrope, simply.

He asked for room in a tree and clambered to the top.

He came down almost immediately.

"Here they are," he said. "Look out!"

And, as he had resumed his trousers, he took them off again, so as to be more at his ease.

Chapter XVI

For two nights, Coriolis had not left his tower.

He had built a sort of belvedere up there, where he loved to spend his time in contemplation. On level ground, in spite of his protecting walls, he did not feel far enough removed from the men whom he despised.

Here, Coriolis had passed two horrible nights and a hideous day. No one will ever know what he suffered, though he was not inclined to exaggerate the importance of a Herment de Meyrentin's disappearance from the face of the earth. When you are first cousin to a gentleman who has written all the nonsense, on the subject of Darwinism and the theory of evolution, with which that pretentious bookworm had filled the learned reviews for twenty years past, you need not expect to be mourned by an old eccentric who has studied nature at first hand, in every latitude, and who has taken her in at a glance, considering her one and indivisible and prepared to prove his views with his pithecanthrope.

When all was said, what had Meyrentin the magistrate wanted with him? As likely as not, he had been sent by the cousin at the Institute, who might have got wind of the pithecanthrope!

It was obvious that this pithecanthrope was going to annoy a lot of people. So much the worse for them! So much the worse for the idiots who do not believe in the doctrine of the evolution of species. Who ever heard of such stupidity! To think that the different species had never been developed on earth! Had the earth itself developed, yes or no, from the iron age to that of the old fossils of the Institute? So their contention was that the earth, which is constantly being transformed and constantly shifting, is covered with species which do not change, do not improve, do not decay with the worlds!...

Oh, how angry Coriolis was, in his belvedere!...Luckily, he was there! Just so! And that prodigious chain of life, arrogantly broken by man, who refuses to know anything of his brothers the animals, he was going to weld for good and all to that rebel's leg! With his pithecanthrope—now that he had turned the pithecanthrope into...a man!—he would say to man:

"Animal yourself!"

But, alas, what a catastrophe!

At the very moment when, after all those years of patient work, he was proposing to make known his masterpiece and to introduce it, as a matter of right, into the great human family, the human child of his genius and his nocturnal studies had behaved like any old wild beast in the Forest of Bandong! For there was no denying it: his dear Balaoo's murderous deed was as unconscious an act of impulse as the closing of any wild animal's jaws upon its prey, in the jungle. What a catastrophe! What a catastrophe!

Yes, Coriolis was having the bad time of his life. Buthe was incapable of vulgar despair. Possessed as he was by his fixed idea of making men out of monkeys and believing that he had succeeded, not an anxious thought as to the dangers involved had ever entered his brain; and his heart had no feeling of pity for the victim. He experienced neither remorse nor indignation. Not for a moment did he reflect:

"What have I done? The murderer is myself!" In his heart of hearts—and who will ever know the heart of hearts of scientific men?—he was not wholly sorry, since there had to be a victim and since you cannot make an omelette without breaking eggs, that this victim happened to be the near relation of a scientist who had never grasped the principles of evolution and who, for years, had horrified sensible men by maintaining his theory of the non-mutability of species!

The thing was quite simple: all the man's grief was due to the fact that he was afraid lest his crime should be discovered and his pithecanthrope taken from him. And I am in a position to add a few words that can only redound to his advantage and his credit: Coriolis suffered untold agonies not merely because it would mean the end of his work, if men learnt what had happened, but also and above all because he was less afraid of prison as a punishment for himself than he dreaded a cage for Balaoo, in which the poor orphan from the Forest of Bandong would have died of a broken heart. Coriolis loved Balaoo with the love of a father for his child.

Besides, to know Balaoo was to love him: so gentle was he, so simple, charming and natural. It was certain that, if Balaoo had only given him time, M. Herment de Meyrentin would have been attracted by him like everybody else; but Balaoo had not given him time.

Chapter XVI

After this, it will be understood why Coriolis sat weeping up in his tower; and why Madeleine, vainly trying to sew by the lamp in the dining-room, cried into the little basket in which she kept her needles and thread; and why old Gertrude, in her kitchen, wetted the knife-board with her tears.

The door between the dining-room and the kitchen was open. Gertrude did not know of the misfortune that had befallen her dear Noël's distinguished visitor; but, as Balaoo had not been seen for five days, she had little doubt that he had been guilty of some villainy. As a rule, when Balaoo took a day off in the forest, the escapade did not last longer than twenty-four hours and Coriolis and Madeleine showed no particular anxiety. But, during the last three days, there was no talking to the master, who had locked himself up in his tower; and Madeleine went about mopping her eyes in every corner of the house. Another extraordinary thing was that, for three days, Gertrude had been forbidden to go into the village on any excuse whatever. Not only that, but all the doors of the house had been barred and bolted. And, on the top of this, they had heard the sound of fire-arms, one night, in the village; and a great light had shot up from behind the Place de la Mairie.

All this mystery was quite enough to make a body tremble. Gertrude dreaded the worst for Balaoo. Nor did her anguish know any bounds when, on the afternoon of the next day, going up to her young mistress' bedroom, she saw the roads black with people and the country filled with soldiers marching towards the forest. In her terror, she called Madeleine, who gave her but little comfort by telling her that she had asked her father what all that crowd and that movement of troops meant and that Coriolis had said that it had to do with the manoevres.

All this was very far from, clear; but one fact was certain, which was that Balaoo did not return.

Gertrude, while cleaning her knives, tried to obtain some little light from the few remarks vouchsafed by Madeleine. But Madeleine hardly answered her questions. And the old servant began to speak of Balaoo with a funereal sadness, as of one whom she was destined never to see again, enumerating his pretty ways, his oddities and all the tricks which he loved to play upon her in her kitchen, hiding the most useful articles and spilling all the salt into the soup when she was making a soup which Balaoo did not like. Gertrude had more than once seen Balaoo's foothands and was acquainted with the great mystery. She loved Balaoo, therefore, not as a human being, but as a dear little pet of her own, that is to say, with all an old woman's immeasurable fondness. Madeleine, on the other hand, cherished the pithecan-thrope as she would a wayward and mischievous brother, whom an elder sister loves to correct and protect; and Balaoo returned every atom of her affection.

The two women could easily have communicated their common sorrow through the open door; and yet they hesitated to do so, especially as they could only expect to intensify their grief. Gertrude was the first to break silence, by speaking of the wedding:

"Have you heard from M. Patrice?" she asked.

Madeleine replied by merely shaking her head. She did not care a straw for M. Patrice at that moment, nor for any sweetheart in the wide world.

"When shall we see him again?" the old woman continued, more or less indifferently.

No reply.

"Will the wedding be here or in Paris?"

A dead silence.

"Balaoo doesn't like it when M. Patrice comes," Gertrude said, more timidly.

This time, she got an answer with a vengeance:

"How do you know, you silly old fool? Has Balaoo spoken to you of Patrice?"

"No, but he becomes unbearable when M. Patrice is here...Oh, where can he be now?...When I think," she moaned, "that, only last Saturday, he was sitting there, on that chair, peeling my leeks for me and telling me his stories of the Forest of Bandong, I feel as if I could die of misery! I am sure that something has happened to him!"

She could not understand why Madeleine did not go out to call him, as she always did when he stayed out too late.

"He must please himself," sighed Madeleine. "If he keeps away for so long, it's because he's lost his affection for us. Papa is right: he is big enough to be a man. He must know his own mind. If he prefers the society of the forest to ours, that's his affair: he will never be anything but a Balaoo of the forest and we must give up the hope, at his age, of making a proper man of him."

"You take it very easily, miss," Gertrude retorted, "and I don't think that's natural. You're keeping something from me, here. You've lost confidence in me. If I'm in the way, you had better say so."

"You're talking like the dear old stupid that you are. No one's keeping anything from you. Balaoo doesn't care about us any more;

and I don't see why I should upset myself: he's only a monkey, after all!"

"You break my heart when you talk like that," said Gertrude, who had a sensitive heart and who once nearly died of grief at the death of a little crook-backed cat which she had shut up in a drawer by accident. "You didn't always say so. You used to say, 'That fellow is extraordinarily clever. He understands all we say and he guesses the rest. He knows more than the mayor and the priest rolled into one.' Did you say that or did you not?"

"Evil instincts always regain the upper hand in the children of wicked parents," replied Madeleine, her little nose all red with weeping and despair.

"He didn't know them long enough to learn their wicked ways," rejoined Gertrude, defending Balaoo inch by inch.

"Oh, he was twelve months old when he left them: that's a lot for a little monkey, my dear Gertrude, a great deal more than you think!"

"I know, of course, that he couldn't talk. He learnt that here; and all his ways are just like yours and the master's. He walks like the master, with a little stoop in his back and his feet turned out. And, when he laughs, he mimics you so exactly, miss, that, if one weren't to see him, one would think it was you!"

"Thank you, Gertrude."

"I'm not saying it to annoy you: there was a time when you would have been pleased to hear it. But you don't care for Balaoo any more; and I can't think what's happened!"

Suddenly, old Gertrude stopped cleaning her knives and ran into the dining-room, for Madeleine had burst into a fit of crying. She sat sobbing, with her elbows on the table and her fair-haired little head between her hands, while her shoulders shook spasmodically.

"Oh, what is it, miss, what is it? Lord above, is it I who've upset you?...Do say something!...You frighten me!..."

"Let me be, Gertrude, let me be!..."

"I see myself letting you be, in such a state! I'll go and call the master."

"No, no, Gertrude, don't do anything of the sort...There...I'm all right now..."

"I feel certain that something has happened!"

"I wish you would stop talking your nonsense! What do you think can have happened? Nothing's happened at all, do you hear, you old fool?"

"I'm sure I beg your pardon, miss," said Gertrude, wounded in her pride and returning to her kitchen.

They sat without exchanging another word. The night wore on.

Gertrude lit her lantern and prepared to go up to her garret. She said good-night, in a tearful voice, to Madeleine, who raised her head and begged her not to leave her:

"You've frightened me with your jeremiads, Gertrude! Come and sleep in my room. We'll put you a mattress on the floor."

"But what's happening? Lord above, miss, I've never seen you like this before!...Aren't you going to say good-night to your father?"

"No, he doesn't want to be disturbed: he's working."

"He's no more working than we are: he's waiting for Balaoo to come back, miss. You can't deceive old Gertrude."

They both lay down in Madeleine's room; but neither Gertrude, on the floor, nor Madeleine, in her bed, was able to sleep. And it was quite two o'clock in the morning when, as though moved by a common spring, they both sat up, with ears on the alert:

"Did you hear, miss?"

"Yes, Gertrude, I heard...I believe it's he, isn't it?"

"It came from the forest. It's as if the forest were sighing."

"That's a bad sign," said Madeleine, in a choking voice. "Those sighs always frightened me."

They were silent...and then, when the sighs in the forest were renewed, they got up, huddled on a few things and opened the window.

And they at once whispered:

"It's he!...It's he!..."

They could see the skirt of the forest, at no great distance, in the moonlight; and, from that near, mysterious, ominous horizon, the sound reached them of a strange growling breath.

The growling increased and became a rolling, like the incipient noise of thunder trying its voice before it becomes a storm. The forest stood poised like an immense, black, tempest-laden cloud upon the earth, upon the fields, which already shook under the as yet distant voice of the thunder. And, suddenly, the thunder burst[11] so furiously that Madeleine almost fainted away as she moaned:

"Oh dear, what are they doing to him? Balaoo never thundered so loud as that before!"

And, when, at the same moment, shots were heard amid shouting, in the woods, the two women flung themselves into each other's arms, stammering in their fright:

"Balaoo! Balaoo!"

Chapter XVI

A fresh report of fire-arms electrified them and sent them rushing madly out of the room, across the house and up the tower. They climbed its shaky stairs, screaming for the doctor. The men were killing Balaoo! They were killing Balaoo!

The two women burst into the belvedere, to find the old eccentric fretting like a wild beast in its cage, tearing from window to window, with fists clenched and mouth afire. Coriolis, who was stifling, had unfastened his neck-tie, his collar and his shirt; and, at intervals, when the shots rang out anew, his nails dug into his bare chest, drawing the blood., With his eyes starting from his sockets, he gurgled:

"They'll kill him!...They'll kill him!...Oh, the scoundrels! The murderers!...The *men*!..."

His overpowering rage could find no stronger expression, nor did it seek one. It was satisfied with that:

"The *men*! The *men*!"

Was it possible, was it possible that they were going to destroy his handiwork, to kill his child?

There was not a doubt left in his mind but that they had surprised Balaoo with Meyrentin's body, that they had tried to arrest him and that, in his madness, the pithecanthrope, forgetting all his acquired human prudence, had revealed himself the monster! This explained both the array of troops and the curiosity displayed throughout the day by all the people of the country-side. Coriolis had reassured Madeleine not long ago, but he himself knew that the thing was certain and that the whole crowd were there for the purpose of storming the forest.

Nevertheless, until two oclock in the morning, Coriolis did not cease to hope that Balaoo, who was an integral part of the forest, would manage to extricate himself by trickery and silence. A pithecanthrope has more than one trick up his sleeve! Every tree is his friend; and he knows how to "move" in the branches!

Alas, the thunder was soon to teach Coriolis otherwise! Balaoo sometimes thundered to amuse himself, but that was always quite evident and Coriolis then knew that the pithecanthrope was making fun of men. Now the thunder of that night was something different, was positively alarming. Never had one of the higher quadrumanes, attacked by a band of hunters in the bush, made the depths of the equatorial jungle ring with a more gigantic anger. And then there were the shots. Balaoo had been discovered! They were giving him a dose of platoon-firing!

Coriolis tore out his hair by handfuls. He took no notice of the women when they entered. Leaning from the tower, he shouted into the night:

"Have at them, Balaoo, have at them!...Defend yourself!...The cowards!...There's a thousand of them to one of you, the cowards!...Have at them, Balaoo!...Kill them! Kill them!..."

Madeleine, seeing his wild condition, tried to silence him, but in vain. He repelled her with the utmost violence. He shook his fist at heaven and earth. He cursed the universe.

Such a work as his! They were murdering his work, the work of a god! For he had proved himself God's equal, that old eccentric, with his pithecanthrope! He had created man; and in less time than it had occupied Him! Where God had taken perhaps five hundred thousand years, he, the old eccentric, had taken ten: ten years and a couple of touches with the scalpel under the tongue! And all that to end...how? In their daring to destroy his masterpiece in the corner of a forest!...O misery! And he wept...

He wept, for the sounds had ceased...The thing must be over...Nothing remained of Balaoo.

Madeleine took her father's head in her lap and petted and consoled him like an old, white-haired child.

He did not reply.

He certainly did not hear her. From time to time, he repeated:

"It's over!...It's all over!...We shall never see Balaoo again, we shall never see him again!"

The scene told Gertrude much that she did not know before. Through her master's ravings, she at last learnt the nature of the "dirty trick" of which Balaoo had been guilty. The dear darling had killed a gentleman visitor! She could not get over it. He who had always seemed to her so gentle...and who certainly would never have hurt a fly!...

Daylight found them all three in the belvedere: they were still there at the hour when nature seems to rise from the mists of the dawn, when thick grey tints enshroud the beauty of the woods, while, far away, on the clearer horizon, the leafless tops of the great trees gleam and sparkle in the light.

With terrified hearts, they assisted at nature's awakening. It was the moment when the earth reeks, when the wind falls, when wild things suck the breath of the earth that makes them strong...Ah, how Balaoo used to love that hour!...And how often Coriolis had caught him, with his nose in the cool grass, sniffing the pungent smell of the morning; how often he had almost to drag him to the schoolroom where his lessons awaited him!...Poor Balaoo, who was so fond of playing truant!...How could they grow accustomed to the thought that

177

he was now probably nothing more than a torn and mutilated corpse, which those brutes of men, who fought a thousand to one, would carry back on a litter of branches, little suspecting the miraculous nature of the game which they had killed!.

But the idea in Coriolis' mind suddenly found utterance on Madeleine's lips:

"If they have killed him," she said, "they will certainly know. They will recognize M. Noël."

"Why, of course! Why, of course! There would be hundreds of people to recognize him; and Coriolis would soon be asked for explanations..."

Well, what did that matter? He would furnish the explanations. He would call to witness everybody who had spoken to M. Noël: Mme. Boche, Mme. Mûre, the small tradesmen in the Rue Neuve and even those rascals the brothers Vautrin, in their prison, for Dr. Coriolis did not yet know of their escape. And people would learn what they had killed, what they had silenced for ever: human speech in a monkey's throat!

When Coriolis reached this second stage of his despair, he saw groups of men emerging from the forest and walking in front of something which he could not yet distinguish, but which resembled a load thrown over a litter of boughs; and he had not a doubt that it was the remains of Balaoo being carried back to the village. Soon he recognized the mayor and the prefect walking ahead: he had seen them, at a distance, on the day before, when already their curious behaviour had caused him no little anxiety. They both seemed now to be talking very excitedly, with gestures expressive of immense distress. Soldiers and peasants followed, making similar gesticulations. And all these people were escorting that sort of bier, over which a long military cloak was thrown. As the procession approached, the occupants of the tower distinguished the details more plainly; and, when it passed the foot of the tower, Madeleine and Gertrude burst into loud sobs, while Coriolis, pale as death, nearly fell over, in his attempt to see. But he saw nothing, except the cloak beneath which lay outlined a human shape that could only be the shape of Balaoo.

When the procession had passed, another followed at once; and here again there were multitudes of people and soldiers around a litter bearing a human figure covered with a cloak...

And then came another...and yet another...making four funeral processions...

"Oho!" muttered Coriolis, who no longer had the strength to stand and who felt as though he were losing his reason for good. "Oho! So Balaoo defended himself!...."

But that was not all...Gradually, the forest belched forth all the soldiers whom it had swallowed up yesterday...but in what a plight! After the dead came the wounded. Of these there were at least a score, limping along in single file, supported by their comrades, with their arms in slings and their foreheads bandaged...Good old Balaoo!...

Yet one more procession brought up the rear. It was formed of a group of people in whose midst a figure which Coriolis seemed to know was struggling in the strangest fashion. Suddenly, he recognized it: Dr. Honorat! But such a Dr. Honorat! Coriolis could not make out the dear doctor's attitude, nor his cries. Honorat's face was covered with blood...and he was singing the Marseillaise!

It was really not the moment to strike up this triumphal anthem; and the others were doing their very best to make him stop, but could not. They also had the greatest difficulty in keeping him on his legs...

At length, this last procession, like the others, disappeared down the Rue Neuve, towards which all the peasants around were hastening with cries and shouts and lamentations, while the bell of the little church began to toll dismally for the dead, with short, single knells that fell from the steeple slowly, one by one, like tears.

Coriolis, remembering at last that he was a member of the human race, slid to the floor at full length, lifeless, icy cold. The women thought for a moment that he was dead. No amount of attention or rubbing was able to restore the warmth to his body. At last, he opened his eyes and looked around him with a startled air:

"Where is Balaoo?" he asked.

They did not reply. He remembered and heaved a sigh that seemed to come from the dark depths of his scientist's soul, the soul that had taught a pithecanthrope to speak. He shook his head and asked:

"How many killed?"

When the others again did not reply, he gave a violent movement of impatience:

"I'm asking you, how many killed, how many killed!"

"But, papa, we don't know," said Madeleine's trembling voice, at last.

"Well, you, Gertrude, go and find out."

She went to the municipal buildings to enquire.

There were four killed and twenty-seven wounded.

Chapter XVI

The first victim was the Vicomte de la Terrenoire, who had died the death of a soldier, at the head of his troops, with his skull cracked like a nutshell. It was his body that lay under the first cloak; and he had been laid in state on the desk in the marriage-registry-office. The three others were private soldiers. Their bodies were placed in a row on the floor of the council-chamber.

In addition to these four heroes, there were a number of men suffering from fractured arms, broken legs, bruised noses; but the wordt injuries were certainly those of Colonel du Briage, who had met with an astounding adventure of which, unfortunately, he was unable to furnish particulars, for the very simple reason that he had returned with his jaws smashed to a jelly, every tooth in his head broken and his tongue torn out by the roots. Moreover, both his wrists were fractured. As for the Three Brothers, not one of them, of course, was brought back, dead or alive. More than that, they had not even been seen; and they had not fired a single shot. The soldiers had discharged their rifles at them, at random, but were unable to say if they had even driven them away. All that they found was Dr. Honorat, tied to the foot of a tree in the middle of the Moabit clearing. Throughout the fighting, he had sung the Girondins' song, *Mourir pour la patrie*, and, afterwards, when the others had tried to make him speak, he had struck up the Marseillaise, which he was singing still. The mayor was utterly dismayed. As for the prefect, he could think of nothing but a telegram which he had received from the government, dismissing him from his post.

From the town-hall, Gertrude went on to the Black Sun. The crowd in the street was so great that she soon saw that she would never reach the door of the Roubions' inn, where generally all the news of the district centred. However, by working her way through the kitchens, she managed to reach the large summer dining-room, now transformed into an infirmary, at the moment when Born-drunk, a sergeant in the second battalion of the 3rd, was describing the terrible, swift and incomprehensible events in which he himself had taken part. He'd had the luck, he had, to get off with a split ear. Now that it was all over, he gave you his word, he wasn't sorry that he'd been there!

Sergeant Born-drunk expressed himself as nimbly with gestures as with words; and often the former were the more easily understood. His hearers could see, as plainly as though they had been present, the little troop under his command, slipping through the tall ferns, noiselessly, amid the silent darkness of the forest; and this merely by the way in which he stooped, bending his body, stretching out his arms, groping with cautious fingers.

And then he pictured the whole mysterious battle, with his chest flung out, his fists cleaving the air, striking at some invisible, retreating form. And then came the firing—Bang! Bang! Bang! Bang!—with his cheek on his arm, as though he were taking aim. Oh, he was there, he was there right enough! But he was no wiser for all that; for, after all, what did anyone know? Why, nothing! Not a thing! They knew that there were so many killed, that was all, and so many wounded. But how did it happen? Ah, that was the difficulty, that was the difficulty!

The colonel alone could have told. But he would never speak again! And, as for writing, they would have long to wait, for both his wrists were smashed! As for Sergeant Born-drunk, he only knew one thing and that was that the whole business had come from above! Yes, the disaster, so to speak, had dropped out of the sky! At the moment when they thought they were going to catch the Three Brothers, when they were not far from Moabit, he had seen Colonel du Briage standing in front of him, right under the moon, in the middle of a little path. Suddenly, the colonel's figure began to rise up from the ground, absolutely like the pictures of the Assumption of the Blessed Virgin. The colonel simply ascended to heaven. Not a word! Not a cry! The "old man" said nothing, but just ascended to heaven, with his arms stretched out, as though to bless the earth!

Sergeant Born-drunk was not the only one to see that wonderful sight: all his comrades around him had seen it...and all were so much struck by it that they thought, at first, that, they were dreaming, that they were the victims of an illusion, an hallucination...And then they had had to accept the fact that the colonel had disappeared: two officers, behind him, had also witnessed that unprecedented piece of witchcraft. And all, officers and men alike, had begun, with their heads in the air, to call out, "Colonel! Colonel!" as though they expected him to drop down from the sky. His figure had vanished through the upper branches of the tall trees...

When the first moment of bewilderment was over, everybody ran forward...They scrambled into the branches, they quickly beat that corner of the forest...But nothing, nobody, no colonel!...

The news soon spread along the whole line, which was closing in upon Moabit. Sergeant Born-drunk was dispatched by his lieutenant to tell Major de la Terrenoire and arrived just in time to see the major disappear, even as he had seen the colonel. But, this time, it was something awful. The major and a few other officers were sitting on their horses under the branches of a great oak. As a matter of fact, they feared that it was coming on to rain; for, though the sky was clear and the moon as bright as a five-franc piece, they could hear the first rumblings of a storm that seemed close at hand.

Suddenly, they thought that the oak itself was struck, for there was a terrible clap of thunder in the tree and the horses shied, reared and neighed with terror. There was no holding them in. Sergeant Borndrunk, if he lived to be a hundred, would never forget the moment when Major de la Terrenoire, sitting his prancing charget, was lifted out of the saddle by something that dropped out of the tree and yet remained hanging to it. It was like a swing in which the viscount was now caught by the feet, while his head swept the ground. It was impossible quite to realize the extraordinary spectacle, in the first place, because it was dark and the moon did not shine clearly through the branches and, secondly, because everybody had lost his presence of mind.

The horses, upsetting everything in their way, bolted, carrying their riders with them or throwing them under the branches. The linesmen ran to the assistance of the officer, who began to whirl round and to come down like a club among the rash group which was trying to rescue him. It only lasted a minute. Two of them, a corporal and a private, were killed on the spot by blows of the viscount, whose own head was no more than a mass of pulp. And the viscount himself, reduced to a useless weapon, was quickly flung by "the swing" into the midst of the dead and wounded.

At the sound of this battle, of the shouts, of the moans of the wounded and dying, some officers ran up and gave orders to the men to open fire, without knowing whom or what they were firing, at the risk of shooting one another point-blank. They next rushed to Moabit, yelling like savages. All the men who were still able-bodied, wild with rage, tearing themselves in the brambles, the impenetrable bushes, leaping into the underwood, maddened by the thought that they were fighting against a mysterious force, a new forest weapon invented by the Three Brothers, had dashed forward whooping as though they were storming a battery. Oh, that assault of Moabit! Sergeant Born-drunk could still hear it ringing in his ears, with the shouts of the infantrymen and the thunder of the trees, for the trees around them growling, rumbling and roaring, as though they were the storm itself. One would have thought that the trees were defending themselves. And, from time to time terrible blows were let fly out of the trees by the Three Brothers, whom they never saw and at whom they kept on firing!...Blows that would fell an ox!...A chap by your side would go down, without so much as an "Ah!" before you knew what was happening!...The most awful bludgeoning blows, raining down from the trees and ending you flat to the ground, with a crash!...

He himself, Sergeant Born-drunk, was grazed by one of those blows, only grazed, fortunately, but enough to split his ear and make him sit on the ground, like a baby, and see stars!

But there were others who wouldn't stir a limb for many a long day and some who would never stir at all...Oh, they would remember the Three Brothers and the siege of the Black Woods!...And nobody would ever know how the forest had managed to defend itself like that!...Not to speak of the animals, which also had fought like mad: animals by the hundred, which seemed to have taken refuge in Moabit as in a fortress and which delivered sallies, rushing upon the soldiers, coming from every side; wild-boars, wolves, running in every direction, spreading disorder in the ranks; herds rushing blindly before them, knocking down and trampling on all that stood in their way.

The colonel was found, at daybreak, in the condition described, at the very spot from which he had vanished. Then they picked up the dead and wounded and came home.

Sergeant Born-drunk finished his story, while the passing-bell continued to bewail this ill-fated and, from every point of view, deplorable expedition.

Gertrude went away, but did not go straight back, first calling on Mme. Mûre and Mme. Bache and on Mme. Valentin's cook, whom she found in tears because of "that poor M. de la Terrenoire, who was so fond of the mistress." And, in this way, she learnt all the events of yesterday and the day before.

Greatly relieved, she returned to Coriolis' tower with a glad heart.

"Well?" asked Coriolis, as soon as he caught sight of her, while Madeleine prepared herself to hear the worst.

"Well, it's nothing."

"How do you mean, it's nothing?"

"Why, it has nothing to do with him. They've been in the forest hunting the Three Brothers, who have escaped from prison and who have hanged the examining-magistrate, just as they hanged Camus and Lombard and that poor M. Blondel! The Three Brothers defended themselves and knocked thirty of them on the head. There, are four killed."

"Nonsense!" exclaimed Coriolis, returning to life, while his heart began to beat with an immense delight. "You don't mean it! And what about Balaoo?"

"Balaoo? Who's talking of Balaoo? Don't I tell you that he was out of it?"

"Oh!" cried Madeleine, in gratitude to Providence. "Oh, can it be possible?"

"It's as I tell you, sure as I hope to be saved!" rejoined the old woman, with amazing effrontery, for she knew quite well what to think of the mysterious defence of the forest and the battle of the trees.

Coriolis and Madeleine embraced. Then Madeleine, hesitatingly, said:

"All the same, he was thundering in the forest last night."

"The soldiers must have frightened him," said Gertrude.

"And then perhaps he is sad," said Coriolis, in a sig nificant tone. "He has been away too long and he dares not come in. You ought to go and fetch him, Madeleine."

Madeleine did not wait to be told a second time. Fifteen minutes later, she was walking, with short steps, through the paths in the forest, calling; in her softest, voice:

"Balaoo!...Balaoo!...Balaoo!..."

And it was not long before she saw Balaoo come timidly towards her, his clothes in disorder, hanging his head, with a repentant face. Sniffing and moaning, he fell on his knees, muttering, as in the days of the Forest of Bandong, when, after perpetrating some piece of mis-chief, he returned to the maternal hut, where a good beating awaited him:

"Woonoup brout!...Woonoup brout!...Brout! Brout!"[12]

"Talk like a Christian, you savage!" said she, with tears in her eyes.

"Mercy!" he sighed, in his gentle, gong-like voice.

She took him by the ear and brought him home.

All the same, he had hanged M. Herment de Meyrentin.

He was given seven days in the black hole, which he fully de-served.

---

[11] In the opinion of every traveller who has heard the orang-utan in the virgin forest, its thunderous voice can be compared only with that of the thunder itself. An angry orang-utan sends the sound of a storm for many miles around, creating a noise that

has deceived more than one inexperienced hunter at the first hearing.—AUTHOR'S NOTE.

[12] *Woonoup brout*, in the language of the larger apes, means "mercy," as Professor Garner tells us.—AUTHOR'S NOTE.

BOOK THE THIRD

BALAOO MAN-ABOUT-TOWN

Chapter XVII

When Patrice arrived in Paris, at 7.15 in the evening, there was no one to meet him at the station. He was surprised at this, although, during the three years since his future father-in-law had left Saint-Martin-des-Bois, Coriolis' behaviour towards him was such that he need not have been surprised at anything.

First of all, he was kept away from Madeleine. True, she and her father paid two or three visits to Clermont; but the young man was never invited to go to them in Paris. After two years, as Coriolis kept on postponing the date of the marriage on inadequate pretexts, the Saint Aubins became curious to know what could be happening at their relations'. They applied to a private-enquiry office, which soon supplied them with information of so absurd a character that they regretted paying for it in advance.

Nevertheless, in course of time, some of this information was confirmed. For instance, it was quite correct that Coriolis never went out without taking young Noël with him and that he appeared, somewhat late in the day, to have acquired an insane liking for that shy and silent lad. He was letting him study for the bar!

Noël studying for the bar! Upon my word! Noël was a law-student and Coriolis accompanied him to all the lectures!

What did it mean? And what was hidden behind this last freak of the ex-consul at Batavia? The Clermon Saint-Aubins were wondering, in consternation and alarm, when, suddenly, the marriage between Patrice and Madeleine was fixed.

Coriolis hurried things in a frenzied fashion. The wedding would be in Paris, but the old eccentric did not allow Patrice any time for the wooing. He considered that a ridiculous and antiquated custom. The young man was not to come to Paris until forty-eight hours before the ceremony, which would take place very quietly, especially as the Saint-Aubins were detained at Clermont by the father's gout and could not be present. On the evening of the wedding, the newly-married couple were to go to Auvergne and embrace the old people before travelling on to Italy, where they would spend the honeymoon.

So Patrice came to Paris by the 7.15 train, as Coriolis had suggested, and found no one at the station.

He felt "hurt."

He had his trunk put on a cab and told the man to drive to the Rue de Jussieu. Here the old eccentric had taken up his abode in an old-fashioned house, on the confines of the Quartier des Écoles, bringing with him his daughter, his old servant, his native "boy" and all his notes and manuscripts on the bread-plant.

Through the windows of his cab, Patrice gazed sadly upon Paris, which was charming to look at on this fine spring evening; but he did not care for Paris. Paris had always frightened him. There were too many carriages. And, even when you kept off the pavement, you were never at peace. Lots of people, even ladies, whom he did not know from Adam or Eve, would accost him and ask him things or offer him things which he did not understand and did not wish to.

When he reached the Rue de Jussieu and the cab put him down outside his uncle's house, the quiet of the neighbourhood appealed to him. It reminded him of the country. The sparse lighting, the pavement echoing under the feet of a distant wayfarer, the solitude around him: all these suggested to his mind certain streets at Clermont where he used to go for a little stroll between dinner and bed-time.

He rang the bell. Gertrude opened the door. She seemed neither surprised nor pleased to see him. She simply said, in an indifferent voice:

"Oh, it's you? Mademoiselle will be so glad."

"Didn't they expect me this evening?" asked the bewildered young man.

"Oh, yes!" replied the old servant. "Your place is laid."

They were standing in a great, cold, flagged hall, ending in an enormous staircase with a wrought-iron baluster. Gertrude pointed to the stairs and a voice from above said:

"Is that you, Patrice?"

"Of course it is! Who else would it be?" replied the young man, somewhat crossly, though he had recognized the voice of his intended.

But Madeleine ran down the stairs and threw herself into his arms. Patrice kissed his cousin, whose demonstrations of affection struck him as being a little put-on. She seemed rather anxious than pleased at seeing him.

He did not think her improved in her looks, because Paris had made her lose her pretty colouring. True, she had developed other feminine attractions, which Saint-Martin-des-Bois would never have given her; but, when you come from the Rue de l'Écu, you don't shake it off easily.

Madeleine, on her side, thought that Patrice looked sulky:

"What's the matter with you?" she asked, pouting. "You seem displeased at something. Is it because you weren't met at the station? You don't know what papa's like. He's not overburdened with politeness and nothing would make him depart from his regular habits. On the other hand, he would never let Gertrude and me go across Paris alone, so late in the evening."

"I'm not complaining!" said Patrice, compressing his lips. "Where's uncle?"

"You'll see him at dinner. Gertrude will show you your room. Be quick: we dine at eight punctually; you have just five minutes."

Patrice' room was a great, bare room on the second floor. There was a little bed, in between high walls and high, badly-closing windows. The walls were covered with the most wonderful panelling, all chipped and worn: he did not even look at it. There was nothing homely about the room, nothing soft. Not a sign of forethought: not a flower; not a photograph; nothing. He would have liked Madeleine to provide something to show that she was interested in the man about to occupy that room. But not a thing! He sighed and felt very lonely.

In what a hurry she had kissed him, pushing and hustling him to get it over! And they were to be married in two days!

He sat down gloomily at the foot of his bed. Gertrude's voice outside the door made him start up:

"Are you ready, M. Patrice? Mademoiselle would like to speak to you."

He paid no attention to his appearance, did not even look at himself in the glass. He washed his hands and found Gertrude waiting for him impatiently:

"Come along, sir!" she grumbled.

And she took him downstairs and pushed him into the drawing-room.

It contained the old set of Empire furniture which he had known at Saint-Martin-des-Bois. Here again there was not a flower in the vases. And the chairs had their covers.

Madeleine was standing near the door. She took his hand and said to him, speaking very quickly, in an undertone:

"Dear Patrice, when we are married, e shall do as we like, sha'n't we? But here we are at papa's and we must not vex him. He has become crazier than ever. We must not be angry with him, for he is very sorry at my going away. He could never bear the thought of my marriage. He made up his mind to it at last, as though he had decided to be operated on for appendicitis. He is very unhappy and he wants to get it over and done with. But, until it is over, he won't have it talked about! So there must be no question of a wedding, at meals or anywhere in the house, That's settled. You will act towards everybody as if you had come to Paris for two or three days on important business which concerns no one but yourself. Is that understood?"

She did not even wait to hear his answer. As he stood there, dumbfoundered, she opened the door of the dining room and went in. He followed her as in a dream.

A young woman of fashionable appearance sat reading by the corner of a window. She raised her head at their entrance. Patrice could not restrain an exclamation: it was Zoé!

It was really true: he saw before him the little gadabout of the forest! This pretty girl who got up and bowed so easily, so quietly, looking so very Parisian in her simplicity and in the modest and assured taste that distinguished her dress, was the Vautrins' sister, whom he had seen running along the forest-paths like an untamed hind, with her hair streaming in the wind or blowing over her forehead! By what miracle did he now find her so greatly altered, looking so "proper"?

When he heard, at Clermont, that Zoé had gone to join Madeleine in Paris, the young man did not conceal his views from his intended. And he wrote to her all that he thought of this latest hobby of his uncle's. But Madeleine replied curtly that she had not been consulted and that, besides, she looked upon her father's treatment of the poor little orphan—Mother Vautrin was dead—as a kind action. Later, Madeleine again had occasion to write that Zoé was making herself very useful in the house, now that Gertrude was getting old. She said that the child had become quite sensible after breaking every link with the past; and she added that Zoé's brothers must certainly be dead, or they would have found means of letting their sister know to the contrary. That was what Zoé thought.

Patrice, while failing to understand how anyone could feel inclined, unless compelled, to be waited on by Mlle. Vautrin, that scion of a too-illustrious family, was delighted with this last communication. The death of the Three Brothers, doubtless slain by the bullets of Major de la Terrenoire's troopers, reconciled him to the sister; for Patrice would still sometimes wake up in bed, with his forehead bathed in perspiration, from a nightmare in which a curious masked driver took him somewhat roughly by the throat and asked him never again to set foot in Saint-Martin-des-Bois. And, as he had dropped the idea of the intervention of a fourth miscreant, of the mysterious accomplice whom the eloquence of the Clermont public-prosecutor had definitely relegated to the realms of legend, he invariably ascribed to the albino the responsibility for the terrible adventures that had nearly caused his death. It was a good thing that Élie was no more; and Patrice had looked forward to hearing the glad tidings repeated by Zoé's own lips.

But he expected to find her in the kitchen.

And he discovered her in the dining-room, where she seemed quite at home, dressed like a young lady, smiling at him with the gracious condescension of a woman of quality who wished to put him at his ease: Zoé, the savage little sister of the three men sentenced to death!

He did not know if he ought to shake hands. But she held out hers to him, very simply, and asked after his health.

He did not have time to indulge in further raptures of wonder. Uncle Coriolis entered the room, followed by a tall and sturdily-built young gentleman, who flung out his chest and displayed a pair of broad shoulders under a well-cut jacket. Madeleine's sweetheart knew that simian face, with the almond eyes, that Far-Eastern type which always surprises us when it is modified by European fashions, such as the hair smoothly plastered down, with a straight parting...and the single eye-glass. Yes, M. Noël was wearing an eye-glass! Patrice, who had never seen him so near at hand, considered that he had improved. The smart cut of his clothes and his frigid bearing made him look almost distinguished. The peculiar ugliness of his face was rather attractive than repulsive.

"He may be quite good-looking in his own country," thought Patrice, reflecting that, after all, looks are a matter of latitude and longitude.

Only he regretted, for that foreigner's sake, the exceptionally powerful build of the animal jaws.

Patrice was astonished by Zoé, but the sight of Noël plunged him into absolute stupefaction:

"He has changed immensely since he worked in the bread-plant orchard," he thought, bowing somewhat coldly in answer to the ex-gardener's curt nod.

And they all sat down to table.

Coriolis had not been at all demonstrative with his nephew. He asked casually after Patrice' parents and, without waiting for the reply, pointed to his place, between Madeleine and Zoé. Noël sat between Zoé and Coriolis.

The soup was followed by an embarrassing pause, which was broken by Coriolis:

"Perhaps, my boy, when you've finished staring like a lunatic, you'll tell us what you're surprised at?"

Patrice was ashamed to be spoken to like that before Madeleine. He had the courage, however, to say, with his nose in his plate:

"What surprises me is M. Noël's eye-glass." Madeleine warned him, with a little kick under the table, that he had made a blunder. But it was too late...His uncle was already going for him:

"Your father wears spectacles; and I don't see why M. Noël, whose left eye is weaker than the other, should not wear a concave glass. Astigmatism is not a privilege of the white race, nor is the use of lenses, to correct it."

This was said in so harsh and contemptuous a tone that. Patrice was crushed. He tried to hide his confusion under a pleasant smile.

"What are you smiling at? You think yourself very witty, I suppose! Don't be afraid: you're not the only one. They're all alike, the young men of to-day who have not left their mother's apron-strings. If you had been three times round the world, as I have, you wouldn't sit gibbering at the sight of a Malay native who looks better in a reefer-suit and a double-breasted waistcoat than you do—you haven't seen him in his dress-things, yet—and who could give you points in Bandy-Lacantinerie[13], solicitor's chief clerk though you may be!"

And, when Patrice, utterly confounded, kept silent: "Ask him questions!" roared Coriolis. "Ask him anything you like!"

"Don't make such a show of the poor young man, sir!" said Gertrude's whining voice, amid a clatter of plates and silver.

She was told, with due respect, to leave the room. Madeleine made the mistake of protesting, whereupon Cariolis closed her mouth too:

"I won't have it, do you hear me, all of you? I won't have Noël laughed at!"

"But, uncle, no one's laughing at him!" Patrice ended by exclaiming, in his exasperation.

"Nonsense! The moment he entered the room, you looked at him like a phenomenon! I won't have it, do you hear? I will not have him looked at like a phenomenon! We can't all be born in the Rue de l'Écu at Clermont-Ferrand!"

"Papa! Patrice hasn't said anything to annoy you. You're exciting yourself about nothing."

"Oh, you'll end by making me ill, among the lot of you: Noël as well as the rest!"

Noël seemed not to hear and went on conscientiously gobbling up a plate of Brussels sprouts.

"Good! Now it's Noël's turn!" said Madeleine, with a forced laugh.

"And Zoé too!" continued Coriolis, growling like anything.

"What have I done?" asked pretty little Zoe's innocent and mellifluous voice.

"You've made four more big mistakes in dictation and you've got bad marks for geography."

"Geography," said Zoé, "simply won't enter my head."

"And spelling? Won't spelling enter your head?"

"Yes, monsieur, but it takes time..."

"Time? What time? You're old enough to be married. You've got to know spelling and geography. When I tell you, Patrice, that I've had more trouble with that little minx than I've had with Noël, perhaps it'll take down your exalted notion of the white race, eh, my boy?"

Patrice nodded his head. He wished his uncle to believe that he shared his opinion; but he could not understand a word of the whole business. So they were now making a blue-stocking of Zoé!

"I want you to understand, child," continued Corialis, turning to Zoé, "that I'm not having you taught a word too much if you want to be happy in your married life." Patrice thought:

"Madeleine put it badly when she forbade me to talk about marriage. When all's said, they seem to talk about anybody's marriage here, except mine."

"I shall never marry," Zoé answered, sadly, casting down her eyes. "Who would have me?"

"That's my affair," growled Coriolis, in a great grumpy voice.

And, as he spoke, he glanced at Noël, who lifted his nose in the air. His indifference to all that was said at that table was gorgeous; and Patrice could not help admiring it.

His uncle grunted:

"It's very bad manners to pretend to be dreaming at table and never to attend to the conversation. I say no more!"

Noël could not have heard, for he took no notice. He made up for it by scratching himself. His sleeve must have felt uncomfortable; for with his left hand he scratched himself vigorously under his right arm, a thing which is not allowed in man's reception-rooms. Uncle Coriolis rapped him smartly over the knuckles with a little ebony ruler which Patrice had noticed on the table, without knowing what it was for. Tap! M. Noël gave a yell, like an animal that is being punished, and let go his sleeve.

"It's disgraceful," said Coriolis. "You forget you're not at Hal-Nan here. It's disgraceful behaviour for a Paris law-student."

"Is he entered?" asked Patrice, jokingly.

"He attends the lectures, with me."

"How far are you, uncle?"

"At the various manners of acquiring property," replied Coriolis. "Noël, just tell us the various manners of acquiring property."

M. Noël, wondering all the time if Gertrude would soon bring the nuts, put his long, aristocratic Hal-Nan hand to his mouth and coughed. Then, in his rather hoarse voice and in the declamatory tone of a little boy saying his catechism, he answered:

"The different manners of acquiring property are by succession, deeds of gift and inheritance; contracts: contracts of sale and contracts of..."

He stopped suddenly.

"Well?" said Coriolis, with a frown. "Contracts of..."

"You know, sir," said Balaoo, watching a fly, "that I dislike that word before strangers."

This with a look of savage hatred at Patrice.

"Oh, indeed!" said Coriolis, putting out his hand for the little black ruler.

Balaoo turned pale, which was his way of flushing, and, speaking very quickly, in a low voice, said:

"And contracts of marriage...of marriage."

He raised his head, pleased at having mastered himself, and now tried to look at Patrice with an indifferent air, like one of the Race who knows how to conceal his private emotions.

"Well, Patrice," said Coriolis, delighted at the result, "what do you think of that?"

Patrice thought:

"Certainly, for a native of Hal-Nan, there's an improvement, the improvement of the little black ruler upon the common-or-garden cane."

But he took good care not to express his thoughts to his uncle, who might have thrown him out of the window, and he said:

"It's wonderful!"

"And, you know, you can ask him anything you like," said Coriolis. "I have given him the thorough education of a young man of family. He knows his classics."

"Does he know Latin?"

"You have no right to make fun of your old uncle, Patrice. No, Noël does not know Latin yet. But you can be sure that, when he does take it up, he'll stump you in less than three months. Ask him about dates and Roman history."

Patrice saw that there was no escape. He would have to "ask":

"Won't it bore you, monsieur, if I ask you it few questions?"

M. Noël, who had just cut himself a great chunk of Gruyere cheese, proceeded to swallow it calmly and made no reply.

"Don't you hear?" said Coriolis. "My nephew Patrice wants to know if he can ask you some questions. Show that you're not a fool."

By this time, Balaoo had cleared his mouth. He knew that he must not speak with his mouth full. Carelessly:

"We should keep our qualities for use and not for show!"

And he dropped his glass from his eye, at the end of its cord.

"Well, that's an answer," said Patrice, grinning like a booby.

"Oh, he's seldom at a loss," said Madeleine. "But you're frightening him, to-night."

Balaoo screwed his glass in his eye again, with a furious gesture.

"Are you vexed?" Coriolis asked Balaoo.

"I know why he's vexed," said Zoé, in a melting voice.

"Why?"

"Because Gertrude hasn't brought the nuts."

"Is M. Noël fond of nuts?" asked Patrice.

"Oh, they're his ideal!" said Madeleine.

"Is that so, monsieur?" asked Patrice, for the sake of saying something. "Are nuts really your ideal?"

"Woe be to him," said Balaoo, "who does not bear himself according to an ideal. He may still be pleased with himself, but he will always be far removed from the good and the beautiful."

Having delivered himself of this aphorism, he looked at the door; but Gertrude was not yet bringing the nuts.

"M. Noël is a great philosopher," said Patrice, with an important air.

And he gave a silly smile.

"You needn't smile like an idiot when you make a statement like that!" said Coriolis.

"Very well, uncle," said Patrice, in a nettled tone.

Balaoo seemed delighted and, of his own accord, remarked, with his eyes still fixed on the door:

"Few men have the wisdom to prefer wholesome blame to fickle praise!"

"What can Gertrude be doing?" said Madeleine, to change the subject.

She rose, went to the kitchen and returned at once:

"I found Gertrude in tears. She made a nice tart for to-night and now she can't find it anywhere."

Balaoo began to shake:

"General Captain must have taken it," he said.

"You lie!" said Coriolis, severely. "General Captain has a broad back and a broad beak. But he is a good and faithful servant. Did you only bring him from the Black Woods to accuse him of your faults? Answer like a man! And don't turn away your head! Why did you eat that tart? You knew that you were doing wrong. Answer me."

"That's true," said Balaoo, swallowing his shame before Patrice and vainly waiting for the nuts. "The clear sense which we possess of our faults is a sure sign of the freedom which we have enjoyed to commit them!"

"Very well," said Coriolis, "you shall have no nuts."

At that very moment, Gertrude entered with the dish and put it on the table. M. Noël's eyes gleamed like carbuncles. But Coriolis' hand was already playing, as though casually, with the little black ruler.

"Papa!" said Madeleine, beseechingly.

Noël thanked her with a moist eye. The eye-glass had dropped out again.

"Papa," continued Madeleine, "you were so pleased with him over the Conference Bottier!"

"Does M. Noël attend conferences?" asked Patrice.

"Young man from the country," retorted Coriolis, "if you had read your law in Paris, instead of in the outlandish parts where you come from, you would know that the Conférence Bottier is a debating-society of young men studying for the bar who meet in the evenings, at the law-courts, to get used to practice and to accustom themselves to public speaking."

"Does M. Noël mean to become a barrister?"

"We'll see about that later. For the present, I am making him study the art of speaking. He is doing pretty well. Oh, the man who cut his ligaments did not waste his time and got good value for his money."

"Has he spoken at the Conférence Bottier?"

"Not yet. I don't want to draw attention to my pupil before I am quite certain of success. But I go there with him; and he sees how a positive is established and how it is met by a negative. The day on which he makes his first speech will be a great day!"

Coriolis uttered this last sentence with such ardour and eagerness that Patrice was struck by it. He felt really sorry for his uncle, who seemed to him to be falling into his dotage.

"Meanwhile," said Coriolis, "by way of practice, I am having him taught Cicero in French."

"Oh, monsieur," said Zoé, shyly, "do ask him to, recite us his story about the *Paladin*!"

"Oh, yes, sir, the story about the *Paladin*!" said Gertrude, stuffing Balaoo's pockets with nuts, unseen by Coriolis.

"Very well," said Coriolis, smiling. "Come, Noël, give us your recitation about the *Paladin*."

Balaoo sulked and sat as still as a stone.

"Come on, you great silly!" said Coriolis, "You shall have some nuts afterwards."

On hearing this, Balaoo stood up, moved behind his chair and rested his left hand on the back, leaving, his right hand free for gesticulation. Then, in his best chest-voice, he began:

"How far at length, O Catiline, wilt thou trifle with our patience? How long still shall that frenzy of thine baffle us? To what limit shall thy uncurbed effrontery boastfully display itself? Have in no degree the mighty guard of the Palatine Hill..."

"Oh, the Palatine Hill!" said Patrice. "I didn't know what they meant with their *Paladin*!"

"Hold your tongue, will you, you villain!"

This objurgation came from Coriolis, whose eyes were starting out of his head, while his fist was almost raised to strike Patrice for interrupting Mr. Noël in his exercise. Patrice instinctively shrank back, half-muttering to himself that his uncle was qualifying for an asylum and promising not to spare him once he was safely married and out of his reach.

Coriolis, a little ashamed at seeing how he had scared his nephew, calmed himself:

"Let him go on," he said. "I wish you wouldn't interrupt him, or he'll forget the whole thing."

"I must begin all over again," said Noël.

"Very well, do."

Standing behind his chair and waving his arms as though in the tribune, Balaoo resumed his recitation:

"How far at length, O Catiline, wilt thou trifle with our patience? How long still shall that frenzy of thine baffle us? To what limit shall thy uncurbed effrontery boastfully display itself? Have in no degree the mighty guard of the Palatine Hill, in no degree the watches of the city, in no degree the fear of the people, in no degree the assemblage of all good men, in no degree this most fortified place of holding the senate, have the looks and countenances of these in no degree alarmed thee? Dost thou not perceive that thy designs are disclosed? Dost thou not see that thy conspiracy is already held bound by the knowledge of all these? What thou hast done last night—last night," thought Balaoo, "I went quietly to bye-bye, to please Madeleine, who does not like me to be out every evening—what on the night before—oh, well, old chap, if you knew what I was doing the night before, wouldn't you just pat me with your little black ruler!—where thou wert—at Maxim's!" muttered the orator, between two breaths—"whom, thou didst assemble—they were drunk as lords!" thought Balaoo,—"what plan thou didst adopt, which one of us dost thou think to be ignorant of? O the times! O the manners! The senate understands these things, the consul perceives them and yet this man lives."

"Bravo! Bravo! Bravo!" roared Patrice, anxious to recover Coriolis' good graces, at least until after the wedding.

Madeleine applauded prettily, Zoé was pale with excitement, Gertrude shed tears; but Gertrude nowadays shed tears on the slightest pretext.

"Yes, br-r-r-ravo!" spluttered Coriolis, choking with gleeful pride. "Did you see how he recited it? The gestures? Weren't they well-felt, eh?...Don't you hear it in the rostra? In the middle of the Forum!...I must take him there. Yes, yes, yes! We'll go to Rome together...The Forum! The rostra!...My Noël standing there, in Cicero's place! Oh, I shall live to see it yet!;" cried Coriolis, raving.

"Does he really understand all he says?" asked Patrice, tactlessly.

He received a tremendous thump in the ribs from Uncle Coriolis, who could have killed him:

"What's that?...What's that?...He undestands better than you do!"

"Well, all the same, there are words...For instance, he never heard of the Palatine Hill at Haï-Nan..."

"Perhaps you can tell us what there was on the Palatine!" bellowed Coriolis.

"There was...there was," stammered Patrice. "I don't know...there were fortifications!"

Coriolis exploded:

"There was a temple, you idiot!"

The tears came to Patrice' eyes. Madeleine interposed:

"Really, papa!"

"Let me be!" said Coriolis. "My gentleman is trying to pull Noël's leg: fortifications, indeed I...I tell you, there was a temple!...And you know the name of the temple!"

"No, uncle, I don't," said Patrice, in a harrowing voice.

"Tell him, Noël."

"The Temple of Jupiter Stator," said Balaoo, without a moment's hesitation, eyeing the nuts on the table and rattling those which Gertrude had put in his pocket.

"It was round the Palatine Hill that Romulus traced the first boundaries of the future capital of the world."

"Well, does that stump you?" asked Coriolis, beaming all over his face.

"Yes, uncle, that stumps me!" said Patrice, hanging his head.

Coriolis, gave Balaoo a friendly pat:

"There, you can eat your nuts!"

M. Noël did not wait to be told a second time. He flung himself on the dish and, with extraordinary speed and dexterity, cracked the walnuts with his teeth, picked them and swallowed them. Patrice had never seen anything like it.

"He can't help that," said Coriolis, good-humouredly.

"I have cured him of any number of bad habits which he brought with him from Haï-Nan; but I have never, no, never succeeded in making him use nut-crackers."

"We all have our hobbies," said Patrice.

"He would sooner die. One would think that it gave him as much pleasure to crack his nuts with his teeth as to eat them afterwards."

"I'll wager," said Patrice, "that M. Noël prefers nuts even to Cicero's orations."

"Answer, Noël," said Coriolis.

Balaoo swallowed his last nut and said:

"We are surrounded by an infinity of real, simple, easy joys. We have but to secure them!"

He screwed his glass into his eye and, after staring at Patrice with a look of utter contempt, turned his head away, obviously unable to bear the sight of the fellow.

Patrice bowed. They rose to go to the drawing-room. Coriolis told Noël to give Zoé his arm, which he did with no great eagerness. On the contrary, he kept his eyes fixed on Madeleine, who had taken Patrice' arm. Then, as though unintentionally, he trod on her dress and tore it right across. He apologized.

Coriolis had not the heart to upbraid him, for he knew the pithecanthrope well and read an immeasurable sadness in his eyes.

Balaoo led Zoé to the tea-table and said:

"I am a little tired this evening, sir. May I ask leave to withdraw?"

Coriolis assented; and Balaoo, after quickly bowing to the company, went up to his room without shaking hands with Madeleine.

[13] The French law-students' treatise on civil law.—AUTHOR'S NOTE.

Chapter XVIII

Balaoo found Gertrude in his bedroom, putting out his evening-clothes and his dress-boots:

"Go away," he said, roughly. "I'm not going out."

"No one will know," Gertrude answered, with a sigh, "and it will do you good to take a little air. Look, here's twenty francs to enjoy yourself with. I'll run down and serve the coffee and I'll come back again. Get your things on."

She went downstairs and returned in five minutes.

Balaoo was lying on the rug by the bedside. He had not changed his clothes and he was crying. Gertrude was terribly upset:

"What's the matter with you? What's the matter?"

"You know what's the matter well enough!" replied Balaoo, pressing his clenched fists to his mouth to check his despair. "What did he come back for?"

"One can't prevent his coming to Paris. He's the master's nephew. He's here on business."

"Oh, I know that, sooner or later, he's bound to come and take Madeleine away. It is man's law, but it will be my death." Craftily he continued, "You may as well tell me if it's for to-day or to-morrow. I swear I won't hurt him. I promised Patti Palang Raing. Man is man; and I have shoe-hands instead of feet. I shall be quite good. I shall go straight to the Seine and drown myself without a word."

"And what will become of me?" sobbed Gertrude.

"That's not what I was asking. Is it for to-day or to-morrow?"

"But I assure you there's no question of that!"

"Then tell me, you old vixen, why they wanted to send Zoé and me to the man's house at Saint-Martin-des-Bois? It was the Bank of France to a handful of nuts that I agreed. They knew what they were doing and that I should love to see the Big Beech at Pierrefeu and the table-rock at Mahon and the orchard of my youth...But I suspected something...and, true enough, 'he' came!...Give me your word that you were not expecting him...You daren't give me your word, eh?...Filth!"

At that moment, there was a tap-tap-tap at the door. Gertrude, flooding her handkerchief with her tears, went and opened it; and General Captain walked in:

"Hullo, Polly!" he said.

"Here's this dirty rotter," growled Balaoo. "What do you want, General Captain?" General Captain gave vent to a whole array of guttural and cackling sounds, that came from his throat as quickly as the words of any old woman in a rage.

"What's he saying?" asked Gertrude.

"He says that he can't understand why we haven't started. I promised to take him to Pierrefeu."

"Pierrefeu! Pierrefeu! Pierrefeu! Pierrefeu!" cried General Captain.

"He's deafening me," said Balaoo, turning over on his rug. "Go and fasten him to his perch, in the kitchen."

"Let's start! Let's start! Let's start!" yelled General Captain, flapping his wings.

"Oh, that's enough of it!" said the pithecanthrope, catching him a tremendous box on the ear.

Gertrude, still weeping, put General Captain out of the room. They heard him, for a moment, on the landing, indulging in a torrent of bad language. Then he went downstairs very carefully, counting every step to the kitchen, where he climbed up on his perch near the door and pretended to go to sleep. As a matter of fact, he observed all that happened, for he was more inquisitive than any man-porter. It was not long before he saw Gertrude and Balaoo come down to the hall, taking endless precautions lest they should be heard.

Balaoo was dressed up to the nines. His light overcoat was open and gave a glimpse of his gleaming shirt-front and the silk lapels of his dinner-jacket. His patent leather boots shone like two black stars on the white flags of the hall.

"He's off on the spree again," thought General Captain. "And the old girl'll kill herself sitting up for him!"

Balaoo allowed Gertrude to kiss him, before he started, and to slip some small change into his hand:

"Ah," he said, with a sigh, "if I had not promised to fetch Gabriel, I should certainly have stayed at home!"

Gertrude pushed him gently out on the pavement and closed the heavy hall-door more gently still. Then she returned to the kitchen and settled down to spend the best part of the night dozing with her head on the table. She rejoiced at having persuaded Balaoo to go out:

"It's a change for him," she thought.

And she congratulated herself on having laid out his things on the bed: his dress-shirt, with the glittering front and the beautiful cuffs, as stiff as steel; his tall stand-up collar: things which no pithecanthrope can resist[13].

"Good night, ma'am," said General Captain, in French.

"Good night, General Captain," said Gertrude, politely.

This politeness was too good to last. General Captain felt a need also to treat old Gertrude as "filth!" But he learnt to his cost that what was permissible in a Balaoo was not always permitted in a General Captain. He got a beating with the tongs and raised such an outcry that Madeleine came running downstairs:

"What's the matter?" she asked Gertrude, in an anxious voice. "Have you been crying again?"

"Yes."

"Is it about Balaoo? Does he suspect anything?"

"Of course he suspects...It'll be terrible!"

"Terrible!" repeated Madeleine, pensively.

Meanwhile, the melancholy Balaoo, with his hands dug into the pockets of his overcoat, his stick under his arm, his shoulders bent, his eyes fixed on the ground, was gliding like a shadow through the deserted streets, wrapped in his own thoughts.

He went down to the Seine by the back streets and turned up stream. On his right were the gloomy buildings of the Halle aux Vins.

What was his dinner-jacket doing in that evil-looking desert?

Well, Balaoo's dinner-jacket was on its way to the Jardin des Plantes![14]

Coriolis had thought himself very clever in removing Balaoo from the bad influence of the forest and transferring the pithecanthrope's abode to the heart of the capital; but he had committed a gross imprudence in taking a house only a few steps from the bears' pit, the monkey-house and the lions' and tigers' cages. A man can't think of everything!

And it was always in this direction, towards his brother-animals, that Balaoo's, dreams led him, almost unconsciously, when his heart was heavy because of men.

On reaching the corner of the Pont d' Austerlitz, Balaoo leant over the parapet and gazed at the rippling water and the shimmering reflections of the gas-jets.

He heaved a deep sigh and felt a touch on his shoulder: he turned round.

"Move on!"

It was an anxious policeman, suspecting a coming tragedy.

"*Tchsschwopp*!" said Balaoo.

"Eh? What did you say?"

Balaoo shrugged his shoulders and moved away in the darkness.

"A foreigner," thought the policeman. "A Russian prince, per-haps..."

Tchsschwopp is east-monkey for something like, "Why can't they leave one in peace?"

Balaoo had slanted towards the right and was now near the omni-bus-office. He quickened his pace, following the railings, in search of solitude.

He found it. Then he pressed his forehead against the railings, the railings round the Jardin des Plantes, that huge cage in which men had shut up his brothers, the animals. Tired and shaking with sorrow as he was, the cold of the bars did him good; and he stood for a long time in that position, with his head against the rails, while his eyes, from which dropped two tears, round and heavy as marbles, glanced down his whole person to the black stars that were his patent-leather boots. That was where the mystery lay, the mystery of his infinite unhappiness, which turned him into something worse than a pariah among men, something like a tamed animal, that is to say, the lowest thing on earth. For the lion is still somebody in his cage, in which timorous men have buried him alive; but Balaoo, what was he, in his patent-leather shoes? A man's plaything, neither more nor less!...

Facing him, beyond the dark clumps of the trees, were the railed dens occupied by the great cats, whose heavy, alkaline scent reached him where he stood. He pictured them, calm, fateful and quiet, with their heads on their paws, sleeping peacefully in their houses. The crocodiles, stretched in their coffin-shaped compartments made no more noise than if they had been stuffed. Near them, under the blankets in which they wrapped their digestive dreams, were the reptiles: the noble families of snakes and Cleopatra's asps, silly little animals, whose fame did not keep them from sleeping. For all these creatures were asleep. The very monkeys, who are never still during the day, were snoring, now that night had come, like brutes: like brutes, thought Balaoo, picturing to himself all that animal population slumbering while he sobbed out his pithecanthrope anguish against the railings.

Even in their captivity, he envied those others behind their bars.

It hurt him dreadfully.

Chapter XVIII

What bliss not to know!...To be ignorant of the "difference!"...Oh, the difference was not so great: it was contained within those patent-leather boots of his; and the passers-by who met that fine young man in dinner-dress would never have guessed what he carried about with him, inside his patent-leather boots!...But he, he, he thought of nothing but that, but the difference...and it spoilt all his evenings. Everywhere, at the café, at the Conférence Bottier, even when he went on to the theatre, his mind was obsessed by the horrible thought of the difference...And his despair led him constantly to the cages of the animal people...There were evenings when he felt so unhappy that he could have longed to have the hard hoofs of the cab-horses in the place of his shoe-hands!...Yes, he would rather have nothing inside his shoes, like a cab-horse, than hide that disgrace there...

One day also, when Coriolis had taken him to see the great pictures at the Louvre, he had come home quite upset. He escaped at the first opportunity and ran to "his" Jardin des Plantes and there spent hours looking at the horny little digits of the stags and hinds and gazelles. There were men with feet like that!...Yes, he had seen them in the pictures of men: men with little horny shoes and two horns on their heads, two pretty horns peeping through their hair; men who played music and made the ladies dance in the forest: beautiful, laughing ladies, in airy dresses...He asked Coriolis if he could not have little horny shoes like those put to his feet, instead of his shoe-fingers; and Coriolis explained that that had not been done since the remote days of antiquity. Coriolis had made fun of him again, of course. Yes, Balaoo was, really and truly, nothing but a plaything for men, for Coriolis, for...for Madeleine!

There was nothing human about Balaoo's sighs that evening; and he had best take care: he had already attracted a policeman's attention; and here came a keeper, on the other side of the railings, going his rounds. The man stopped, without seeing him, and listened to hear where those extraordinary gasps came from. Was it the hippopotamus moaning in his sleep? The elephant trumpeting? The panther bored to death?...No, keeper, resume your rounds: it is Balaoo weeping. And Balaoo has nothing to do with you!

The keeper moved away; and Balaoo, under his breath, murmured the following plaint, which was rather a complaint and which he always carried with him, deep down in his sad heart:

"Patti Palang Kaing! Patti Palang Kaing!

Could not the God of Christian man
Say that these fingers bound should be,
The toes on the shoe-hands of me?

"Patti Palang Kaing! Patti Palang Kaing!
Why did the God of Christian man
Alter the language of my song
From my native Forest of Bandong
And teach me to weep at right or wrong,
If He could not also bring His mind
The toes of my shoe-hands to bind?

"Patti Palang Raing! Patti Palang Kaing!
Appeal to the God of Christian man
To restore the language of my song
From my native Forest of Bandong!
And give me back my mangrove-trees,
With my hands that were not as these!"[15]

Poor Balaoo! Luckily, he had Gabriel left to console him, Gabriel, who was waiting for him now.

But it would not do to attempt anything before the time for the keeper to finish his round. The clock struck. Balaoo wiped his wet eyes with his handkerchief, spat in his hands—a thing he never used to do before he saw the acrobats at the music-halls—and, with a very careful movement of his loins, so as not to crease his shirt-front, jumped inside the gardens.

Balaoo feared nothing on earth but dogs. He no longer dreaded the man's rounds, the hour of which had passed; but he was afraid lest the dogs, who could feel him coming even in their sleep, should wake. Fortunately, they were tied up in the little yard near the lion house. Nevertheless, there was the question of the scent to be grappled with. But Balaoo had a capital trick, which always succeeded when he went to visit his friends, at night. He used first to call on the polecats, in the rotunda by the entrance, and would come out simply reeking of pole-cat. Then he was able to walk about anywhere and to go as near as he pleased to the buildings watched by the dags. The smell of polecat does not make them bark: it is a natural smell in the Jardin des Plantes;

whereas the smell of man and the smell of pithecanthrope—"The same thing," thought Balaoo—always makes dogs bark.

Balaoo knew where the keys of his friends' houses hung, in the man's house, near a little fanlight which you had only to push open. Then you just put in your hand. There was no danger.

He made no noise walking. He had learnt to walk silently even in his patent-leather boots. Besides, no feathered animal on his road, sleeping on one leg, would have been silly enough, even if wakened with a start, to cry murder. It would have known at once that friend Balaoo was passing. No animal wauld give the alarm: he could be easy, quite easy, as long as the dogs smelt the scent of pole-cat.

The Abyssinian goats, in their sheds, bade him good evening with a little beat of understanding which he alone took in and which he answered by just breathing through his nostrils, without stopping in his walk. The great waders, the tall herons played him a stealthy little tune on the castanets of their long beaks.

But he would not go near the horrible tribe of low-class monkeys, otherwise known as the monkeys with prehensile tails, who were the scum and the disgrace of the animal world. Every race has its scandals. Among the members of the Human Race are disreputable troglodytes, who live in stone caves, squatting on their hams, with hair coming down to their heels, even as there are astounding Esquimaux, with sealskin legs and thighs, and niggers, niggers who absolutely dare to wear white shirt-collars. If Balaoo ever rose to any sort of position among the members of the Race, if he woke up one morning with proper shoe-feet, he would give lectures all over the world in favour of forbidding niggers to wear other than black collars.

But the low-class monkeys with the prehensile tails were the greatest disgrace of all! A pithecanthrape can mix with all creation, from the highest to the lowest, without losing caste; but not with those!...If he, a pithecanthrope from the Forest of Bandang, were to do such a thing as that, no oriental anthropoid would ever forgive him; and Gabriel, if he came to hear of would spit in his face...flatly!

Balaoo, after calling on the pole-cats, exploring the surroundings and parading his pole-cat scent, returned to the lion-house. The inmates knew that it was he, by the way in which he turned the key in the lock. And there was a general commotion in the cages even before he set foot in the corridor. However, if they expected, that evening, to have a good old palaver with Balaoo, who always told them such extraordinary man-stories, they were mistaken. His visit was brief. They had hardly time to say how-do-you-do and good-bye. Balaoo walked out again, leading by the hand a companion of almost his own size.

It was Gabriel, the great Asiatic ape.

At first there was not a word exchanged between them. Gabriel could judge by Balaoo's attitude and silence that his friend was full of sorrow. He squeezed Balaoo's hand gently, to convey to him that, without knowing the cause, he felt for him in his grief. As they turned by the sea-lions' pond, Gabriel tried to ask a question; but Balaoo closed his mouth with a curt and impatient "*Woop!*" which means, "Please, I beg of you!" And Gabriel, seeing his friend so upset, squeezed his hand once more, harder this time.

"*Tourôô!* 'Tis good to feel the grasp of a friend's hand," thought Balaoo.

Balaoo had no friends, no chums, among men. He dreaded familiarity as the greatest danger that threatened him. He hid his shame under an uncompromising pride.

Latterly, especially during the last two months, it had seemed to him as though the time which he spent with Madeleine was being measured out to him grudgingly.

When he was not with Coriolis, who was his master, with Gertrude, who was his servant, or with Zoé, who was his little slave, he was all alone...all alone with the thought of Madeleine and his own shame.

The nights were terribly hard. Once, when he had been finding consolation in the company of the great cats in the lion-house, Gabriel, a new-comer behind the bars of civilization, had lent a flattering ear to all that Balaoo said; and the thought occurred to Balaoo to make a friend and comrade of the ape. He got on well with him, had much less difficulty than with the others in translating what he called his man-thoughts into animal language. They had common turns of speech, common idioms that delighted them and brought them within a mile of their Forest of Bandong. Java, their wild and mysterious mother, had sent the same blood flowing through their veins.

Another thing that attracted Balaoo was that the pithecanthrope realized, at the first glance, all that could be made of an ape, properly dressed by a smart tailor. To begin with, there is a closer resemblance between your anthropoid ape, with his straight nose and his long, oval face, and a Western man than between a Chinese, for instance, and a gentleman from Tunis. But this particular ape is found only in the Far East, near the Forest of Bandong, and is a cousin of the pithecanthrope.

Chapter XVIII

Of course, the pithecanthrope is his superior, for he unites within himself the three greatest qualities in the world: the dexterity of the Java ape, the strength of the gorilla and the intelligence of man.

"The pithecanthrope is as handy as the Java ape and as powerful as the African gorilla, but not as clever as man," thought Balaoo, quite rightly. "But he is cleverer than the Java ape."

Gabriel believed everything that Balaoo told him and accepted his lead without question. This, moreover, was the only condition on which Balaoo consented, occasionally, to take Gabriel out, in the night of men, to amuse him. And Gabriel was not to growl when he got, back. Once, when Gabriel did growl on returning to his cage, Balaoo gave him a good shaking and swore that he should not see him again for two months.

Balaoo did not want to have any bothers. He could not take Gabriel to Coriolis', could he? And Gabriel, once outside his cage, was helpless without Balaoo. So no nonsense! Settled, once and for all. *Tourôô!* All right!

Balaoo was still holding Gabriel by the hand. Together they stole to the dead-butterfly-house. The two of them had spent hours here chatting, sure of remaining undisturbed. It was here that Balaoo, before venturing to let Gabriel take his first steps in the night of men, gave him his final instructions and imparted his last lessons in behaviour before a pier-glass that dated back to Mme. de Pompadour. And it was in an old wall-cupboard, in which Cuvier[16], as likely as not, had kept his things, that Balaoo hung up the very smart suit of clothes with which he had presented Gabriel and in which Gabriel proudly arrayed himself before their escapades.

They made their way in by methods of their own, methods connected with windows and gutter-pipes. And they came out again without soiling their clothes.

Balaoo was no longer the scapegrace of the Big Beech at Pierrefeu, who used to return to the man's house with the seat of his trousers torn. His trousers, whatever the exercise in which he indulged, never had any other crease than that which they were meant to have. And Balaoo was anxious that Gabriel should take the same care of his things that he did.

They both wore the little soft, black-felt hats that were then the fashion. Lastly, Balaoo had made Gabriel a present of a magnificent pair of spectacles. The one with his eye-glass and the other with his spectacles could go where they pleased, without fear of molestation. But they must mind the dogs.

Balaoo and Gabriel, dressed like smart man-youths, waited behind the entrance at the corner of the Rue de Jussieu, without hurrying, for there was no smell of keeper.

Suddenly:

"Now!" said Balaoo.

One, two, three and over the railings! But they did not loiter in the Rue de Jussieu. Three bounds brought them to the Rue Lacépède, where they stopped to take breath. And, staidly and sedately, they turned up the well-lighted pavement of the Rue Monge.

They walked along very nicely, still holding each other by the hand, and nothing particular happened until they reached the Rue des Écoles. Here Balaoo said:

"Listen, Gabriel, I shall let go your hand now, because we are coming to a swagger part where people of our age don't walk hand-in-hand. But be very careful. Don't leave me. Do everything that I do; and none of your tricks, mind!"

These injunctions were superfluous at the time when they first went out together. Gabriel, trembling all over with anxiety, was then content to imitate all Balaoo's movements; in fact this caused them to be noticed one evening and taken for larking foreigners. But Gabriel was beginning to acquire a certain freedom from restraint; and Balaoo dreaded his impulses:

"None of your tricks!" he repeated. "And mind the dogs!"

For, once mere, Balaoo feared nothing on earth but dogs. The word fear is not strong enough: he was terrified of them. When he saw one, he would turn pale and fly, jump into a tram, or fling himself into a passing cab and tell the driver to go to the first address that came into his head: Bandong, for instance! He lost all his presence of mind. The moment a dog saw him, the first thing it did was to look at Balaoo's feet. One would think that it knew, that it guessed what was inside Balaoo's boots; and, however much that dog might respect the boots of anybody else, it knew no peace, unless Balaoo was clever enough to retreat in time, until it had tried its longing teeth on Balaoo's shoe leather.

"The fear of dogs," Balaoo explained to Gabriel, in quick and comprehensive monkey-language, accompanied by a facial and manual pantomime which means as much to monkeys as to men, who themselves emphasize their words with gestures and grimaces, "the fear of dogs is the first stage of wisdom. Patti Palang Kaing classes men and dogs together. He says, in his book of the forest, 'Do not trust their animal appearance, their hanging tongues, their arched tails, their whole air of being out for their own enjoyment, sniffing the good smell of the earth. They work for men without seeming to, like the traitors that they are, and they will dig their fangs into your throat, straight away, for a mere "Thank-you" from man.'"

"Patti Palang Kaing speaks of the big sporting-dogs, not of the little dogs you meet in the cafes," said Gabriel, scratching the tip of his nose.

"Don't do that!" said Balaoo, hitting him with his stick. "The little dogs in the cafés, on the ladies' laps, are very troublesome too. They never stop barking while one's in the room. I never sit down without first looking round to see if there's a little dog about."

Just then, as they were passing the Brasserie Amédée, a little dog, on the lap of a lady sitting outside in the street, began to yelp like mad.

"Come away!" said Balaoo.

And he took Gabriel's hand to drag him to the opposite pavement.

But the little dog was too quick for them and, leaping from the lady's lap, fastened its teeth in the calf of Gabriel's leg. Gabriel, in his irritation, gave it a kick on the jaw and killed it.

The thing happened so rapidly that Balaoo had no time to interfere:

"And that's not the end of it!" he thought, as he realized the damage done. "A pretty business, this is!"

A crowd gathered round them in a moment, while the lady uttered heart-rending cries and stirred up the whole neighbourhood against them.

The customers outside the café had risen as one man and were abusing them for wild beasts and savages. The girls on the students' arms broke their sunshades and umbrellas over the two friends' backs. A gentleman tried to hand Gabriel his card.

Balaoo did not let go of Gabriel's hand. Gabriel stood trembling and chattering his teeth. He was especially terrified at the eyes of the gentleman who was holding out his card.

"The dirty aliens!" cried somebody.

"Don't answer," said Balaoo, who seemed to have some experience of this sort of riot, having no doubt more than once, quite unintentionally, provoked the anger of the populace in the course of his nocturnal escapades. "Don't answer. Fall back." He fell back step by step, dragging Gabriel with him. "Fall back, without a word; and, whatever you do, don't touch them."

But the crowd followed their retreat. And the gentleman with the card hung on to them and persisted in thrusting his pasteboard under

Gabriel's nose. Gabriel could not help breathing on the card, which tickled him—breathing through his nose—and then there was the devil to pay. The gentleman shouted that that villain, that murderer, that coward who refused to fight had spat in his face!

The arrival of a number of students, marching down the Rue Champollion in single file, added to the uproar and confusion. Balaoo, still retreating—for he knew where he was going—and still dragging Gabriel him, had the happy thought of taking the lunatic's and telling him that he would hear from their seconds in the morning: he had seen this done at the theatre in a play by M. Georges Ohnet. Still yielding before the impact of the crowd, they soon found themselves with their backs against the Musée de Cluny. This was was what Balaoo was waiting for:

"Hop!" he said. "Hop!"

"Hop" means "jump" in monkey—as well as man-language. Gabriel understood. An ivy creeper hung from a gargoyle. Balaoo and the anthropoid ape were in the museum garden before the others knew what had become of them. When they understood, they redoubled their din. A window of the museum opened and a poet, M. Haracourt, put out his head to declare that they were making it impossible for him to work.

The people explained that there were two ruffians in his garden. Thereupon he woke all the attendants, but no one was found hiding behind the stone relics of Julian the Apostate; and the crowd, emitting a variety of opinions on the event, went back to the Brasserie Amedée for more drinks.

Meanwhile, Balaoo and Gabriel were far away, sitting outside a café at the corner of the Avenue Victoria and the Place du Châtelet, ensconced in a dark corner where you can drink at your ease, that is to say, with your fingers. And Balaoo said to Gabriel:

"You see what dogs can bring you to. I had a system with them at Saint-Martin-des-Bois. To save bother, I hanged them all. The people believed in an epidemic of dogs; no one in the neighbourhood ever kept a dog again; and I was left in peace. But there are too many of them in Paris!"

"Last time we went out, you promised to take me to Maxim's. Are there any dogs there?"

"No, but you won't be, able to drink with your fingers."

Balaoo, at the beginning, had intended to take Gabriel's education thoroughly in hand; but this was only a momentary good-natured impulse. And, whenever they were certain that they were alone, in the shade outside a cafe, with their hats over their eyes, they would straightway, both of them, drink their lager-beer with their fingers: you dip your fingers into the glass and suck.

This relieved Balaoo of no little constraint. His excuse was that he thought that no one saw him. And, before throwing a stone at him, we should first make sure that we know a single member of the Race who never, in the seclusion of his bachelor dining-room, thinking himself unobserved, eats his fried potatoes with his fingers or rests his elbows on the table. And we have all read how M. de Vigny[17] used to take his meals in private, so as to eat more at his ease.

All went well on the Place du Châtelet until the man with the pea-nuts arrived, when Balaoo had the mortification of seeing Gabriel leap at that worthy merchant and rob him of his wares in the twinkling of an eye.

The pea-nut vendor, mad with terror and thinking that his last hour had struck, contented himself with picking himself out of the gutter into which he had rolled and running away at full speed in search of a policeman. He found one and brought him stalking to the café where the tragedy had been enacted.

The scared and peaceable customers told the man that his assailant had gone away with a gentleman who said that he would "make himself responsible." They had tried to keep them back, so that they might offer some explanation, but in vain. The brutal lover of pea-nuts had left without a word, on the pretext that he did not speak French. Paris is full of foreigners who consider that they can safely take any liberty.

Some members of the audience at the Théâtre Sarah Bernhardt, who had come out during the interval for a drink and witnessed the attack, had ventured under the emotions aroused by *Angelo Tyrant of Padua*, to express the opinion that "it is not necessary to go to the theatre to see dishonest people." Whereupon the gentleman who was with the lover of pea-nuts and who had "made himself responsible" declared that "it is not dishonest when you pay for things" and, before departing with his friend, laid a penny on the table.

Then, as they had not settled for their bocks, the manager and the waiter had run after them; but the one carrying the basket of pea-nuts under his arm turned and showed two such formidable and threatening rows of white teeth, under his spectacles—you saw nothing but teeth and spectacles in his face—that the two men stopped, feeling sure that that indelicate customer had meant to bite them.

While the policeman was taking notes in his little book and asking the people to "speak in turns" and while the plaintiff was mourning the goods which he would never see again, Balaoo and Gabriel had long been "moving on," in the familiar phrase of the minions of the law. Seated on the top of the tram-car that runs from Montrouge to the Gare de l'Est, they enjoyed the mildness of the weather, the beauty of the young leaves on the trees along the boulevard, the charm of that spring evening and the excellence of the pea-nuts.

Balaoo waited to "remonstrate" with Gabriel until the basket was empty, which was when they reached the Saint-Lazare prison. Gabriel was proposing to get down and walk along the cafés in search of more pea-nut vendors; and Balaoo felt that the time had come to enlarge upon the danger of his conduct. He put on his severe voice to tell Gabriel that, if he went on stealing pea-nuts, he would go to prison. And, pointing to the walls opposite, he explained to him what a man's prison was.

Gabriel could not help shuddering at the sight of that horrible building. He thought of his bright and airy cage in the Jardin des Plantes, among the trees and the flowers, where he was visited daily by man-children's nurses and by scarlet-legged warriors. He promised Balaoo anything and everything, if Balaoo would only take him to Maxim's. Balaoo had told him that it was the best cafe in Paris for pine-apples and bananas, only you must behave properly there and keep quiet, because it is visited by the best people. Balaoo himself had been there two or three times, having heard it well spoken of, between the positive and the negative, at the Conférence Bottier.

"I don't mind taking you to Maxim's," said Balaoo, "but you understand that, if you go for the bananas and pine-apples as you went for the pea-nuts, we shall be in for trouble. You must wait to be served and not imagine that every dish that passes before your eyes is meant for you."

Gabriel swore by Patti Palang Kaing that he would keep his hands in his pockets.

Half an hour later, they drove up in a taxi-cab and walked into Maxim's. As the driver of the taxi had not been paid, he waited for them, as in duty bound, outside the door.

Balaoo and Gabriel felt a little shy and had not the courage to disturb all the fine people who blocked up the middle passage between the tables. Moreover, Balaoo had his own little favourite corner, on the left, as you go in, behind the door. You attract less notice there and can eat your pine-apples and bananas in peace and comfort.

"Oh, here's the Hindu professor!" said Henry, the manager, as Balaoo and his friend entered the restaurant. "Baptiste, take a pine-apple to the Hindu professor. And some bananas."

In first-class establishments, a customer has but to visit the place twice for the waiters to remember all his tastes and little ways. Baptiste went to execute the order and returned almost at once:

"The Hindu professor wants to speak to you," he said. "I can't make out what he's saying."

"But he speaks French."

"Yes, only he's asking for raw rice. I can't serve him with raw rice!"

"Raw rice?"

The manager walked to the table at which Balaoo and Gabriel were seated and bowed:

"Have you given your order, gentlemen?"

"It's like this," said Balaoo, cutting up a pine-apple for Gabriel. "I've brought a friend with me. My friend would like a little rice. Can you give us some rice?"

"Certainly, sir," said Henry, with his usual perfect manner, which never betrayed the least astonishment.

"How would you like it served? With milk? Or in a soup? Or rice-croquettes or cakes? Would you care for gravy-rice?"

"We should like it raw," said Balaoo, giving one half of the pine-apple to Gabriel, whose head was hidden under his soft felt hat.

"Quite raw?"

"Yes, quite raw, in a salad-bowl. It's very easy: you take a large salad-bowl and, fill it with rice. You bring it to us; and we pour in some champagne."

"Ah, I see," said Henry, "an Indian dish! It ought to be delicious."

And he hurried off to give the order.

"Try and eat decently," said Balaoo to Gabriel, "They're staring at us. It's not difficult to eat a pine-apple decently."

"There are no dogs here," said Gabriel, speaking with his mouth full, "but lots of ladies."

"Be careful with the ladies," said Balaoo. "They're almost as big a nuisance as the dogs. If they speak to you, don't kick them; leave it to me to answer them."

Gabriel, who had finished his pine-apple, started eating the tooth-picks, unseen by Balaoo:

"Tourôô!" he said. "Rely on me!"

At that moment, a "lady" passed and said: "Hullo, there's the Hindu professor! He's brought his monkey with him!"

Balaoo turned white with rage:

"*Goek*!" he said, following her with his eyes. "She smells of buffalo-hump."

But the sight of that brazen woman who smelt so strong carried his thoughts back, by a fatal contrast, to a young man-woman who smelt like the spring when the violets sprouted among the mossy roots of the Big Beech at Pierrefeu. In vain he tried to divert his mind with the incident of the pea-nuts, the dead dog and all the comical situations caused by Gabriel's inexperience and charming innocence: the sad and anxious thought of Madeleine seared his inmost heart, even as his inside was scorched when he ate a whole jar of pickles by himself.

Meanwhile, Gabriel had finished not only the pine-apple, but all the bananas and all the tooth-picks:

"Is there nothing more to eat?" he asked.

"I'm out on the spree to-night," said Balaoo. "I'm standing you a bowl of rice-and-champagne. It's coming." To the wine-waiter, "Bring a bottle of champagne. A very light wine, please," he added, pointing to Gabriel, "because of my young friend here."

"Is champagne nice?" asked Gabriel, who was now eating the matches.

"It pricks your nose and makes you walk crooked," said Balaoo, gloomily.

"How sad you are, Balaoo!" said Gabriel, finishing the matches and beginning to eat the box.

"The man from Saint-Martin is back!" said Balaoo, ominously.

"*Phoh! Phoh*!" said Gabriel, sympathetically.

Balaoo discreetly wiped his eye with a corner of his napkin:

"Wonoup! Wonoup!"[18]

Gabriel, with lightning rapidity, seized upon the swizzle-sticks which the waiter brought to free the champagne of its superfluous gas:

"I could see that you were sad," he said. "*Phoh! Phoh*!"

"Sweet is the warmth of your hand," said Balaoo, ready to burst into tears. "*Tourôô! Tourôô!*[19] I am very unhappy, Gabriel...What are you eating?"

"Nothing," said Gabriel, turning pale.

"Show me!" said Balaoo, opening Gabriel's mouth and closing it again. "Oh, those swizzle-sticks! You're quite right. They're no good with champagne, they take away all the prickly feeling in the nose. It's better to eat them by themselves."

Chapter XVIII

"Look at the things on that lady's hat," said Gabriel. "Are they good to eat?"

"You must learn to exercise a little self-control," said Balaoo. "I used to eat hats myself when I was a youngster: all Madeleine's summer-hats; for winter hats are no good. And then I grew up and left her hats alone...I used to wait until she fed me out of her hand...*Wonoup*!...Where are the days when I ate out of Madeleine's hand, the days when I saw her enter the orchard of my youth, looking like a rose-bud? She was also like the partridge running to her brood; but the partridge has not so shapely a figure, nor so light a gait. Her voice was as sweet as the Bengal warbler's song."

"I don't understand all you say," said Gabriel, "but my heart is in your breast."

"*Tourôô*! Thank you!" said Balaoo, pressing his hand under the table. "What have you in your hand?...Where did you get those cigars?"

"Out of the box, when the gentleman wasn't looking."

The waiter had taken the box and was walking away, discreetly counting the cigars.

"What do you mean to do with them?"

"Eat them."

"Yes, for dessert. You must give me half. Ah, here comes our rice-and-champagne!"

Henry had made a point of bringing the salad-bowl himself:

"I've done as you wished, gentlemen," he said. "It's raw."

"That's right, Henry," said Balaoo. "Stir it as you would a salad, while I pour in the wine."

And he stretched out his hand for the bottle of champagne which the wine waiter was uncorking. Unfortunanately, the man was put out by Gabriel's grimaces and allowed the cork to pop and strike the ceiling with a noise like a gun. Gabriel, in his terror; leapt at one bound across the space between the table where he was sitting and the bar opposite and hid himself behind the bar, yelling:

"Brout! Brout! Wonoup! Brout!"[20]

"What's happened? What's happened?" cried a chorus of customers.

"Why, it's the monkey from the Folies Bergère!" said a lady.

"It's very like him," said different voices.

The lady went up to take a better look at Gabriel, whereupon the excited ape suddenly snatched off her magnificent hat and, obeying his instincts, began to devour it upon the spot. Seeing that masterpiece of

216

the Rue de la Paix disappearing between Gabriel's teeth, the lady, the lady's friend and the waiter uttered piercing yells. But Balaoo shouted the war-cry, the rallying-cry of the Forest of Bandong. One more bound; and Gabri joined him. The two were outside on the pavement when Maxim's best customer arrived, just in time to calm the bewildered staff:

"It's the Maharajah of Kalpurthagra," he said, "out for the night with his monkey!"

Meanwhile, the taxi which had brought them was carrying them away. The driver, who had hardly seen the faces of his fares, considered them a bit "on."

On reaching the gate of the Jardin des Plantes, Balaoo made it clear to the driver that the Maharajah of Kalpurthagra had painted the town so very red that night that he had hardly a sou left in his pocket. The driver was quite satisfied. He declared himself the maharajah's humble servant, said he would call for his orders at eleven o'clock in the morning and disappeared, after taking off his cap to his highness.

Had Balaoo been really merry that evening, he would, not have failed to shout after the driver:

"Ask for M. Gabriel! Third cage on the left!"

But Balaoo was not really merry...

After climbing the railings with Gabriel, he walked with downcast head, sadder than ever, in spite of their great evening. They came to the sea-lions' pond at the moment when the dawn was beginning to dispel the darkness of the night. Gabriel, who was afraid of being scolded, said nothing. But Balaoo was not thinking of rating Gabriel. He made him sit on the ground beside him, took his hand and shivered and sighed. And he spoke men's words which Gabriel did not understand. But he spoke them so sadly that the tears came to Gabriel's eyes:

"Listen, Gabriel," he said. "In the spring, I brought her the first flowering branches. Then she looked at me and said, 'My poor Balaoo!' And that was all. Yes, indeed, poor Balaoo!" And Balaoo began to weep. "Balaoo is the most to be pitied of all Patti Palang Kaing's creatures."

"*Woop!*"[21] said Gabriel.

"There is none on earth that understands me but you," said Balaoo, pressing Gabriel's hand. "I will tell you a thing, Gabriel, that I have never told to any one, not even to her. But we weep together, you and I. Thus do the feeblest plants entwine to resist the storm."

"*Wonoup! Wonoup!*" sighed Gabriel.

"It's a song which I have written. Listen. Put your ear closer. It is a song in man-language. But you will understand it, merely by the beauty of the words."

"*Wonoup! Wonoup*!" said Gabriel. And Balaoo whispered into Gabriel's ear:

"Patti Palang Kaing! Patti Palang Kaing!
Hear how my sorrows flow!
I roamed through the garden of man
Like one of the race in woe.
Not one of them saw my tears:
Not she whom I love the best,
Though she heard how I beat my breast
In a grief that none can know.
To the other, who strolled with his nose on high,
She said, 'It is thunder passing by.'

"Patti Palang Kaing! Patti Palang Kaing!
Hear how my sorrows flow!
If only there were bands
To the toes of my shoe-hands,
I should say, in accents low,
To Patti Palang Kaing:
Keep Thou, across the seas,
Thy plantains, mangroves, mango-trees,
Since Thou hast put me bands
To the toes of my shoe-hands!
Patti Palang Kaing!
Balaoo knows no pang!

"And I should say to Madeleine,
In the softest voice of men:
'Madeleine, my fair,
I fain would kiss thy hair!
If only there were bands
To the toes of my shoe-hands! '

"Alas, did not the other say:

'I would kiss her hair to-day!'
Silent I watch and stand,
Waiting to kiss her hand!'"

"Poor Balaoo! Poor Balaoo!" said Gabriel, wiping away Balaoo's tears.

[13] Negroes also are mad on well-starched white linen.—AUTHOR'S NOTE.

[14] The Paris Botanical and Zoological Gardens on the south side of the Seine.—TRANSLATOR'S NOTE.

[15] For the translation of these and the other verses in the present volume I am indebted to the willing assistance of Miss D. Eardley Wilmot.—TRANSLATOR'S NOTE.

[16] Georges Cuvier (1769-1832), the famous French naturalist.—TRANSLATOR'S NOTE.

[17] Comte Alfred de Vigny (1797-1863), the author of Cinq-Mars. He spent the last twenty years of his life in retirement.—TRANSLATOR'S NOTE.

[18] "Alas! Alas!"—AUTHOR'S NOTE.

[19] In the secondary sense of "Thank you!"—AUTHOR'S NOTE.

[20] "Mercy! Mercy! Alas! Mercy!"—AUTHOR'S NOTE.

[21] In the sense of "Please, please, calm yourself!"—AUTHOR'S NOTE.

Chapter XIX

Patrice, on his wedding-day, was garbed in evening dress, with a white tie, by eight o'clock in the morning. As there was nothing more for him to do in his bedroom, he left it; but, on the landing, he found Gertrude, who very civilly begged him to go back to his room, as the master was coming to see him.

Coriolis arrived soon after; and the first thing he did was to rail bitterly at Patrice' attire. He told him that he looked "like a village bridegroom" and asked him to put on a frock-coat or a jacket, unless he wanted to have the Paris street-boys "chi-iking" after him. He added that it was bad enough to have the stupid fashion that compelled girls in the twentieth century to dress up for the altar like virgins of antiquity going to the sacrifice. In short, he found a pretext for venting his temper, which had been execrable during the last forty-eight hours. The young man took off his dress-coat, but, like a good little solicitor's clerk from the Rue de l'Écu, kept on his white tie. He had resolved never again to be astonished at anything. He ascribed the odious snubbings which he was constantly receiving at the hands of his future father-in-law to Coriolis' excessive grief at the prospect of losing his daughter; and he explained in the same way all the curious mystery, all the incredible reticence which had hitherto surrounded the preparations for the ceremony.

During the two days which Patrice had spent at his uncle's house previous to his wedding, he had not caught a glimpse of a ribbon, a parcel, a bandbox, a dress, a flower. A nosegay which he had brought home from one of his walks was seized, the moment he entered the hall, by the furious hands of Gertrude, who flung it into the dustbin without a word of explanation.

He excused the old servant just as he excused the father:

"I am robbing them of a pearl," he said to himself. "It is easy to understand that they can't forgive me."

In reality, knowing that he was improving his advantage hour by hour, he took a secret and malicious pleasure in his humiliation and deliberately made himself smaller and more insignificant at the thought of his coming revenge.

All the formalities were settled. Patrice had seen the family-solicitor, the mayor and the parish-priest. But he had seen very little of Madeleine, on the day before, and nothing of Mlle. Zoé or of the formidable law-student.

But the absence of Zoé and Noël from meals did not trouble him unduly. He had gathered from a few sentences exchanged in a corner between Gertrude and Madeleine that M. Noël had taken the liberty of spending a whole night out and had not come home until ten o'clock in the morning, in such a state that he had to be carried to his room, where he had since been looked after like the prodigal son of the house.

This little escapade did, not seem to vex Madeleine particularly; but Coriolis was like a bear with a sore head.

The civil marriage was fixed for ten o'clock and it was now a quarter to ten. Patrice timidly mentioned the fact to his uncle, who was still in his indoor jacket. Lastly, on looking out of the window, the young man was astonished to see outside the door none of those extraordinary hired landaus in which the felicity of newly-married couples is usually paraded through the streets of the metropolis.

"A carriage?" asked Conolis. "What do you want a carriage for?"

Patrice turned pale:

"Why, isn't it time to go to the town-hall?"

"The town-hall's not so far as all that!" retorted his uncle. "We shall walk."

The young man gave a start: was that how the old eccentric hoped to escape observation? By walking along the pavement, with his daughter, in white and orange-blossoms, on his arm?

Feeling half-stifled, Patrice opened his mouth, if not to utter a sound, at least to breathe. Coriolis gave him a friendly push that sent him breathing out on the landing:

"Come along," he said. "We're only waiting for you."

Nevertheless, he stopped at the top of the stairs and Patrice saw him lean over the baluster to ask, in a hushed voice:

"Can we come down?"

Gertrude's voice replied, in the same key: "Yes, it's all right."

Then they went down one flight and entered the drawing-room. Madeleine was there with Gertrude. Patrice stepped back in dismay: Madeleine was in black!

Chapter XIX

He could not believe his eyes. There she stood before him, his young bride, wrapped in a dark cloak, with a hood to it, which she wore when she went shopping with Gertrude on rainy days.

Having stepped back, Patrice stepped forward. This time, he was trembling with rage. He felt like tearing everything and everybody to pieces: the uncle, the niece and Gertrude. But, even as a ray of sunshine will suddenly appear in the darkest and stormiest of skies, so Madeleine's smile beamed from under the hood, while the cloak parted to reveal the prettiest little bride that Patrice could have imagined in his fondest dreams. At the same time, a delicious smell of natural orange-blossoms—a present from Gertrude, who had crowned her young mistress brow with it—pervaded the whole room.

Patrice fell on his knees before Madeleine and kissed her dear little feet, which, shod in white-satin slippers, were hidden in ugly rubber galoshes. The poor young man sobbed aloud:

"Why," he asked, amid his tears, "why do you hurt me so? Will you ever tell me why?"

Coriolis raised him and pressed him to his heart:

"Madeleine will tell you, my boy," said the old man, whose agitation seemed to have reached its height. "Yes, Madeleine will tell you and you will forgive us. Come, kiss your wife, Patrice, and let us hurry to the mayor's. You are quite right, we are late. Let's get it over."

"Yes, yes, I want it over," whispered Madeleine, herself moistening Patrice' kind cheeks with her tears. "I want it all over..."

"I quite agree with you," said Patrice, in all sincerity, blowing his nose. And he added, lyrically, "It would have been over quicker with a carriage!"

But already Madeleine was dragging him to the staircase. She had taken his arm and, with a swift movement, wrapped herself once more in the folds of her ill-fitting cloak.

His uncle slipped on an old, worn frock-coat which Gertrude handed him. The old servant was the only one who appeared dressed for the occasion. She had squeezed herself, with some difficulty, into a puce coloured silk which she had had specially made and which not even a furious display of anger on Coriolis' part had induced her to take off. The four of them were going down the stairs, when a door above their heads opened and Patrice heard hurried footsteps. He turned round and saw Mlle. Zoé standing behind them, looking paler than a wax statue. She hardly had the strength, in the excitement that fluttered her shapely breast, to utter words of which Patrice vainly strove to discover the full dramatic sense:

"He is at the window!"

Coriolis, on the other hand, the moment he heard them, cried:

"Oh, dash it all, dash it all! Let's go by the back stairs."

For the house had a servants' staircase leading to a little door that opened on an adjacent lane. Only, the doors of that staircase and the staircase itself had remained unused for years without number and the descent by this narrow and gloomy passage, as steep as a well, was a tragic enterprise. They had to battle not only with rusty bolts and hinges, but also with time honoured accumulations of dirt and dust. Fortunately, the antiquated lock that fastened the door on the lane was almost falling to pieces, but for which fact the wedding-party would never have emerged from that awful pit of darkness.

When they were at last outside, they all looked at one another. The two men were horribly dirty, but the two women had passed through all that dust as by a miracle, without getting a speck of it on themselves. The uncle shook his nephew, not to brush the dust off him, but to make him hurry up. He took the lead and only turned to mutter:

"Come along! Come along!"

He walked with his back bent and hugged the wall as though he were trying to hide from observation. But the extraordinary thing was that Madeleine and Gertrude copied this curious attitude. The two women had gathered up their skirts and were hurrying along with hunched shoulders. Patrice in vain tried to obtain an explanation. It seemed that they had no time to answer him; and if he stopped for a single instant, the uncle, or Madeleine or Gertrude would pull him by the hand like a lazy child whom they were afraid of leaving behind.

"What a funny wedding!" thought the young man. "To look at us, people would say that we were a pack of suspects under the Terror, trying to avoid the agents of the Committee of Public Safety."

At last, they reached the town-hall, by strangely circuitous roads. If Patrice had not taken care, on the previous day, to remember the mayor's poor, that functionary would certainly never have waited for him so long. The ceremony was rushed through, as they say, "in five secs."

Coriolis had told Patrice not to trouble about witnesses: that was all arranged. And the cobbler, the porter and the commissionaire from the corner duly put in an appearance. As soon as they arrived, Madeleine threw off the dark outer garment that concealed her fresh and youthful charms; and Patrice might have thought that she had dressed only for those rapscallions, had he been capable of thinking of anything at so impressive a moment.

Chapter XIX

To go from the town-hall to the church, they took a closed cab. Their ragamuffin friends followed in an open fly. Coriolis was beginning to do things handsomely.

A low mass was quickly said; and, as soon as the register was signed in the sacristy, the witnesses paid and the young couple lawfully married in the sight of God and man, their thoughts turned to breakfast.

Coriolis took his party to a celebrated little riverside restaurant which he used to visit in the days of his youth. The old servant had previously taken a bag there, containing an ordinary walking-dress for Madeleine. The trunks, it appeared, had been sent on to the station.

The uncle asked for a private room, took Patrice by the arm and tried to lead him into the passage:

"Let's leave the women," he said. "Madeleine is going to change her dress."

But Patrice kicked at the suggestion:

"Look here, uncle, you must admit that I have always done what you wanted; but let me look at my dear Madeleine in her bridal dress for a few minutes longer. It will be the brightest memory of my life."

Coriolis grunted a few words which Patrice did not catch; but he dared not, thwart the young man; and Madeleine kept on her beautiful white dress and her wreath of orange-blossoms for the wedding-breakfast.

Patrice sat beside his young wife:

"She's so pretty, one could eat her, uncle!" he said.

"Eat your radishes, in the meantime!" growled Coriolis to his lovelorn solicitor's clerk of a nephew, while Gertrude, who was in a melting mood, shed tears.

An unspeakable feeling of peace, tranquillity and calm was shed by that deserted corner of the embankment and that out-of-date, neglected restaurant. After all the tribulations of that memorable morning, Patrice felt entitled to give a sigh of relief. He sighed with happiness over Madeleine's hand, which he raised to his lips, and he was beginning to express the delight which so sweet a moment gave him, when the waiter brought in "the shell-fish."

While handing round the oysters, he informed the gentlemen that there was some one asking for them downstairs who seemed very eager to see them.

Coriolis rose, looking very pale:

"Who is it?"

"Oh, I don't know!" said the waiter, with a gesture which obviously meant that the person's identity was a matter of supreme indifference to him.

"But...but is it a man? A woman?"

"It's a woman."

"It's Zoé!" cried Madeleine, in a great state of excitement.

"Send her up! Send her up at once!" said Coriolis.

And, when the waiter had gone, the father and daughter exchanged anxious glances that worried Patrice more than he could say.

"What can have happened since we went out?" thought Gertrude, aloud. "She must have her reasons for coming."

Then Zoé made her entrance. She was bare-headed; her hair had come undone; and she tried in vain, with a feverish movement, to twist and put it up again. Her face expressed the most intense anguish; the dark rims round her eyes told of some great sorrow; and the corners of her mouth trembled.

"Goodness gracious, what's the matter?" asked Coriolis, Madeleine and Gertrude, in one breath.

"He's looking for you"

"What!"

"He's escaped!...He knows everything!...He ran out of the house like a madman!...Take care!...He is capable of anything!..."

And Zoé, panting and exhausted, dropped into Gertrude's lap.

"But who, who?" shouted Patrice, failing to understand the terror of those around him.

"Who? Noël, if you want to know! Noël!" roared Coriolis, who was holding his head between his hands, as though he were afraid of its dropping off.

"But perhaps he will come here," said Gertrude.

"Let us fly."

"But where, papa? Where are we to fly to?" moaned Madeleine. "It would be. better not to go down to the street, if he is on our track."

"He has lost the track," gasped Zoé, who was stifling, but who dared not ask Gertrude to loosen her stays before Patrice.

"Aha, he has lost the track!" cried Coriolis. "But hasn't he followed you? Are you quite sure of that?"

"I followed him...I took a cab...Oh, it's awful, awful!'...He's quite mad!..."

"But mad about what?" asked Patrice, whose irritation was reaching its height.

"Mad on Madeleine, if you insist on knowing!...Yes, he is madly in love with your wife...He writes poetry to her...Now are you satisfied?"

"And are you all in such a state because a gentleman chooses to write poetry to Madeleine? Let the fellow come here; and I'll talk to him: a pretty thing, indeed!"

And Patrice showed his fists. Coriolis' shrugged his shoulders and Gertrude shook her sad and obstinate old pate:

"Poor Noël, he will never get over it!" she said. Patrice could have torn her eyes from their sockets:

"But what do we care about Noël?" he kept on exclaiming in his fury, bewildered by this inexplicable bomb which had burst in the midst of his new-born happiness.

Alas, no one bothered about Patrice! Not knowing what decision to take, after cautiously closing the doors and windows, the others feverishly questioned Zoé, who, in short, abrupt sentences, broken by sobs, told so fantastic a story that Patrice wondered if he was not dreaming that he had found his way into a lunatic asylum where the words which you hear spoken have no sense even to those who utter them. "I expect," sighed Zoé, "that he was pretending to be dead-drunk for two days on purpose, so as to be left alone: he was up so quick this morning, suddenly, and so soon dressed. And the noise he made: bang, bang! A kick at the cupboard! A kick at the chest of drawers! Kicks everywhere! Bang, bang, bang! A kick at the door when I asked him, from outside, what the matter was. He answered that man-women disgusted him and that Patti Palang Kaing had forbidden him to marry a man-woman, but that the laws of the Forest of Bandong did not forbid M. Noël from attending so fine a ceremony, as long as his honour was not at stake! 'O rot, rot, rot!' was all he said. And that it was no use my dressing in Paris fashions, that I should never be as nice-looking as a female monkey in the huts on the swamps! However, the worst was that he kept on going to the window, while he dressed—I peeped through the key-hole and saw him moving about—as though he were watching for something in the street...Oh, some one must have told him...and yet it seems hardly possible!...What comforted me was that you had already started...He went back to the looking-glass and knotted his tie quite three times over, saying unpleasant things to me, all the while, through the door...Then, when he wanted to put his boots on his shoe-hands, he was seized with a fury that made me shake on the landing where I stood...I heard him gnash his teeth and fling his boots all over the room...Oh, I was sorry that we did not follow our first plan!...But he deceived us by pretending to be dead-drunk...Yes, I ought to have taken him at once to the Jardin d'Acclimation[22]. He knows nobody and forgets everything when he is at the Jardin d'Acclimation. We would have lunched there quietly, he and I together, and I would have invited the giraffe."

"I beg your pardon, I beg your pardon," said Patrice, venturing to interrupt, "but I don't quite under..."

"Hold your tongue and listen!" shouted Coriolis.

Coriolis was walking up and down the room, kicking the furniture as angrily as M. Noël had done. He turned to Zoé:

"But, after all, what was the matter with him? He could not suspect..."

"Nonsense!" said Zoé. "If he had not suspected something, would he have made such a row? He threw a pair of boots into the street. I asked him what was the matter. He answered, in an awful voice, which I shall not forget, if I live to be a hundred, 'Don't you smell orange-blossom?'...I could have dropped! I smelt nothing on that storey...no one of the Race could have...and then it was long since Madeleine had run down, ever so fast, and gone out...Well, he, with his nose from the Forest of Bandong, smelt the orange-blossom through the floors, the stairs, the doors and the walls!..."

"Excuse me, uncle," Patrice interrupted again, "excuse me if..."

But Patrice was unable to continue. Coriolus had made a rush at Gertrude and was shaking the charms and trinkets which she wore round her neck, over her puce dress, until the young man and Madeleine had to interfere to save that old friend of the family from being nearly throttled. Uncle Coriolis could not forgive the servant for rousing M. Noël's scent with a flower which would not have smelt at all, if Gertrude had not taken it into her head to present Madeleine with a wreath of real blossoms. At last, Patrice triumphantly took Gertrude in his arms. She promptly renewed her expressions of pity for M. Noël; and the bridegroom as promptly dropped her in a chair, where she sat, a poor, moaning thing.

No one had so much as touched the oysters. And, at Madeleine's request, while Coriolis continued to kick at the walls—without disturbing the neighbours, for that once famous, but now neglected little restaurant had no other customers but themselves—Zoé resumed her narrative in the face of the bewildered Patrice:

"So he must have smelt the wreath of orange-blossoms through the door. Then he opened the door. I never saw him look so pale in my life. 'It's a scent,' he said, 'which people wear on their wedding-day. I have read that in men's books. Is anyone in the house being married to-day?' I must have been very much upset, for he stared at me with a sad smile and said, 'Poor Zoé, you're looking none too well yourself!' And he went downstairs, pushing me gently out of his way and lifting his nose in the air to sniff the orange-blossom. He went straight to the drawing-room, where Madeleine had sat waiting for Patrice. When he came out again, his face was terrible to see. He had the strength to ask me a few questions with his trembling lips: where was Madeleine? I said that she had gone out. Then he wanted to know about M. Patrice and you, sir. I did not know what to answer and was making up a story, saying you would all be home soon, when he put on his terrible Bandong gong-voice: 'The scent of orange-blossoms is what people wear at monsieur le maire's!' he said. And, with that; he rushed down the stairs and into the street and I after him...At first, he was rather at a loss. He hunted for the scent, without finding it. It was not on the pavement. He sniffed the air in every direction. At last, he walked round the house, went up the lane and picked up the scent near the side-door...He took no notice of me at all, did not hear a word I said to him...He was soon out of the lane and I had the greatest difficulty in following him. He went along at a mad rate, with his nose still in the air, pushing against the people, the horses, the carriages and even stopping the omnibuses...I saw him, from the distance, go into the town-hall and come out again almost at once...Knowing that you were going to take a cab at the town-hall, I said to myself, 'Perhaps he'll lose the scent-because of the cab...'"

"I beg your pardon," Patrice broke in once more, "I beg your pardon. I know the smell of orange-blossom is very strong, but I can't understand..."

"That'll do!" shouted his uncle. "You will never understand anything...Go on, Zoé....He left the town-hall..."

"Yes, he left the town-hall and, still with his nose in the air, still knocking up against the people in the street, he went to the church...From there, he took the road that seemed to lead here...This time, I caught him up and tried to speak to him. He threw me at the foot of a wall, like a bundle of washing, and started running, running, running...I jumped into a cab, meaning to come and warn you in time, if I could, when I saw him, at the corner of the Boulevard Saint-Germain, go straight ahead, instead of turning down the street that leads to this place...I thought I must find out where he was going...He ran along the boulevard, ran on, with his nose in the air, jostling people aside, and, without a moment's hesitation, walked into a very 'swagger' lunching place, the Restaurant de Mouilly, I believe...'What does he mean to do there?' said I to myself...Suddenly, I understood: there was a whole row of landaus, with a wedding brougham, drawn up along the pavement!...On leaving the town-hall and the church Noël had smelt another wreath of orange-blossoms, had pitched upon another wedding-party!...What he did to them I do not know...I heard them screaming like mad...I saw people rush to the windows and shout for help as if the house was on fire...And that's all I can tell you...I came on here...You are safe, for the moment...But the poor fellow is out of his senses...I never saw him like it before...trembling from head to foot and rolling his eyes...Oh, how they must have 'caught it' at the other wedding!"

Thus spoke pretty little Zoé, in her despair; and, when she had done, she gave free play to her tears. "If only nothing happens to him...at that wedding party!" muttered Coriolis, stopping his perambulations for a minute.

Patrice bent over Madeleine, who appeared to be sadly and silently pursuing some distant thought:

"What are you thinking of?"

"I think as papa does: if only nothing happens to him at that wedding-party!"

And so there was no thought, no care, in that room, for anyone except the wild lunatic who had crossed the path of Patrice' happiness like a dangerous beast!

"It's too bad!" he protested.

Zoé interrupted him:

"I don't think you need fear anything on that score; you know it's impossible to catch him...He comes and goes and disappears as he pleases!...No, I am much more afraid that, when he discovers his mistake, he will go back to the town-hall and the church and find the real scent. If he keeps cool, he can do anything with his nose!"

"What do you mean, he can do anything with his nose?" yelled Patrice, struggling against the state of stupefaction into which Zoé's queer speeches were beginning to plunge him.

Zoé stared at him in amazement: why, didn't he know yet?

Patrice read both grief and mischief in her eyes.

"Ah," she said, without replying to his astonished outburst, "we none of us look like people at a wedding, considering that this is a wedding-day!...The best thing you could do would be to take the first train and not to wait until the evening. That's my advice to you!"

"But why, why, why? I want something to eat!" protested Patrice, "I want to eat in peace and quiet! Don't you want to eat in peace and quiet, Madeleine? It's no reason, because a maniac..."

He did not finish his sentence.

"There he is!" cried Zoé, who was leaning out of the window.

Oh, what a flight!...Coriolis dragged or rather carried in his arms the fainting Madeleine. Gertrude hustled Patrice, pushing him in front of her, digging at him with her fists. At the corner of a little staircase which Coriolis seemed to know of old, he turned and, tearing the fatal wreath of orange-blossoms from Madeleine's forehead, in spite of Patrice' yapping expostulations, flung it to Zoé:

"Here, stay here, you, and stop him! Lock him in!"

And, roughly thrusting Zoé back, he shoved the rest of the band down the well of the little staircase.

Meanwhile, M. Noël, with quivering nostrils, was climbing the main staircase of the once-famous little restaurant. Patrice and Madeleine, accompanied by Coriolis and Gertrude, arrived at the Gare d'Austerlitz in time to see the Auvergne express steam out of the station. The next was a slow train, stopping at every suburb on the line. Patrice declared that his wife and he would go by it. He was eager to leave Paris, to be alone with Madeleine and question her and get rid of all the horrible thoughts that oppressed his heart.

Then, suddenly, Madeleine, who had not spoken a word since their headlong departure from the restaurant, closed her eyes and fell in a dead faint on the platform.

An indescribable confusion and excitement ensued. Madeleine was still wearing her wedding-dress. The sight of this bride swooning at a railway-station attracted all the passengers and emptied the trains that stood waiting to start. The guards and stokers left their posts, the porters dropped their loads, the waiters came running out of the refreshment-room. Above the stir of the crowd rose Gertrude's yells and the angry shouts of Coriolis, who distributed kicks all round.

Soon the rumour ran that a girl had been married against her will and poisoned herself, there, before everybody, on the railway-platform, rather than accompany her husband. Men glared at Patrice, who, in his white tie, was obviously the bridegroom, as though they could have murdered him.

Fortunately, Madeleine opened her eyes and gazed at the young man with a look of fond affection which con tained as it were an entreaty that he would pardon her for the outrageous wedding-day which they had given him. And Madeleine's lips also parted to emit a word that gave poor Patrice the shudders:

"Home!"

"Yes," growled Coriolis, who was as red in the face as his daughter was pale and who seemed threatened with an apoplectic stroke, "let's go home: I can't let you leave in this state of weakness."

"My poor young lady!. My poor young lady!" whined Gertrude. "It'll be the death of her...Indeed it'll be the death of her...and of him too!"

At these words, Patrice, who knew to whom that cry of pity referred, lost control of himself and, going up to Gertrude from behind, bit with all his teeth and all his might through the sleeve of puce-coloured silk that covered the tough arm of the old friend of the family. Gertrude howled with pain. Patrice assumed an air of innocence and begged her to moderate her grief. As far as he was concerned, he said, he objected to Madeleine's returning home. Thereupon, the crowd all went for him, threatened to do for him, treated him as a savage and loudly pitied the young and charming girl who had been "sacrificed to such a brute!"

A lady gave Madeleine her smelling-salts; a gentleman who declared himself to be a doctor stooped down to unlace her stays. Patrice made up his mind to die like a hero. Snatching his wife in his arms, he rushed through the crowd and out of the station. He had the luck to find a taxi and put Madeleine into it amid a chorus of execrations.

"Where to?" asked the driver.

"Down the Auvergne Road!" shouted Patrice. But Coriolis, running up, ordered: "Rue de Jussieu!"

And he called Patrice' attention to Madeleine, who had closed her eyes again.

Gertrude, before taking her seat, gave a last word of warning:

"Rue de Jussieu?...But suppose he's there, sir?"

To which Coriolis replied:

"If he is, you know there's no one like Madeleine to bring him to his senses."

And Madeleine's lips opened once more:

"Yes, he will listen to me."

The taxi moved off. The crowd began to thin. Someone observed:

"They had much better drive to the nearest chemist! Marriages like that ought not to be allowed!"

Patrice was fool enough to show his face at the window and was greeted with boos and jeers:

"Ugh!...Bluebeard! Bluebeard!"

[22] The Jardin d'Acclimatation, which Zoé calls "the Jardin d'Acclimation," is the Zoological Garden on the north side of the Seine, in the Bois de Boulogne; the Jardin des Plantes is the Zoological Garden on the south side.—TRANSLATOR'S NOTE.

Chapter XX

But Patrice bore the crowd no ill-will. The person for whom, at that moment, he entertained a feeling devoid of all affection was his Uncle Coriolis. The young man swore that he would make the crack-brained old rascal pay for the wretched time which he had given him. The feeling aforesaid was made up, first, of the hatred which any placid young gentleman cherishes for the man who upsets his composure and, secondly, of the vague dread that Madeleine and himself, Patrice, were about to become the victims of some extraordinary and perhaps criminal machination on the part of that dangerous eccentric. Whatever happened with Noël, Patrice had made up his mind that Coriolis was responsible for the catastrophe.

The observations which he was able to make during the swift taxi-drive only increased his grave and overwhelming anxiety. Coriolis held Madeleine's drooping head on his breast. The young woman opened her eyes from time to time, gazed silently at her father and then shut them again, retaining the picture of the old man's face under her closed lids.

Coriolis had lost all his excitement of the morning. He wore an expression of stern reflection, but his sternness seemed directed against himself, for he uttered a strange sentence:

"Perhaps I am on the verge of punishment. God's will be done, if I have offended Him."

Madeleine could not hear these words without shuddering; and her frail arms hugged the speaker closer to her. As the cab turned into the Rue de Jussieu, Madeleine said:

"Don't be frightened, papa. He is no longer a wild beast. I shall talk to him; and he will understand. Our mistake was to run away from him as though he were a wild beast; and that is certainly what he resents. But, if I speak to him as one would to a man, he will behave like a man."

Gertrude said, simply:

"Yes, he will kill himself like a man!"

Madeleine, Gertrude and Coriolis sat and looked at one another. Patrice saw that the same inexplicable anguish united them; and Noël began to assume the figure of a monster in the young man's awe-struck brain.

But Patrice was still unable to understand; and that queer incapacity to understand frightened him more than anything else. Now that the others were talking freely before him of things relating to the mystery, the mystery itself appeared to him all the more unfathomable, with dizzy depths of gloom and horror into which he dared not peer.

They reached the house. It was almost incredible, but Madeleine seemed to have recovered all her strength. She was the first to alight, entirely unaided. Patrice stared at her in bewilderment: she was as white as her dress, all the same.

Patrice insisted that the taxi should wait. They stood on the pavement and examined the front of the house: everything was shut up. Coriolis had his latch-key; they went in. The young man almost forced Madeleine to take his arm. He felt it trembling under his own. She was afraid! She was afraid! Then why had she cotne back? Why had she wanted to come back?

She said aloud, after listening to the silence of the house:

"He is not here!"

Then it was for "him" that she had returned. Patrice felt horribly hurt; and yet he did not doubt Madeleine's love for him.

All three were straining their ears for the least sound. Madeleine said, with a sigh:

"They have not come in. Perhaps Zoé has made him listen to reason. Oh dear, if only Zoé has persuaded him to go for a stroll in the Jardin d'Acclimatation!"

Coriolis had definitely forbidden Balaoo to go to the Jardin des Plantes, which he considered too near. Gertrude said:

"It's funny, but I don't see General Captain."

As she spoke, General Captain appeared on the top stair of the first flight. The bird-porter wore a very peculiar air. To begin with, he did not say:

"Hullo, Polly!"

He said nothing at all, he did not speak, which was very unusual in General Captain. And be kept on wagging his small green head in a most distressful fashion.

"There's something the matter with General Captain," said Gertrude, who knew him well.

Still silent, he went upstairs as they approached, hopping backwards, constantly wagging his head, constantly keeping his eyes fixed upon the party.

"There's something the matter, there's something the matter," Gertrude repeated.

Patrice felt Madeleine's hand tremble still more violently on his arm. She agreed with Gertrude:

"Let us follow him," she said. "You can see he's calling us."

The whole thing was childish and uncanny. That green bird, with the mysterious backward gait and the incessantly wagging head, appeared to them, in the middle of the great staircase which their anxious feet hesitated to climb, as the evil spirit of that cold and echoing house.

He led them through the passages to the head of the servants' staircase which they had taken that same morning to escape M. Noël's curiosity; and there they discovered, lying at the top of the stairs, with her arms outstretched and her face covered with blood, Zoé! They cried out with terror. Coriolis flung himself upon the lifeless body and raised a scared face:

"She has received a terrible blow on the head," he said, "but she is not killed."

They carried her to her room and laid her on the bed. Coriolis held some ether to her nostrils. She opened her eyes.

At the sight of the young woman in the bridal dress who was tending her, she was convulsed as though with an electric shock:

"I'm not dreaming?" she cried. "It's you, Madeleine? You, here? Oh, go away! Go away! Madeleine darling, go away!"

They tried to silence her, to calm her, but in vain. She seemed endowed with an incredible strength to push Madeleine from her:

"Go away! He's coming!...He's coming and he will kill you!"

They could see that she was delirious, but the words of her delirium terrified them:

"Yes, he will kill you!...When he saw that you had gone off with Patrice, that you had run away from the restaurant, there was no holding him. I locked the door of the private room, the moment he was inside, and hid the key. He struck me, dragged me by the hair, weeping all the time, saying that he hated me, that he would kill me if I did not at once tell him where you were...I gasped that you were at the Gare de Lyon...Then he gave one bound to the window...He went out by the window...But he will come back, he will come back!...And, as I have told him a lie, he will kill me!...I don't mind: I only came back for that...But my strength...my strength failed me at the top of the stairs...and I fell on the stair...I thought I was going to die...but I don't want to!...I want him to kill me...himself; with his tremendous fist, because he will never, never love me!..."

And Zoé, who had half-raised herself, fell back upon the pillow and closed her pretty eyes.

Madeleine wiped the blood tenderly from her little friend's young and sorrowful face, kissed her on the forehead and wept bitterly.

"Let us fly!" said Patrice. "Let us fly from that monster whom you have taken into your house and who has nothing human about him!"

"Yes, go," Coriolis' gloomy voice commanded. "Go, both of you...You see, Madeleine, what he has done to Zoé.... Go."

"But, father, you know that he won't mind Zoé's voice, but that he has always obeyed mine!"

"Patrice, take your wife away," commanded Coriolis.

"Then have you no faith left in your work, father?" asked Madeleine, in her calm, harmonious voice.

Coriolis stalked across the room, a prey to some mysterious agitation; but he stopped opposite Madeleine and, looking her straight in the eyes:

"What if we have not killed the beast?" Madeleine did not lower her eyes:

"I swear to you that the beast is dead! Why would you not believe me? All this would never have happened. He has the right to be spoken to like a man!" But Zoé's voice was raised in frenzied appeal:

"Go! Go!... He will come back and do murder!...He will commit murder with his tremendous hand!..."

"No," said Madeleine, sitting down by Zoé's bedside, "he will hot commit murder, because I shall remain and speak to him."

But Zoé, avoiding the arms that tried to restrain her, slipped from the bed and, on her knees, entreated Madeleine and Patrice to flee without delay:

"He will murder you both!" she cried. "You don't know all, you don't know all!...It is not his fault that Patrice is not dead already!...He will kill you as he killed Blondel...as he killed Camus...as he killed Lombard...and...and another...another whom you know of!...It was he...it was he who killed them all!...I lied to you, Madeleine; it was not Élie who cried in the night, 'Pity! Pity in the man's house!' It was...it was Balaoo!..."

Raving wildly, she dragged herself on her knees; and Madeleine retreated before that awful voice, that voice which Coriolis was now trying to silence by main force, yes, by main force, with his hands crushed against Zoé's mouth:

"Hold your tongue!...Hold your tongue!" he railed, hoarsely.

Coriolis, with his white hair, looked a hundred. Madeleine, wild-eyed, open-mouthed, horror-stricken, seemed mad. But there was no stopping Zoé's mouth:

"He will kill you!...He will kill you all, all, all!" she cried.

And Zoé's hands clutched Madeleine, drew her outside, pushed her into the passage, flung a cloak over her shoulders:

"Kill you! Kill you!...Go! Go!...you have just time!...Kill you!" screamed Zoé, clamouring for the others to assist her.

And Zoé's hands, Patrice' hands, Gertrude's hands, Coriolis' hands all pushed Madeleine out of the old house...

The newly-married couple fled, fled through the sullen night, through the storm bursting over Paris. Leaning back in the taxi, Patrice seemed to hold a dead woman in his arms, while, through the hum of the motor, the throbbing engine seemed to repeat, everlastingly:

"Balaoo!...Balaoo!...Balaoo!...Balaoo!..."

Those three syllables roused the utmost depths of his tragic memory. He banged at the window: the cab pulled up outside a shop. Five minutes later, Patrice stepped in again.

"Where have you been?" asked Madeleine, who had come to herself at the sudden stop of the taxi.

"I have been to buy a revolver."

"What for?"

"To kill your Balaoo."

"That was quite unnecessary. You can't kill a pithecanthrope with what you have bought!"

"A what?"

"A pithecanthrope."

Seated, alone with Madeleine at last, in the train that was hurrying them southward, Patrice listened to her story. She told it to the end, with a white, scared face, and Patrice now knew all. Stooping over his hands, which clutched his poor head and hid the shame upon his face, he let words slip through his fingers, words that came and struck at her heart—"Tack! Tack! Tack!"—like tiny taps of a hammer:

"That comes," said Patrice, in a hard and metallic and ever-so-distant voice, "that comes of having an uncle who thinks himself a genius."

Madeleine fell back on the seat, gasping for air, swooning. He did not even see her, and finished saying what he had in mind:

Chapter XX

"We shall all have to stand our trial...Your father is a murd..."

Something rolled between his legs like a bag that might have fallen from the rack. It was Madeleine's white body, tossed about by the jolting Auvergne express.

"Dinner is served," said the restaurant-car attendant, fortunately without looking into the compartment!

As the man had seen nothing; Patrice was able, without scandal, to proceed with the various experiments calculated to restore her who, since that morning, was his wife: air, salts, a window let down, a bodice unlaced, kisses and tears. All Patrice' love returned as soon as he felt between his arms the adorable and throbbing burden which it was his mission to defend against the savage enterprises of a pithecanthrope. And, when Madeleine began to return his kisses, he felt that there would yet be happiness for them both on earth, despite that dire adventure. When he had yielded to his first impulse and failed to control his temper, it was because he really did not expect to find that sort of rival installed in a respectable family.

"Oh, Madeleine darling, why did you not tell me of those terrible things earlier?"

"My love, my love, I swear that, if I could have dreamt for a moment that that horrible Balaoo was capable of committing the crimes which Zoé spoke of, I would have told you all before consenting to be your wife! And, if I believed that he had committed them, I would have refused your hand! But I do not believe it, no, I do not believe what Zoé said. Zoé was trying to be revenged on Balaoo: I would never have thought it of her!"

"But she said that he also killed some one whom you know of!"

"Oh, that was an accident! He squeezed a gentleman's neck too hard; and the gentleman died of it. Balaoo does not realize the strength of his hand. He has the hand of a murderer, without knowing it. We had to train him to give up habits for which he was not morally responsible; and we really thought we had succeeded...You mustn't believe all that Zoé says, dear. Balaoo once committed manslaughter, through carelessness: that's a thing that can happen to anybody. Now, since he has been in Paris, he knows that he must not touch men's necks with his terrible hand: he knows what it costs...Papa took him to see an execution and he came back quite impressed, I assure you...Patrice, my own, what are you thinking of now?...You look quite pensive!"

"I'm thinking that I've let myself in for a nice thing!" said Patrice, brutally.

Madeleine's tears began to flow once more. Patrice made an attempt to console her, but she pushed him away. No, no, he must not touch her: it did her good to cry...And if Patrice regretted his marriage as much as all that, the thing was easily remedied: he could divorce her!...Then he would be quite happy, wouldn't he?

"I adore you!"

Oh, the power of love in the golden days of youth!...

Here are two young people, the victims of the most frightful adventure that ever crossed what lovers call a honeymoon; and it is all forgotten in a kiss! Patrice fears nothing now: he loves!...He is mightier than the racial mysteries!...The placid little solicitor's clerk from the Rue de l'Écu feels within himself the pride and courage of an archangel wherewith to fight the monster.

"Second dinner, gentlemen."

The attendant's voice brought them back to earth again; and the two young people exchanged a pleasant smile, a pleasant smile that expressed their single thought: the two young people were hungry. They had not lunched. It was eight o'clock in the evening. And there is nothing like excitement to give you an appetite!

A quick wash and brush-up; and soon they were laughing at their rig-out, at their appearance, at their swollen eyes, at that wedding-dress which Madeleine had been obliged to wear all day, at that cloak of Zoé's which was much too short for her and which covered the dress without concealing it.

They laughed at everything, at everything; they laughed at their own fears; and they went to the dining car to make a hearty meal.

They had to walk through the whole length of the train; and the jolting knocked them about and set them giggling afresh: they were a little unnerved since the morning. Right at the end of the car was a little table for two, where they would be very comfortable and able to laugh, by themselves, at all around them and at themselves and at everything, I tell you, at everything, at Balaoo himself, yes, and at the veal and spinach and the chicken and mushrooms: we all know what de-licious cooking we find in railway dining-cars!

"Some more salad, sir?"

"Yes, please...Two dinners, darling; they have two dinners on this line: such a lot of people travelling at this time of year..."

The second dinner had filled the two compartments of the restaurant-car, which were separated by a sheet of ordinary plate-glass. The other was the smoking compartment; but people were dining at all the tables.

"Oh, Madeleine...if you could only see...it's too funny!...No, don't turn round...you can look presently...Over there, at the end, there's a lady in a hat: such a hat! It would be just the thing for General Captain!...You'll see her: it's a lady on the right, sitting next to...next to...to...Oh...Madeleine!..."

"What's the matter, Patrice, what is it?...Are you going to faint now?"

Patrice was no longer laughing:

"Madeleine," he said, in a hollow voice, "I believe the person next to the lady in the hat...is Balaoo!"

"Ah!"

"Don't turn round!...Don't turn round!...He's bending forward!...I can't see plainly...his felt hat is over his eyes...Ah, he's raising them!...He's looking at us!...It's he!"

Madeleine could not help turning round. Patrice was right. It was Balaoo. He lowered his head as soon as he saw Madeleine look at him. She made a sign to her husband to change seats with her. As he did so, her fingers met his. Patrice' hand was moist and shaking. She tried to give him confidence:

"Don't be frightened," she said. "He is tamed now. His violent fit is over, he is lowering his head, he dare not look at me."

Patrice, who had turned extremely pale, said:

"The reason I'm trembling is that I want to polish off that loathsome brute for good and all."

"Hush, dear, and pass me the bill of fare."

But Patrice, who now had his back to Balaoo but could still see his image in a glass behind Madeleine, continued:

"If he comes, I shall know what to do."

"If he comes, you will let him come," said Madeleine, in a curt tone which the young man disliked exceedingly.

"A good bullet in the ear would settle his business as easily as anyone else's."

"Patrice, if you love me, you will do what I say..."

"First of all, keep your revolver in your pocket."

"Well? And then?"

"Then, when dinner is finished, go back with the other passengers and leave me alone with Balaoo."

"That, never! Have you forgotten what Zoé said?"

"Balaoo was mad this morning; he is perfectly quiet now."

"Why did he follow us here? Do you think it's with a good intention? Zoé was perfectly right. We must be on our guard!"

"I am not taking my eyes off him and the poor fellow daren't even look up at us...He does not know what to do: he is hiding his face behind the bill of fare, putting it down, taking it up again. Now he's pretending to give an order to the waiter. Now he's moving the bottles on the table. It's pitiful...Listen, Patrice dear, you must leave me alone with him for a moment and I'll scold him. He will get down at the first station, I promise you."

"You can do as you please, but I sha'n't leave you."

"Oh!" exclaimed Madeleine, anxious but dignified.

"He's getting up, he's going, he'll escape us...You can see he's afraid. Let's go after him. I must speak to him, at all costs, I must know what he wants!"

"Yes," repeated Patrice, "we must know...know what he wants...We can't continue this journey with that thing about us."

They stood up. Patrice tried to pass in front of Madeleine, but she pushed him behind her with some violence and they hastened through the two compartments of the dining-car with the staggering gait of tipsy people quarrelling. They were the object of general curiosity and of some laughter. Balaoo, who was on the foot-board joining the dining-car to the next coach, turned round angrily, thinking that the people were laughing at him.

Patrice was almost blinded by those fierce and flashing eyes...and he shuddered to the marrow of his bones. He had recognized the eyes of the monster in the black mask who had nearly strangled him on the top of the diligence, by the Wolf Stone.

Madeleine hurried after Balaoo, who had now reached the corridor. Patrice, behind her, cocked his revolver; and the three ran one after the other, in Indian file. Madeleine called, in a faint voice:

"Balaoo!...Balaoo!..."

The other must have heard, but no longer turned his head, seemed wholly taken up with his flight along the corridor. He slipped like a shadow throllgh the astonished passengers, who, with staring eyes, watched a pursuit that looked to them like a game.

"Balaoo!" said Madeleine, in a voice of command.

But her voice in vain adopted a tone of authority, like that of a lion-tamer preparing to lash his animals: the other no longer obeyed. Then, as he was gaining ground, Madeleine's voice became gentle and beseeching and she uttered the "Balaoo!" that had always brought him back, moaning, to her feet, at the worst and most rebellious hours of his savage brain. But Balaoo seemed not even to hear and rushed into the corridor of the third carriage. When they arrived there, he was gone; and they ransacked the whole train to no purpose, in a galloping anxiety. Balaoo had disappeared! And this seemed to them even more terrifying than to have him in front of them in the restaurant-car, stealthily dining at a little table, deceitfully mimicking the actions of one of the Race ordering his dinner, while, underneath the table, the sinewy thighs of one from the Forest of Bandong were preparing for a murderous leap!

Patrice and Madeleine retreated half-dead to their compartment, locking and bolting it, though that made but a poor defence against an enterprising Balaoo. Since her voice was powerless, even when raised in entreaty, they were at the monster's mercy. What was going to befall them, with that hateful thought of the pithecanthrope around them? They realized that everyone of their movements was spied upon, from some place, which they could not discover, where the anthropoid's malice had found a refuge. And it was only now that Zoé's voice, proclaiming all Balaoo's crimes, reached Madeleine's ears with its full, dreadful force:

"He will kill you as he killed Blondel...as he killed Camus...as he killed Lombard...and another whom you know of!"

Ah, yes; yes, yes, she knew!...She had seen him at work!...She had seen his terrible hand at work!...She was forewarned, she knew what he was capable of and, if he killed yet another—another who was sitting beside her, fingering the revolver in his pocket with a trembling hand—she could say to herself, with absolute certainty, that that fine piece of business, the business of educating a pithecanthrope, was hers!...Oh, the anarchists need not think that reversible bombs alone are delicate and dangerous to handle; there are other receptacles; such as brain-pans, which, when manipulated a little too roughly by old professors or a little too heedlessly by young ladies, also have a way of going off at a moment when you think them quite safe, brain-pans of pithecanthropes and the like, which reverse of their own accord upon the shoulders of thoughtless young persons!...

Patrice and Madeleine cast haggard eyes above, below and around them. Where was he? It was frightful not to know where he was; for they could feel his eyes!

The train was travelling at a speed which would have frightened them, if they could have felt frightened, at that moment, of anything but the eyes that watched them...Unconsciously, instinctively, they sat closer together...They embraced each other with timid arms, shuddering under the eyes that were slowly killing them...The train rushed through station after station with a whistle that rent the black veils of the night like silk. Sometimes, the train made a noise like thunder: that was when it was passing through a tunnel. And here again came the noise of the thunder, at the moment when they were most afraid. Then...then...they saw the eyes watching them behind the glass, the glass of the carriage-window, which was pitch dark in the tunnel and formed a black frame for the terrible head of Balaoo watching them!

Patrice made the movement that would set them free. His hand darted forward like a spring, his hand armed with the revolver, and Madeleine uttered one last cry of pity and compassion:

"Don't shoot!"

And Patrice aimed between the two eyes and fired.

The train made such a noise of thunder in that tunnel that they alone heard the shot that was meant to kill Balaoo. No one, therefore, would come to disturb them in their murder of a poor pithecanthrope who had strayed from the Forest of Bandong. But had they murdered him as much as all that? Did not Madeleine say that you can't kill a pithecanthrope with a revolver? Madeleine looked out with every sign of despair. She made a rush at the window, tried to open the door, at the risk of being dashed to pieces in the tunnel. Patrice had to exert all his strength to hold her back. And now, panting, they watched the drama enacted behind the pane.

The bullet had made a very clean' little hole in the window-pane and another little hole, not so clean, because of the blood, at the root of Balaoo's nose, behind the window, to which he was clinging desperately. Balaoo gazed at Madeleine with, his fast-closing eyes; and never had Madeleine seen a more human look, at the moment of death, even in the eyes of the tamest animals, even in the eyes of sporting-dogs when they die in the arms of their masters who have shot them through awkwardness...And Balaoo let go the carriage-window and disappeared in the black rumbling hole.

"Balaoo! Balaoo! Balaoo!" cried the despairing Madeleine, imprisoned in Patrice' arms. "Balaoo! Balaoo!"

Poor Balaoo must be in a thousand pieces by now. There is nothing like a train in a tunnel to kill a pithecanthrope.

Madeleine was stifling. But Patrice began to breathe. Alas, how often do we not find, at the moment when we think ourselves safe, at last, from the pursuit of fate, that it turns against us with the most deadly cruelty! Even so with Patrice Saint-Aubin. Seeing his dear little Madeleine for the third time nearly expiring on that wretched wedding-day, he resolved to shorten this first part of the journey. They left the train at Moulins and drove to the old Hôtel de la Gare.

Chapter XX

Here, Patrice engaged a suite of rooms of which he had not time to appreciate the full comfort, for, when he went downstairs to give some orders to the proprietor, he heard an appalling cry from Madeleine's lips:

"Help!"

All the terror that a cry can express was contained in that one cry. The hotel-keeper and Patrice felt their hair stand up on end. They flew to the unhappy girl's room. She was no longer there; but the window was wide open on the night.

Madeleine must have made a supreme effort to defend herself. The marks of her bloodstained fingers were found on the sheets torn from the bed. And a trail of blood led from the bed to the window.

Chapter XXI

We shall now see the memorable circumstances in which the private misfortunes of the Saint-Aubin family assumed the proportions of a public calamity.

Let me first quote two paragraphs which appeared in the *Patrie en danger* and the *Observateur impartial* respectively and which passed unnoticed at the time. It was not until later that people thought of connecting them with the extraordinary incidents that upset the whole existence of the capital. The *Patrie en danger* wrote, in its "Paris Notes:"

"The impudence of foreigners knows no bounds. They treat Paris like a conquered city. This is a fact which we have all observed for ourselves. They expect the best seats at the theatres; and the tables outside the cafes are theirs as though by right. Yesterday evening, two Roumanian students stopped in front of the Brasserie Amédée in the Rue des Écoles and, finding a little dog in their way as they were going to sit down, calmly fired a revolver at it[23] and killed it. They were pursued by the indignant crowd and only just had time to climb a gutter pipe of the Musée de Cluny and thus escape the punishment that awaited them. M. Haracourt, the genial keeper of our national museum, in vain interrupted his work to look for the offenders, who were able to make good their flight by means of a gargoyle from which any respectable man would, nine times out of ten, have fallen and broken his neck."[24]

Chapter XXI

On the same day, the *Observateur impartial* contained the following, under the heading:

NOT EVERYBODY CARES
FOR PEA-NUTS

"If the long-suffering ratepayers who constitute the Paris public would occasionally take the law into their own hands when tired of the multitudinous annoyances thrust upon them, life in our much overrated metropolis would perhaps become endurable. A few years ago, a man could still sit outside a cafe without being pestered by peripatetic street-vendors, hawkers of every kind, newspaper-boys and dealers in picture-postcards and transparencies; he could take his cocktail without having his table invaded by the latest thing in toys or by a keg of olives. Things, unfortunately, have changed; and we can well understand that people suddenly lose their tempers in the face of the obstinacy of a pea-nut vendor whose wares they have already respectfully refused. Yesterday evening, at the Cafe Sara Bernhardt, two young attaches of the Japanese Legation, weary of a torment to which they had doubtless never been subjected in the streets of Nagasaki, sent a too-enterprising dealer in pea-nuts flying into the gutter. The incident occurred during the interval between the acts and caused some little commotion; and the representatives of the prefect of police were preparing to draw up a report, when the young Japanese were clever enough to vanish with the agility of monkeys, clinging to a passing tram-car and scrambling to the top by sheer force of muscle, without using the steps, no doubt so as to show the passengers on the Montrouge-Gare de l'Est tram that people are pretty resourceful in the Empire of the Rising Sun."

On the following Sunday, this paragraph appeared among the society-paragraphs in the *Gaulois des dimanches:*

"H. H. the Maharajah of Kalpurthagra, who has come to France to study our habits and customs and the advantages of wireless telegraphy, sups every night at Maxim's. His Highness has brought with him, from his own country, a recipe for raw rice in champagne which is highly appreciated by the customers of an establishment where it is still the fashion for a very 'Parisian' set to seek relaxation from the labours of the day. Henry, the popular manager, recommends that this exotic, but succulent dish should be prepared exclusively with the *minimum brut* of the well-known Singsong brand."

My next quotation is from a very curious report that appeared in the theatrical columns of the *Bigarro* on the day after the wedding of Mlle. Arlette des Barrieres, the celebrated musical-comedy-actress, and M. Massepain, the tenor:

"Contrary to the custom which has lately been introduced and which entails the disappearance of the husband and wife immediately after the light lunch that follows upon the marriage-ceremony, the newly-married couple had resolved to spend their wedding-day among their friends. These are many in number; and the large banqueting-room of the Restaurant de Mailly was called into requisition to hold them all, or nearly all. For every theatre and every branch of artistic talent was represented around the charming Arlette, who looked perfectly exquisite in white and orange-blossoms. The breakfast promised to be one of the most successful on record and a general gaiety was arising round the tables spread with a Gargantuan banquet, when a most grotesque and deplorable incident came and spoilt everything.

"A practical joker—if that be the word, for I really do not know how to describe the dismal wag—whom no one was able to recognize under his perfect make up as 'Prince Charles' of the Folies-Bergere, eye-glass and all, appeared at the entrance to the reception-rooms and asked to speak to the bride. His manner was so peculiar and his excited demeanour seemed so threatening that the servants left him in the hall and went to inform M. Massepain, who, at once, in great astonishment, quitted his seat in search of further particulars.

"The popular tenor found himself confronted with a visitor who refused to give his name and who, without for a second ceasing to swing, sway and waddle from side to side, after the manner of 'Prince Charles,' the famous chimpanzee aforesaid, declared that he would not go until he had spoken a word to the bride. He added, to the intense amusement of all who heard him, rudely sniffing the air as he spoke:

"'Oh, I know she's here! It smells of orange blossoms!'

"M. Massepain, impatient of a sort of jest that threatened to be prolonged indefinitely, tried to take his visitor by the arm, but was flung back with such violence as to draw cries of indignation from the guests who had gathered round him. Some of them wished to interfere and give the clown a good hiding; but M. Massepain pushed them aside and, going up to the man, who was slouching round and round the hall like a bear in its cage, said:

"'Sir, I don't know you.'

"'Nor I you,' said the other, 'but I know that the bride is here and I will not go away without speaking to her.'

"'Sir,' retorted M. Massepain, quite calmly, 'my patience is nearly exhausted.'

"The other replied, with unparalleled insolence, ceasing his sort of dance:

"'A man without patience is a lamp without oil!'

"'Sir,' cried M. Massepain, angrily, 'this farce has lasted long enough. Go away! You only excite our pity.'

"And the other, who seemed to grow cooler as M. Massepain became more heated, replied:

"'Pity is the finest and noblest passion of mankind!'

"'That's enough of it! He's getting at us! Turn him out!' shouted the guests, while the bride was surrounded by friends who prevented her from going to see what was happening and who were determined to protect her from that madman. 'What does he want? Who is he? Why doesn't he give his name, at least? He has no courage!'

"'Courage,' rejoined the irritating visitor, screwing his glass into his eye, courage is the light of adversity!'

"The guests did not know what to do under this rain of apophthegms; and the visitor held his ground. The waiters were sent for and tried to force him down the stairs. He pushed them back with an incredible display of strength and cried, in a voice of thunder that was heard all over the establishment, from top to bottom:

"'I will go when I have spoken to the bride. You need only say a word to her, just one word, and she will see me at once.'

"The scandal was attaining such proportions that M. Massepain, to put an end to it, asked the visitor:

"'What word do you want said to her?'

"'Say, "Bilbao."'

"'Bilbao?'

"'Yes, Bilbao, she will understand. Go on.'

"'Bilbao!' repeated the guests, laughing and humming,baloo! 'You bet, he'll grow, for he's a Spanish lad!'[25]

No sooner did the horrible fellow perceive that they were making fun of Bilbao—native place, no doubt—than he went quite mad. Pushing and overturning all who tried to oppose his progress, he entered the banqueting-room. The bride had taken refuge in a private room, but it was a useless precaution, for the intruder guessed where she was and, while the others ran to the windows on the Boulevard Saint-Germain and shouted for help, he made his way, upsetting the tables and chairs and smashing the glass and crockery, to the door between himself and 'Our Own Arlette' and broke the hinges with a tremendous kick. When he saw the bride fainting in the arms of her bridesmaids, he seemed quite astonished. He at once begged her pardon and said, aloud:

"'I must have made a mistake!'

"Then he returned, with calm steps and knit brows, to the banqueting-room, where, as is easily understood, disorder and uproar reigned. Some policemen, who had hurried up the stairs, tried to take him by the collar; but he gave one bound to the window and jumped into a tree. An enormous crowd, attracted by the clamour that came from the restaurant, was standing on the boulevard. Loud shouts greeted the appearance and flight of the man, who sprang from branch to branch and tree to tree with a supernatural velocity which enabled him soon to escape the policemen in pursuit.

"The general opinion is that the trouble was created by a sort of music-hall acrobat—as everybody knows,

250

Mlle. Arlette des Barrieres began her career on the variety stage—or, at any rate, a low fellow who thought that he had some reason to be revenged on our charming little actress. M. Massepain has furnished the police with full particulars and we shall soon know what is at the bottom of this unpleasant affair. Meanwhile, we offer our sincere sympathy to Mlle. Arlette des Barrieres and her popular husband."

Here is another note inserted in the *Gaulois des dimanches* of a week later:

"H. H. the Maharajah of Kalpurthagra has written to us to say that he has not been to Maxim's since his arrival in Paris and that he has no connection with the person who introduced the fashion of raw rice and champagne (*minimum brut* of the famous Singsong brand) into that first-class establishment. We have telephoned to Henry, the well-known manager, who regrets this usurpation of rank on his customer's part, all the more as he has not seen him since and as no one has yet called to pay the bill."

A few other papers copied these paragraphs and embellished them with more or less witty comments, in the latest Boulevard style; and the various incidents seemed wholly forgotten, until, one day, the *Vie à Paris* published, in its evening edition, a paragraph headed, in large capitals:

"THE SHAM MAHARAJAH AGAIN."

After reminding its readers of the first appearance of this worthy at Maxim's, the newspaper went on to say:

"There was great excitement yesterday in the Rue Royale. A taxi-cab driver who had been victimized by the sham Maharajah of Kalpurthagra recognized him outside the Cafe Durand, where he was quietly drinking a bock, with the serenity begotten of an easy conscience. The driver at once pulled up beside the pavement and made a rush for his would-be Hindu Highness, clamouring for his fare for driving him all night through the gayest streets of the capital. However, the 'Maharajah' appears also to have recognized his chauffeur; for he hastened to leave his table, relinquishing his beer and of course forgetting to pay for it. The waiters joined the driver; and their shouts soon collected the usual crowd of onlookers. The police appeared upon the scene; and our 'Mahajarah' would undoubtedly have spent the night in the cells if, by some mysterious feat of gymnastics, he had not disappeared in the thick foliage of the trees on the boulevard, where it became impossible to find him."

This peculiar manner of escaping pursuit resulted in establishing a natural connection in the minds of M. Massepain and his friends between the sham Maharajah of Kalpurthagra and the strange visitor to the Cafe de Mailly. There are not so many people in Paris capable of running away through the tree-tops! Lastly, a local paper published in the Quartier Latin suggested that there must be a relation between the incidents on the Boulevard Saint-Germain, those in the Rue Royale and the climbing of the walls, railings, gutter-pipes and gargoyles of the Musée de Cluny.

The newspapers promptly jumped to the conclusion that all the queer things that had happened in Paris for some months past must be put down to the score of a mysterious acrobat whose eccentricities, pointing to a mind tainted with madness, threatened to endanger the safety of the inhabitants.

And it was then that the press gave way to the panic to which I have alluded at the head of this chapter and lost that presence of mind which it should have communicated to the people of Paris, who were soon to be driven mad by the fantastic and criminal enterprises of the elusive Maharajah. But, between ourselves, it is no use protesting against the "scare-lines" in the evening papers.

The first article to spread consternation was headed:

"GIRLS, DO NOT QUIT YOUR PARENTS' SIDE!"

This scare-line was followed by an account which stated that the mysterious acrobat who walked in the trees had been seen in a chest-nut-tree in the Tuileries Gardens and that there was reason to believe that he was not alone. Persons whose word could be trusted declared that they had seen him carrying a young girl in his arms, like a savage.

But this first scare-line, which caused excitement, was nothing compared with the second, which caused absolute terror:

"DISAPPEARANCE OF FOUR GIRLS.

"A monster, unworthy of the name of
man, drags them by the hair through
the trees and, carries them, like a
prey; over the roofs of the metropolis."

This was the alarming and tragic heading that appeared in the four o'clock edition of the *Patrie en danger*. The newspaper-vendors who excited the crowd with their mad rushing and shouting sold their cop-ies up to five sous apiece. The father and mothers, above all, wanted to be informed and did not look at the cost, that day. People stopped drinking outside the cafes, stopped walking on the pavements. They read instead. Everybody read, or listened to others reading. The story was simple enough: since that morning, four girls had disappeared, carried off by the monster. One had vanished at the corner of the Rue de Médicis and the Rue de Vaugirard, another in the middle of the Boulevard Saint-Germain, a third near the Square Louvois, while the fourth was picked off the top of a tram-car going along the Quai du Louvre. Note that all four had disappeared in places where there were trees. The monster hid himself in the trees and suddenly put out his hand, pulling the girl's hair with invincible force. The girl followed, loudly screaming, and so rapidly that no one had time to hold her-back. A young person who had just been discharged from hospital and who was resting on a bench in the Square Montholon owed her safety to the fact that her head had been shaved during her illness. Only her false chignon remained in the monster's hands. As for the monster, he was endowed with infernal speed; and people would still be looking for him in the trees; when he appeared on the other side of the street or boulevard, on a roof, to vanish then and there with his prey.

In conclusion, the *Patrie en danger* advised ladies and young girls not to walk under the trees. And, in a moment, the pavements of the boulevards were emptied and the roadways crammed with a crowd that blocked the traffic, all walking with their noses in the air.

On the evening of that memorable afternoon, an unfortunate lamp-lighter, who was cleaning a gas-lamp, standing on a ladder against the trunk of a tree, was nearly torn to pieces by a wild mob that stupidly took him for the mysterious acrobat who walked in the trees.

The prefecture of police was on tenterhooks.

The Municipal Council was called upon to take exceptional measures. Certain idiots, of the class that always turns up at difficult moments when people are not inclined to make fun of them or any one, certain idiots contended that the only way to get rid of the mysterious acrobat who walked in the trees was to cut down all the trees! The families of the girls who had disappeared were interviewed by the newspapers and photographed down to the fourth generation. The Ville Lumière was losing its head.

But the incredible scandal fell in all its horror on the panic-stricken city with the famous head-lines in a late edition of the greatest paper for news in the world: the *Époque*. Here is the gruesome heading:

PARIS A PREY TO THE MINOTAUR.
THE MONSTER IS KNOWN.
AN ANIMAL WITH A HUMAN BRAIN.
A TALKING PITHECANTHROPE.
FORMIDABLE INVENTION OF PROFESSOR CORIOLIS SAINT-AUBIN

And here is the article which was copied into every newspaper all over the world:

"There are no mysteries to the *Époque*. Its news service, which is unique in the journalistic world, has already enabled it to render the most signal services to the cause of humanity.

"History repeats itself. At the critical hour, when the metropolis is living in terror of the monster who seems to have established his empire on the roofs of Paris, the *Époque* has succeeded in penetrating the secret of the strange and formidable personality of the kidnapper of young girls. And we can tell the mothers' to take comfort; for, the police authorities, informed by the *Époque* as to the nature of the enemy to be vanquished, will soon be able to rid us of this horror.

"It was by following step by step the fantastic appearances of the creature who was long taken for a music-hall acrobat gone mad that we were enabled gradually to ascertain the space to which the monster usually confined his evolutions. We were thus led to the Quartier Latin and thence to the Rue de Jussieu, where we knocked at the deserted house of his owner, a man whose name will ring through the ages, M. Coriolis Boussac Saint-Aubin.

"In this house, which we entered by a window, everything was in the greatest disorder. The building seemed to have been hastily abandoned. We were received, however, by a parrot which, for more than an hour, never ceased screaming out a word, or rather a name, which at first conveyed nothing to us, but which also will remain famous in history. This word was:

"'Balaoo! Balaoo! Balaoo!'

"'Balaoo is the animal-name of the monster who, in the life of Paris, has his man-name: M. Noël. Balaoo is the name of the first monkey, the first ape to speak the language of men.

"M. Noël is well known in the neighbourhood, where his odd ways, his curious ugliness and his characteristic waddling gait did not pass unperceived, while the faces which he was in the habit of pulling around his eye-glass have more than once excited the laughter and witticisms of the little ragamuffins in the streets. But no one ever suspected that this somewhat eccentric, but, until recently, well-behaved person was a Javanese pithecanthrope or ape-man. For M. Noël was a customer of the Café Vachette and the Brasserie Amédée! M. Noël attended the lectures at the law-courts! M. Noël belonged to the Conférence Bottier! M. Noël dressed like a respectable man! M. Noël spoke French like anybody else! And yet, O unfathomable mystery of the races, M. Noël is not a man! M. Noël is only an anthropoid ape! He has four hands! He is directly related to the orang-utan and the large ape of the forests of Java, the archetype of which can be seen, at the Jardin des Plantes, in the ape Gabriel!

"And now what is this mystery which will throw all our readers into commotion? How did we succeed in discovering the secret? How did we find Balaoo's master? It all happened very simply, but still it had to be thought of! We began by seizing the files filled with papers in M. Coriolis Saint-Aubin's study. Here we discovered the most curious documents imaginable, relating to the transformation of Balaoo into M. Noël. These documents, we admit, do not belong to us. Judging by their importance, we may say that neither do they belong to M. Coriolis Saint-Aubin, their natural owner. They belong to universal science; and it is to universal science that we propose to dedicate them, day by day, by publishing them in our columns from to-morrow onwards, changing nothing, adding nothing, respecting the truth in accordance with the reputation which we have acquired among our readers.

"From the moment when, in the empty house in the Rue de Jussieu, we first glanced at those immortal notes, many incidents connected with the famous acrobat who walked in the trees, incidents which had seemed incomprehensible, became illumined with an unexpected and dazzling light; and we were able to understand the most curious actions and observations which, until then, had appeared to us, for the most part, to be invented by the maddened imagination of the crowd.

"Our object thenceforth was to find, with the least possible delay, the man whose scientific recklessness had let loose that monster upon humanity. There was no doubt in our mind, judging by the objects surrounding us, that this man, this gifted, but dangerous scholar, had fled, fled from the hateful consequences of his daring, fled on hearing of the crimes committed by his terrible pupil. He had to be found; he must, by fair means or foul, be set on the track of the great Java pithecanthrope. He alone was perhaps capable of instilling sense into that unique creature outlawed-by men and animals alike; he alone could save us!

"We at once embarked upon a close enquiry into the last public acts of M. Coriolis Saint-Aubin and we learnt that, a few days ago, he married his daughter to his nephew, M. Patrice Saint-Aubin; that the ceremony was performed in the strictest privacy and almost incognito; that M. Noël was not present; and that the young couple hurriedly took the train for Auvergne, while, almost at the same moment, the mysterious acrobat who walks in the trees was creating a disturbance at the wedding-breakfast of Mlle. Arlette des Barrieres and M. Massepain, the tenor.

"The coincidence between those two events, the flight of the newly-married pair and the disturbance on the Boulevard Saint-Germain, gave us ample food for reflection. The result of our reflections was not long in doubt. It slightly altered our first view of M. Coriolis Saint-Aubin's flight. As M. Noël was pursuing the bride, we considered that the father must be chasing M. Noël, with a view to saving his daughter. He was bound to fear a tragedy. Did he arrive in time? Had he come up with them? We hastened on his tracks and we are now, unfortunately, in a position to say that M. Coriolis Saint-Aubin arrived too late! He found only his son in-law, under lamentable conditions which were certainly, so to speak, the prelude to all the crimes, all the abductions under which the capital is groaning to-day!

"The responsibility of that madman of genius is really terrible: terrible in the eyes of history, in the eyes of science and in the eyes of the law. We are not using this last word because we think that it behoves us to draw down the vengeance of justice upon a man who believed that he was accomplishing a great work: we are simply conveying a piece of news. M. Coriolis Saint-Aubin is at this moment in custody! He gave himself up two hours ago. We ourselves, at his own request, took him to our new prefect of police, M. Mathieu Delafosse.

"All these incidents, occurring at the moment when we are about to go to press, cannot be related with all the desired detail; but we shall publish in a few hours a special edition in which we shall continue to ex-pound to our readers the formidable racial mystery in the Rue de Jussieu. For the present, we shall consider that our work has not been in vain if we have helped in any degree, however small, to dispel the morbid terror that was beginning to overcome the bravest of us and if we have restored some little peace to family-life. The wild beast is known; the tamer is known: it is only a question, let us hope, of bringing them face to face. But let the Cage be prepared, the cage in which to shut up the new minotaur, who, since he speaks French, will perhaps consent to tell us what he has done with his living prey.

"We will conclude by saying that we discovered M. Coriolis Saint-Aubin on a Bourbonnais road, hunting, with his son-in-law, for the traces of his child, who had been kidnapped by the monster. He thought that he was his pupil's only victim. He did not know that there were other fathers groaning, mothers in tears, sisters trembling, brothers thirsting for vengeance; concerned only with his private tragedy, he knew nothing of all the tragedies in Paris. When we informed him of what was happening in the capital, he was thunderstruck, for he had no idea that the pithecanthrope, for whom he was looking in the country, was back in town.

"STOP-PRESS NEWS.

"Two of our reporters telephone that they have just found the monster's tracks on the roof of the Hotel-de-Ville, where he is walking about in all security. Our staff will organize a pursuit without delay."

This was the article that sent all the journalists of the capital flying to the prefect of police, only to learn that M. Mathieu Delafosse, the new prefect, whom the advent to power of an ultra-radical ministry had relieved of his disgrace, was at the Place Beauveau, where the minister of the interior had called an urgent meeting of the cabinet. I cannot do better than publish the official statement dictated, after the cabinet-council, to the journalists present:

"The prefect of police made a statement yesterday to the ministers assembled in cabinet-council. He declared as follows:

"'A man of whom I had never heard, M. Coriolis Boussac Saint-Aubin, sent in his card to me, requesting me to see him at once. I sent to ask his business, but he replied that he would only speak in my presence and that there must be no delay, because it was a question of life and death. I had him shown in.

"He did not strike me as mad. Before I had time to speak, he said in a clear, deliberate and exceedingly sorrowful voice:

"'Monsieur le préfet de police, I am a wretched and unhappy man. I have come to give myself up to the police. I alone am guilty of the crimes which are horrifying Paris and for which it would be vain to prosecute a poor creature to whom I have not succeeded in imparting a sense of responsibility. I have been hideously punished for my pride and folly. God is chastising me in my heart and in my brain, in the child of my flesh and the work of my mind. It was I that made the mysterious acrobat who walks in the trees. I made him out of an animal, for hatred of mankind. The work of hatred can never be fruitful," my strange visitor continued, "and the worker is the first victim. I am a wretched man and an unhappy man. I have lost my daughter, who may be dead by now, herself kidnapped by my pupil. And, in trying to turn an inferior creature into a civilized being, I have only succeeded in inventing a monster, the horror and terror of mankind. Yes, monsieur le prefet de police, I have done that, I have made an ape talk! I have made an ape talk like a man, but, for all my efforts, I have not succeeded in giving him a human conscience. Therefore, I have not made a man; therefore, I have made a monster; therefore, convict me, sentence me, imprison me, torture me: I deserve every form of punishment! I am accurst!...God has smitten me as I deserved!...I wanted to reform or to accelerate His work. To accelerate the work of God is the pride and the crime of man; and it has caused my downfall. My scalpel, by cutting a nerve under the tongue and allowing me to bring another close to it, forestalled the work of the evolution of species by a hundred thousand years; but, not possessing the requisite instruments, I could not supply the hundred thousand years of consciousness necessary to enable my pithecanthrope to move among men without danger...without danger of his committing unconscious crimes; for, as regards the others, monsieur le prefet de police, men see to that!'"

"After these words, which were accompanied by tears and every evidence of despair, the prefect of police put a series of direct questions to M. Coriolis Saint-Aubin, who replied in such a way as to leave no room for doubt regarding the nature of the monster in question.

"Of course, if this declaration had not been preceded by all the incidents that have been alarming the capital for some days past, it would only have been received with the utmost reserve. But it is impossible to resist the proofs, as the prefect of police impressed upon the council, after hearing the evidence of certain persons acquainted with M. Coriolis Saint-Aubin and his household.

"In the circumstances, it has been decided that every measure shall be taken to capture the monster at all costs, alive or dead; and the instructions on this point give full powers to the prefect of police. At the same time, we may mention the desire expressed by both the minister of public instruction and the minister of agriculture that the monster should, if possible, be taken alive, as they consider the study of this phenomenon to be of the highest value to universal science. But the prime minister's orders were formal:

"'There are too many mothers in tears. The capital must be rid of the monster, at the earliest possible moment, by any and every means.'"

The town, pending the discovery of the mysterious hiding-place where the new minotaur had secreted his collection of girls, the town, I say, lived, more than ever, with its nose in the air. The monster was tracked over the roofs of the Hotel-de-Ville by the journalists, the firemen, the clerks and also by the members of the central division of police, which force was called into requisition because of its celebrated physique. The police had instructions to capture the monster alive; and, for a moment, they thought that they had him.

As a-matter of fact, the chase was conducted with an energy that partook of both anger and despair. The ape was hunted from garret-window to garret-window, from chimney to chimney, to the roof of a little outhouse opposite the Caserne Lobeau. The central police, equipped with ropes and lassoes that seemed very much in their way, were ready to spring upon him, when Professor Coriolis himself was brought out on the gutter and perceived that, in spite of the horror of that tragic struggle, the monster had retained a little of the veneer of civilization which he had been at such pains to bestow upon him. The pithecanthrope, in fact, showed himself, for a second, between two chimneys, leaping from one to the other, with an eye-glass in his eye!

"Balaoo!...Balaoo!" cried the professor, in a soft voice of distress containing less anger and reproach than the despair that yearns for consolation. "Balaoo!..."

But, at the sound of this voice, this cry, the other, instead of replying to the one who called to him, seemed to discover a fresh energy. The fear which, but lately, had made him run away now turned into fury; and, rushing like a meteor upon a group of policemen and town-hall clerks—the latter armed with their paper knives!—he butted them out of the gutter and sent three or four of them flying into space.

The luckless men crashed on the stones of the square below, in the midst of the populace who came crowding up with a thousand cries of horror. Then a score of shots were fired at the monster, who received them point blank, without seeming to mind them, and re-entered the Hôtel-de-Ville by a garret-window, after knocking down a stalwart policeman who had showed his head at that window.

And the monster rushed down the corridors. He was seen to dart like an arrow through every department. Ratepayers, who had been waiting for hours to receive attention, fled howling and were never seen again.

For Balaoo was now no longer being pursued: everybody was fleeing before him. He seemed to be everywhere at a time, on every floor. He reappeared in every corner, bumping against groups that vanished like smoke.

He had a way of his own of descending a staircase, sliding down the well, like an eel in its trap.

Through corridors and staircases, he made his way to the council-hall, where M. Mathieu Delafosse was vainly striving to reassure a score of ædiles who had not yet left the sitting, thinking, perhaps, in their hearts, that they were safer there than elsewhere. Here too there was a general *sauve-qui-peut*, but the other had passed and was out of sight long before their fright was over.

For twenty-four hours, no one knew what had become of him. The police hunted everywhere. They went to the length of burning straw in the cellars of the Hotel-de-Ville, so as to smoke the monster out if he had found a refuge there. A cordon of troops, with ammunitions of war, surrounded the municipal buildings. Five detectives dragged Coriolis with them wherever they went; and the professor, tangle-haired and wild-eyed, allowed himself to be led from cellar to attic, calling:

"Balaoo!...Balaoo!..."

But Balaoo did not reply. Where was he? No more girls had disappeared in Paris, through the agency of Balaoo or any other, and this was explained by the fact that the girls were all kept carefully immured in their parents' homes. The sittings of the municipal council were suspended until further orders; and the anguish, increased by the mystery of that complete disappearance, was greater than ever, when the monster suddenly reappeared on the top of the Tour Saint-Jacques. The clerks of the meteorological office were the first to see him and fled, after informing the police. This time, there was little doubt that the end of the drama was at hand.

The Tour Saint-Jacques, which was at once isolated by a circle of police and troops, was a very small and dangerous refuge for Balaoo. He himself seemed to realize as much, for, seeing himself hard pressed by a crowd of armed men and a mob of people loading him with curses, he worked himself into an uncommon state of fury, even for a large Java ape. His prolonged, rolling, rumbling cries were heard from the Place de la Bastille to the Louvre. The traffic in the Rue de Rivoli was of course interrupted. The tops of the omnibuses and tramcars were thronged with people shaking their fists at the Tour Saint-Jacques and yelling for the death of the pithecanthrope.

Sometimes the monster's figure was seen dancing and turning somersauts at the very top of the tower; but he would disappear at once, to reappear swinging from a scaffolding. Already over fifty shots had been fired at him, with no other result than to increase his rage. Sheltering himself behind the scaffolding, he began to hurl blocks of stone at the crowd.

Chapter XXI

A regular hail of stones came down, striking, wounding and kill-ing the onlookers. The monster was not long in clearing the Rue de Rivoli and the Square Saint Jacques. The troops and the police were driven back; and still the square continued to rain with stones. The pithecanthrope was actually demolishing the Tour Saint-Jacques in self-defence; and this so rapidly that there were wags ready to suggest that, after three or four days of that siege, there would be nothing left of the Tour Saint-Jacques but its scaffoldings!

This, of course, was an exaggeration. But, all the same, it was manifest that the most exquisite gargoyles were lying in fragments on the roadway and that, taken all round, the monster was destroying the famous monument faster than the city architect could hope to repair it. And this lasted all the night through.

In the morning, M. Mathieu Delafosse arrived, together with the five detectives who were still dragging M. Coriolis Saint-Aubin about with them. The new prefect of police was in at least as deplorable a condition as the ex-consul at Batavia himself. He was suffering from less despair and grief, but greater exasperation. A sort of diabolical fatality seemed to dog his career; and he could find no better compari-son for his present curious and tragic difficulties than the unprecedented incidents of the siege of the Black Woods, at the time when he was prefect of the Puy-de-Dôme.

Had he been able to suspect the undoubted relation between those two catastrophes and that Coriolis was the sole cause of both, he would certainly not have deprived himself of the satisfaction of stran-gling that ill-omened prisoner with his own hands. But the rapid succession of events and the quick action of the drama had not yet given the police time to institute an enquiry which would have ex-plained many things by referring them to first principles in the shape of the French education of Master Balaoo.

M. Mathieu Delafosse came straight from the prime minister, who had threatened him with his dismissal within twenty-four hours if the pithecanthrope's business was not settled that same day. And it was with a view to settling it that he arrived accompanied by Coriolis and the five detectives and also by a colossal sportsman in a pair of yel-low-leather leggings, with a rifle over his shoulder.

The attention of the crowd was at once fixed upon this new fig-ure. He was a giant. He stood head and shoulders over everybody else. Soon, his name passed from mouth to mouth, for the man was famous. He was the celebrated lion-killer, Barthuiset.

If the legends told at certain cafe-tables were to be credited, that man had killed more lions in Africa than the Atlas Mountains ever contained. It is not a good thing, even for real heroes, without fear and without reproach, that legend should exaggerate their exploits too lavishly. People at certain other, more sceptical cafe-tables began to believe that Barthuiset had never killed anything at all; and it was perhaps because of this that M. Mathieu Delafosse had not at once applied to him in circumstances where a first-class rifle-shot might render the most signal service.

Astonished and a little vexed at this neglect, Barthuiset might never have offered to save the situation for monsieur le prefet de police, if the lion-killer, whose heart was twice as big as that of ordinary men, had not at last taken pity on the good city of Paris. Donning his trusty hunting-leggings and his trusty hunting-belt and taking his trusty hunting-rifle and his trusty cartridges with the explosive bullets, Barthuiset waited on M. Mathieu Delafosse at the moment when M. Mathieu Delafosse returned from the prime minister's, scared and dejected by the ultimatum of the government.

The prefect of police, like everybody else, had heard of Barthuiset the lion-killer. He looked hard at him. Barthuiset, in all the actions and at every hour of his life, resembled a fat Dutchman digesting a first-rate lunch. This phlegmatic attitude in the midst of the general excitement rather pleased M. Delafosse than otherwise. He tapped Barthuiset on the shoulder and said, simply:

"My dear M. Barthuiset, if you don't kill that pithecanthrope, I'm a dead man myself."

Barthuiset replied, with a wink of his left eye:

"Show me your pithecanthrope, that's all I ask. There will be time enough to make your will afterwards."

These words did not comfort the prefect of police particularly:

"You can't be sure of your shot," he said.

"If it were a lion, I should never forgive you for saying that, monsieur le prefet de police. But I have never killed a pithecanthrope. There's no harm in trying. There's a first time for everything."

The prefect, therefore, brought him with him, but took care also to bring Coriolis. The little band entered the Square Saint-Jacques, amid the silence of the throng, bravely, at the risk of being crushed by a projectile broken from the historic pile. Balaoo had not given a sign of life that morning; but people were wary and no one had yet ventured to approach the scaffolding.

When they were within ten yards of the tower, M. Mathieu Delafosse said to. Coriolis, who seemed to be wool-gathering and quite daft:

"Call him."

"What for?" asked Coriolis, looking more stupid than ever.

"To parley with him!...Understand, we sha'n't kill your pithecanthrope except in the last extremity," explained the prefect, "though he's led us no end of a dance. As you say that he listens to reason, speak to him, coax him, say something to him, show us that he is not quite a savage."

Coriolis allowed himself to be taken in by these words. For, as the prefect guessed, the terrible thing was that, in spite of Balaoo's crimes and Madeleine's abduction, Coriolis instinctively wished to save Balaoo. His hails on the roofs of the Hotel-de-Ville were, above all, warnings, entreaties to fly!

The moment that it was no longer a question of killing Balaoo, Coriolis would call to him in different terms; and, in fact, he ceased to address him with a man's shout and cried, in monkey language:

"Tourôô! Tourôô! Tourôô!...Gooot!...Woop!"[26]

Then and there, the monster was seen to put his head cautiously between two planks of the scaffolding and anxiously to look down upon that numberless and, for the moment, silent crowd.

This silence, after the late tumult, seemed to surprise and alarm him. With a hesitating movement, he screwed his eye-glass into his eye and leant still further forward, bending almost his whole body over the group whence came the friendly words of his native tongue:

"Tourôô!...Gooot!...Woop!"

And bang! The shot was fired, the shot from the rifle with the explosive bullets of Barthuiset the lion killer.

An immense, prodigious and prolonged shout, made up of thousands and thousands of cries, rose up from the town, from the streets of the delivered capital.

The pithecanthrope had toppled over and, in his turn, fell at the foot of those walls of which he had been the terror. But he fell upon a mound of soft earth and did not succumb for the first few minutes. And the citizens of Paris were able to hear the dying agony of the monkey, of the great anthropoid ape, of the great ancestor, as it is heard in the depths of the equatorial forests and as it lingers in the expiring bodies of our mysterious brothers the animals, even among those which are not exactly pithecanthropes.

The citizens heard that despairing wail, of which Louis Jacolliot, the traveller, has written:

"At the supreme moment of death, the terrible brute gives forth sounds that are very nearly human...Its last wail gives you the impression of something higher in the scale of nature; and you feel as though you had committed a murder."

Coriolis, as that shot rang out, felt his heartbreak; and it was, for a moment, as though he himself had been shot dead. He saw the great body spin through the air, he rushed forward as if to catch it in his arms. Fortunately, the creature crashed to the ground beside him, without touching him. Coriolis flung himself upon those dying remains that lay groaning like a man.

He bent over the body...and, suddenly, he rose to his feet, with a mad yell of triumph: it was not Balaoo!

[23] In spite of all the care which the press, as a rule, takes to tell the precise truth, it is liable, like all of us, to be mistaken; nor is anyone exactly to be blamed for this. It is an inevitable result of the tendency to "pad" the news received.—AUTHOR'S NOTE.

[24] I am not quite sure that it is necessary to point out to the English reader that, in this and the following "cuttings," M. Leroux deliberately (and very skilfully) reproduces the stilted journalese of the news-columns in the Paris papers.—TRANSLATOR'S NOTE.

[25] "Il grandira, car il est espagnol:" the well-known duet in La Périchole (1868).—TRANSLATOR'S NOTE

[26] "All right! All right! All right!...Come!...Please!"— AUTHOR'S NOTE.

Chapter XXII

No, that big dead monkey, dressed as a man and wearing an eyeglass like Balaoo, was not Balaoo. A few hours later, it was known that he was Gabriel, the big Java ape from the Jardin des Plantes. As he had played many a prank in his time and repeatedly shown signs of temper, his formidable vagary was easily explained: he had made his escape by taking advantage of the boozy negligence of the keeper, who was always slipping away to the wine-shop round the corner.

Was there any reason to be surprised that, with his irresistible instinct for mimicry and assimilation, he had prigged a suit of clothes and put them on? No, from this point of view, we need be astonished at nothing, in monkeys.

Gabriel's cage, like many others at the Jardin des Plantes, was a double cage, with a railed open-air compartment and another railed compartment inside the lion-house. The communicating-door was usually left open, so that Gabriel could seek sun or shade according to the temperature and the time of day. As the keeper or the visitor can see only one compartment at a time, each must have thought that Gabriel was in the second when he was looking into the first and vice versa. And this explained how Gabriel was able, for several days and nights, to scour the roofs of the capital and frighten the town with his sinister exploits before his absence from the Jardin des Plantes was discovered.

But then where was the famous pithecanthrope, the monster, half man and half brute, who spoke the language of men? What had become of Coriolis' invention? The police were much too glad to be rid of one monster to saddle themselves with another. They declared, without delay, that Coriolis' invention was a figment of that diseased brain, treated the professor as a monomaniac and asked him to go and cloister his monomania in his house in the Rue de Jussieu, holding himself meanwhile at the disposal of the police.

The day that saw the deliverance of Paris saw also that of the missing girls. They were discovered by the greatest of accidents, at a moment when people were despairing of ever learning what Gabriel had done with them.

Maddened by the hue and cry, the great ape had ended by carrying the poor things to the roof of the Louvre and had managed to fling them more dead than alive into an attic, where he locked them up. They were all found safe and sound, though obviously very ill. Nevertheless, the ape had done them no harm.

The books written by travellers in the equatorial forests furnish us with examples of this kind of rape in which the "wild men of the woods" take a futile and childish pleasure and which can only be compared with the passion of the thieving magpie for collecting objects which it accumulates in hiding-places known to itself alone.

The girls owed their life to the scientific and naval curiosity of a certain M. Benezebque, a schoolmaster in a small parish not far from Montauban; for they would all have died of hunger and thirst in their sequestered attic, if M. Benezecque, driven by a wish to inspect some models of ships, had not climbed to the top floor of our famous old palace, where a long series of dull blows informed him that some one was calling for help, blows struck against a door near the thirteenth-century gallery which you can see to this day, between the hours of eleven and four, on Mondays, Wednesdays and Sundays.

Professor Coriolis was returning to his house in the Rue de Jussieu when an evening edition of the *Patrie en danger* acquainted him with the fortunate delivery of the victims of Gabriel's demoniacal freak; and he was not at all astonished not to find Madeleine's name among those of the missing girls. He well knew that Madeleine had not been carried off by Gabriel.

When he entered his hall, feeling so despondent that he thought of suicide, he saw a letter lying on the floor.

The letter bore the postmark of Saint-Martin-des-Bois and was worded:

"I am waiting for you at the Big Beech at Pierrefeu.
"Balaoo."

Chapter XXIII

For hours, Coriolis, with his clothes torn, his hands and face lacerated by the thorns and brambles, pushed branch after branch aside in his vain search for the Pierrefeu clearing, overtopped by the Big Beech which he knew so well in his youth.

He was lost in the forest. He had come alone, not wishing to mix up others in his terrible family-history and not knowing what last fatal surprise might await him at the strange meeting-place fixed by Balaoo.

Besides, who was there to come with him? Was he not alone on the earth from this day forth? Patrice, who was being nursed at Clermont, had refused to see him and kept accusing him of every possible crime in a delirium that threatened to destroy his reason for good. Little Zoé, whom he had tried to make into a young lady for Balaoo, at the time when, in his extraordinary madness, he hoped to obtain a civic status for the son of the Forest of Bandong, little Zoé, struck to the heart by Balaoo's criminal love for Madeleine, was dying in the arms of Gertrude. Both had left his roof and would have nothing more to do with him.

And his daughter: where was his daughter? Was it true that the monster had killed her rather than be parted from her? And was Coriolis on the point of being faced with his child's corpse? Had Balaoo, bewildered with remorse, sent for him to weep over a tomb? Why had he not mentioned Madeleine in his letter? O tragic silence! O hateful uncertainty! O Madeleine! O Balaoo!...

For hours, the unhappy Coriolis had flung those two dear names to the echoes of the forest; and none but the echoes had replied.

Time after time, he seemed to recognize the paths that led to the Big Beech of Pierrefeu; but his footsteps became involved and perhaps only turned around themselves. The sun was now sinking in the sky and piercing the tall trees with its slanting rays. The twilight was at hand: Balaoo! Madeleine!

Balaoo, you who loved your little mistress so well, can it be true that you carried her off as a wild beast would and lent a deaf ear to her voice?

Despite the horror of that murderous abduction, Coriolis did not yet quite despair in the depths of his being. Certainly, Balaoo must have been terrible at the first moment and, thinking of nothing but the hideous thing that Madeleine's voluntary departure meant to him, he must have listened only to his instinct to retain possession of the beloved object and carried off the young woman in his arms with the same recklessness with which he would have stolen a lifeless thing. But, afterwards, it was impossible that Balaoo should not have yielded to Madeleine's voice, which for the pithecanthrope had the same fascination that serpents find in the voices of flutes.

Thus did Coriolis argue, or try to argue, as he continued to tear his clothes and flesh against the brambles on his path. It was the last hope that he built upon an hypothesis frail indeed, in the face of Balaoo's prolonged silence in his Pierrefeu clearing. Alas, if the charm of Madeleine's voice was so potent, the young woman would have ceased to be a prisoner from the first day! Poor Coriolis! His thoughts strayed like his footsteps; and, as the golden beams of the sun now reached him horizontally through the leaves, he struck the lower branches with his crazy forehead and cried, in the falling night:

"My daughter is dead! My daughter is dead!"

Then, dropping on his knees and lifting his hands to heaven in an attitude that implored both pity and forgiveness, for the first time he regretted his handiwork.

As his eyes, filled with an immense despair, rose to the sky, they encountered a thick circle of crows, chattering horribly, as birds and men do after a great banquet. The circle flew up, then down again and at last disappeared into the forest, with a mad accompani ment of hoarse and strident cries, like the hiccuping laughter of surfeited birds of prey.

Coriolis' heart turned icy cold. And suddenly his gaze fell upon a white veil clinging to a young branch. He rose and staggered to that veil or rather to that shred of material white as a bride's veil. He had not a doubt but that it was Madeleine's veil. He recognized it. His terror told him that he was not deceived. He snatched it from the forest with fevered hands and, sobbing, raised it to his lips.

A few steps farther, he found a piece of the satin of the dress...and then a little slipper...It was Madeleine's little white slipper...He covered it with frenzied kisses...

Chapter XXIII

And he called out, with all the strength of the sorrow that filled his breast:

"Madeleine!...Madeleine!..."

He called in the way in which you call not upon a living, but upon a dear dead woman, in the hope that she may appear to you. For there are moments when human sorrow does not dread ghosts and when it conjures up shades to press them to its heart, without trembling on the threshold of the great mystery; moments when love would have the dead come forth from the dark and when it is astonished—so loud has been its call—that the spirits do not come and kiss its lips!

"Madeleine!..."

The cawing of the crows was his sole answer. And, guided by the cawing of the crows, he continued his progress through the clustering branches. When he had pushed aside the last from that corner of thick timber, it was as though there had been a fire on the level of the ground and of the holes in the ground and as though he had come upon the centre of the furnace. He recognized the Moabit clearing. Over a thousand crows were there and did not so much as turn their heads, being busily engaged in devouring the carrion of three great men's corpses lying on the grass with outstretched arms.

And, though their foreheads were smashed in and much of their flesh eaten, Coriolis recognized the Three Brothers, who, for so many years, had been the terror of the country-side. Their guns lay beside them; the biggest of the three, red-bearded Hubert, still held his in his clenched hand.

The ferns and bushes all around were torn and broken and trampled. The struggle in which these had suffered and the three Vautrins met their death had created a sort of circus, a sort of flat ring. It must have been a terrible battle.

Who had been strong enough to defeat the Three Brothers, armed with their three guns? And what all powerful weapon had laid low those three huge bodies on the blood-soaked earth? Oh, it was simply a weapon made of wood! It also lay there, resting on the grass, after performing its work. It was a fine young tree, which might have reckoned on long years of glorious forest-life and which, trusting in the future, had dug its roots solidly into the fostering soil. And behold, a hand had torn it out of the earth as though it were not fastened there; and it was this birch-trunk, whose silvery whiteness was splashed and stained with the brown blood which it had brought spouting from the three men's heads, it was this birch-trunk that had done the killing.

What giant, what hero had waged battle here? What archangel's hand had wielded this flaming sword of wood?

On a branch of that tree, Coriolis saw yet another strip of the white veil that sent his heart beating in his chest like a drum; and also, after disturbing the crows, which protested and staggered around him like a black, drunkenband, he saw yet another piece of the white dress clutched in the fingers of one of the albinos.

And he no longer had a doubt but that his child was the coveted booty of that wild men's battle. His troubled brain, burning redder than that flaming forest at eve, pictured in a flash all the phases of that tourney of blood and death.

It was here that Balaoo must have hurried with his prey, to this friendly solitude of the forest where men would not come to rob him of her whose presence was as necessary to his life as the air he breathed. And then, no doubt, he had come upon the three men, the sole inhabitants of that solitude and the sole masters of that corner of the forest. The brute men had risen against the animal, on seeing him the possessor of so fair a prey, and they, in their turn, had tried to snatch it from him.

They were dead; and Balaoo had carried elsewhither the sacred object of that battle of the gods. Balaoo!...Balaoo!...

Moabit suddenly fell into pitch darkness; and Coriolis collided with the living walls of the clearing, which closed their branchy arms and leafy hands upon him. And, having reached the last stage of his despair, he sank down to the ground, like a child in its cradle.

In the morning, he woke and thought that he must still be dreaming when he saw Balaoo's sad and serious face bending over him.

He tried to cry out. Balaoo, with his finger to his mouth, enjoined silence:

"Take care!" said the pithecanthrope, whose voice seemed to reach him through a lake of tears; "Take care!...Don't wake her!..."

"Is she dead or alive?"

"She is asleep...Hush!..."

"Is she dead or alive?"

"She is asleep and we must not wake her."

And, walking straight before him, with his finger to his mouth, looking round from time to time to make sure that the other was following him, Balaoo led the way, a very long way, through the forest. Everything was silent as they passed. The birds interrupted their singing, the leaves ceased to quiver with joy in the morning breeze.

Balaoo's finger raised to his mouth seemed to command all nature to hush and not disturb the rest of her to whom they were going.

Was she dead?

Was she alive?

Was she at rest for all time?

Balaoo himself perhaps did not know.

They reached the Big Beech at Pierrefeu. Balaoo pointed to the upper storey of branches and to the road which Coriolis was to take. Coriolis went up it, obeying Balaoo as Balaoo had once obeyed him and not even wondering whether he could resist the pithecanthrope's gesture of command, accompanied by that extraordinarily human and divine look of sadness which he had not yet seen in his eyes, having never seen anything there but childish looks.

They climbed into the tree, which was as large as a little wood that might have surrounded Balaoo's private dwelling.

And they came to the private dwelling, to the hut built in the style of the Forest of Bandong which Coriolus, remembering the huts built by the pithecanthropes on the mangroves in the swamps, was not at all surprised to find there. Only, this hut had a door, as in a man's house.

He opened the door, while Balaoo, more and more sad and more and more polite, like any man inviting a stranger to cross his threshold, stood modestly behind him.

He opened the door and found himself in the presence of Madeleine lying on a bed of dry leaves and decently covered with a rug which he remembered once missing from his pony-chaise.

Madeleine was pale as death, but not dead. At the noise which her father made on entering, she opened her eyes; and two syllables came from her bloodless lips:

"Papa!"

Coriolis fell on his knees' before his child, raised the dear head, pressed it to his heart and bathed it with his tears:

"Forgive me!...Forgive me!..."

"Forgive you for what, papa?...Hasn't Balaoo told you?...Embrace him: he saved me!"

Coriolis' eyes wandered from Madeleine to Balaoo, who, standing in the doorway, turned aside his head so that he might not be seen to weep:

"What! He *saved* you?"

Then Madeleine, putting her shapely, trembling arms around her father's neck, told him the terrible story of her abduction from the room at Moulins by Élie the albino. Mother Vautrin's son must have heard of the marriage of her whom he had never ceased to love and of the contemplated arrival of the newly-married pair at Clermont-Ferrand.

His sudden resolution to go and lie in wait for them, like an animal lurking for its prey, spoke volumes for the mental attitude of the Three Brothers, who, definitely outlawed from human society by their conviction and sentence, had for years led the lives of wild animals in the depths of the forest.

But, whereas Hubert and Siméon lived only to eat and breathe in their lair, Élie's fierce heart was still, from time to time, roused by the memory of a white figure that used to appear to him, in the old days, when he returned of a morning from his clandestine hunting-expeditions, at the edge of the dawn-swept fields. The image of Madeleine lingered deep down in that brutal brain; and, if he had sunk so low as never to speak a word, never to reply to his brothers' call, it was because he never ceased to converse with Madeleine's image and to say things to her that could be confided to none other.

When prowling with his brothers like a jackal around the villages which they still terrorized, at intervals, with their plunderings, Élie heard of Madeleine's approaching return to Clermont with her young husband. He said nothing to his brothers, went to Clermont, made enquiries in the neighbourhood of the Rue de l'Écu and went back to Moulins.

His aim was to kidnap Madeleine before her arrival at the capital of the Puy-de-Dôme. There, he might have had to abandon his sinful plan; whereas, if he carried off Madeleine in the open country, he could undertake, by travelling only at night, to reach his haunt in the forest undisturbed.

To get into the train, take advantage of a stop at an intermediate station, or even of the slowing down of the train at certain places on the line of which he knew, and rush into the night with the young woman in his arms: this was the exceedingly simple plan that suggested itself to his brute brain.

Events turned out in such a way as to simplify things even more. At Moulins, he saw Madeleine and Patrice alight from the train. It was all that he could do to refrain from seizing her on the platform, in the midst of the passengers. He might have made the attempt then and there, had she not passed so quickly, on Patrice' arm. He felt his heart seething, his brain afire, himself trembling with impatience to effect his rape.

Chapter XXIII

At the hotel, he walked straight in behind them and then made his way, with watchful eyes and ears, to the courtyard. A light appeared in a window; and he saw Madeleine's shadow. Ten minutes later, Madeleine was in his arms. He stopped her screams by thrusting his hand into her mouth and flung her half-dead into a cart. He jumped on the box and did not stop until the horse dropped between the shafts. By this time, he had covered a long way on the Paris road, going in the opposite direction to the Cerdogne country; and this, a few hours later, must have thrown first Patrice off the scent and then Coriolis.

Lastly, the coincidence of the events for which Gabriel was responsible completely restored his ease of mind and he proceeded to travel by short and careful stages to the Moabit clearing.

He did not speak a word to Madeleine, but he terrorized her into eating and drinking. She hoped, for a moment, that the pursuit of which she was bound to be the active and desperate object would end by dicovering her before she was imprisoned for good and all in one of the horrible Moabit quarries for which they were making. She knew the terrible legend of those quarries, all peopled with ghosts and corpses, lined with skeletons and treasures. But the forest closed in upon them before help came; and they arrived at Moabit.

The two brothers received the albino and his white prey in silence. Élie said:

"This shall be my wife, the wife of Élie of Moabit."

The others stepped towards her with eyes of flame. She saw that they were armed and that all the three looked at one another with a great hatred. She realized that the Three Brothers were going to fight and that she would be the victor's booty.

And, as the three were snatching her from one another with their terrible arms, as she felt their monstrous fingers tearing her, she gave a loud scream that echoed far through the forest:

"Balaoo!...Balaoo!..." And Balaoo appeared.

Oh, it was a battle of giants, a mythological contest, with the thunderbolt of modern fire-arms superadded! But, whether because the pithecanthrope gods watched with a jealous vigilance over their terrestrial hero, or because nature had endowed him with a flesh impervious to the vulgar lead of men, the human thunderbolt was powerless to stay the onslaught of those avenging limbs.

The forest itself armed him with its terrible weapon; and the weapon whirled around their heads.

Balaoo! Balaoo! He had come! He was striking for her! For her he was killing his three forest brothers!

She had called to men in vain: none had come. But she had only to utter his name, for him to rush into the fray and come out victorious, the dear, formidable, gentle, terrible Balaoo!

And all for her, for her who had seen Patrice fire at Balaoo nor sought to divert his hand, for her who looked like a white lily, on her knees, in the centre of Moabit, while the battle was raging around her.

Ah, did ever doughtier knight enter the lists? Cut, Balaoo, and thrust! Use your hands and your shoe-hands! A Balaoo, a Balaoo!...Strike! Fell!...Here's for Siméon!...And there's for Élie!...As to Hubert, you must keep your hardest blow for him.

They have danced around you with their empty guns, which they are now using as clubs; but you have your trusty tree-club and you have shown them all the colours of the rainbow: red above all!

Oh, what blood on cheeks and arms!...Hop, hop, Balaoo! She had but to call your name and you came! Tourôô! Tourôô! Bang! One more good blow in the ribs for Élie, who will never stand on his feet again and who is dragging himself in the grass like a hare with its hind-legs broken!

And their skulls are cracked and stream with blood; but they are sturdy fellows, for all that, and not to be demolished with the first blow of a tree-trunk! They are as tough as pithecanthrope flesh-and-bone itself! Have at them again! *Woop! Phch! Phch*!... A blow here, a blow there!...

The warriors are as though drunk, dancing round Balaoo like bears, and it is you, Balaoo, who make them dance like that, as a gipsy does his bear. *Goek! Goek!*...Patti Palang Kaing's hell awaits them!...Oof! They breathe no more!...They moan no more!...They move no more!...

They are dead all three, with arms outflung on the red grass. But you, you are in a sad plight too, my poor Balaoo!...

However, this is no time to coddle yourself, when the white lily of Moabit sinks down softly to the ground, exhausted, after beholding your victory. It is your turn now to carry the white lily in your arms, with precautions worthy of a man-child's nurse, by the Lord Patti Palang Kaing!...

And you laid the lily on the cool bed of leaves in your lonely dwelling in the Big Beech at Pierrefeu!...Blessed be Patti Palang Kaing, who watches over stout hearts from his throne in the Forest of Bandong and who rewards brave forest battles; blessed be Patti Palang Kaing, inasmuch as he has blessed your dwelling, O Balaoo!...

Chapter XXIII

That is the story of this last episode: bloody, tragic, heroic and beautiful as the fights of antiquity.

Madeleine, with her poor, faint voice and her pale breath, the breath of an expiring lily, was not able to tell all these glorious feats of war to the weeping Coriolis. But the few words which she whispered in his ear, together with what he had seen—the corpses and his humble Balaoo's wounds—all this made him sob for joy, made his heart leap with pride; for Madeleine was saved and Balaoo had acted like one of the Race in the days of the blameless knights.

Balaoo was still turning away his head in the door way of his forest dwelling, lest he should show his eyes full of tears.

Madeleine, sighing, said:

"We must beg his pardon, very earnestly. We were wrong not to treat him as one of the Race. He said to me, 'I wanted to see you once more, Madeleine, before you went away with a husband of your Race. What did you think and of what were you afraid? One with fingers to his shoe-hands will always be a true friend to the daughter of men; and, if you knew the law of the forest, laid down by Patti Palang Kaing at the beginning of the world, you would know that the daughter of men can walk without fear in the forest; but it is not forbidden to touch the tracks of her footsteps with one's lips, nor to lick her hand!' That was what Balaoo said, was it not, my Balaoo? He told me all that, beside my bed of leaves, waiting for you to come: he even told it me in immortal verse, for Balaoo is a great poet, are you not, Balaoo?"

Balaoo, at the door, nodded his head in assent, but kept it still turned away, for his pain was more than he could bear and threatened to burst like an untimely storm...And he held himself in, lest he should seem ridiculous, and tried to swallow his sobs and keep his thunder to himself...

Poor Balaoo, who knew that Coriolis had come to take Madeleine away!...Poor Balaoo, who had himself summoned his master, by order of his little mistress, and who had himself gone, after himself writing the letter—for Madeleine was then too ill—and posted it at night in the box of Mme. Godefroy the postmistress and been very nearly recognized by that confounded old mole of a gossip of a Mother Toussaint, who had not yet forgiven him for his theft of the Empress' dress!.......

A few days passed; and it was over. Madeleine was gone. She had gone to join her husband and Balaoo would never see her again. His master would come back, but not she, because of the man's law that told her to follow her husband. She had but just gone; and, after a leave taking that made all who lived in the Cerdogne country believe that a great storm was raging in the woods and on the mountain, he remained there, at the door of his forest dwelling in the Big Beech at Pierrefeu, remained there motionless, with his arms and legs hanging and his head on his chest, motionless as a pithecanthrope of wood.

And he stayed like that while the tinkling carriage bells tinkled against his heart, now dry and hollow as a drum; for he had nothing left in his heart now, nothing: she had taken it all. At least, it produced that effect upon him, a sense of emptiness; it was as though he had an empty box there, which naught would ever replace: naught but memory, O Balaoo!...

And you shall see, Balaoo, that memory does fill the heart, ay, even to bursting-point!...

There was not a sound now under the greenwood. Balaoo went indoors and lay at full length on the bed of leaves that had kept the shape of her body...and, incredible to state, Balaoo still had tears to shed.

Then, when the last were spent, he lay for two days and two nights on the bed of leaves, lying without movement, like a pithecanthrope of wood. Old forest friends climbed up to him, peeped through the crack in the door; and he did not move a limb. Old As, who now had a broken leg, looked in and saw and went off without a word, shrugging his shoulders. Balaoo knew none of them now.

At the end of the second day, when Coriolis returned, he found Balaoa sitting at his door, with one shoulder in the sun and a consumptive look in his face.

Coriolis had told his daughter that he was going to retire for good to Saint-Martin-des-Bois; but he lied in his thought: it was to the Big Beech at Pierrefeu that he meant to withdraw, far from a society that could but curse him, alone with his divine masterpiece, with the man from Java whom his genius had brought into the world. At any rate, he must see what he could do. There were unpleasant rumours in the department, stories about a pithecanthrope. Coriolis considered that he was best-off in the forest guarded by the memory of the Three Brothers and of the battle in which so many brave officers and soldiers were slain...It was a very nearly safe and inviolable retreat, very nearly...

Coriolis' first thought was how to overcome Balaoo's sadness. He was right, for the poor fellow was extremely ill and, if he went on moping like that, without mov ing, at the top of his tree, would surely fall into a decline.

Coriolis took him for walks in the forest. To divert his pupil's thoughts, he told him of the pranks of a certain Gabriel, whom many people for a moment believed to be Balaoo. In fact, Coriolis himself was taken in by a trick which Gabriel had of wearing his jacket open and suddenly thrusting his fingers into the pockets or arm-holes of his waistcoat; and, lastly, because of an eye-glass.

"I knew Gabriel well," replied Balaoo, making an effort to follow his master's train of thought. "He used to copy everything I had: my clothes and even my way of wearing them. I once made him a present of a pair of spectacles; and I see he managed to make an eyeglass out of them, because I wore one. Those monkeys are never happy unless they are mimicking people!"

They walked for a time without speaking; and then Balaoo resumed:

"While all these horrors were being put down to me, I was on my way to Pierrefeu, in despair. I merely wanted to see Madeleine once more. I saw her through the window of the railway-carriage; but the other tried to kill me; and I am very sorry that he did not succeed."

Coriolis fondly pressed Balaoo's arm. Balaoo humbly returned the pressure and lowered his head, as he concluded:

"Yes, my only wish now is to die...to die in this forest which has known her, which has heard her soft voice calling, 'Balaoo!...Balaoo!...Balaoo!...' My only joy henceforth will be to see the trees at the foot of which we used to sit when she wished to teach me some fresh story...Here I shall find her image everywhere...Patti Palang Kaing is kind...He will let me die here..."

Coriolis tried in vain to silence him. Balaoo thought of nothing but Madeleine and took a mournful pleasure in confiding his thoughts to all the branches on the road. He was visibly pining away. He emerged from his dreams only to speak of Paul and Virginia, which his master had read to him. The story attracted him above all others because he found in it a likeness to his own misfortunes. And, like Paul after Virginia's departure, he visited all the spots where he had been with the companion of his childhood; all the places that reminded him of their alarms, their games, their picnics and the loving-kindness of his dear little sister; a young birch which she had planted; the mossy carpets over which she loved to race; the open spaces in the forest where she used to sing and where their two voices had mingled their two names: Balaoo!...Madeleine!

In five days! time, he took to his bed; and Coriolis began to fear that he would never leave it again. One morning, Balaoo woke from his coma and saw Zoé and Gertrude standing by his side. He betrayed neither anger nor the least ill-humour. Nay more, he let Gertrude kiss him tenderly and begged Zoé's pardon for all the pain which he had caused her since he first knew her. His voice was gentle and soft; he allowed himself to be nursed and petted. He was as weak as a child at the point of death. Coriolis, kneeling behind him and supporting him, though he was no stronger himself, ventured to use the "word-remedy" which little Zoé, with her fond heart and quick intelligence, had suggested of her own initiative. He leant over and whispered two syllables in Balaoo's ear:

"Bandong!"

At once, Balaoo's eyes kindled, his frame stiffened, his chest breathed more firmly and he repeated:

"Bandong!"

Then Zoé asked:

"Would you like to go back to the Forest of Bandong, Balaoo?"

"Oh," said Balaoo, with a terrible sigh, "oh, how I should love to see it once again before I die!"

"Well, we will take you there, Balaoo!...We will all go together!..."

Balaoo put his great, quivering fists to his lips, as was his habit when he wished to restrain the too-noisy expressipn of his joy or grief:

"Let us go!" he said. "Oh, let us go!...Far from men's houses!...Take me back to my Forest of Bandong!..."

There was no reason nor room for hesitation. It meant salvation not only for Balaoo, but for all of them, especially Coriolus; for Zoé had returned from Clermont with the most grievous news. M. Mathieu Delafosse now knew for certain that the smart officers and brave men killed in the attack on the forest had fallen under the blows of Coriolus' pithecanthrope. The official enquiry had ended by clearing up that gruesome business; and the police were once more hunting for the master and his terrible disciple.

There was only just time to fly.

They crossed the frontier and took ship for the East.

They fled to the Forest of Bandong.

Epilogue

Balaoo was saved on the day when he set eyes once more on the place where he had seen his mother for the last time. It was three days' march from Batavia, a few hundred yards from the mangroves which, for a thousand years and more, had been digging their roots to the very heart of the earth. He recognized the disposition of the glade and the thick leafy vaults that cast the same shadow and the same light; for it takes hundreds of centuries to alter those landscapes created by the last upheavals of the world and the first vigour of the universal sap.

"This is it," he said, stopping his companions. "This is my Forest of Bandong. These are the woods of my childhood. Here I played with my mother and my little brother and sister. I was strong and lusty even then, though still a baby, scarcely three or four years old. My little brother and sister were only just beginning to walk, while I gambolled and frisked about and called and beckoned to my little brother and sister and invited them to come and share my sports...The little fellow tried a skip or two, to follow me, but they were vain efforts. I can still see him tottering on his little legs that were hardly strong enough to bear his weight. He fell; and my little sister fell also; and our mother picked them up tenderly and encouraged them with word and gesture...What followed I shall remember to my dying day. My mother, seeing the little ones so clumsy and so tired, took them in her arms and began to sing them to sleep, rocking them and crooning a sweet lullaby of the swamps. O Patti Palang Kaing! Then they of the Race arrived. And they threw a net over me, in which I struggled while my mother fled to save my little brother and sister, flinging me a cry of farewell, the cry of a pithecanthrope mother, which is like nothing else in the world: it rings in my ears even now...It was lucky for them of the Race that my father was engaged elsewhere in the forest that day...Yes, this is it. This is my Forest of Bandong. O Patti Palang Raing, shall I ever see them again: my father, who thundered so loud; and my mother, who watched over our games; and my little brother and sister, who rolled and tumbled in the grass, like awkward little kittens!"

Balaoo did not find his relations. And he came to the conclusion that he had long since been forgotten by his friends. The village in the swamps had disappeared. But Balaoo rebuilt the huts on the triangles formed by the three roots of the giant mangroves. And all the four of them—Gertrude, Coriolis, Zoé and he—lived at that spot in peace and quietness.

Gertrude had grown very old and no longer budged from her seat, busied eternally in knitting socks which Balaoo never wore, for he now went about on his unshod finger-toes. Zoé had become the active and more and more untamed servant of her two masters. She never addressed Balaoo except in the third person of the monkey language. She had forgotten her Paris fashions and dressed in leaves. And she was glad to learn no more geography. Coriolis had lost the habit of talking man language and confined the expression of his thoughts to a few anthropoid monosyllables. He took a keen delight in returning to what he considered the starting point, the source of human life, the monkey race. The unhappy man no longer had the cerebral force to conceive that this set-back was perhaps sent to him as a punishment from Heaven for daring to amuse himself with the sport forbidden by nature, the sport of mixing the species!

Balaoo, who went to Batavia every six months to fetch a letter from Madeleine at the poste restante and who was constantly reading Paul and Virginia, Balaoo alone retained nearly all his acquired civilization. In this he was greatly aided by the memory of Madeleine. He lived with the thought of his young mistress ever before his mind.

She was now a solicitor's wife at Clermont-Ferrand and had two little boys, who played in the house in the Rue de l'Écu with that contemptible General Captain.

"If ever those two youngsters want anything in this life," said Balaoo, "they have only to make a sign: I'm there!...*Tourôô!...Woop!...Tourôô!*"

I have said that Balaoo retained nearly all his acquired civilization, in his Forest of Bandong. But he did not become proud on that account. And, when the denizens of the forest, the real wild brothers of Bandong, gradually drew closer to the new family in the mangrove village and, on spring evenings, formed a circle around Balaoo and listened to his tales of men, Balaoo would say in their language, after a short prayer to Patti Palang Raing:

"Animals are animals and gods are gods, but men are nothing at all!...In short," Balaoo concluded, putting his fingers up his nose, after the insulting fashion of pithecanthropes, "men are gods spoilt in the making!"

A PLAINTIVE HYMN TO PATTI PALANG KAING,
GOD OF ALL THE ANIMALS IN THE
FOREST OF BANDONG

By

BALAOO

(Dedicated to Mlle. Madeleine Coriolis Boussac Saint-Aubin.)

Voopwooooppwooooppwoooopp![27]
Patti Palang Kaing! Patti Palang Kaing!
Could not the God of Christian man
Say that these fingers bound should be,
The toes on the shoe-hands of me?
Patti Palang Kaing! Patti Palang Kaing!
Why change the language of my song
From my native Forest of Bandong
And teach me to weep at right and wrong,
If He could not also bring His mind
The toes of my shoe-hands to bind?
I roamed through the garden of man
Like one of the race in woe.
Not one of them saw my tears:
Not she whom I love the best,
Though she heard how I beat my breast
In a grief that none can know.
To the other, who strolled with his nose on high,
She said, "It is thunder passing by."
If only there were bands
To the toes of my shoe-hands,
I should say to Patti Palang Kaing:
"Patti Palang Kaing! Patti Palang Kaing!
Keep thou, across the seas,
Thy plantains, mangroves, mango-trees,

Since thou hast put me bands
To the toes of my shoe-hands!
Patti Palang Kaing!
Balaoo knows no pang!"
And I should say to Madeleine,
In the softest voice of men:
"Madeleine, my fair,
I fain would kiss thy hair!"
If only there were bands
To the toes of my shoe-hands!
Alas, did not the other say:
"I would kiss thy hair to-day!"
Silent I watch and stand,
Waiting to kiss her hand!
Patti Palang Kaing! Patti Palang Kaing!
Appeal to the God of Christian man
To restore the language of my song
From my native Forest of Bandong!
And give me back my mangrove-trees,
With my hands that were not as these!

[27] This exclamation is equivalent to the "Ororororoi!" of the Greek tragic author and means "Alas!"—AUTHOR'S NOTE.

Also from Benediction Books ...
Wandering Between Two Worlds: Essays on Faith and Art
Anita Mathias
Benediction Books, 2007
152 pages
ISBN: 0955373700

Available from www.amazon.com, www.amazon.co.uk

In these wide-ranging lyrical essays, Anita Mathias writes, in lush, lovely prose, of her naughty Catholic childhood in Jamshedpur, India; her large, eccentric family in Mangalore, a sea-coast town converted by the Portuguese in the sixteenth century; her rebellion and atheism as a teenager in her Himalayan boarding school, run by German missionary nuns, St. Mary's Convent, Nainital; and her abrupt religious conversion after which she entered Mother Teresa's convent in Calcutta as a novice. Later rich, elegant essays explore the dualities of her life as a writer, mother, and Christian in the United States-- Domesticity and Art, Writing and Prayer, and the experience of being "an alien and stranger" as an immigrant in America, sensing the need for roots.

About the Author

Anita Mathias was born in India, has a B.A. and M.A. in English from Somerville College, Oxford University and an M.A. in Creative Writing from the Ohio State University. Her essays have been published in The Washington Post, The London Magazine, The Virginia Quarterly Review, Commonweal, Notre Dame Magazine, America, The Christian Century, Religion Online, The Southwest Review, Contemporary Literary Criticism, New Letters, The Journal, and two of HarperSanFrancisco's The Best Spiritual Writing anthologies. Her non-fiction has won fellowships from The National Endowment for the Arts; The Minnesota State Arts Board; The Jerome Foundation, The Vermont Studio Center; The Virginia Centre for the Creative Arts, and the First Prize for the Best General Interest Article from the Catholic Press Association of the United States and Canada. Anita has taught Creative Writing at the College of William and Mary, and now lives and writes in Oxford, England.

www.anitamathias.com
wanderingbetweentwoworlds.blogspot.com (General and Culture)
thegoodbooksblog.blogspot.com (Reading and Writing)
theoxfordchristian.blogspot.com (Christian)